Yours

by
KIM LOVE

WORDS MATTER
PUBLISHING
OUR WORDS CHANGE THE WORLD

Dedication:

To Matt.
There is not enough space in this world
for all the thanks you deserve.
You have always supported me in every crazy idea
I have ever had.
You have given me words, inspiration, love, and
tons of hope.
And because of that, my dream became real, and WE did it.
You might not read romance, but you created it in my life.
And I will always be thankful to be Yours.

To all those who encouraged and cheered for me,
this is for you.
Especially for Laura W. for being my very first fan and for
crying and laughing with me as I made these characters
come to life.

Chapter 1

Sitting in the chair by the window, I watch little raindrops rush down the glass like tiny racecars. "It looks miserable out there. I hate it when it rains this hard." Kasey meows in agreement as he circles through my legs, letting his head rub against me in affection. My mind and body struggle against going out or staying in to cuddle into the blankets on the couch with my furry best friend. It is cold, wet, and pretty much a normal early November day in Chicago, but knowing I have a million things to do finally forces me from the warmth of the house. A string of grumbles escapes as I trot to the car and into the gloomy day.

Now, as I sit in traffic with the heavy rain dancing on the rooftop, I truly wish I had just stayed home. "Why do I always wait until the last minute to do everything? Why did I even say I would go this weekend? Why am I questioning myself out loud?" *Because I can,* I think to myself before my thoughts start to wander to other things while waiting for traffic to move.

My ringing cell phone vibrates loudly in the cup holder, breaking through the silence of the car and bringing me back from my daydream into reality. I notice Paul's name across the screen, and it just adds to my already crappy mood. I can only imagine what he wants.

"Hey, Paul." I hit the button, knowing full well if I don't answer he will just keep calling.

"Miranda, I hate to bother you, but I am hoping you can swing by the office and pull those files for the Williams case before you head out. It seems like we are going forward with the case, and I need all the info we have. Leave it all on my desk, and I can take it from there when I return this evening."

Letting out a deep breath, I force a smile and answer in my perfect assistant's voice, hoping he doesn't notice. "Of course, Mr. Lester, I would be happy to." Even though it is my day off, I should be anywhere but in the office. He never believes in fully embracing the day off.

"Great. I appreciate it. Have a nice trip, and thanks." He hangs up without a goodbye, and all I can do is shake my head.

I love my job and my boss most days, but seriously, just one day off is all I am asking for. Guess there goes my day of peace.

Deciding to go into the office before shopping, I make a quick right onto Fifth to circle around and notice the traffic is not so bad this way. Well, that is a plus. Turning up the radio, I decide to focus on the positive of the day. I am going home for the weekend to see my family and celebrate my niece's birthday. And that is exciting. I miss them all like crazy.

Cranking up the radio, I choose to let it guide me as I sing along and smile at the people in the cars next to me. See, all good. Music is my release. Thoughts of my sweet little niece pop into my head. Yes, happiness is way better. No one is going to take me down.

When the light changes to green, I pull into the intersection, but a flash of gray on my right catches my eye, and all I can do is scream as bright light and searing pain tear through me before I pass out.

Faint voices talk somewhere in the background, but as I try to move, pain radiates from everywhere, and I struggle to focus. My eyes don't want to open, and my body feels trapped. I'm not sure where I am or what is going on, but fear is starting to seep into my mind, and I struggle more to understand what is happening.

"Hey, it's okay. Please don't move. The ambulance is on its way." A strong male voice comes from beside me.

I don't know who it is, but it is comforting knowing I am not alone. I try to move again, but the voice tells me it is okay, so I wait, hoping my body will respond quickly.

Now the rain is starting to hit my face, and it makes me uncomfortable. I need to move.

"Please don't move." The voice is clearer now, closer, but I still can't open my eyes. My right arm is pinned, and panic stirs in my chest until a hand lays on my shoulder, and a calm, soothing warmth takes over.

I can hear more talking from around me, but nothing makes sense. "Where…I have to move…" The words won't come out as I struggle to stay conscious.

"No, you need to stay still. You are hurt. Please." His voice holds concern, and as I start to understand, my body tenses, but his hand is still there. I need to wake up.

Finally, I get my eyes to flutter open, and when I look up, I am met with bright green eyes that are staring down at me. Down. I am down. I have to blink to focus, and I can now see they are full of fear, which makes a new level of panic flow through my pain-riddled body. Everything hurts. Warm tears run down my face as I try to form words, but nothing is working.

"Shh, please, it's going to be okay. Just stay with me. Stay still. What's your name?" His voice is so close, but as much as I try, I can't talk.

I can't focus; the pain is too great. My vision is blurry, and the raindrops running down my face are not helping. "Miran..." I try, but this time, I lose myself to the darkness.

More voices. My eyes fly open, and new pain burns through me like a bolt of lightning. I realize I am stuck completely, and there are now people shouting around me.

"Hey, it's okay. I'm here. You will be okay."

Turning slightly, I meet those same green eyes from earlier. I still can't figure out what is going on, but I try to focus on him.

"The paramedics are almost here. Just hang on."

I focus on his face, his black hair, which is soaked from the rain, and the way his green eyes seem to glow in the grayness around us. My eyes move higher to his eyebrows, and I notice he is hurt.

"You're bleeding." My words are like an echo in my own

head, but I am pretty sure I am talking out loud, or at least I hope I am.

I watch as he reaches up and touches his forehead, pulling back bloody fingers. "I'm fine." He nods before looking me over again, this time with more concern.

"I, I'm…confused…the rain…it's in my eyes…" My throat is tight and is causing my voice to strain.

He moves over me, shielding me slightly as his eyes search my face. "It's not the rain. Please, you need to stay still." He squeezes my left hand, and I feel its warmth even through the pain.

And then, I understand. Fear like I have never felt before lances through me, cutting me to my very core. It is blood. My blood. And there is a lot of it. I can tell by the look on his face that I am right. Dear God, how bad is it? I need to know. "How bad?" My voice is barely a whisper, but I know he hears me by the way he flinches.

"You are going to be okay. Just hold on. Keep talking to me. What is your name?" His eyes search mine as his grip tightens around my hand. If he is not telling me, it must be bad.

My mind is getting cloudy from the pain, and I am trying to think hard to remember what happened, but it is almost impossible. Nothing makes sense. I just want to figure out where I am.

"Miranda." My name slips from my lips when he asks again. My voice sounds so small, so weak. I try to tell myself not to panic, but it isn't working. I am panicking.

Sirens. I can hear the sirens, lots of them. I need to listen to them and focus, but the coldness is starting to creep in, causing my body to shake. "Please. I'm scared. Please don't leave me." Darkness tugs at my vision, and I fight, but I can't stop it, and it starts to take me under as his grip tightens on my hand.

"I'm right here. I'm not leaving. I promise." There is a new deepness to his voice, but it is low and calm. Too calm. Or maybe it is me. Maybe this is the calm before it is over. Before I can ask, though, my eyes close completely, and I give in.

Pain forces me back awake, although I don't know how long it has been. I realize someone is moving me. Shifting me. Paramedics maybe? I can hear them. Thank God. My left arm now moves freely, and I feel the warmth of someone's grip. His hand is still around mine. He is still here. I try to turn to see him, but something stops my movement. Think, Miranda. Stop and think. Okay, it's a neck brace, I was in an accident. A tear slips out of the corner of my eye as I search for my bearings.

"Ma'am, I'm here to help you. My name is Ben. I need you to stay calm. We are going to get you out of here, but it is going to take us a minute. I need you to focus on me and do what I tell you, okay?"

"Okay." My voice is so hoarse.

"I need you to stay perfectly still. I know it hurts but stay still for me."

Terror causes me to grip the man's hand harder, and he responds by placing his other hand on my shoulder.

"I'm still here." His voice washes over me and brings a

small bit of comfort. There are more voices now, and people are talking and moving around me as I watch.

"Sir, we need to get you looked at." Someone tells the man that is next to me.

"No. I promised to stay with her, and I'm not moving."

"Okay, but just until she's in the ambulance, then you need to be checked."

"Just get her out." The man seems angry, or maybe it is fear and pain, too. The voices get louder, then start to fade again before I suddenly feel a soft surface, and then I am moving. I am free. I squeeze, and he squeezes back, then darkness again.

"Miranda?" My name floats around in my head. "Miranda, open your eyes for me." A different voice, not the earlier paramedic. Slowly, I force them open and realize I am now in the ambulance. My arms and legs are strapped down, and nothing is moving. Everything is foggy, but I can hear, and that helps.

"Ma'am, easy. You have been in an accident. Can you talk to me?"

I give a painful nod in response.

"Do you know your name?"

"Miranda Michaels." I croak out. My head is pounding, and the bright light hurts my eyes.

"Don't close your eyes, Miranda. Stay awake."

"Too bright." I try, but it is no use, I have to close them.

"Can you tell me where…" I can hear the paramedic, but I cut him off as I try to sit up.

"Easy." He tells me.

"No, where is…" I did not get his name. "The man…" I try to think of what to say, and suddenly, a hand slides back into mine and squeezes.

"Still right here." The warmth of his voice settles my body and lets me relax. Exhaustion is setting in, and a shiver goes down my back. I am so cold. So tired.

"Hang in there." The man's soft voice whispers as his thumb rubs over my knuckles, but it isn't enough, and I slip back into the nothing.

Voices…movement…noise. I struggle to open my eyes against the bright lights.

"Ms. Michaels, I am Dr. Shay. Can you wake up and talk to me?"

There is now a doctor leaning over me, looking into my face. "Where am I?" Which is a stupid question since I know where I am. And with the flurry of people around me, I can only guess it is not good.

"You are at the hospital. You were in a car accident, and we need to take some X-rays and then get you into surgery. You have a broken arm that needs to be repaired immediately. Understand?" The doctor is still looking down at me, but his sweet smile eases some of my fear.

"Okay. My head hurts a lot." I can barely speak, but I get another smile from the doctor.

"You have a pretty good bump and are going to need some stitches in your head, but we can talk about that in a bit. Right now, I want you to try and stay still for me." All I can manage is a nod before a shiver runs through me, bringing back the cold and the darkness.

Chapter 2

I try to stretch, but the pain has been replaced by stiffness and an all-over body ache. The room is quiet around me, except for the steady beep of the machines. Hospital. Right, I am in a hospital. I am still alive. Gently, I open my eyes and am surprised to see a nurse standing over me.

"Well, good evening, Ms. Michaels. Glad you could join us. My name is Nancy. Do you know where you are?"

"Hospital."

She stops messing with the machines and focuses on me. "Yes, you are. Do you know what happened to put you here?"

"I think, no, I know…a car accident?" Tears well up in my eyes, fighting to get out.

"Yes, you were in an car accident, so I need you to take it easy. Let me get your vitals, and then we will let the doctor know you are awake." Nancy's gaze moves across the bed, and I follow, where my eyes land on an unknown man standing by my bed. His hand squeezes mine, and immediately, I know who it is.

"Hi," I force out.

"Hi," he whispers back as we stare at each other. Those bright green eyes are locked on mine, and I can't remember much, but I remember them. I take a moment to look at his face and dark hair, realizing that I never had the chance to see him before. Maybe he is an angel.

The nurse interrupts our staring contest, causing me to blush. I should not be looking at him like that anyway. I turn back to Nancy and try to sit up, but she lays a hand on my shoulder to stop me.

"You had quite the knock to the head, and since you just had surgery, you need to take this very slow. Okay?" Nancy gives me a look to not question her, and it just brings on another pang of panic.

"How bad?" I ask, struggling to keep the fear out of my voice.

"We can let the doctor go over everything with you."

"No, please, tell me, how bad am I?"

Nancy glances over at the man and then exhales. "Well, you have a bad concussion to start. You have a broken right arm, bruised ribs, twelve stitches to close that cut on your head, a very nasty bump, and a whole lot of bruises." She pauses to give me time to process.

"Oh." It is the only thing that comes to mind as I look over my battered body, and the cast catches my attention, but my body is so weak that it is too heavy to lift.

Starting at my toes, I make slight movements to make sure everything works. Definitely, all are still there.

"Do you have any pain?" Nancy's question halts my inventory of injuries.

"No. Just sore, and I am very thirsty."

"I will let the doctor know you are awake, and we can work on getting you some ice chips to start." She pats my shoulder, causing me to scrunch my very sore nose.

My hand immediately goes up to my face as my eyes water. "Is my nose broken?"

"No, just bruised. The top of your head took most of the force of the airbag." Nancy raises her eyebrow as she looks at my face.

"Oh. Can I sit up?" I already want out of this bed. She agrees, and after a bit of adjustment and a pillow fluff, I feel better, but my stomach takes that moment to growl.

"Sorry." My embarrassment flushes my cheeks.

"Don't be. That's a good sign. Let me go speak with the doctor, and I will be back with something." Nancy gives me a reassuring smile before she leaves the room, and now it is just me and the stranger standing by my bed.

I look up at the man and take in his appearance. He is tall, maybe six foot two or three. It's hard to tell from the bed, but he is at least that much. And younger than I expected. Although I don't know what I was expecting, he just seemed older before. He looks around my age, maybe twenty-eight or thirty. His jet-black hair is a mess, falling over his forehead where a bandage sits, and by the look of it, he is going to have a black eye tomorrow. He must have been in the accident also, as I remember his forehead bleeding.

My eyes take in his handsome face before traveling down and noticing his white t-shirt stretched over his chest. It is untucked from his suit pants, wrinkled, and covered in blood. I try not to linger there too long, letting my gaze continue down, following his arm to where it meets mine, and he is still holding my hand.

"Um, hi." The words are barely more than a mumble from the embarrassment I suddenly feel.

"Hi." His answer is soft, but when I chance a look up, he is still staring down at me.

"Are you all right? Did you get hurt badly?" My voice is hoarse, but not from thirst this time. It is from this stranger who is still by my side.

Without a word, he reaches up and touches his head where the bandage sits and flinches as he visibly swallows hard. "I will be fine. You are the one that I am worried about." His fingers wrap tighter into mine, taking our attention down to our joined hands.

"I'm tougher than I look. I will make it. I just wish I could remember what happened. I only have bits and pieces, and not very much. I think some jackass ran the light." Raising my other arm, I am finally able to hold up the cast. "Broken arm is a first for me."

When I look back up at his face, he has a look that is maybe sad or angry. I can't tell, but I am more interested in why he is still here. I don't even know him, but I am curious. "I have to ask, have you been here the entire time?"

He nods slowly in answer, and suddenly, I feel terrible for asking a complete stranger to stay with me.

"You didn't have to stay."

A small smile appears on his lips for a moment, and I am not sure why, but it makes me feel a little better.

"You must be sore, too. Do you need to go? You probably should. Not that I want you to, but you need to rest. You should rest." Oh God, my mouth. I feel stupid immediately as the words tumble from my lips.

"I'm okay." His words are flat as he looks away.

"You are not okay. All that blood on your shirt says otherwise. You probably need to go rest and recover yourself."

He glances down at his shirt and then back to me but doesn't speak right away.

"Since it's not my blood, I think I am fine. And a promise is a promise." His hand squeezes mine, and I am once again thankful to not be here alone.

That is until it hits me that if it isn't his, it's mine. Shit. "Oh God. It's mine. I'm so sorry for bleeding on you." I bite back a gasp as it all sinks in. I bled all over him, and yet he stayed. That must be awful to have to sit here in that.

"It's just a shirt." When he speaks, his voice is deeper, and I notice that his breathing has quickened as he watches me. I say nothing as we just stare, letting the silence fill the quiet room. I have no words to make it okay, and clearly, he is not looking for me to explain, so we just wait for someone to speak as we continue to watch the other. The air thickens between us, but still, he stands there, holding my hand.

The nurse takes that moment to enter, causing us to break eye contact, and I am a little thankful.

"Ice chips to start. Once you keep it down, we can move on to Jello." I have no choice but to let go of his hand and take the offered cup of ice chips. I hate it immediately. It has been my constant through this entire ordeal, but the ice chips win out.

My mind is a whirlwind of emotions as I look at the cup, wondering how I am possibly going to do this one-handed. I lift my broken arm, but my fingers are still too numb to hold the spoon.

And as I contemplate just eating straight from the cup, his gentle voice comes from next to me.

"May I help you with that?"

He pulls over a chair and gently takes the cup from my hand, causing my cheeks to heat up again.

"Thank you."

"Of course."

He holds the cup while I try to eat the ice chips with my left hand, but I fumble. Sensing my frustration, he takes the spoon from me, and I let out another embarrassed "Thank you."

At first, it feels awkward as he offers me a spoonful, but the coolness on my lips is so soothing that I ignore the awkwardness and savor it. He quietly offers another spoonful. When I glance up at his face, the corners of his mouth lift slightly, and I respond with a shy smile.

"Um, I'm sorry, but I don't remember your name." I watch the small smile spread across his face, making him even more handsome than before. Not that I am looking, but not that I am not either. I mean, how can I miss it…okay, I need to focus on eating the ice, not him.

"Ethan." His name is so soft as it floats off his lips that it seems unnatural for his size.

"Thank you, Ethan, for being my hero."

"I am not a hero." Suddenly he looks away, his voice flat, and all the sweetness is now gone.

"To me, you are." I feel so shy as I give him a glance through my lashes, which only causes my cheeks to burn more.

"Just eat your ice chips." With a shake of his head, he leaves it, and it is back to silence between us.

After Ethan has fed me the last of the ice, which still makes me blush to think of it, he leans back in his chair as I fuss with the bandage on my head. I can see him watching me out of the corner of my eye, but I pretend to ignore him and pick at the little pieces of stuff in my hair. Oh, joy, it's dried blood, and I'm not even sure what the other stuff is. Gross.

"Leave it alone." Ethan's voice makes me jump.

"What?"

"Your head, stop messing with it." His smile has all but faded, and it makes me pause. He is so serious, and all the sweetness is gone from his voice.

I wonder what happened? Did I do something? He must have mistaken the look I give him because he repeats himself, and I suddenly feel the need to explain.

"It itches." I glare, and this time, he smiles, even though he is trying not to.

"You need to leave it be."

"I can't." I am momentarily distracted when Nancy comes back in with a tray of goodies, forgetting that I am currently being sassy with him.

The tray contains chocolate pudding, orange Jello, apple juice, and a cup of water. I go straight for the chocolate before Nancy even has the tray on the table. "Just start slowly. Don't eat too fast or too much; you might get a tummy ache."

"You got it." I agree after taking a long, slow drink of the ice-cold water from the straw.

"I mean it, slowly. You make sure of it." She points to Ethan, who looks a bit surprised, before leaving me to my buffet.

Holding the pudding in my left hand, I silently determine the best course of action to take and if using my teeth would be too inappropriate in front of Ethan. I mean, I barely know the man, and I don't want him to think I am a heathen.

Choosing to not be odd, I give him a sweet smile. "Would you pretty please open this for me?"

"Of course." His chuckle sends goosebumps down my arms as he takes it from me and pulls it open before reaching for a spoon.

"I might actually be able to do this one on my own."

He nods before handing it over and leaning back in his chair to let me do it as requested.

It takes me a hot minute to figure out the coordination, but getting that first bite into my mouth without a mess is worth the struggle. "So good. I'm so hungry." The words come out louder than I expect, which makes me blush yet again.

"Well, it is almost six o'clock, so I imagine you are hungry."

That information makes me pause as my foggy brain races. "Shit!" Suddenly, I realize it is dark outside, and I was supposed to go by the office. "SHIT!" I repeat when I also realize that I am not in the car headed to my sister's! She is going to freak!

"What is it?" He is suddenly by the bed as I frantically look around.

"My boss. My sister. My family. Everyone is probably worried and wondering where I am."

As I start to search the little stand beside the bed, my heart races in panic. I need a phone, any phone. Something. "Do you know if…"

Without a word, Ethan reaches past me to the drawer next to me, stopping me mid-question, and pulls out my purse, which he hands to me.

"I made sure to grab it and your cell phone from the car. I have already talked to your sister." He looks up at the window uncomfortably, avoiding my gaze. "The same number kept calling, so I thought it might be someone looking for you. I explained to her what happened, and the police have already spoken to your parents. They are on their way." Now, he is the one who looks embarrassed.

"Oh." It is all I can manage as my brain processes. "Thank you," it comes out as a whisper, but only because I am stunned that he would answer my phone and think of someone being worried about me.

"I did ask your sister if there was someone else that I needed to call for you. A husband or boyfriend, and she said no." He looks directly at me with a question on his face.

"Oh, no, no boyfriend, it's just me and my cat." I push the Jello container around, unsure if he is asking for himself or just to be nice.

"May I open that for you?" His voice has softened again, and when I shake my head no, he clears his throat and again looks up at the dark windows.

"Ethan, you don't have to stay. I mean, I'm sure you have a family and life to get back to also." I don't want him to go, but he doesn't need to feel obligated to stay here.

"Nowhere else to be." His voice is flat and emotionless, and I am starting to pick up that he does that when he doesn't want to talk about whatever it is at that time. "I just want to make sure you are okay." He adds; again his voice is softer when he looks back at me.

"I'm okay." It doesn't sound as convincing as I mean it to be because I really am not okay, but I choose to keep that to myself for now.

After I eat a little more, I can feel him watching me, and when I glance up, I am met with his sweet smile. Before I can say more, though, a yawn escapes, and suddenly, I realize how tired I am. My eyes feel heavy, and I want to rest. As my eyes close, I yawn again and know I need to sleep. It came on so quickly.

"Sleep. Rest," Ethan says from next to me, his hand on my shoulder, making me warm with his touch.

"Ethan, you are my hero no matter what you think. Thank you for staying with me." I whisper, and I feel his hand in mine before I drift off to sleep.

When familiar voices surround me, I open my eyes slowly and carefully, unsure if this is a dream. I know that voice, it's my sister, and she's here.

Once my eyes are open, she sees me, and a rush of emotion is all over her face. "Thank God you are okay!" Emma is sitting on the bed next to me and gently leans in to hug me, holding on tight and a bit longer than necessary. She brushes the hair from my face as she looks me over, and I realize just how much I have truly missed her. It seems like it has been months. "How are you?"

"Sore, but I'll make it," I speak a little slower, giving her a smile to show I am all right.

"You don't look okay."

With that signature mom look glare, I almost cave in, but instead, I swat her hand away and tell her I am fine. I don't need to be babied.

Mom is the next to fuss over me. "My God, Miranda, we were so worried. What can I get you? What do you need? I was so sick trying to get here. We went as fast as we could." Mom holds my hand and runs her fingers over the side of my face, very gently tracing the bruise I can feel there.

I know she is worried, but I have never been one for all the attention.

"Hey, baby," Dad speaks up from the end of the bed, and that makes me genuinely smile.

My dad gets me. "Hey, Dad." And that's all he says before patting my leg and glancing to his left. My eyes follow and find Ethan by the window, arms crossed, watching me. When our eyes meet, that familiar warmth in my cheeks is back. What is it about his glance that makes me go all school girl!?

"Still here," he answers as if reading my mind. He stayed. My heart beats a little faster at the thought of him watching over me as I sleep.

Emma turns to look at him and gives him a huge smile, which he nods back.

"I am guessing you have already met Ethan," I announce to my family, but my eyes are still on him.

"We did." Mom is still fussing over me as she answers, but I still do not look away. My eyes stay on him.

"He told us he stayed with you at the accident and then here in the hospital. I am very thankful someone was with you." My mother continues to straighten my pillow and the blanket, and it is distracting, but I don't want to look away.

"Mom, I'm fine."

"Hush, you are not fine." And she continues on. I let her because, knowing my mom, this is how she feels useful.

"Ethan told us you were in a car accident, but what happened?" Emma has gotten serious suddenly, taking my attention away from Ethan.

"Actually, I don't really know." I turn to face Ethan again, hoping he can shed some light on my memory loss. "Did you see what happened? I mean, all I know is the light was green, I went, and then there was a flash of gray. I remember bits and pieces of being told to hang on and stay still from you, but nothing more."

"Some asshole ran the stop light and hit you. Thank God for airbags." He looks sad as I touch my head; it still hurts a lot.

"I hope the other driver wasn't hurt too badly." That is more out loud than I expected, and now everyone is looking at me in surprise.

Before I can explain, though, Ethan continues. "Not as bad as he should have been. He walked away." Ethan's voice is very flat, and clearly, he is angry. He must be upset about being wrapped up in all this, too.

I wonder how bad his car is. I wonder if my car is okay. The thought depresses me. I love that car. I worked really hard to get it.

"Hey, you're okay. That's all that matters." Emma has moved up the bed to lay next to me and is holding onto me as I start to cry.

There is something about her embrace that just breaks the dam. I've been holding it in all day, but now, it's open, and my emotions are out. Closing my eyes, I relax into her, feeling the comfort she brings. A warm hand lays on my shoulder, and I know who it belongs to without looking. Although, when I do finally open my eyes, Ethan is standing by my bed, smiling down at me, with a bit of worry in his eyes.

"Are you all right?" His voice is tender as his eyes search mine, but I just nod yes so that I don't break down more. "I'm going to go home and freshen up since your family is here now. I will be back to check on you later." He takes my hand and squeezes it, and somehow, I know he will.

"Okay," I manage through the tears and the sob I am holding back.

I watch as he picks up my phone, works on it for a minute, then lays it back down on the tray. "I put my number in. If you need anything at all, please call me. Get some rest." He takes my hand back and gives it another squeeze, causing me to almost melt into the bed.

"Thank you." My words turn to mush when he does that slight smile of his, and I get that head nod in return before he lets me go. It's like we just understand each other.

Emma sits up and shakes his hand, thanking him again and again for taking care of me.

"The same goes for all of you. Miranda has my number; if there is anything I can do, please let me know." He tells us goodnight, and I watch as he walks to the door, where he pauses and turns back around to smile at me one more time before closing the door.

As soon as he is gone, I miss him immediately. Although, it only lasts a second because Emma starts in as soon as the door is closed. "Now that we are alone, you need to fill me in. Where did he come from? Did he save you? How did this all come about? Are you a couple?"

"Emma, stop. There's not much to tell. I know his name is Ethan and he was there at the accident. I was semi-conscious, but he held my hand and stayed with me, keeping me calm until the paramedics arrived. Well, I sort of asked him to stay with me since I was terrified, but that's beside the point. He stayed. He was in one of the cars because I remember them telling him that he needed to be checked out, too, but he stayed with me anyway. Even in the ambulance and then here. That's all I know." With a quick glance at the door, I am hopeful that he will come back.

"He's gorgeous." Emma giggles, which makes me giggle too.

"I know. And those eyes." I bite back my grin, which causes us to start laughing, but the pain sears through my side. "Ouch. No laughing. It hurts." But we both laugh again.

"Girls, not the place." My mother chimes in.

"Sorry." Emma mouths at me before laying back next to me, and I realize how tired I am again. When Emma wraps her arm around me, I thank her and drift off to sleep.

Chapter 3

When I wake, the sunshine is pouring through the window, and I try to move, but I am sore and stiff. It hurts everywhere. Wincing as I move, I roll slightly to the side and find my sister asleep on the couch. There is no way I can get up alone, so I hit the button for help instead of waking her. That's when I notice the huge bouquet of flowers in the corner and the get-well balloons on the other side of my bed. I assume they are from my family, and that makes me smile.

When I am back in bed, Emma rolls over and sits up quickly. "Morning," she mumbles, half awake.

"Morning."

"How are you?" She is now up and at my bed as I am getting situated back to a comfortable position.

"Sore. Very, very sore. Everything aches." Tears well up in my eyes before I can control them, and she is right at my side, making it better. Thankfully, the nurse arrives with my meds and orders my breakfast which takes my mind off how miserable I am this morning.

Emma notices me looking at the flowers, and without asking, she walks over to them and returns with the small envelope. I open it and read the little white card inside.

I hope these make you smile.
Get well soon.
~ Ethan

Ethan sent them.

Emma pulls the card from my hand and looks at it with a giggle.

"They are from Ethan," I announce, and the smile isn't going to leave my face.

"I already knew that. He came by early this morning and delivered them himself and the balloons." She reaches up and touches the shiny balloons, catching my attention. He brought me balloons too. My heart pounds in my chest at his sweetness.

"I was mostly asleep when he came in, but I noticed his snazzy suit and tie. We thought he was hot before; wait until you see him all cleaned up." Emma giggles as she tells me about his visit and describes his outfit in more detail than necessary.

"I think he might have the hots for you," she adds.

"You think? It's so weird, I like him, but I don't even know him." The giggling between us starts again, but I wince as pain goes down my arm this time.

"Sorry."

"I'm fine. It always hurts worse the next day, right?" I try to pretend it doesn't, but it does. "Where are Mom and

Dad?" Changing the subject, I just want it off me so my mind doesn't register the pain.

"I sent them to your place to rest last night."

"Good idea. They did not need to sleep here." I shoot her a disapproving look, but she ignores me.

"I wasn't leaving you alone. And it wasn't that bad." She shrugs and then starts to clean up her blankets, leaving me to think about everything.

After breakfast, Mom and Dad are back, and we send Emma to my house to shower and rest. I need rest, too, so after a short visit, my parents go off to relax somewhere other than my hospital room, and I nap. I need the space. They are amazing people, but they overdo it sometimes, and it's overwhelming.

However, after tossing and turning and not being able to sleep, I decide to make some calls and get ready for some out-of-bed time per the doctor. Just as I am getting up, though, Ethan appears in the doorway, surprising me, but before I can invite him in, he steps back and announces very politely that he will wait in the hallway.

Getting to my feet and walking is a bit of a struggle since I am still a bit off, but the nurse is with me, and I am determined. And as he stated, we find Ethan right outside my door, and we exchange a smile and a hello as I pass by. I also notice he is in a suit with his hair combed and freshly shaven, which Emma was right, it does make him look even hotter than before. Although I do like the messy hair, it adds to his mystery.

The nurse makes me focus on walking, which is harder than it should be as I shuffle along. Sadly, I don't make it very far before the dizziness overwhelms me. I try to stay standing, but I am losing the battle, and I just want to sit. The nurse who is holding me up calls for the other nurse who is following to bring the wheelchair, but before she can get there, I feel strong arms around me, lifting me, and I know it is Ethan.

"Can I help?" I hear him over my shoulder and feel his warmth against me as he holds me up. His scent drifts over me, and he smells incredible as he helps me into the wheelchair. So incredible that I want to snuggle into him but turn back to the nurse to stop the thoughts going through my head.

"Sorry," I grumble to the nurse, but she gives me a genuine smile.

"Honey, we don't expect you to run a marathon yet."

"Don't expect that even after I recover either." I tease, and with a hearty laugh, she pats my shoulder, and I don't feel so much like a failure.

Once I am nestled back into the bed, the exhaustion is almost too much, but I am not giving in just yet. Ethan has just come back in and is again standing right by my bed.

"Hi." He gives me a beautiful, bright smile.

"Hi." I smile back sleepily. "Thank you for the flowers and balloons."

"You are most welcome." He takes my hand in his, and it feels so good, like it belongs there. I missed it, and him, even though it has only been a few hours.

"And thank you for holding me up," I add with a yawn.

"Again, you are welcome. I am happy to help where I am

needed." I can't keep my eyes open, but I want to talk with him. I want to get to know more about him.

"How's your head?" he asks softly.

"It's been better, but I'll live." I try to make it a joke so it isn't serious between us.

"I really hope that you do." His green eyes shine, and dammit, I feel the deep blush creep into my cheeks.

"Me too," I add as I look down, way too embarrassed to keep looking at him. He raises my hand, and I feel the slight brush of his lips across the back of it, sending shivers down my entire body. I honestly want more, but he pulls away.

"Get some rest." He gently lays my hand down on the bed.

"You don't have to go. I mean, you don't have to stay either, but you are welcome to." That sounds so much like I am asking, and I blush darker.

"I'll be right here." Pulling over the chair, he sits next to me, and with that knowledge, I drift off to sleep with a smile.

My body does not want to wake up, but I hear talking, and I am curious. My dream was wonderful, and I feel warm and safe, but I want to know who is here. I know one is Ethan, but I can't make out the second voice. Someone is messing with my IV, which is distracting. I try hard to open my eyes but can't; my head hurts too badly.

The bed shifts, and immediately Ethan's scent floats over me. He takes my hand in his, making it all better. I feel myself relax until he speaks to me.

"Miranda, are you awake? There is an officer here to take a statement from you for the accident. If you think you can or want to try, just wake up." I only mumble, not even sure what I say or if it makes sense.

"Miranda, can you wake up?" I try to shake my head no, but again, my head hurts too much. I hear Ethan again, and this time, he is telling the person to leave. Then Ethan's hand squeezes, and I return it before I drift back off.

When I do finally manage to wake up, I am not sure how long I have been sleeping, but I feel better. I feel rested. However, my stomach is growling loudly, and I know I need food. When I open my eyes, Emma is talking quietly to Ethan on the other side of the room. Mom is reading on the couch, and Dad is next to her, watching TV. It makes me happy that they are all here.

"Hey, sleepyhead, I was getting worried. You have been out for almost five hours now." Ethan's smile greets me, and I didn't even realize he had walked over to the bed.

"My head hurt, and I didn't want to wake up. I heard you asking me to, but I just wanted to sleep. Sorry." I offer an explanation.

"Don't be. It wasn't important. An officer left his card and wants you to call him when you feel like talking. Once you are well. There is absolutely no rush." His voice is a little stern and deep, and I like it.

"And you need to rest, so go back to sleep if you want." Emma has moved over next to Ethan, as they stand at my bed.

"No, I'm good. I'm hungry." Before I can ask, Ethan has the menu and is reading off my choices. He is so serious about it, but it is adorable. His voice is deep and sexy, and I know I could listen to him read all day.

"Grilled cheese. Pickles, fries, and whatever sherbet they have. I prefer green or orange." His eyes are on me as I rattle off my order, and it feels like it is just us, not a room full of people. I watch as he picks up the phone and orders my food without hesitation. Emma, who is still next to him, is grinning like a fool and shaking her head. Yeah, I know, I am thinking it too.

After I have thoroughly stuffed my face, Emma updates me on Kasey and the house, and we all sit around talking about how the weather has turned colder and how much rain we are getting. It is a normal conversation with my family and Ethan. He seems to fit right in, and it is strange to me, but I am happy he is here.

Finally, I have the nerve to ask Ethan about my car. Now that he's been here a while, it doesn't seem so intimidating, especially as he is laughing at Emma's jokes.

"Ethan, I was wondering if you might know how bad my car was?" He glances at Emma, and everyone stops talking immediately. I can see him visibly take a deep breath before he reaches over and takes my hand, but it isn't bringing me comfort this time.

"I'm afraid it might be totaled. I would almost guarantee it. All the cars involved were." The look of sadness in his eyes is unmistakable, and I am sure he has lost his car, too.

"I loved that car." The news has taken me down, but his hand squeezes mine, helping to dull the ache.

"Miranda, we will get you a new car. Insurance will cover it, and the person that hit you will cough it up for all of this. I will make sure of it." Emma is suddenly mad as she straightens up the bottom of my bed.

"Yeah, I'm sure it will be taken care of. Did the officer leave anything about the accident or maybe who it was? Or if they even have insurance. God, I hope they have insurance. Maybe they were drinking. Did anyone get hurt badly? Or did anyone die?" A shiver runs up my spine. What if someone else is hurt worse than me? What if it's a kid, or an old man that doesn't have family?

"Easy. It's okay. No one died. The man walked away. And other than you, no one else was hurt badly. You took all the impact." By the tone of his voice, I can only imagine he is upset, too. His words are tight, and I can almost feel his anger.

"Of course, he did. Asshole will pay for it all." Emma is so angry, and I know if she has anything to do with it, he will pay. She will hunt him down.

"I didn't even find out where you were in the crash and how you were hit. How's your car? And how is your head? I have been so concerned with myself that I didn't even check on you." Although it is very brief, I notice his grimace before he looks down at our joined hands, where he squeezes and closes his eyes. I hope he is okay.

"Mine is a total loss. I already know that. And my head is fine." His thumb brushes lightly over my knuckles, but he doesn't look at me.

"I'm sorry," I whisper an apology, not that it will help, but maybe he will feel a little better. And really, I am sorry he lost his car too.

"You have nothing to be sorry for. Nothing at all." He looks right into my eyes, and my heart skips a beat as I hold my breath for whatever he is going to say next. I can see in his eyes that whatever it is, is hard on him.

"I am…was…I…" He swallows hard, and the look of pain crosses his face again. "I wish it…" He is struggling, but before he can finish, my food arrives, and he quickly moves away from the bed, letting go of my hand and leaving me worried about what he is going to say. Emma and I exchange a look, but she shrugs and comes over to help me with my tray as Ethan stands looking out the window.

We sit and talk about Emma's kids, the upcoming holidays, and all the other meaningless crap that sisters talk about. Mom continues to fuss about cleaning and keeping herself busy while Dad just sits and watches TV, not saying much at all. It's nice. I need normal right now. Well, as normal as a hospital room can get.

Ethan is quiet. He has been since before my food arrived. Whatever he is worried about must still be on his mind. I have caught him looking at me a few times, but he always looks away, and he only speaks up briefly when a question is thrown his way. Otherwise, he is keeping to himself until he excuses himself to the hallway to take a call.

As soon as he is out the door, Emma starts in again. "Girl, he's so into you. Even sitting over there, all quiet, I see him watching you. Maybe it's love at first sight. Whatever it is, it's so romantic." Emma is all dreamy while I just roll my eyes.

"Emma Lynn. Control yourself. Poor Miranda has been through hell. Don't start your interrogations." My mother tries to keep my sister in check, but it never works.

"Mom. I'm not." Emma whines, making me laugh. She is the older sister, but sometimes I think she is the more immature one. I wouldn't change it, though. She is perfect the way she is.

"I have no idea what he is thinking. I barely know him. You already know what I know."

"Maybe he's a stalker then." Emma giggles, making my mother slap her arm and scold her again.

"Will you two stop fussing over her? She's a grown woman." My dad pipes up from his chair but barely looks in our direction.

"Thanks, Dad." Now, I am the one giggling.

"Admit it, though, it's strange that he's just here hanging around like he's known you forever. He even bought you a huge vase of flowers, ordered your food, and keeps asking if you needed anything. The man is infatuated with you. I think it's love already." Emma's eyebrows wiggle before she makes kissing faces, and of course, Ethan walks in at that exact moment.

"Knock it off," I growl at her, but it just makes her giggle more. Ethan pulls over the other chair and is back to sitting next to us.

"Did I miss the party?" His smile makes me feel a little lighter as he looks between us. Whatever was bothering him seems to have passed with the phone call.

"Not at all." I slap Emma's arm, but she just kept laughing. Thankfully, she does change the subject and asks Ethan what he does for a living. Which makes me almost spit water out of my nose, causing me to cough. I kick at Emma, but she is ignoring me. Witch.

"I'm in publishing." His answer is short, not much there to go on.

"Do you write?" My curiosity is now piqued.

"No. I work in an office. Not a creative bone in this body." Emma giggles again at his response, and I kick her again as he gives me that little half-smile.

"Oh, what, like newspapers or magazines?" Emma asks sweetly, trying to recover. I hate her.

"Books and some magazines. I, along with a group of editors, decide who and what we publish." For a moment, he looks proud, and it looks good on him. Really good.

"Miranda's a lawyer." Emma throws out, and Ethan looks surprised.

"Not quite yet. Working on that, though," I add quickly.

"Close enough. She's amazing. So smart and talented. And fiercely determined, too. She was always winning our arguments growing up."

"Emma, stop." I know what she is doing, and I wish she wouldn't.

"I will have to remember that." With a half grin, Ethan looks over at me, and once again, I am flooded with embarrassment. I hate her right now.

"Don't listen to her." I try.

"Oh, always listen to me, I have the good gossip." Emma blocks my kick this time, and everyone laughs, making me feel even more foolish.

"We can trade stories later. What I need now is some dinner. I will be taking Mom and Dad to get some good food," Emma announces, and before I can argue, Dad has agreed, and they give me hugs and are out the door, leaving me alone with Ethan.

"Sorry, my family makes me crazy."

"I understand, mine does, too." He reaches over and takes my hand, leaving me a bit breathless at the look on his face. "I can leave too if you want to rest." His eyes are soft as his thumb rubs over my knuckles in that now familiar way.

"No. Please don't go. I mean, you are welcome to stay, but you can go if you want." Words rush out even as I try not to be a dork.

"Nowhere else I want to be." He whispers, and my entire body warms as his eyes travel over me. Silence stretches between us until he finally clears his throat and changes the subject, asking if I need or want anything.

"No, you have done so much already." I glance over at the beautiful flowers, and when I return to his face, his grin widens, and his smile is infectious.

I can't take my eyes off him, and as he looks back at me, I feel the electricity, almost a pull between us. I can't ignore it, and I sense he feels it too, as his thumb rubs bigger, faster circles across the back of my hand and then up my wrist. My mouth is dry, too dry. I slide my tongue over my lips, causing his eyes to widen slightly at the motion. My breathing increases, and all I can focus on are his pink parted lips.

His hand moves up my arm, but I don't look away from his entrancing green gaze. His fingers move all the way to my cheek, and my body automatically leans into his warm hand against my face. His thumb traces my lower lip as it quivers under his touch. Which is so…good. Exhaling, I can't help but close my eyes. It feels so right, him here, touching me. Warmth is everywhere, and I shouldn't, but I want him to keep doing it.

Suddenly, he mumbles and moves away. My mind wants to yell no, but it is too late. As I open my eyes, he is still watching me though, and I can't look away from him.

"Ethan…" My words are barely a whisper, almost a plea. I want him, but it is so quick. I don't even know him. But somewhere deep in my soul, I feel like I already do. I open my mouth to say something, but nothing comes out. All I can do was watch him.

Those green globes shine with some unknown emotion as they stay locked on me. I can't look away, and I am not sure how I want this stranger so badly, but I do. I want to taste his lips, feel his touch. My heartbeat jumps into overdrive, and I want to ask him to kiss me. He doesn't move; in fact, he doesn't even touch me again before he clears his throat and drops his eyes. The moment is lost. Again.

"I hardly know you." My mouth decides to speak up before my brain catches up. I need to gather my wits here and control myself.

"Not much to know." His smirk tells me otherwise, and it's adorable. "I doubt that." I smile getting his grin in return. Suddenly, our eyes are searching each other's again, and this time, I reach out with my good hand and find the soft skin of his face as my body moves forward. The corners of his mouth turn up as he moves to get closer. My lips part in anticipation, but he hesitates, barely an inch away. I can't wait. I close the gap between us, and the breath leaves my body as his lips touch mine.

His hands find my face and hold me as our lips brush over each other. It is slow at first, gentle and unsure, but the growing tingle in my lips causes me to gasp. He takes it as an invitation, one I don't fight. I accept him, and every hair on my body is on end with the electricity between us. His lips are soft, but the intensity between us increases with each stroke of our tongues. Leaning in, wanting more, I am stretching to get closer, to get more, but I flinch in pain as fire races down my side. I try to fight it, but he notices and breaks the kiss gently but doesn't move far from my lips.

"Wow." His breath brushes the word over my lips as his fingers move slowly down my cheek. Yes, definitely wow! We just stay there in silence, breathing in each other until he stands, and I feel shy, not knowing what to say or do.

"I've been wanting to do that since I walked into this room." His grin is so sexy it almost makes me whimper. I'm shocked into silence, though, and I just sit and watch him for a minute before agreeing. He gives me the most beautiful smile in return, and I think I see the relief wash over him. Maybe he is nervous, too.

My hand is back in his as he makes small circles with his thumb. It is funny how comfortable I feel around him for barely knowing him. Closing my eyes, I think maybe Emma could be right. There is something here. He is gorgeous, but that isn't it. I can't even describe it; it's just…awesome. He brings me comfort, and I feel safe when he is near, even more so when he is holding my hand.

"Miranda?" I hear him say my name as more of a question.

"Mmmmhmmm?" I mumble, but I am starting to doze off. I feel so good with his kiss still fresh on my lips.

"I need to tell you something."

"Hmm?" I respond, but I feel sleep overtaking me. I hear him talking, but I can't understand his words as I drift off into dreamland.

Chapter 4

When I wake, it's very quiet, and late in the day by the absence of sunlight. I squint at the clock to see it is 7. I don't like sleeping all day; it turns me around. My eyes scan the room, and there he is, asleep in the recliner next to me. He is still here. Watching him breathe silently for a few minutes, I wonder how this happened. He is almost too perfect to be real.

My body forces me to stretch, taking my eyes off him, but then I notice the note on the table in front of me. It is from Emma; I know that handwriting:

> Hey, you were out cold when we came back
> and didn't want to wake you. Your man was
> asleep, too. I don't think he is sleeping much.
> We decided to just go crash at your place, but
> I will be back up later tonight. Call me if you
> want me to bring you anything. Love you.

My man? I look back over at Ethan again. I don't even know his last name, where he lives, works, or anything. He could be a serial killer, for all I know. Although he probably would have killed me by now. Looking at how peaceful he is, I doubt he is psycho, but he is crazy for spending days up here with someone he barely knows.

Yesterday he had on a suit, and he did say he was an editor or something, so he is at least employed. And by the size of those flowers, he isn't broke. Not that it matters, but he isn't some bum off the street, either.

My mind is reeling with all the possibilities. How is someone so hot and employed, and incredibly sweet, single? Wait, what if he isn't single? Or what if he is divorced? Does he have kids? Is he a slob? Really crazy? My mind is moving faster than I can keep up, but the doctor arrives and pulls me out of my frantic thoughts.

"Ms. Michaels, how are you feeling?" the doctor asks as he checks my head.

"Sore, but better than I was this morning." When he touches around my stitches, I flinch from the pain. "Still hurts," I say more as a plea for him to stop touching it. Moving on, he checks my arm and cast, then moves down to my ribs. It is all still very sore.

"Any new pain?" He asks as he pushes on my ribs, causing me to jump.

"Ow! That is very tender, doc." He nods and keeps exploring, mostly ignoring my grumbles of pain. I see that Ethan is now sitting up and is rubbing his face, but I try to focus on the doctor.

"Let's take a look at your eyes." He shines a light in my eyes then asks me to follow his finger. "Well, you don't look any worse this evening. I'm sure more bruises will come up, and tomorrow will probably be a worse day as far as soreness, but you should make a full recovery." His smile is reassuring.

"Well, that's good to know." Humor is my coping mechanism.

"I think we will take a look at the concussion symptoms tomorrow and decide when we can let you out of here."

"That sounds great, thank you."

"Okay, I will stop by sometime tomorrow afternoon." He looks at the bump on my head again and then the side of my face, where it is bruised. "We do need you to get up and walk before you can leave, though." He turns to the nurse who has come in and tells her what he wants, offering to try to walk again tonight once the halls quiet down. Then he excuses himself with the nurse, leaving me to process.

"So, another night in here." Ethan offers me a sleepy smile.

"Looks that way. It's okay, though. I think it is for the best."

Ethan looks a bit confused as he glances around the empty room. "Did your family not come back?"

"They did." Holding up the note for an explanation before I elaborate. "We were both sleeping, so they went back to my place to rest. Emma said she would be up later." I watch as Ethan puts the recliner all the way down and stretches.

"That's good. I heard Emma talking about kids. She has two, right?"

"She does. Sophia and Tristen. I don't get to see them often. They live about seven hours away, just outside of St.

Louis. I moved here about two years ago, and it's been tough being away from them and my parents. I was actually headed to their place for Sophia's birthday before the accident."

"No kids of your own?" His question surprises me, but it isn't unexpected. I mean, we barely know each other, and the only way to find out is to ask. "Or boyfriend?" he adds with interest.

"Um, kind of established I'm not attached to anyone. And no, no kids." Messing with my straw, I feel a bit shy.

"We did, didn't we?" He grins so freely that my face heats.

"What about you?" I can hardly stand to look at him without my breath catching. That kiss has changed me. I want more.

"No kids. No attachments. Just work." Aww, one of those guys. He is a workaholic, putting his career over relationships. That explains everything.

"What?" He cocks his head.

"Nothing." Giving him a smile, I purposely avoid his eyes.

"Not nothing. That look gives you away."

"What look?" Now, I am curious as to what look I give off.

"The way you tilt your head and furrow your brow." His grins only gets bigger.

"I do?" I must look surprised because he laughs at me.

"Yes. I have seen you do it a few times. So, what is it?" He is playful, and I am already adoring it.

Shaking my head, I don't want to answer.

"Come on." He coaxes me, and there is no way I can stop myself from telling him now. Hell, with a smirk like that, I will tell him all my secrets!

"Just wondering if you are a married to your job kind of guy?"

"Yes. You could say that." He sits back in the chair and nods as he watches me. I'm guessing that's why he is single then.

"What about your family?" I ask, hoping he will elaborate more about his life.

"Mom lives about 30 minutes from me. Dad passed a few years ago, and I have two younger sisters. One travels the world, and the other is here. Isabella is in college and lives at home with Mom. You? Other than Emma?"

"Nope, just Emma, her husband, and two kids. And my parents. I had always hoped to be married and have a bunch of kids by now, but hey, life had other plans." I wish I would not have said it the minute it is out of my mouth.

"I think that happens to all of us at least once."

"Seems to happen to me a lot." Picking at the blanket, I don't want to look up and give anything away, but Ethan talks right on past my bitterness.

"What made you move up here?" He asks as he takes out his phone.

"Work. I wanted a change." I don't want to elaborate, but he looks at me with interest.

"A change? That usually means a bad breakup." With a quick glance, he puts his phone away and gives me back his full attention.

"No, well, not prior to moving." I continue to play with the string, hoping he won't ask, but he does.

"You moved here with someone, and it didn't work?"

"Something like that." I roll my eyes. It is a miserable story that I really don't want to share as it makes me seem weak.

"Sounds like it was not your choice." His smile makes me relax, and I can tell he isn't judging.

"The move was my choice. Finding out he was here for another woman and not my happily ever after was not."

"I see. Well, it's his loss." Ethan sends me a wink, and although it is playful and sweet, we have already opened this can, so now I need to finish.

"He didn't think so. He kicked me out on the street and moved on. Literally. But hey, that was two years ago, and I'm over him." I still sound bitter.

"So, was the job worth it, at least?" He picks up on my mood and moves on.

"Most days. I mean, it was in the beginning, but some days I want more." Actually, most days, I do.

"Why is that?" He has now leaned forward out of curiosity.

"I work for Lester & Associates. I was hired as a legal assistant to work my way into a full paralegal position. However, these days, I am more like the boss's secretary. I work directly for Paul Lester now and haven't seen a courtroom in over four months. I wanted to finish college and become an actual lawyer, but that changed with my new location and job." I huff. Damn men.

"So why don't you find a new position somewhere else?" Good question.

"I like the people and Paul. Mr. Lester is a really good boss, plus the pay and benefits are amazing. It's not something I would get somewhere else just starting out. And with an apartment, student loans, and living expenses what they are here, I can't afford to start over." He nods as if he understands. Maybe his life is just as complicated.

"What about you? You said you were an editor?" He looks at me for a minute, then smiles that sweet smile.

"In a nutshell, yes." Now, I am confused.

"Not giving much away there, Mr. Editor." His laugh makes me smile as he adjusts in his seat.

"I'm a little more than just an editor. I make a lot of the major decisions at the company." A chuckle escapes, and mixed with that half-grin; it is sexy as hell.

"Like a senior manager?"

"Very senior." He now looks a bit uncomfortable, so I choose not to dig.

"Sounds like a great job. I mean, being around books all day sounds like heaven. I love to read." Smiling, I try to bring him back to the playful side again. I want this conversation to be easygoing and to learn about each other, not make it weird.

"It is. Although not as exciting as being a big-shot lawyer." He teases.

"Not a lawyer, still have lots of work to do for that. Just an assistant."

"Well, that's a mighty prestigious law firm that you work

for. I know they have some major corporate clients, and they don't just let anyone in there." Now, I am a little surprised that he knows that.

"They do. And that is the other reason I don't want to leave. I have my foot in the door there already. Paul teases me that it was my hard-headedness that got me in there, and I don't want to lose that." He nods again in understanding. I guess being upper management, he would know the firm. I wonder what company he works for. Maybe they are clients. Wouldn't that be a kicker?

"So, where is your apartment?" He stretches again in his chair, letting his long legs out in front of him. I am so thankful I moved last year from that dump I was in, so now I don't have to be embarrassed anymore.

"Arkadia Tower. On the west side." I squeak out in pride.

"I know where that is. Nice place. It's about 15-20 minutes from me." Good, he lives close.

"It is nice. I moved there last year. It's a little expensive for my space, but I like the building. And you?"

"I'm over on the north side." He doesn't elaborate, and curiosity is killing me. His jaw has tightened, so I know he doesn't want to talk about it. I have noticed he doesn't share many details of his life, but I will hold back my additional questions for now.

"So, would you like a better meal than hospital food? I think your family had the right idea to eat out. I can go get us something." He is already on his feet, ending our question session.

"I'm okay with the food here. I can't do anything with a

fork." Giggles escape me as I hold up my arm and wiggle my fingers from the tip of my cast.

"Then it's either handheld or I feed you." His wink brings back the familiar blush to my cheeks. "Really, what would you like? Anything. My treat." He moves over to sit on the edge of my bed, waiting for my answer, and I could think of a few other things I want beside food right now.

Instead of answering, though, I have a question. "Ethan, can I ask you something?" Immediately, he tenses.

"Sure."

I find the string on the blanket again. "Why are you doing all this? I mean, I'm very happy that you are here, but I don't know you, and well…I don't know; I just feel like I am dreaming." He visibly relaxes as if my question is not as crazy as I think it was. "I don't mean to be ungrateful, but I don't even know your last name, and you have barely left my side. It's weird and strange but comforting at the same time, and I'm going crazy not knowing why."

His fingers run over my blanket-covered leg, and I can feel that tingle of electricity through my body from his touch.

"It's Bradley. And honestly, I stayed with you at first because I had made a promise to you. Then, something about you drew me in, and suddenly, I found it hard to leave your side. I wanted to make sure you were all right, so I stayed longer. Even after you were awake, and I knew you were going to make it, I kept finding reasons to stay. And that smile of yours, I can't even explain it. I just don't want to go." He shrugs his shoulders as if it were not a big deal.

Umm, okay. Wow. I have no words at first. That is a lot

of admission there, and I have only known him for a few days, but I have to admit, I like him. A lot. Like more than I should. It isn't normal. It is crazy. Maybe I am as crazy as he is. My body warms again, and I look up into those beautiful eyes of his.

"I kind of like you too. I'm glad you stuck around." My hand slides over the blanket to take his, and I can feel the heat burning in my cheeks. How is he doing this to me? I have never acted so shy. Instead of a response, though, he looks away, and I think I see pain cross his face.

"Are you okay?" My voice cracks slightly, wondering if I have said something wrong. However, when he looks back at me, that smile of his is incredible, and all my worries fade away. Damn, he is gorgeous.

"Anyway, thank you. And boy, am I glad you aren't into looks. I am sure I look hideous. Last I checked, I looked like I had been run over by a truck." I try to lighten the mood as I make a face, but he doesn't laugh. "I mean, I'm not model material on a good day, but usually I look at least slightly average. Or normal. Well, as normal as I can get." This time, I giggle, and I finally see that slight smile on his lips.

"Miranda, you are much more than average. I find you very attractive." His statement shocks me, but I want to keep this conversation light for my own sanity.

"Even with stitches across my face, blood in my hair, a broken arm, and a knot the size of Texas on my head? I think you need to have your vision checked." Again, I smile but barely get a grin.

He takes my hand and gives it a squeeze. "Even looking a mess, yes. And I have perfect vision." He is so serious. I am again silent as his eyes travel over my body. "I think you are incredibly beautiful." His voice is soft, but still, he looks troubled.

"Ethan, are you okay?" I ask, but he doesn't look at me this time, just down at our joined hands.

"Miranda, I need to tell you something." And here it comes. I brace myself, but he doesn't speak right away, and my stupid mouth keeps running to fill the space.

"Please just tell me you are not married. Or gay. Or worse, belong to a traveling circus." I am teasing, and this time, he actually laughs.

"No, no, and definitely not." I give an exaggerated exhale and act relieved.

"Thank goodness, I hate clowns." I am dramatic and he laughs freely, making me feel better.

"Okay, if it's not those things, then I'm cool." I give him a goofy smile, and he laughs again as he shakes his head at me.

"I'm glad you have a great sense of humor." He chuckles again.

"More than I should sometimes." I can't help but laugh at myself. It is one of the only things that have gotten me through the bad days.

The nurse takes that moment to come in with meds and instructions to walk, ending our conversation, but I am happy to see it is Nancy.

"Keep that thought. We will finish this conversation when I am done." I give him a pointed look, and his hands raise in defense as he agrees.

"I will step out while you get up and ready. Think about dinner." He points back at me as he leaves the room.

"Quite the boyfriend you have there. Has he even left your side?" Nancy's laugh is sweet as she helps me out of bed.

"Not my boyfriend. And no, he really hasn't." We exchange a look, which makes me blush as she shakes her head. I'm surprised my cheeks haven't caught fire with all this blushing!

"Young love is always the best." She announces as she puts a belt around my waist, making me flinch.

"Not love either. Funny thing is, I just met him. He was in the same car accident and held my hand to keep me calm until the paramedics arrived. I didn't even know his last name until about 20 minutes ago. He was just there, like an angel. I was terrified, but he made me feel safe. We just clicked." Biting back my smile so it doesn't take over my face, I try not to be giddy.

"Well, sweetie, that is how love starts. It just hits you in the head one day." Her belly laugh causes me to giggle. Maybe she is right. And with sweet thoughts, I venture into the hallway for my walk.

Chapter 5

One complete circuit around the floor, and I am exhausted, but I make it! It feels like Ethan is hovering the entire way, but it is nice to have him here with words of encouragement. Nancy just laughs at him, though, as he worries each time I pause. I even catch her wink at me a few times when he is "helping." He is adorable and the main reason I am able to finish.

I can hear the commotion before we even get back into my room. "My family," I announce as we reach the door.

"I'll wait out here." Ethan brushes my arm with his fingertips, causing goosebumps to pop up everywhere.

"Only for a minute, then you come back in." My response earns his super sweet smile, which makes him even more gorgeous than he already is. While I am returning that smile, I notice he is almost a full foot taller than me. And muscular. Wow, I never noticed before how tight this sweater is across his chest. Damn. Nancy nudges me, and I realize I am staring. Oops.

"Sorry," I whisper as she guides me through the door.

"Honey, I am older but not blind. He is definitely a looker," she laughs.

"Aunt Rana!" My niece jumps up as soon as we clear the door. I immediately hold up my hand to halt her from knocking me over with her hug. She starts to cry as she looks me over.

"I'm okay, Soph. Promise. Just need you to be gentle." Emma pulls her into her arms, and I notice Tristen and Joe in the back. I say hello to everyone and notice more flowers and balloons adorn the room. Yep, my family.

"Okay, family, I need you to all step out while I get her settled in; then, you can give her all the hugs you want," Nancy announces. Thankfully, they listen and file out past us into the hallway.

"I left you new PJs on the bed," Emma whispers as she passes, and I am thankful she always takes care of me.

"Bathroom first?" I ask Nancy, and she agrees.

"Of course. We can get you freshened up and put you in some clean clothes."

"I would love that. Can I wash my face if I keep it away from the stitches?"

"Yes. Let me help you. We will have you cleaned up in no time."

Nancy gently washes my face, and I am stunned at how much blood is still there. She brushes my hair and wipes me down from head to toe. I feel like a child but am happy to get clean, so I don't protest too much. In the bag that Emma left is a sleep shirt, underwear, lotion, and a pack of hair ties.

"God love my sister," I announce and hand a hair tie to Nancy as she softly pulls my hair up into a ponytail.

"Thank you for helping me," I acknowledge through a foamy mouth of toothpaste. I had no idea how much I needed it. And to finally be able to wash my hands, well, one of them and my fingertips, is almost tear-inducing. It feels so good to be up and clean.

"My pleasure." Nancy's smile is warm and motherly.

"I feel so much better."

"Just wait until you can take a shower. It will feel like heaven." Her laugh makes me want to hug her.

"Now, let's get you back in bed and get some meds. I am sure you are exhausted, and you have a whole lot of people waiting for you."

"Not too bad, but yes, I am anxious to see them all."

Once I am back in bed, in comes the mob. Mom immediately starts fussing over me, and both kids sit on either side of the bed, asking a million questions before they even give me a chance to answer.

"Will you two let her be for a minute," Emma scolds, but not without a smile. I think she is happy to have them here, too.

"Leave them be. I am so happy you are all here." And I am. My family always makes me feel better, even if they drive me crazy.

"Where is Ethan? Did he not come back in?" I look around for him, hoping he didn't leave with all the commotion.

"He went to grab you guys dinner. He said to tell you he would be back shortly." Emma is searching through another bag she brought in and pulls out some Sharpies in various colors. "To sign your cast," she announces as she hands them off to the kids.

"Oh. Okay. Well, thank you for the info and the markers." I laugh as Sophie pulls my arm onto the table and starts to work.

We talk for a while, and I tell the kids what happened, as much as I can remember, while Sophie continues to draw. They ask more questions than I have answers to, but it doesn't bother me. I know it will all work out.

"Emma tells me the man that hit you walked away unhurt. Is he in jail?" Joe asks.

"I don't know anything more than that about him. I have to call the police officer and give my statement, but I haven't felt like it. I just remember a flash of gray and then being out of it most of the time."

"Well, I hope they lock him up. Did you call your insurance agent? Maybe you should get a lawyer." Mom adds in her two cents.

"Yes, I called them, gave them my information and the report number, and they are handling it. I also talked to my boss, Paul, earlier, and he said whatever I needed was at my disposal. I don't know if I will need a lawyer; I hope not, but Paul already assured me he would take care of it." Mom shakes her head at the information, and I just wish this was all over.

"His insurance, assuming he has it, should pay for your medical bills, loss of wages, and a new car. If they don't, you lawyer up right away. You get everything that is coming to you," Joe adds.

"Okay, everyone, I know you are trying to help, but I don't know much yet. I just want to heal up. I am too exhausted to deal with it all right now."

"Honey, we are all just concerned for you. This was a serious accident." Mom pats my leg.

"I know, and I appreciate it. I will get it all sorted out. Right now, I have to rest and worry about getting out of here."

"Miranda, I can stay up here as long as you need me." Mom now has my hand in hers.

"Thanks, Mom." I just hold her hand as she brushes the loose hair from my face.

"I don't want you alone." Mom's sweet moment is over, and she is fussing again.

"I'm fine. Really, I look worse than I feel. And I'm sure in a day or two, I will be back up and running." At least, I hope so.

Emma and Mom are discussing who can stay until when and what I will need like I am not even in the room. Sophie is drawing out a pretty design around the end of my cast and up around my thumb, and Tristen is back to being engrossed in his phone. The silence is killing me.

"Emma, where are you guys all planning to stay? Did you book a hotel? You know you are all welcome to crash at my place. The sofa pulls out, and I still have the air mattress. I know it's small, but it's free." I don't mind them being there; at least the cat will not be alone.

"We will find somewhere. Let us worry about that." Mom brushes me off.

"I can call that little Comfort Inn place we stayed at last time. It was nice." Emma offers.

"That is like 45 minutes away with no traffic. No. Seriously, you guys don't need to spend the money; just stay at my place."

"Don't fight with me. And what happens if you come home tomorrow? You will need your space. Besides, we won't all fit there. Just let us call them." Mom waves me off and I know it's a losing battle with her.

I want to argue, but there is a knock at the door, and it is Ethan with a literal cart full of bags. And I can only guess by the amazing smell that it is food. My mouth is watering, and I don't even care what it is.

Ethan leaves the cart on the other side of the room and comes over to my bed with that sweet smile plastered on his face.

"I brought dinner for everyone. Hope you all are hungry." Ethan's beautiful green eyes are shining down at me.

"That is very sweet of you to do. Thank you." Returning his smile makes me feel all flushed again.

"My pleasure." His eyes are fixed on mine for what seemed like minutes. Then something passes between us, and I watch his eyes widen slightly as if he feels it, too.

"No room," Emma announces loudly from next to me as she hangs up the phone, effectively breaking our trance.

"Nothing available at my place either." Mom pouts as she puts down her phone.

"I have another here." Emma clicks something on her phone and puts it to her ear as Ethan looks at me, a bit confused.

"They are trying to find a hotel for the night, even though I offered my place," I explain and get a look from my mother.

"Mrs. Michaels, there is a convention this weekend, and everything local will be full. Let me make a call. I have a few friends that can pull some strings. Give me just a minute." Ethan gives me a wink and takes out his phone as we all just stare at each other while he makes his call.

"Mark, Ethan Bradley. I need the big suite for the next few days. Can you make that happen?" There is silence while he waits. When he looks up and around the room, he asks my sister, "Six of you, correct?"

"Yes, but we don't need a suite." She tries, but he shakes his head no and answers the man on the phone, ignoring her response.

"Yes, six. Perfect...Yes...Everything...Michaels Family...Thank you." He hangs up and smiles like he just solved all the world's problems. I am not sure what he has just done but watching him do it was sexy as hell.

"Taken care of. I have a suite for you at the Ritz-Carlton." He explains, and my mom immediately looks panicked as she glances at Emma. I know exactly what she is thinking because I am thinking it, too. It is way too expensive. Ethan must also understand her look as he smiles at my mother.

"Mrs. Michaels, it is all taken care of. There is nothing to worry about." He nods at her, and she starts to relax but gives a glance toward me instead.

"Thank you, Ethan, that is very kind of you, but we can take care of the cost." Mom tries.

"Nonsense. I have it covered. In this town, it helps to know the right people. Now, who is hungry? I brought enough for everyone. That is if you like Mexican." We all agree that it sounds great, but I can still see the worry on my mom's face. I will just tell him I will cover it later, then she will be ok.

Ethan pulls the containers out of the bags and announces, "I have tacos, chicken quesadillas, nachos with beef, salsa and chips, the works. Help yourselves." He grins proudly. The kids jump up without hesitation, but Emma stops them.

"Stop right there, you two. Mind your manners. Miranda first." Emma snaps, and the kids step back to wait.

"Aunt Rana, can I make you a plate?" Sophia asks politely.

"Yes, please. It smells amazing. Thank you." I adore her so much.

"Thank you, Ethan, so much." Sophia surprises him with a hug, but he gives it right back. I reach my hand out and take his, giving it a squeeze to get his attention.

"Thank you." I mouth up at him.

"You are welcome." He squeezes back, and I notice that hint of a grin that I like so much.

Emma and Sophia dish out the food, and he even thought to bring bottled water. He squeezes my hand again, and I exhale.

"My hero again," I whisper.

"Eat," he says as Sophia puts down a plate for me, trying to ignore my statement.

And we do. We eat and talk, and I almost forget I am in the hospital. It is so nice to just be with all of them. Nancy has even helped herself to a taco after giving me meds. I notice Ethan watching me throughout the meal, and it makes me feel special. When I bite back a small smile, he gives me another wink as I shove the rest of my taco in my mouth and giggle in embarrassment.

After we are done, Emma cleans up the mess and bags up the trash as I lean back in my bed, full and happy, with a huge yawn.

"Okay, folks, I think someone needs to get some rest," Emma announces.

"You guys don't have to go so soon." I have had a good time with them today, but Emma is having no part of it as she packs up her kids.

"All you need to do is check in at the front desk. The suite will be under Michaels. If you have any problems, Emma has my number. Just call me." Ethan shakes my dad's hand before my mom smothers him in a hug. Joe and the kids exchange their goodbyes, and I get tons of hugs and kisses. Mom tells me she will be back bright and early as Emma kisses my cheek and whispers, "Keep him." But I can only shake my head at her as they leave.

"Well, nothing like meeting the rest of the family after knowing me for all of a few days," I tell Ethan, trying to keep the mood light.

"You have a great family," he answers as he falls into the recliner in front of me.

"Thank you for all of this. The food, the hotel, and your support. You really are too much." I swing my legs out from under the cover and sit up to stretch and see him better.

"I will be paying you back for the hotel. I know that wasn't cheap." I can only imagine how much a suite at the Ritz costs. Probably more than I make in a month.

"First, you are welcome. Second, I like your family. Third, you will do no such thing. Fourth, it really is my pleasure. And fifth, where do you think you are going?" He raises his eyebrow in question as he looks at my legs that are hanging off the bed.

"Ethan. You barely know me. I can't let you pay for my family's hotel stay. I'm sure that place is expensive!" I scoot to the edge of the bed.

"Miranda, I might not know you well yet, but I will. And I can help your family and you while you are in the hospital. I have connections, and they come in handy." His grin says more than he does.

"Ethan, I can't let you pay for that. I do appreciate you not making a huge deal when my mom nearly passed out at the mention of the Ritz, but I can pay you for it." Ethan sits up on the edge of his seat and looks at me with a sudden seriousness that nearly takes my breath away.

"Please, don't argue, just let me do this." His eyes plead with me.

"Ethan," I say his name while I get ready to argue, but the look he gives me next makes me not want to argue, so I bite my bottom lip to keep my mouth shut.

"Fine."

"Thank you." He exhales loudly. I wasn't in the mood to argue anyway. And when I stand, he stands also.

"Bathroom," I answer his earlier question as I start to move slowly. "And no, I can do it on my own." I glance at him, but he still follows me to the door.

"You are welcome." He gives me one of those bright smiles as I turn at the door and shoo him away.

It feels good to walk and move freely, even though I am still stiff and ach in places I didn't know could hurt. When I finally come back out, he is relaxed back in the chair, watching me.

"I do appreciate it all," I add as I make my way back to bed.

"I'm happy to know that." His eyes droop closed, and he looks so calm but very tired sitting there.

"Why don't you go home and rest?" I offer.

"I'm good."

"Ethan, you are exhausted." I try to be a little more forceful.

"No, I am fine. Lay down and rest." His eyes are closed, but that grin plays on his lips.

"Go home and rest," I say one more time.

"You just have to have the last word, don't you?" He shakes his head.

"No." I can't help the smile that spreads across my face.

"Miranda?"

"Yes?"

"Lay down and rest, and I do not want to hear another word." I can hear the humor in his voice, which makes me giggle, but I don't dare speak. I like it when he is playful.

My phone buzzing wakes me up from my nap, and when I open my eyes, it is dark in the room. It takes me a minute to adjust before I pick up the phone from the table and see it is Emma.

"Hey?" I am hoarse from sleep, but I hope they made it to their room okay. I glance over and notice Ethan is gone, making me a bit sad.

"Miranda, we are in the Presidential Suite! This place is huge! I mean, HUGE. We have food in the fridge, a fully stocked bar, wine, soda, the works. Everything. And it's all included. We have special cards and even had a guy bring up all our bags and show us how to work everything in the room. You wouldn't even believe this place!" She takes a breath, so I take my chance to talk.

"Wow, Em, that's awesome."

"I know. I am sending you pictures. I don't know who this guy is, but marry him now." She is laughing, and I can hear my mother agreeing in the background.

"Em, slow down. I don't even know his full name." I am dizzy from her conversation and excitement already.

"Miranda, I don't care. He's awesome. I want to jump on the bed! It's so fluffy!" I laugh at the thought of her doing it. I know she would if Mom wasn't there with her.

"Make sure you give him a huge kiss and a thank you from us!" She adds, and I think she really is jumping on the bed now.

"I will let him know your appreciation." I am so happy as I hear everyone talking and laughing in the background. I'm so thankful Ethan did this for them. I know being here has to be stressful for them, too.

"I hope you guys have a great evening there."

"Oh, Miranda, you have no idea. I can't even explain it."

"Pictures. I will wait for them."

"You got it. Okay, I know you were sleeping, so go back to it. I need to go soak in this massive tub." We laugh some more, and I look up to see Ethan standing in the doorway, backlit by the hallway lights.

"OKAY, love you all."

"Love you more. Seriously, kiss him like three hundred times."

"I will. Night."

"Night!" Emma calls out. With a shake of my head, I hang up, and Ethan walks back into the room.

"I was worried you left without saying goodbye." Why am I so embarrassed every time I open my mouth to talk to him? Ugh.

"Of course not. Just went for a coffee." He holds up the cup as proof as he sits back in the recliner.

"Ethan James Bradley," he announces with a grin.

"What?" I am sure I look as confused as I feel because he chuckles loudly.

"You told your sister you didn't even know my full name. It's Ethan James Bradley."

Oh.

"You heard that." I am totally embarrassed.

"I did. And by the blush on your cheeks, I'm sure it was quite the conversation."

Oh, if he only knew.

"She was thanking you for the suite. Apparently, it is impressive." I shift uncomfortably as he chuckles again.

"It is, and she is very welcome." He sips his coffee, and just the sight of his lips curved around that cup turns me on.

Instead of going back to sleep, we end up talking about nothing for another hour until I am wiped out.

"Why don't you go home and get some rest? I'm sure you are tired of sitting here. It's almost 11, and I'm going to crash anyway."

"Are you sure? I don't mind staying if you want me to." Ethan moves from the chair to the edge of my bed, and instantly, my body warms with a need to touch him.

"I'm sure. Go. I will be fine." I watch as he gives me the sexiest grin, and I want to take it back.

"I'm sure you will be. I'm not sure I want to go, though." And with that, he leans in and kisses me.

The moment our lips touch, I feel my entire body come alive. Again, my breath leaves my lungs as his hand finds my face, and he gently holds my head to him while his tongue caresses my lips. Instinctively, my lips part, and he accepts my invitation and deepens the kiss. My hand moves to his shoulder, and I use it to steady myself as I lean into him more, causing him to groan at my touch. Slowly, I slide my hand up into his hair, and it is so silky and soft, just as I had imagined it would be. I feel his other hand on my back, pulling me closer, his fingertips like fire through the coolness of my pajamas.

My body craves him. His touch, his kiss, they make me feel alive like nothing before. He has my entire being responding in ways it hasn't in almost two years. I want him. I want him so desperately. I don't care where we are or who he is. I just want more. I need more.

The kiss deepens as his hand travels up my side, and I flinch as my ribs protest his touch, making him immediately stop.

"Are you okay? I did not mean to hurt you." He is inches from my lips, and it is too far.

"I'm fine. Please." I lean forward to reconnect us, but he stops me with a gentle brush of his thumb over my cheek.

"As much as I want to continue this, and trust me, I do, I think a hospital bed is not the place." He grazes my lips briefly with his and then leans back so I can look into his beautiful green eyes. My fingers run over his stubble, and he leans into my touch this time. Even the softness of his cheek and the roughness of the hair there are just as I have imagined.

"Your eyes are incredible." I didn't mean to say that out loud, but it causes him to grin.

"Yours aren't too bad either." He whispers as his eyes lock onto mine.

"They are just brown."

"And yet, so special. I think they might just hold the answers to all of life's questions." He is serious again, and it makes me blink in surprise.

"Or it could be a lot of secrets," I add with a giggle, trying to break the trance he has on me.

"Could be. Might have to kiss them out of you." He brushes my nose with his, and my body wants to arch back into him. He makes me feel like a giddy little girl with his sweet words. And we won't even talk about what his touch does to me.

"When you get out of here, I would like to take you on a date. To a dinner that you have to eat with a knife and fork." He winks at me but doesn't move too far away as his fingers tug at a loose piece of hair that has fallen from my ponytail. He then pushes it back behind my ear and runs his finger down the side of my face causing a shiver to run down my spine.

"I would like that. In fact, I might even be up for bowl-ing, or who knows, maybe ice skating." I am giggling again, and I hate it, but it makes him laugh.

"Maybe we should stick to safer things, like a movie." His response makes me laugh harder.

"What fun is that? I'm sure I could kick ass in left-handed bowling!" We laugh until it hurts, and I can hardly breathe. He is hilarious tonight.

"Well, Ms. Michaels, I think I should add to this work of art you have going on here on your arm. Then I am going to tuck you in and let you rest." He takes the five Sharpies off the side table and holds them up.

"Hmm, what's your favorite color?" His question comes with that sexy grin.

"Red."

"Blue it is." He pulls the blue Sharpie out, and I laugh hard again. He turns my arm around to find a good spot, then lifts it so it is pointed up, with my elbow on the table. He shoots me a sexy grin before he starts to draw on the inside of my arm, above my elbow, his eyes shining with mischief.

"Don't watch me." He grins as his fingers brush the skin on my arm at the top of the cast, making me shiver.

Ethan is concentrating so hard, but I sneak a peek, even though I can't see what he is doing.

"No peeking." He growls deeply, and my body reacts to the sound. He is going so slowly that my arm is starting to ache from holding it up, but I don't dare move. Watching him is worth it.

"Done." He finally announces as I tilt my arm to look.

"It's so cute!" There on my cast is a little drawing of a guy made from boxes, hugging my cast. One hand has a little flower, and there is a little heart by his signature. Ethan. I love it. It is perfect. He is perfect.

"I love it." The smile on my face is so wide it almost hurts.

"I do not draw much, but he always makes me smile." He taps my cast with a chuckle.

"Thank you, it's perfect." I beam and he nods slightly, but his eyes catch mine, and we watch each other for two long breaths.

"Okay, if I don't leave now, I might not leave at all." He reaches up and tucks that same bit of my hair behind my ear.

"I wish I wasn't in this mess right now. I don't want you to go." The words come out in a whisper.

"Me either. I need to, though." He pulls me into another electric-filled kiss. His hands on my shoulders, and mine on his biceps. His lips almost burn mine with the heat between us. It doesn't last nearly long enough as he reluctantly pulls away and stands while I look over his beautiful face, wondering what the hell I am doing.

"Goodnight, Miranda." He bends down and puts a kiss on the top of my head.

"Goodnight, Ethan." My tongue swipes over my tingling lips as he walks toward the door. When he reaches it, he turns and holds up his hand in a wave, then he is gone. The content smile on my face is not going away anytime soon. I am so lucky to have met him. He is amazing. I say a little thank you to the ceiling, then curl up and drift off to sleep.

Chapter 6

The next morning, the nurse wakes me up just after 5, fussing over my machine that seems not to be working right. It's too early, and I know I won't be able to go back to sleep, so I just lay there, letting my mind drift back to the blissful moments I shared with Ethan. Ethan. I wonder what he is doing this morning.

I manage to rest a little before breakfast arrives. Afterward, I take a walk, clean up, and settle into the recliner. It is barely 8 am when I notice my phone light up with a text from Ethan.

Morning Beautiful. I will be up around 11 am.
I have some business to attend to.

Morning! Take your time. I will be here all day.

He called me beautiful. My heart fills just a little bit more. I wait for another text, but nothing more comes. Before I can be sad about it, my family arrives and starts telling me about the hotel room and the wonderful night they had. I had a great night, too, but I don't want to tell them all about it yet.

After what seems like hours of chatting, exhaustion hits me hard. The kids are happy to leave and go back to swimming at the hotel, but Mom decides to stay with me. After she ushers everyone out, I thankfully fall asleep quickly while she reads in the chair.

My phone ringing wakes me up a short time later. Against my body's protests, I roll over and pick it up. "Hello?" I answer sleepily.

"Ms. Miranda Michaels?" a man asks.

"Yes. Who is this?"

"Officer Daniels, ma'am. I was one of the officers at your accident on Friday, and I need to get your statement and ask you a few questions. Is now a good time?"

"Of course." I move the bed up to a sitting position to better focus. Mom looks at me expectantly and I tell her it's an officer about the accident, and she nods, returning to her book.

"Thank you for taking the time to speak with me. I know this is a difficult time, but I hope you are recovering."

"I am, thank you. And, of course, I am sorry I didn't call you sooner."

"It is understandable. Now, Ms. Michaels, do you re-member anything about the accident?" he asks. My brain goes back to that time, but I don't remember much more than the pain.

"Please, call me Miranda. And no, I don't remember very much at all. The doctor told me the airbag and impact knocked me out quickly. I know that it was raining, and the light had changed to green. I started to go through the intersection when I saw a flash of gray out the right-side passenger window, and my car was hit. I passed out or was knocked out right after that and don't remember more than bits and pieces." I wish I knew more.

"Are you sure the light was green?" the officer asks, and I want to yell that, of course, I knew. I am a very observant driver!

"Yes, I am 100% sure. The other car definitely ran a red light." I answer rather grumpily. "The other driver better not be thinking this is my fault," I add.

"No, ma'am. We just want to make sure we have your side in the report," he says politely.

"I'm sorry, it's just been a miserable few days here, and I did learn that the other driver apparently walked away, which makes me a little bitter," I try to apologize.

"I can understand that."

"Honestly, I don't remember much at all, but maybe Ethan Bradley can help. He was in the accident also and stayed with me until the paramedics arrived. I think he saw everything, though I'm not sure where he was, but he was hit, too. I have his contact info if you need it." I offer to help.

"Yes, Ms. Michaels, we know who he is. He has already given a statement and is cooperating with us," he answers but seems to stumble through his words. What did Ethan tell them? Was someone else hurt? My mind races. With my background, I know the officer will not tell me anything, though.

"I wish I could be more help, but I didn't see the other driver. Ethan told me that it was a man, and he walked away, but I didn't see him or even the car. That's all I know." The officer is quiet and doesn't answer. "Are you still there?" I hear him clear his throat.

"Um, Ms. Michaels, Ethan Bradley was the other driver."

My heart stops dead, and the room darkens around me as his words repeat in my head. The room starts to spin, and my mind gets fuzzy as tears run down my face. My mom shakes me and calls my name, but I can't even speak. The phone drops from my hand, and I hear her talking, but I can't process it. Not Ethan, no. He's my hero, not the villain. My world goes gray as it all makes sense now. My heart is shattered.

After a few deep breaths, I compose myself enough to finish the conversation and hold out my hand for the phone. "She's right here, hold on," Mom says into the phone and hands it back to me.

"I'm sorry. I felt really dizzy and lost my focus." My heart is racing, and I can hardly breathe, but I need to finish this. I struggle through the last of his questions, hoping to make it through before my heart breaks completely.

"Okay, I think that is all that I need from you. Please get some rest. I will get this report completed today. And if it helps, Mr. Bradley has taken full responsibility for the accident and is cooperating with us. Thank you, Ms. Michaels, for your time. Have a nice rest of the day, and I hope you mend quickly."

"Thank you." I don't even know what to say. I can only hang up the phone.

"Miranda, what is it? What's wrong? Do I need to call

the nurse?" Mom is holding my chin, forcing me to look at her.

"I'm fine."

"No, you are not fine. What did he say? Your eyes glazed over, and all the color left your face." I cannot even look at her, knowing what I know. He was the cause. My sweet, beautiful Ethan. It was him.

"MIRANDA!" Mom snaps, and I look back up at her. "That's it." She reaches over and calls the nurse.

"I'm okay." I try to say again, but the room is spinning. How is this possible? I start to shiver, and the next thing I know, the nurse is there, checking my vitals and asking me questions while another nurse is putting warm blankets on me.

"Miranda, how are you feeling? What happened? Can you talk to me?" The nurse is in my face.

"I don't know." My voice sounds distant and shaky. How can I tell anyone this and break them, too? As I start to cry again, Mom takes my hand, but it feels all wrong, and it brings more tears, not comfort. It takes all that I have not to lay down and curl into a ball. I can hear my mom speaking with the nurse, telling them I was on the phone and then went pale and almost passed out, but I don't care. I don't care about anything right now.

"Miranda, did he tell you something bad? Sweetheart, you need to answer us." Mom is now rubbing my arm to calm me.

"Yes. The other driver..." I can't even say it.

"Alright, shhh." Another nurse is there, talking over me,

and that makes three of them. I'm still shivering and can't focus. My heart is aching. I kissed him. I wanted him. He didn't even tell me. All those moments he could have told me.

"I'm tired. I want to sleep." It's all I can manage to blurt out as I roll away from the nurses.

"Okay, just lay still. We have some medicine on the way. It will help you relax." One of the nurses tells me as I close my eyes against the pain. It's so much worse than the accident.

"No more visitors. Just you, Mom. No one else. Not today." I whisper as I try to hold back the sobs.

"Okay, we will take care of that. Miranda, I'm going to give you meds in your IV that will work right away. Just relax." The nurse's calm voice washes over me before the warmth enters my arm from the IV.

Mom squeezes my hand, making more tears roll down my face. How could he not tell me? I just don't understand. I try but sleep never comes. I am completely heartbroken.

I'm not sure how much time has passed, but the tears have stopped for now. Mom is now in the chair across the room, on the phone with my sister. I wish I could tell her, but I just can't bring myself to do it. Admitting it out loud will make it real, and I already feel so defeated. He was my hero. My savior. My comfort in the darkness. And now it makes sense. He did it because he was guilty. A single tear slips from under my closed eye, and I try to force myself to sleep.

There is a knock on the door, but I don't move. I don't care. I just want to be alone. I hear my mom open it, and I try not to listen, but I can't miss it.

"I'm sorry, she doesn't want to see anyone right now." Mom announces.

"Can you tell her it's me? I'm sure she will." It's Ethan. A whole new set of tears rock me, and my heart breaks more.

"I'm sorry, Ethan. Something happened, and she's not well." Mom tries to explain, but she has no idea just what it is. I haven't told her. I can't.

"Is she okay? Is she sick? What can I do to help?" I can hear the concern in his voice, and it only tears me up more. Damn him.

"She was on the phone with an officer about the accident. Something about the other driver, I don't know. She just went pale and got sick. The nurse had to give her something to relax. She's resting and doesn't want visitors."

I can't hear what he says because it's muffled, but I don't care. Nothing he can say will change it now.

The door opens, and I hear footsteps before Mom is at my side.

"Miranda, are you awake? Ethan wants to talk to you." Her voice sounds strained.

"I don't want to talk to him. Ever." My face is soaked with tears as I move it back into the pillow.

"Please, Miranda, can I explain?"

My body freezes. He's here.

"Please." He is almost pleading, but I can't. Not after all this time.

"Go away." I keep my eyes closed tightly and will the tears not to fall. His hand brushes over my arm, and I jerk it away. "Leave. I have nothing to say to you." I choke out as my body starts to shiver again, and I pull the blankets up closer to my chin. I don't want to look at him for fear it will destroy me.

"All I can say is that I'm sorry and ask for your forgiveness. For all of it. I have been sorry from the moment I saw your beautiful face and held your hand in mine. It was wrong, and I should have told you, but I couldn't. I wanted to, please, believe me, I did. I swear, all I have ever wanted to do was make you better. Please, Miranda." His fingers brush over my hair, and I turn my head away. I can't let him see me cry.

Quietly, his hand runs down my arm to my hand, where he takes it and squeezes it. A sob escapes as he pulls my hand up and kisses it.

"There are no words that I can say to show just how sorry I am. I know I was wrong, but I hoped…I just thought I had more time to tell you. I really am sorry, Miranda. Please let me fix this." After a moment of me not responding, he asks me again. "Miranda, please. Don't shut me out. I can fix this." He tries again, but I can only cry more.

"I'm sorry. So very sorry." His voice is strained and full of emotion, but I can't. He lied to me. And after I don't respond, he gives my hand one more squeeze. When I don't squeeze back, he lets go of my hand, and I hear him walk out of the room. My poor heart doesn't have anything left, and I feel like my chest will cave in any second.

"Miranda." Mom is at my side immediately and takes my hand. "Ethan told me. I'm so sorry, honey." She strokes my hair, but it is of no comfort.

"He almost killed me. He feels guilty; that is what all this is. Probably some sort of game, so I wouldn't sue him. I was starting to have feelings for him. Mom, I kissed him!" The tears roll down my face uncontrollably now.

"Oh, honey, he really does like you. Maybe he was wrong not..."

"MAYBE!?" I cut her off. I am fuming mad.

"OKAY, he was wrong not to tell you, but maybe he is telling you the truth. Have you ever considered that he didn't have to stay here? He could have taken off once you were in the ambulance?" She tries to soothe me.

"Not buying it. And whose side are you on anyway?" I snap and then regret it. "Sorry, Mom. I just need to sleep and forget about him." I apologize again and roll over as the tears fall hard on my pillow.

Mom wakes me for dinner, and I realize the day is almost over. I would roll back over and sleep, but my stomach is growling, and I need to use the bathroom. Mom helps me and then tucks me back in while I wait for food. I have no energy to even talk to her, even though I can see she has so much to say. Thankfully, she leaves me be.

The food on the tray in front of me doesn't even look appetizing, and after I push it around for a while, she tells me that Dad came by for a bit. She didn't think I would mind. And a florist was here and delivered more flowers. She points out the vase of pink roses.

"They are from Ethan." Her smile tells me she doesn't hate him as much as I do, and that angers me more.

"There is also a very pretty plant from your office. And Aunt Cindy and the girls sent some flowers, too."

My room is starting to look like a florist shop. The windowsill, the two side tables, and the extra bed table are all covered. Plus, the huge plant on the floor and all the balloons.

"I may have Emma take some of these to my apartment tomorrow. It's a little much." I groan.

"Everyone just wants to show you they love you." Mom brushes my hair off my face, which does little to help my mood.

My phone has vibrated a few times, so I finally look at it, seeing fifteen texts and a few missed calls. Emma, Sophia, Emma, Paul, my best friend Nicole, and of course two from Ethan. I hover, deciding if I want to read them, and of course, my finger moves on its own.

> *I know you hate me. I am truly sorry. I should have told you.*

Delete.

> *No matter what you think of me, I really do like you.*

He likes me. Do I even care now? Before I can help myself, I respond.

> *I don't know what to think. You could have told me the numerous times I asked about the other driver. I'm not sure what game you are playing. Do you really like me, or is it just some scam to keep me from suing you? For the record, I wouldn't. Still won't. Don't fight me with regard to what insurance needs to cover, and I will walk away and leave you be.*

As soon as I hit send, I stare at the message I wrote. It sounds so cold.

He answers right away.

> *I promise this is not any type of scam to get you to not sue me. I wanted to be there with you. I still do, more than anything. I know I should have told you. I wanted to. And all of this is my fault. You won't worry about anything. I promise to take care of it all. It's all on me.*

I re-read it as another text comes in.

> *I do not want you to walk away.*

Damn it. I want a fight. I want to hate him. I want him to be heartless and evil and make me want to ignore him!

> *I appreciate all that you have done, but I'm done. It was all based on a lie. I can forgive most things, but lying is not one of them. Please do not contact me. I am deleting your number.*

As soon as it's sent, I feel an immediately loss. At that moment, I realize just how much I like him, and it is a devastating feeling. He made me feel life again. No. He's a liar. I can't. I won't. I will never do that again. He doesn't deserve me.

> *I am sorry, Miranda. I hope one day you will forgive me. I will not be deleting yours. I do not want to ever forget you.*

What? Seriously, why does he have to be all sweet? I groan.

"Everything okay?" Mom catches me off guard.

"Yes. Just answering some texts." All I can do is grumble and keep it all to myself. I don't want discussions or lectures. I just want to be left alone.

The evening passes with nothing new. The doctor won't let me go home, and it sucks, but it is what it is at this point. I send my mom back to the hotel so I can be alone. I miss Ethan, and it's miserable. Nancy is back on, and I'm thankful for a friendly face.

"I heard what happened earlier. You doing okay?" Nancy asks as she checks on me.

"Yes. I found out who the other driver was. It was Ethan."

Nancy looks startled at my response. "You mean that sweetheart of a man that is head over heels for you?"

"Yes, the very same. I don't ever want to see him again." I expect Nancy to agree with me, but instead, she sits on the bed and lays her hand on my leg.

"Are you sure about that? He seems to care a lot about you. The way he fusses around here after you. And I'm pretty sure I saw that same glint in your eyes for him."

"I'm sure he was feeling guilty," I grumble.

"That wasn't guilt I saw, but I'm just a silly old lady." She pats my arm, and I see the compassion on her face.

"Well, let's get you up and see how you do. Maybe you can go home tomorrow. Home always feels better." She gets me up, but I'm still cranky.

"Somehow, I doubt my lonely house is going to do much for my mood, but maybe you are right."

"Honey, I'm always right." She winks, and that makes me feel slightly better. She knows it, too, as she smiles brightly and attaches my walking belt.

After we have made a lap, I'm feeling more stable, so I ask for a second lap. It feels great to be moving, and when we are done, I want to celebrate, but my room is empty. I sent everyone home, and my heart aches.

"I'm a horrible person, aren't I? I sent everyone home so I could pout in peace, and now I'm alone when I want to celebrate." I slump on the bed.

"I'm here, honey. You want some ice cream?" She smiles brightly.

"Yes. Chocolate. Can you have some with me?"

"Of course!" She scurries out of the room, returning shortly after with two cups of ice cream and spoons.

As we sit and eat, I start to feel better. "You know, Ethan has called up here at least three times tonight to check on you." Nancy looks at me out of the corner of her eye.

"Really? I'm sure he's..." I'm not sure what he is doing.

"Miranda, I'm not trying to stick my nose in, but maybe he is sorry and really does care. God brings people together in funny ways sometimes."

I contemplate her comment and wonder if maybe I am wrong.

"You know, I might tend to believe that if he would not have lied to me for days. I asked about the other driver more than once, and he ignored it. If he would have told me in the beginning..."

"You would have kicked him out sooner." Nancy raises an eyebrow in that motherly way that makes you question everything.

"Maybe." I huff. "I just need to focus on healing, not some silly man." That's it. I'm done with this.

"Alright." Nancy smiles, but under it, I know she doesn't agree with me.

We finish our ice cream, and I tuck back in for some TV. Mom calls to check on me, and I talk to her and Emma for a bit before Emma finally brings it up. Of course, Mom told her everything. And she reminds me how much he has been there for me and how much they all like him. I try to express my thoughts on the matter and move on, but she gives me grief.

Eventually I convince her to leave it and that I want them all to come back up in the morning. And I tell her that she needs to take some plants home because it is starting to look like a jungle in here.

At some point, I finally fall asleep, although it is a restless one, filled with images of Ethan and those amazing green eyes.

Chapter 7

The doctor and nurse are in, wanting me to wake up for vitals and a check, and when I glance over, I notice that it's almost 8:30. Dang, I guess I was tired. We go through some tests, and they check me over and determine that I can go home after lunch, with a list of restrictions, of course.

I call Mom and order breakfast. The day passes with people in and out, texts of well-wishes as word spreads, and another round of flower deliveries from friends. The kids bring me a teddy bear as they say their goodbyes to go home with Joe since they have school tomorrow. It is Monday already, which is hard to believe. And I miss them as soon as they are gone. Emma and Mom are staying, and I'm thankful for that, as I am going to need some help for a bit.

After my grilled cheese lunch, the doctor comes in again to release me. I'm so happy to get out of here. Emma has already made a trip back to my apartment with flowers and brought me back fresh clothes and shoes. Nancy made me promise to come visit, and after bundling up in the car, we head home.

Home is just what I need, and it smells amazing with all the flowers. They are everywhere. Some even look new. I decide to plant myself on the couch with a large cup of hot chocolate that Emma bought on the way back and let the two of them set out to tidy up and get me settled in. It's nice. This apartment hasn't seen this much activity since I moved in. It's comforting to have my family here.

After my rest, Emma helps me wash my hair and combs out all the tangles and blood, and God knows what else. That is when I really get to see myself in the mirror, and I almost cry again. The stitches across my forehead are dark and bruised as they travel up into my hair. My two black eyes and nose are more green than purple now, and although the scrapes and scratches don't look as bad, it is still awful. Pretty much, I'm a mess.

My light brown hair still looks limp and miserable, and I'm upset at the small, shaved patch over my left temple where the stitches are. I touch it and flinch; it's still sore, but thankfully, the bump has gone down. Nancy told me I must have hit the door frame. Even though the airbags protected me, I still hit something hard.

"This better all heal." I think out loud as I continue to touch and poke all my injuries.

"You will be back to your almost beautiful Rana self in no time." Emma winks at me through the mirror.

"Haha." I try to punch her, but she moves past me. She always teases me that she got the looks and I got the brains.

As I settle back on the couch with Mom, the doorbell rings.

"Got it," Emma yells as she steps away from the laundry area. "Miranda, this gentleman needs your signature." She announces from the front door. And when I look up, there is a man in a suit standing in my kitchen. Mom notices my concern and walks with me.

"What is it?" I ask him as he stands there.

"I am just here to deliver it, ma'am." He hands me a clipboard to sign and then gives me a large tan-colored envelope. Emma shows him out as I gently open the envelope.

"It's from a lawyer's office. Ethan's lawyer, to be exact." I can't help but laugh as I read the name.

"What?" Mom asks as she looks at the paperwork in my hand. "It's from Baker and Baker. Our biggest competitor." It causes me to roll my eyes. Of course, he would be using them.

"What do they want?" Emma stands closer to read over my shoulder.

"Not sure." But I am a little worried.

As I scan through the document, I start to relax.

"It says that they are working directly with the insurance companies and that all my expenses stemming from the accident will be paid in full. My vehicle will be replaced, including all taxes, licenses, and fees. All medical bills, lost wages, and living expenses while I am out of work will be covered as well. Apparently, I just have to send my bills, receipts, and rent statement to them, and they will cut checks as expenses are incurred." I read through the lists of covered items, which is pretty much everything.

"It looks like I am not going to need anything, and I do

not have to rush back to work to pay my bills. However, all communication regarding the accident must go through his lawyer. I am not to discuss it with anyone outside of their legal team or my own attorney." I give the paper another glance and shake my head.

Mom takes the papers from me and looks over them. "This was really quick," Mom says out loud as she reads.

"Oh, I guarantee Ethan helped push it all along," I grumble and roll my eyes as I head back to the couch while Mom and Emma go over the papers again.

Emma stops me. "Miranda, there is another envelope here."

Emma holds up the plain white envelope and hands it to me. On the front is my name in very nice, neat cursive handwriting. Inside, there is a handwritten note from the same person and a check. A check from him. My eyes grow huge before Emma takes it from my hand.

"Miranda!" My Mom gasps as she looks at it, but I have already seen it, and I'm still processing it.

"Miranda, this is forty thousand dollars." Emma's hand is over her mouth.

"Nope. I will not take that. No way." I put my hands up when Emma tries to hand it back.

"What does the note say?" Mom asks. I didn't even read it after I saw the check. I pick it up and read it out loud to them.

Miranda,

You have every right to hate me. In fact, I do not like me much right now either. I did not tell you the truth, and for that, I am incredibly sorry. I never wanted to hurt you. I swear that I was not planning on hiding the information; I just did not know how to tell you, especially after developing feelings for you. That single moment when you asked me to stay with you and your beautiful eyes met mine, nothing else mattered but you from then on. I wanted to make sure you were okay and to take care of you. You are very special, Miranda, and after spending the weekend with you, I would do anything to change things between us. All I can say is that I am truly sorry and hope that one day you will forgive me.

The enclosed check is for you. I know that your expenses will be covered, but I do not know how quickly that will happen. You will need to replace your car and have money for daily expenses. This was my fault, and I want to fix it. I want to make sure you are taken care of.

I don't know how else to say I am sorry. If it helps at all, I was not drinking or on drugs, as you thought. It was not my cell phone that distracted me. I was simply late to a meeting and thought I could make the light. I never made the meeting, but I met you. I wish it would have been different, that I would have met you in a coffee shop instead, but I am still thankful that I did. Thankful for those few wonderful days I had with you. I wouldn't change those for anything.

My offer of dinner stands indefinitely.
Anytime. Anyplace. Always.
Ethan

My heart aches as my eyes fill with tears. "Um, that was quite the apology," Emma says softly from beside me. They watch as I stand there in silence, letting my heart run through all the emotions.

"It was. But the money? Is he trying to buy me off?" Suddenly, I am angry.

"Miranda, I'm sure…"

I cut Emma off. "NO. I don't want it. I want nothing from him." Tossing the letter on the counter, I leave it there where I don't have to deal with it.

"Miranda Grace! That man is head over heels for you. I'm sure he means well. He is probably hurting as much as you are." I am shocked at my mother's outburst.

"Means well? Running a red light and almost killing someone is not meaning well. What would have happened if I had died?!" Immediately, I regret yelling, but I am angry as they stare at me. My head is throbbing, and my arm hurts from my clenched fists.

I stomp my foot, pull out my phone, and hold it. I have no idea what to do. I want to yell at him, to throw it back in his face, to scream. Instead, Emma walks over and directs me to the couch.

"You need a time out." Her smile is sweet, almost teasing, but I'm not having it.

"No. I need to punch something. In fact, I want to punch him. Right in that beautifully sculpted nose of his! UGH!"

My sister laughs at me, and I realize how childish that sounds.

"I'm sorry." She tries, only to start laughing harder. My Mom joins in, and I can't help myself. It does sound pretty stupid.

Emma is now sitting next to me and has taken my phone.

"What do you want to do? Mail it back? I can do that. Or would you feel better if I drove you over to punch him in the nose? Maybe a nut shot would be better." Emma giggles.

"Emma Lynn!" My mother scolds her, which makes us all laugh harder. Wouldn't that be a show worth seeing?

"Personally, I think you should deposit it and go shopping. You work so hard and have so little. What would it hurt to spend the man's money?" Emma shocks me.

"No. I want no part of it. No." Crossing my arms in protest, I hold back my flinch from the pain of my ribs.

"I think you pout better than Soph." Emma teases as she pulls out her phone and looks at a text. I see it before she can hide it, and my blood instantly boils.

Does she hate me?

"ARE YOU FREAKING SERIOUS?!" I snap out loudly. It is a text from Ethan, and she turns green under my now red-hot, angry stare.

"Miranda! Mouth!" My mother chimes in, but I completely ignore her to focus on my traitorous sister sitting in front of me.

"Are you seriously texting him? I can't believe this!" I stand up and stomp into the kitchen, so angry I can't see straight. How dare she text him!

"Rana! I'm sorry! I sent him a text this morning to let him know you were going home. I just thought he would like to know." She looks sorry, but it doesn't help. I am pissed.

"That wasn't a thank you for the information text!" I yell back at her.

"No, but he asked how you were. I told him. And now he's asking if you hate him." Her shoulder shrug tells me she is not taking this as seriously as I am.

"Tell him yes, I do. And he can take that fucking check and shove it up his ass!" I stomp into my room and slam the door. How dare she! How dare he! God, just my luck, I finally meet someone, and he's a liar and a pig. A gorgeous pig. My mind instantly thinks about his silky, soft black hair and his bright green eyes looking down on me. Which only deepens the ache in my chest. Falling onto my bed, I cry myself to sleep.

Chapter 8

Emma shakes me awake and jumps back as I glare at her. "Don't hate me. I love you. It's time for dinner. Mom wants food." She holds her hands up in defense as she backs away. I try to move, but I'm so stiff I can hardly sit up, and Emma notices. "I am just going to help. Don't hit me." Emma reaches for my arm to help me, and I only let her because I need it.

"I'm not mad anymore. Well, not at you. Just don't text him anymore. He doesn't deserve to know how I am. I'm just mad, cried out, and exhausted. Just give me a minute." I explain, and she does, following at a distance as we go into the kitchen.

"Feeling better?" Mom asks me with a raised eyebrow as she sips her coffee.

"Yes, and I'm sorry to both of you." I sit on the chair at the island and run my hands through my hair to make sure it's not too wild.

"Good. I was wondering if you felt like going out. You do not have any food in the house, or I would cook something." Mom looks down her nose at me disapprovingly.

"Yeah, I know. I don't buy a lot of groceries when it's just me. Usually, I just pick something up on the way home." Why do I feel like a kid getting scolded? "We could go out if it's not too far or too much. I don't have the energy to sit through a fancy meal."

"Why don't we pick something up instead? Is there something close?" Mom asks.

"My other medicine needs to be picked up, so why don't we do the Chinese place down the street. I can eat that easily." We agree, and then I disappear into my room to clean up.

Standing in front of the mirror, looking at the mess I am, makes me want to cry. Nothing fits over the cast, and I'm frustrated and mad and just want something to work right! After ten minutes of searching, I finally find a hoodie that will work, and as I slip it over my cast, I notice the little box man on my arm. Damn him. Why did he have to be so perfect? My heart hurts right along with my head.

Thankfully, my mom and sister make the rest of the evening better with dinner, a chick flick, and ice cream. And when I finally crawl into bed, I have a restless night of sleep. Between pain and heartbreak, it's a long night.

The sun is barely starting to peak through the window when I finally wake up. I'm still deciding on what to do with Ethan. I do know that his outrageous check will go back. The insurance money will pay for my expenses and bills, so it's not needed or wanted. I let out a long exhale and Emma rolls over to face me as I stare at the ceiling.

"You awake?" I hear her whisper in the dark.

"Yes," I mumble.

"I can't sleep either. You know it's only like 5 am. Why are we awake?" She groans.

"I know why I can't sleep, but you should be out. My bed is comfortable and it's quiet, so you should be snoring." I roll towards her.

"Are you in pain? Do you need me to get some meds for you?" She sits up a little with a hint of worry in her voice. She knows I'm not okay, and I won't be able to hide it from her for long.

"No, just a lot on my mind." Even in the dark, I can feel her studying me.

"You thinking about Ethan?"

"Actually, I was thinking about how shitty my luck is." I let out an uncomfortable laugh.

"Well, that's new." Emma props herself up against the headboard and tells me to start talking as she crosses her arms. She means business.

"Em, I am so screwed up. I mean, who else has luck like me? I follow the man of my dreams to Chicago, only to get left at the curb a month later. I find the job of my dreams, only to lose it to a snot and end up a freaking glorified secretary. I pull myself back up and am finally in a good place, only to get mowed down in an intersection and nearly killed. Then... wait for it... I meet the most gorgeous man alive, who I think has a heart of gold, only to find out that he's the one who almost killed me. And if all of that isn't bad enough, I get a call from said man of my previous dreams to tell me he's marrying the bimbo he left me for." I pause, waiting for her to catch up.

"Wait, what? When did the scumbag call you?" Emma figured it out quicker than I expected.

"Last night at the hospital." Emma is shocked into silence.

"He called to tell me he was getting married. To her. Didn't even ask how I was. Just told me, so I didn't hear it through our social circles. If you can even believe he came up with that trash." Just saying it out loud feels like a slap in the face.

"What a dickhead. Those two deserve each other. Did you tell him you were in the hospital?"

"Hell no. I don't want anything from him. Besides, he will hear it in our social circles." I give her air quotes, and she tries not to laugh as she covers her mouth.

"Well, you still have the job, and you could have the gorgeous guy." She pokes me in the arm.

"Ouch. Yes, on the job, but I don't think I want the guy. I mean, I feel like the whole start of whatever this is, was based on lies. How do I know he wasn't there for other reasons? I mean, the man obviously has money because he's retaining a hell of a law firm. Are they doing this to keep it under the rug? What insurance company pays for all of this without a fight? That's hush money." I swallow back the tears that are now brewing again. I hate him for making me feel something again.

"Are you sure? That note sounded pretty real." Emma takes the fingers of my broken arm and laces hers with mine.

"I was barely home for an hour, Em. He had to have or-chestrated all that pretty fast. It was the weekend. And why so much? I could see a few thousand, but forty? What does it look like to you? I want to send it back."

"I see your point." Emma strokes my hair, then adds, "I'm sorry Sis. He seemed like such a good guy." I roll onto my back, but the tears just roll out from the corners of my eyes.

"If I would have just gone to the store first, instead of the office, I would be sitting at your house eating breakfast with the kids." The heartbreak is clear in my voice.

"You can't think like that. You are just upset. Everything..." She pauses, and I shake my head.

"I know, everything happens for a reason. I just wish I knew this reason." I finish her sentence for her.

"Me too." She pulls me over into a gentle hug letting me relax into her as the tears fall.

"Let's get some breakfast, go shopping, and figure out how to return that check. But I do have to ask, are you sure? That could make the difference between eating steak and ramen noodles in the next few weeks. Who knows when the insurance company will cough up the funds?" She has a point.

"I just feel wrong about it. Why so much?"

"Well, you could always ask him." Emma stares at me, waiting.

"You're serious? You want me to call him? Didn't the letter say to call the lawyer only?" She's quiet for a minute.

"Well, nothing said that I couldn't contact him."

She reaches for her phone and dials, but I panic. "Em, it's only 6am!" I screech in horror.

"And I bet he's up." She smiles before tilting the phone

so I can hear. My heart is frozen while it rings. I hear two rings, three...and then...he answers.

"Emma. Is everything okay? Is Miranda alright?" The nervousness in his voice is heart-wrenching, and he's out of breath.

"She's fine. Actually, she wanted to know something, but the letter your lawyer sent made it sound like she should not contact you directly." Emma is confident, but he is silent. My heart breaks more. I knew it. I try to move away, but Emma holds my arm to keep me in place.

Finally, he speaks softly. "My lawyers demanded it for protection. Emma...she can call me anytime, for anything." He's silent again, and I close my eyes, not wanting to listen to his breathing.

"I will pass that along," Emma whispers as she looks at me.

"She won't call me, will she? She's never going to." He sounds so sad that I almost break.

"I don't know Ethan. She wants to know why you sent so much money." His pause is all I need to hear, I've had enough, but Emma holds me in place. "Ethan, she thinks you are paying her off."

"What! NO! That was not it at all. I just want to make sure she has money. I..."

"I don't want your money!" I shout into the phone, cutting him off. I can't take it anymore.

"Miranda. Please, let me explain." He sounds surprised.

"NO. I don't want your money. I'm not some charity case." The tears stream down my cheeks as a new wound opens in my heart.

"No, that's not what I meant. I want to help." No more, I move away, and this time Emma lets me.

"Miranda?" He is calling my name, and it's too much. I can't.

Emma takes the hint. "Ethan, she doesn't want to talk to you."

"Emma, please. Help me here. What can I do? I never meant it that way." Emma looks at me and I shake my head no. I can hear him, but I won't talk to him.

"Thank you for clearing it up. I will let you know if she needs anything else." Emma nods at me and hangs up.

"Sorry, Miranda." I cry into her hug as she holds me. "Why am I so upset?"

"Because you like him, and he hurt you. Although, I don't think he meant the money that way. I really think he wants to help." Emma is trying; I know this, but it still makes me mad.

"You are probably right, but I don't want it. Can you take it back to the lawyer's office, please?"

"Are you completely sure?"

"Yes, I'm going back to work on Monday, and I have paid time off. I don't need it. " I sit up and wipe my eyes. I'm done with this.

My forehead burns where the stitches are. "I need pain meds, food, and shopping." Is it too much to wish for things to be back to normal because I feel like shit. "I'm going to clean up. Take a shower, and let's go out." I head to the kitchen for meds.

Mom is already up and ready and has made coffee. She

looks at me in complete surprise, or maybe it's my appearance. "Rough morning?" She asks over her cup.

"Yes." I get a glass of water and take my meds as she continues talking.

"Miranda, honey, I never intervene, but that man is trying. They aren't all perfect." Her comment makes me roll my eyes. Her best talent is intervening.

"Mom, he doesn't need to be perfect. Just not a liar or a cheat." Taking the offered cup of coffee, I don't continue with her conversation. Instead, I head to my desk to write out my own note to return with the check. I sit at my desk and pull out my special stationery, the light pink stuff that I rarely use.

> Ethan,
>
> As asked, I am going through your lawyer. I don't want or need your money. I'm not some broken little girl that needs your help. I am perfectly fine on my own. In fact, I am more than fine.
>
> Thank you for holding my hand and staying with me. I am grateful for that. Even if it was your fault. And thank you for the flowers.
>
> Miranda

It's not pretty, but I wrote it. I slip it and the check, into the envelope and write Mr. Ethan Bradley c/o Mr. Jason Baker on the outside and leave it on the counter.

There, he can have his money back and I get the final word. I giggle, remembering his comment about that. He was right, I will this time, too.

 Chapter 9

We have breakfast at the diner on the corner and then decide to drive to Baker and Baker to drop off the envelope. Emma pulls up out front in a visitor space and parks waiting for instruction.

"Are you sure you want to do this?" Mom asks from the backseat.

"Yes," I almost choke out from the pain in my chest.

"You two stay here, and I will take it in." Emma goes to take the envelope, but I stop her.

"No. I want to take it in. Alone." Taking a deep breath, I steel myself. I have to do this. I need the closure.

"Miranda, that's a long walk and what happens if you get dizzy?" Mom asks.

"I will take it slow, and I will be fine. I want to do this myself."

With my ponytail swinging with purpose, I walk up the steps, in the front door, and up to the security desk, fully intending to make it quick and painless.

"Good morning, Ma'am." The guard smiles.

"Good morning. I need to drop this off for Mr. Jason Baker, please." I hold up the envelope to show my intention.

"Do you have an appointment?" He asks.

"No, just need to leave it." I lay it on the desk and turn to leave, but he stops me.

"One moment, ma'am, I will call up to his office." I start to argue, but he ignores me. "Hello, this is Dale in security. I have Ms..." He looks at me expectantly.

"Miranda Michaels," I state.

"I have Ms. Miranda Michaels here. She has an envelope for Mr. Jason Baker." He listens and then nods. "Thank you." He answers the person on the other end and then waits. "The secretary is checking if he is in," Dale informs me. Of course, he is in. I know the man; he's never not here.

"I don't need to see him. I just want to leave this." I try, and Dale nods but keeps talking into the phone and thanks the person again.

"Mr. Baker will be down in a moment to meet you. He has asked that I escort you to a conference room." He comes around the desk and waits for me to follow.

"I don't need all of that, I just want to leave this," frustration fires me up.

"I understand, Ms. Michaels, but Mr. Baker has asked me to have you wait here."

"Fine. Okay. Thank you." I am in no mood to argue.

He leads me to a small conference room and tells me to take a seat, which I do. A young lady enters and offers me something to drink, which I decline. I just want out of here. Why didn't I just let Emma bring this? While I am kicking myself, the door opens, and in walks Jason...with Ethan. My body freezes as our eyes meet, and I take in his beautiful face and those perfect emerald eyes. I notice what I am doing and quickly look away. What the hell is he doing here?

"Miranda. An unexpected visit. How are you feeling?" Jason approaches me, and I stand to greet him. We have always been friendly to each other, and I don't see the need to change that now. He takes a moment to look me up and down before pulling me into a gentle hug, surprising me.

"Um, been better." My voice is husky at the shock of seeing Ethan and the hug.

"I was very upset when I learned that you were hurt, but I didn't think it was in good taste for me to visit." I relax a little at his sincerity.

"I appreciate that, Jason. Thank you." I nod and then add, "You know you would have been welcome." I notice that Ethan is shifting his weight. He's uncomfortable. Good.

"We are friends." I give Jason a sweet smile, which he returns.

"Yes, we are." His professional appearance slips as he hugs me again.

Ethan clears his throat. Time to deal with the elephant in the room. "Ethan." I nod at him, and he gives me that gorgeous smile, and for a second, I almost fall for it.

"Miranda," he breathes out. Jason glances back and forth between us as my eyes take in Ethan's appearance. He looks amazing in his dark gray suit. So dominating and professional. Why is he so damn hot? He doesn't take his eyes off me either, and now I shift uncomfortably.

"Please sit. What can we do for you?" Jason brings me back to the conversation.

"I wanted to drop this off for Mr. Bradley. The documents I received stated that all communication must go through you." I hand Jason the envelope, and he looks at the pink stationery, which suddenly makes me feel stupid.

"Is this personal?" He asks, surprised as he looks at Ethan again.

"Yes, just returning what belongs to him." I avoid Ethan's gaze as Jason takes it and hands it to Ethan, who turns it over a few times and then opens it.

"Read it later," I state, but he reads it before I can stand.

"No. I gave this to you." His voice is louder as he pushes it back across the table at me. Jason looks confused, but Ethan is stone still.

"Jason. Please instruct your client that I do not want his money." I almost spit out. Jason looks at the envelope, then at Ethan.

"You gave her money?" Jason is very surprised and by the looks of it, angry.

"No. I gave her a gift." Ethan is stern.

"I do not want it," I say just as sternly. I glare at Ethan and hope he can feel the fire in my eyes.

"Miranda, please excuse us for a moment." Jason stands.

"Of course." I watch as he walks into the hall with Ethan, I'm sure giving him an earful. The envelope sits on the table in front of me, and I am not taking it back. I cross my arms in defense and to keep myself from shivering. My sweater isn't enough in this place. I need to go, but as I move towards the door, it opens, and they reenter. Jason looks frustrated.

"Miranda, I am sorry for the interruption. Ethan has informed me that he gave you that as a friend, not due to the accident." The shock must show as I exhale.

"No. It was due to the accident, and I don't want it." I glare at Ethan again as Jason picks up the envelope and holds it out to me.

"Jason, I'm done with the conversation. Please don't."

His eyes soften as he looks at me. Mentally, I am pleading with him, and it works. He winks and pulls the envelope back. "Thank you," I say relieved, and he nods.

Now, as we all stand staring at each other, I decide to move, and they both flinch at the same time.

"I'm sorry, I have to go." The sudden change makes me sway, and in a flash, Ethan is at my side, holding my good arm. His touch vibrates through me, causing the breath to leave my lungs, just as it always has. Concern is etched all over his face, but he doesn't move or speak.

"Miranda, are you okay?" Jason asks, and he's next to me also.

"Yes, just moved too quickly. I'm good. Thank you." I pull my arm away from Ethan, and briefly, he looks hurt but recovers quickly.

I turn and hug Jason goodbye. "It was good to see you," I say, and he whispers in my ear, "I'm sorry about this. I'm here if you need me." His lips brush my cheek, and for a moment, I don't move away.

Ethan clears his throat again. He's so close I can feel him. Did he see Jason? Well, if he didn't, he will see me. I lightly kiss Jason's cheek back. My stubbornness gets me into trouble every fricking time.

As I turn back, Ethan's concerned face is my weakness, and my hardness softens. He stands there, waiting. His green eyes pleading with me.

Dammit, Ethan. I can't finish my thought as I exhale loudly and almost give in to the pull between us. His lips start to curve up in a smile, and it breaks my trance.

"No. No way, I can't do this. I just want the insurance to run its course, and we can all move on. I appreciate the gesture, but I don't want it." His smile fades instantly, and I know I need to go.

I start to step around Ethan, but he gently takes my hand from my side and squeezes. Just like he did all those times before. I pause next to him, fighting the urge to stay, but he lets go. My body shakes as I glance up at him.

"Goodbye, Ethan." I force out as I nearly run out of the room.

I just make it out the doors as the tears start to fall, and while I run to the car, Emma jumps out when she sees me.

"What happened? We were just getting ready to come in after you. Why are you crying?" She holds me back to look at me.

"I should have let you do it. Ethan was here. Jason, his lawyer, had to come down and get the letter. It wasn't fun." I cry on Emma's shoulder as she holds me.

"Did he try anything? I will beat his ass." Emma is mad, but I don't care.

"No, just wouldn't take my no on the money."

I feel Emma nod and put her hand up, which makes me turn back, and there he is, standing ten feet away. He nods back at her but doesn't move.

"I think he was making sure you were okay," Emma says softly. He looks solid and strong standing there, but his face says otherwise. I hold his gaze for what seems like minutes, then turn back to Emma.

"Let's go," I say, wiping my eyes. My makeup is smeared across my hand. Great, now I look like a fool. I get in, and when I look up, he's still there.

"Miranda, honey," Mom says from behind me, but I just shake my head no and let more tears fall as Emma pulls away, and I lose sight of him.

After shopping and lunch, I try to have a good time, but it's too tough. Finally, I was able to convince them to let me go home and rest.

"Miranda, honey, you haven't smiled all day. You need to snap out of this. If you want him, go after him. If not, move on." God, my mother can be so blunt sometimes.

"Yeah, not such an easy choice." I push the elevator button for my floor and look at the floor as I wait. As we come down the hall, I see more flowers and a plant sitting outside my door.

"You would think I would be out of friends by now," I announce as I unlock the door and pick up one of the vases. I set them on the counter and go back for the other vases and the plant that sits out there while my sister and mom carry in the bags.

"Plant is from a client," I announce as I read the card.

"This vase is from some friends," I drop the card on the pile with the others that I have collected. And when I open the card for the huge bouquet, I blush with embarrassment.

It was good to see you today. Heal quickly.
~ Jason.

I smell them and smile. The last vase is from Ethan. Nothing on the card, just his name as the sender. I roll my eyes and move them to the last open spot on the end table. Jason's vase stays on the island. I pick up the plant and set it on the floor by the TV.

"Anyone we know?" Mom asks as she walks into the kitchen.

"A client, friends, and Ethan, again," I say flatly.

"That man must be loaded. He is spending a fortune on flowers." Emma wiggles her eyebrows.

"I don't care," I comment as I flip through the mail. A few cards and some bills. Nothing exciting.

"Loaded is an understatement," Emma calls from my desk where she has parked herself.

"What?" I walk over and see his beautiful face on the screen.

"EMMA!"

"What? I wanted to google him yesterday but didn't get a chance." She gives me her mischievous grin. I want to walk away but give in and lean down to see what she has found.

"He's the CEO of Bradley Publishing. Along with the owner of numerous other companies." Emma rattles off, and she sounds impressed, but I don't care.

"So?" I mumble, but then there are the pictures. Emma scrolls through screen after screen, and I can't look away. His green eyes have captured my attention, and I feel like each one is looking at me. It makes me shudder.

"He's hot." Emma mewls.

"Very," I whisper. She nudges me as she clicks on one of him standing in swimming trunks. He looks like he is on a boat, his hair whipped around from the wind. My mouth dries, and I lick my lips.

"Why Miranda, I thought you loathed him." Emma giggles.

"I do, but damn." My brain won't let me look away. Now I see more than green eyes. There are also his soft hands that held mine, his mouth, his lips...no! I've had enough.

"Enough. You research all you want. I'm taking a nap." I swing by the kitchen for meds, shut my bedroom door, and crawl into bed. Once there, I check my phone, and he has texted me. Twice.

> *I just wanted to make sure you made it to the car. I hope you are resting.*
>
> *I miss you.*

I run my finger over the text but then toss the phone to the side. Nope. I don't want another mess. My screen goes dark next to me, and I close my eyes and drift off to sleep.

The rest of the night and the next few days pass without incident. We make a trip to the doctor, the grocery store, Target, and a few times we eat out, but mostly we stay in. Mom cooks and Emma cleans. I just sleep. There is no more contact from Ethan. No more flowers, texts, or letters. I'm happy he got the hint, but I miss him terribly. I just go through the motions of the week and try to get over him.

Saturday afternoon, we decide I am well enough that Mom and Emma should go home. Of course, they don't want to, but it's time to get myself back into life.

"Honey, are you sure? I can stay as long as you need me and fly home later." My Mom fusses as we stand in the lobby.

"Mom, I will be fine, I promise. I feel better, and I need to get ready for work on Monday." She hugs me hard.

"You don't have to rush back. The doctor said he'd write you off another week."

"I know, but I want to try. And I promise, if I need you, I will call." I try to reassure her, along with myself.

"Okay. You will come home for Thanksgiving, right?" Mom pulls me back and looks at me.

"Yes." She lets me go with another kiss.

I watch them drive away, and I miss them, but I'm glad to have my apartment back. My couch is calling my name. What should I do first? I don't really have much to do since Mom and Emma cleaned and bought groceries, so I decide to watch TV but end up flipping through channels for an hour until I find a movie I haven't seen yet. Back to normal, I think, as I settle in for the night.

# Chapter 10

The alarm wakes me up at six am Monday morning, and I'm excited to go back to work. I did absolutely nothing yesterday; I just rested up for today. After a quick bath, I get myself dressed and do my hair and makeup. I'm getting so much more comfortable with my left hand, and thankfully, now I can use my right fingers, too. I bought a new suit jacket that fits over my cast, and with my slacks and heels, I look like my normal self. My face has almost healed, except for the place where the stitches were; that still looks angry but better than before. Thankfully, my new hairstyle covers the shaved spot, and as I stand in front of the mirror, I feel good.

I glance at my watch, noting that the cab should be here in about 5 minutes. After making sure my meds and supplies are tucked into my large new purse, courtesy of Mom, I grab my phone and keys and head down to the lobby.

As I step outside, the sun is shining, so I tilt my head back and feel its warmth. I am ready. I can do this. Someone calls my name and pulls me from my internal motivational speech.

"Ms. Michaels?" There is a man holding a car door open.

"Yes?" I answer as I glance around.

"Good morning, ma'am. I am here to take you to the office." He smiles warmly.

"I have a cab already." Looking around, I don't see the cab yet, but I am sure it will be here.

"The cab has been sent on, ma'am." He just stands there holding the door. I glance back, then consider if I should get in.

"Ms. Michaels?" The man's smile is so sweet.

"Okay." I smile. I will make sure to thank Mr. Lester personally for this. He was so worried about me driving this week that it was overly sweet of him to send a car. I slide into the black sedan, and it is warm and cozy as the man shuts the door.

After he is in, he asks if I would like music on. "Sure, anything is fine with me. Thank you." He nods and turns on some classical music. This is nice and soothing. I watch as the traffic flows by, and in just a few minutes, we are in front of my office. Front door service. No parking and walking for me today.

The driver gets out and comes to open my door before I can, and I feel like a celebrity as people stop to look. I say thank you as I pull my bag over my shoulder.

"My pleasure, Ms. Michaels." He nods and shuts the door before waiting for me to go inside.

People start to welcome me back as soon as I am through the door, and it feels so good to be back. It takes me a bit to get through the greetings, but I make my way to my desk, and there sits a large vase of flowers. I open the card, and it's from the firm, welcoming me back.

April, our secretary, who has covered for me, welcomes me with a tight, warm hug. "I'm so glad you are back." She laughs and hugs me again. "I don't think I can keep up with Mr. Lester again this week." She whispers. *Amateur.*

"Well, let me get settled, and you can fill me in."

"Oh, Mr. Lester and Mr. Lester Sr. are in court this morning and not sure if they will be in. Paul told me to make sure you take it easy this week and ease back in." She admits with a blush.

"Thank you, April." She nods and walks back to her desk.

Once my computer starts, I notice most of the emails have been gone through. There are only a few marked with flags for me to deal with. I check the calendar and see that it is, thankfully a light week. After I check my voicemail and reorganize my desk, I feel better being here.

At 11:30, April interrupts me to ask if I want lunch ordered in, but I decline. I want to get out and walk, and maybe I will go down to the deli.

It's a beautiful day, and the fresh air does wonders for my soul. There is a short line, and after ordering my sandwich, I find a seat by the window to people-watch, a favorite pastime of mine. I am engrossed in my sandwich and watching a couple across the street embrace when I hear his voice and freeze mid-bite.

"I am happy to see you are out and about. I heard you returned to work today." His smile is small, but those eyes still look exactly as I remember and seem to hold me captive.

"Yes. It feels good to be back." I whisper, not sure what else to do.

"You look lovely." He pauses before wishing me a good rest of the day and then turns to leave.

"Thank you." My words are weak, and I feel shy as I watch him walk out the door and disappear down the street. He doesn't even look back. The breath I am holding releases loudly, and I sit there confused. Is he over me already? That makes me extremely sad, even though it shouldn't. I should be over him. My sadness kills my appetite, and I head back to the office with a heavy mind and an even heavier heart.

Back at my desk, April delivers a UPS envelope that came while I was gone, along with a few messages. I look through the message and decide they can all wait. I see the package is from his insurance company and open it to find a check for my car and some paperwork. Finally, the check seems to be for the full replacement value on my Camaro, which shocks me, but that's great. I guess I will go car shopping soon.

"Shit," I say out loud.

"Everything okay?" April asks as she walks past with some files.

"Oh, yes. Sorry." I cover my reaction with a smile. How am I going to shop for a car without a car? I guess I will call my friend Nicole, or I might have to take a cab. Ugh. I slide the papers back into the envelope and slip it into my purse to be dealt with later.

At 5 pm, I turn off my computer and tell everyone good night. I realize how tired I am as the elevator takes me down to the lobby, and I hope that I can catch a cab. As I step outside though, there stands the driver from this morning waiting for me.

"Ms. Michaels." He smiles.

"Oh. Service home, too?" I am surprised.

"Of course, ma'am." Well, this is perfect. Dang it, I completely forgot to thank Mr. Lester. I will need to do it first thing tomorrow.

As we pull up in front of my building, the driver gets out to open the door.

"Same time tomorrow, ma'am?" He nods his question.

"Oh, you don't have to do that. I can call a cab."

"No trouble. I will see you at 7 am." He smiles and waits for me to get into the building before he leaves. I admit it will be nice to have a good car ride with a safe driver. Cabs around here can be crazy.

At 7 am, I am in the lobby, and there is my car.

"Good morning, Ms. Michaels."

"Good Morning." I go to slide in and stop. "I'm sorry, I don't know your name." I wait for his answer.

"Charles, ma'am, but most people just call me Charlie."

"Well, Good Morning, Charlie." We exchange smiles, and he shuts the door. We enjoy the silence as we drive to the office, and he informs me he will be here at 5 to pick me up.

April is waiting at my desk. "Good morning, April."

"Good morning, Miranda. Mr. Lester wanted me to let you know that he will be out in court again today. He sent you an email with all the info he needs pulled for the next case. If you need help, please let me know." She hands me a coffee and walks back to her desk.

"Thank you." She rarely gets me coffee, but it's much appreciated.

I have my head down, working on documents, when my cell phone rings and I notice it's Jason, which makes me smile. "Hello?"

"Hey, Miranda. I hope it's okay that I call you."

"Of course. What's up?"

"First, I wanted to check on you and see how getting back to work was. And second, to apologize for the show that developed on Tuesday at my office. It was uncalled for, and it won't happen again."

What? Why was he apologizing? "No need to apologize, Jason. Ethan's a grown man; he can apologize for himself. Don't worry about it; it's over. And I am great. I love being back at work. Thank you for checking on me." I feel a little bit of heat in my cheeks. He hasn't called me in ages.

"Actually, I wanted to apologize for my behavior." His voice is soft, and it makes me pause what I am doing.

"You didn't do anything wrong." I am not sure what he means.

"The kiss on the cheek, the way I held you. I am not sure what came over me. You're involved in a case with my client, and I shouldn't have crossed that line. I am very sorry."

"Wait. I'm not upset at all. And I'm not involved with him. He crashed into me. I am just trying to move on."

"I understand that, but I have to keep his best interest at the forefront."

"Oh. Okay, I honestly didn't think anything of it. You and I are friends, and you were concerned for me. That's it. I am not in any way upset or think you crossed a line. And thank you for the flowers. They were beautiful." I smile at the image of them.

"You are welcome."

I can hear him exhale, which makes me smile again.

"Jason, there is a personal and professional line. You are allowed to be my friend. I'm not the enemy." I hear his laugh of relief.

"Well, Mr. Bradley didn't like it too much." And there it is.

"Really? Is that what this is about? Ethan?" Anger starts to boil in my veins.

"No, he just wanted to make sure we weren't dating. Client attorney stuff. I assured him we weren't. Just old friends. Correct?" I hear hope in his voice, and again I smile.

"That is correct. Always friends. Even when we are on different sides of the table."

"Glad we are okay. I hoped I hadn't offended you."

"Never. And maybe after this case is over, we can grab dinner and catch up." Did I just say that out loud?

"Sure, it's a date. I mean, not a real date. Just a friend date. Okay, I'm going to go now. Bye, Miranda."

"Bye, Jason." I hang up, and April is standing over me, staring. I didn't even realize she was standing there.

"Who was that?" April leans against my desk, curious for information as always.

"Just an old friend." I smile, but my blush gives me away.

"Sounds like you just asked said friend out on a date. Did he say yes?" She sits down on my cabinet, clearly wanting to chat.

"He did say yes, but just to dinner. It's not like that at all."

"Uh-huh."

"April, he's just a friend."

She winks at me and gets up to leave.

"Oh, Mr. Lester would like you to meet him for dinner tomorrow night with potential new clients. Something about a woman's perspective or something. He will email you directly with details." She skips back to her desk, leaving me to wonder about Jason's intentions.

That reminds me, I need to email Mr. Lester. I send a quick email to him thanking him for the car service and how easy it made the commute yesterday and this morning. I let him know that I have received the insurance check and that I will be getting a car sometime this week. After I hit send, I notice that it's past 12, and I need to eat.

I walk down to the deli again and grab a sandwich to bring back. As I'm walking out the door, who should be walking in? I think I startle him when I pause in front of him.

"Miranda."

"Ethan." We just stare at each other for a minute, then he moves to the side to let me through, breaking eye contact. I take that as a cue to go, and once I am past him and out the door, I step to the side and exhale.

Why is he in my part of town again? It is my part, right? I don't even know where his office is. Maybe he's close. Maybe I've passed him before? No, I think I would remember, wouldn't I? I will just have to find a new place to eat. I can't handle bumping into him daily.

Thankfully, the rest of the day goes smoothly, and when I leave for the night, I find Charlie waiting just outside the entrance for me.

"Charlie." I smile warmly at him.

"Hello, Ms. Miranda." He smiles back.

Once he's in, I ask if he wouldn't mind swinging by the bank since we have time.

"Of course. Anything you need, I'm happy to take you."

"Thank you." He's such a sweet man.

He offers to take me to pick up dinner, but I decline and just go home. It's another lonely night of food, TV, and fitful sleep. Seeing Ethan again today keeps those hurt feelings at the surface and makes me dream. Both good and bad.

I wake before the alarm today, determined to have a great day. I'm up and ready to go on time, and decide I want a good coffee this morning, so I ask Charlie to go through Starbucks, where I order one for myself and one for him. He is very grateful as it is colder and overcast this morning. We make small talk until he drops me off at the door.

"Thanks, Charlie. I'm supposed to have dinner with Mr. Lester tonight, and since I'm not sure what he has planned, I may not need a ride home."

Charlie reaches into his jacket pocket and pulls out a card. "Just give me a call, and I will be there. I am happy to take you or pick you up as needed." He smiles as I take the card.

"Oh, great. Let me find one of mine." I start to look through my bag for my case, but he stops me.

"No need, I have it already."

"Great. Thank you." I thank him again and head into work with a smile. I do really enjoy his company.

As I come off the elevator, to my surprise, I see Jason

talking to Paul. I smile brightly, but it doesn't last as I see Ethan step around April's desk. Oh, joy.

"Good morning, gentlemen." I plaster on my brightest smile, and they all return their versions of good morning.

"Miranda, Mr. Bradley, and Mr. Baker would like to borrow you in the conference room for a little bit. Is that okay?" Paul looks concerned as he looks between us.

"Of course." I look at Jason, and he shrugs before April shows them to the conference room while I drop off my stuff in my office.

Paul knocks on my door almost immediately. "Hey, kiddo. Do you want me to sit in as your lawyer? Jason called me last night and told me he was representing Mr. Bradley in the accident. I thought you said the driver that hit you was at fault, and this was settled? You also never told me it was Ethan Bradley." He leans against my doorframe.

"Honestly, Mr. Lester, I didn't know who had hit me until I was out of the hospital. And until a few days ago, I didn't even know who Ethan Bradley was. He was just Ethan, the nice guy that saved me at the accident. I'm rather confused about it all myself. And yes, as far as I knew, on Tuesday, it was all settled." My nerves are on high alert as I quickly put away my stuff.

"I see. So, do you want me to sit in with you? Just for support?" His relaxed demeanor tells me he is in friend mode, not necessarily lawyer mode.

"Actually, I think I would like that. I'm not sure why they are here, and I'm a little concerned he has changed his mind about not fighting me." I try to smile, but my fear has me rattled. The thought has crossed my mind on more than one occasion that he might change his mind. And after the cold shoulder this week, I wonder if he is going to be difficult now.

I watch Paul's face soften. "Come on, kiddo, let's go make him sweat." He buttons his suit jacket and changes his stance. On days like this, I adore him completely.

We walk into the conference room, all business. Jason looks surprised as they both stand. "Miranda, Paul." Jason nods and looks directly at me for direction.

"Mr. Lester is here on my behalf as my lawyer. I wasn't sure what this was about, and so I decided to include my own attorney." I smile sweetly as I sit.

I immediately notice Ethan flinch, which makes my smile widen. "Mr. Bradley." I nod to him.

"Miranda." His eyes are cold, and his face is stone. It makes me shiver when I see nothing of the sweet man I knew in the hospital. Maybe this isn't a friendly visit after all.

"There really wasn't a need for all this, as it was just an informal meeting. Mr. Bradley just wanted to make sure Ms. Michaels was doing well and that all her needs were taken care of." Jason is sweating as he stumbles over his words. I have never seen him sweat before, and I am alarmed.

"Well, then, there will be no harm in me sitting in to make sure." Paul smiles at Jason, who visibly swallows hard. Ethan doesn't even bat an eye. I glance at him, and he doesn't look my way. As much as I want to punch him, it still hurts to be ignored. I feel crushed that he doesn't at least acknowledge me.

"Ms. Michaels, do you have any expenses that need to be paid as of yet? Medical...missed wages?" Jason is stumbling as he glances at Ethan.

"I submitted, via email to you, my receipts for my medicine yesterday. That is all I have so far." I am even timid in the presence of cold Ethan. And just like the hospital blanket, I find myself picking at the edge of my notebook.

"Well, Mr. Bradley has informed me that he would like to cover your rent and your missing wages this month." Jason starts to get his cool back.

"That's not necessary. I have..." Paul puts his hand on mine to silence me.

"Ms. Michaels would be happy to submit her rent statement to you. She has missed five days of work so far. I will have April type up her wages and hours and send them over to you." Now I'm the one that is sweating.

"Of course. I will look forward to those documents later today." Jason glances at me and I nod but feel so small suddenly. I chance a look at Ethan; he's so…angry looking as he stares at Jason with something unknown to me. I watch him for a minute and really miss his smile. I don't like this man that is sitting across from me.

"There is also the issue of Ms. Michael's car." Jason starts to talk again, but I speak up.

"I received the insurance check yesterday for my car. It will cover the cost of a new one." I glance at Paul, and he nods in agreement.

"Mr. Bradley would like to reimburse you for all taxes, license, fees, and expenses in purchasing your new car as stated in the documents you have received." Jason puts a piece of paper on the table. "He would also like a list of all your utilities, insurance, and other daily living expenses for the month." He places more pages in front of me.

My anger suddenly takes over all my other thoughts. "No," I say louder than I expected, and all heads turn to me. I stand up and slap down on the table, making everyone jump. "This testosterone show is over. I will not submit every detail of my life to you. I do not want your money. I made that very clear to you when I returned your check. You can cover the normal expenses that were caused by the accident, but you will not invade my life." I realize I am yelling now as I watch the shock hit Ethan's face, and he slowly recovers. Paul takes my hand to calm me down.

"I think Ms. Michaels is under a lot of stress and may need to take ten minutes." Paul stands and starts to guide me out of the room. I meet Ethan's eyes, and they soften briefly before I think I see hurt on his face, and immediately I feel tears. Shit. I hurry out of the room with Paul.

"Okay, deep breaths. I'm sure you understand how this negotiating thing works by now. They offer, we ask for more, we settle, they pay, and we all shake hands and go home. You don't worry about anything." Paul holds my shoulders as he looks into my face. "Are you okay?" He seems concerned as he watches me.

"No," I answer in a daze.

"No, you are not okay?" He is closer to my face.

"Yes, I'm okay. No, I don't want his money. You don't understand." I say softly.

"You are right, I don't understand. Where's my tiger that fights for every last cent?"

"I don't want to explain it right now. I just want to go back in there and tell them to go back to their offices and leave me be." I exhale loudly as I close my eyes.

"Okay, if you are sure. I trust you. Let's go." Paul agrees.

When we return to the room, both men stand again. Ethan doesn't look as cold, but he still stands still, barely registering my movements.

"Miranda, are you okay?" Jason asks without a second look at Ethan.

"Ms. Michaels would like to end this meeting," Paul announces as he stands at my side. This gets Ethan's full attention as he looks directly at me.

"Are you sick?" Ethan finally speaks.

"No," I can't look at him, nor do I want to.

"Well, then, let's finish this, and we can be on our way," Jason says, laying a pen down next to the pages on the table. No one else notices, but I hear the quiver in his voice and wonder what Ethan has told him this time.

Taking a deep breath, I look directly at Jason as I answer. "No. I don't want his money, or his help, or anything else from him." Ethan is staring hard enough that I can feel it as I speak, making me uncomfortable.

"Ms. Michaels, I don't think Mr. Bradley is asking. He feels this is his duty," Jason tries to explain.

"It's not his duty. I don't want it. Just pay what we agreed upon, and let's move on." I am getting tired of this. I just want to go back to work and put this entire thing behind me.

"It is my responsibility," Ethan speaks loudly, surprising me, but I recover quickly, spinning around to face him.

"No, it is not!" I say louder. My own anger is very clear.

"I will do it, and you will accept it," He's stern, his voice deep as those eyes bore into me.

"NO! I am not some poor little girl who needs you and your money. I am a grown-ass woman!" I can't help but yell back at him. He's infuriating!

"You are acting like a child!" He yells back. I see Jason moving out of the corner of my eye, but I don't give up.

"WELL, ETHAN BRADLEY, YOU ARE ACTING LIKE AN ASSHOLE!" I yell again, but this time, I feel Paul's hand on my shoulder, and I try to shrug it off. I am beyond angry now.

"You are not in your right mind. I am trying to help you!" He is really loud now.

"I. DO. NOT. WANT. YOUR. HELP!" I scream.

"TOUGH!" His voice is thunderous now, but it doesn't stop me.

"YOU ARE A LIAR AND A...." I can't even think of the words.

"People, if we could just settle down a bit." Jason is trying to calm Ethan down as I stand fuming. Paul is standing behind me with his hands on both my arms, almost holding me back.

"WHY? WHY WON'T YOU LET ME HELP YOU?" He yells, his voice echoing off the walls and I notice Jason flinch.

"I DON'T WANT YOUR HELP!"

"TELL ME WHY!" He is so mad that I am sure there is steam coming off his red face.

"NO!" I yell back. Jason and Paul are doing everything they can to calm us down, but I am so over this game.

"MIRANDA!" He glares at me in warning like that is going to stop me.

"NO!" I stand taller. I will not back down.

"If you two will settle down, we can talk this through!" Jason is mad now. I ignore him and Paul, who is trying to pull me back. I will not let him win.

"YOU ARE IN DEBT UP TO YOUR EARS! TAKE THE FUCKING MONEY!" He yells and then stops. I blink. The room is deathly silent as his words settle among us. Did he really just go there?

"FUCK YOU!" I yell and turn to leave. Suddenly, he moves across the room in two steps and grabs my arm, spinning me around. I pull back my arm and stumble, but he grabs me by both arms and pulls me to him, crashing his lips into mine. I try to fight it at first, but my body betrays me, and I lose the battle, letting my lips push back into him.

As his tongue swipes over my lips and invades my mouth, I come to my senses and push away from him.

"Mr. Bradley!" Jason yells, and Ethan lets me go. We all stare at Ethan in disbelief. His eyes are wild, and I can physically see him breathing hard. My own body is in flight mode, but my legs won't move. And I still feel the pressure of his lips on mine.

Paul takes my arm and turns me to him. "Miranda, are you okay? Are you hurt?" I can hear compassion in his voice as I try to bring myself back to earth.

"No," My own voice is small and weak now.

"Mr. Bradley, if you put your hands on my client again, you won't have to worry about her accepting your money freely. She will get it all." Paul is furious. "This meeting is over." He pushes me towards the door, and I move, needing to be out of this room.

I hear Jason chastising Ethan as we get out the door, but I'm stunned into silence. What just happened? What did I do? Why did I scream like that? Holy hell, I hope I don't get fired. "Mr. Lester, I'm so sorry. I lost my head in there. Please forgive me." Tears start down my face, and I am not even sure why.

"Shhh, don't you worry. This was not your fault." He pats my back as we walk to his office, where I sit on the small couch in the corner, and April appears with a cup of coffee. After breathing deeply for a little bit, I finally compose myself enough to look up at Paul.

"I'm okay," I reach out and take his hand to reassure him as he sits in the chair across from me.

"I think you should pack up and call it a day. It's been one hell of a morning already. Everything here can wait until tomorrow. April can pick up the slack." I think about it for a minute and decide it is probably for the best.

"Okay," I mutter.

"How are you getting home? Do you need me to have someone take you?" Paul asks as he gets up and pulls out his cell phone.

"No, I will call Charles. He said he'd be around all day.

He's a sweet man. Thank you for doing that for me." I rub my face a few times to control my temper. I need to get it together while I am here.

"Doing what?" Paul looks lost.

"For sending Charles to bring me back and forth to work." Paul looks at me like I've grown two heads. "You didn't send a driver, did you?" Realization sets in.

"I did not. I was wondering what that email meant this morning. I haven't had time to ask you."

My blood instantly boils, and I jump up from the couch, kick off my heels, round the corner, and run down the hall full force. I see that they are still in the room, and I rush in before anyone can stop me. I hear Paul calling after me down the hall, but I don't stop. Jason looks up in surprise as I run in. I am sure I look like a hot mess.

"Who hired the driver?" I spit out angrily, but they both just stare at me and then look at each other. "Who was it? I want to know right now. It wasn't my boss." I stand my ground as Jason comes around the table to me.

"Miranda, calm down." Jason tries to put his hands on my shoulders, but Ethan doesn't say a word.

"It was you, wasn't it?!" It's more of a statement than a question. I already know it is Ethan.

"Miranda, it was my suggestion." Jason's voice wavers. I look at him, and he has his hands up in defense now, but I know it wasn't.

"Who is paying him?" I glare at Jason, who glances back at Ethan, and I have my answer. Slowly, I drop my head back and exhale out to the ceiling.

Paul enters the room behind me, mumbling and huffing for breath. I just stand there with my eyes closed, taking deep breaths. I need to control my temper. When I start to speak, it is calm and slow as I address them. I will be the rational person here.

"Why am I the only person in this room that finds this whole situation offensive? I do not understand, for the life of me, why you won't take no for an answer." I have turned to face Ethan. "I do not want your money. I do not want a driver. I do not want anything from you. You have done enough damage already. Just leave me alone. Please." I expect another argument.

"I can't," Ethan says sharply.

"You can. You just choose not to." My anger starts to build again, and I realize I have started to shake. I feel the blood starting to leave my face as the room tilts, and I reach for a chair. Jason yells my name, but I start to pass out. Ethan's green eyes are over me as the edges of my vision go dark.

"MIRANDA!" Paul yells somewhere behind me, but all I see are those green eyes filled with fear as my own close. There are hands on me as I am lifted. I feel like I am floating in a bubble of warmth.

Ethan's voice is near. "Stay with me, Miranda. Please, don't go to sleep." He's close to my face, but I'm not sure where. People are yelling. So many voices. I'm confused, but I feel safe and drift off.

I hear my name and open my eyes. Ethan is holding me against him, and we are moving. I tilt my head and see Paul, Jason, and April following behind.

"Miranda. Stay with me, please, dear God, stay with me." I hear his voice. It's so soft and full of concern.

"Where are we going?" I think I manage to say and I feel his arms tighten around me, so I'm sure he heard me. I'm still somewhere between awake and asleep, so nothing makes sense.

"I'm taking you to Paul's office." His words are soothing, and I pull the blanket up. I'm cold.

"Okay." I want to close my eyes again.

"Don't close your eyes, Miranda. Stay awake."

"Okay." I am so tired, and my head hurts, but I feel him quicken his steps.

"I'm going to lay you down," Ethan says to me, and all I can do is blink as I try to focus on him. His face is blurry, but I know it's him. Then I feel the soft sofa under me, but I'm still so cold. I pull the blanket again, trying to stay warm, and notice it smells so good. Inhaling, I realize it smells like Ethan. I smile. Ethan.

"Miranda, the paramedics are on their way." Jason is talking to me now, and I nod, but then understand what he says and suddenly start to panic. When I try to sit up, hands hold me still.

"Stay down. You passed out." Paul adds, and I reach out and find a hand. His hand. Comfort washes over me, and I relax back on the couch. The three of them keep talking, but I am so tired that I just have to close my eyes, just for a minute.

I try to move but can only move my fingers. They brush against something—a blanket, maybe. My eyes won't open, no matter how hard I try. I don't want this, not again.

"Miranda, honey, it's Mom. Can you move your fingers again?" Mom? Am I dreaming? I move my fingers.

"Yes, Miranda, do it again." Okay. I do it again and hear her cry. "Honey, can you open your eyes?" I try, really try, but they won't budge. Only my fingers move again. "It's okay, baby. Just move your fingers again." I do, and she touches my cheek.

Now I can't move my fingers. I hear talking, although I can't make out what they are saying. Suddenly, a bright light hits my eyes, but I can't flinch or turn my head.

"Miranda, it's Dr. Shay. Do you remember me? Can you move your fingers again?" I try hard, but nothing moves. Mom is talking, and I feel touching, then nothing, just blackness. Quiet blackness.

My fingers move again, but it's quiet around me. No one is asking me to move now. This time, I can move my arm a bit, and when I do, I feel softness, like silk between my fingertips, but then it's gone too soon. A hand grabs mine and squeezes. Ethan. I can't squeeze back or move, and I start to panic.

"Miranda, can you hear me?" Ethan's voice is quiet, and I feel his breath on my cheek. I will my fingers to move as his thumb brushes over my knuckles. "Can you open your eyes? Please, for me?" He sounds so sad, and I try but nothing is moving. Again, he squeezes my hand, and I want to scream. Why is this happening to me?!

"Come on, baby, you have to wake up. Please. I will do anything if you just wake up." His breath dances over my ear as he speaks. I really try, but still nothing happens. No tears fall from my eyes, and no sound comes from my lips. It's like I am frozen in time.

"Please." Anguish is thick in his voice as he moves closer. I feel his breath, and then his lips brush across mine. I remember the feel of his lips and struggle to find them again. Quietly, his fingers touch my cheek, and I hear him saying he is sorry before I drift back off into the blackness.

Beeping? Yes, I hear beeping this time, and my fingers move. Then my hand moves, followed by my arm, and I can open my eyes. Oh, thank God! It's dark and quiet, but I can move my hand more now. I feel silk again, but this time, I can look down. It's Ethan. His silky black hair is on my fingers, and his head is lying on the bed next to me, his hand on my leg. He's sleeping on his arm. It must be late.

Reaching over, I touch his hair again. It's so soft. As I am trying to figure out if this is real, he moves, and his hair glides through my fingers. He lifts his head, and when his sleepy eyes meet mine, relief washes over his tired face, and he smiles.

"Miranda. Thank God." His hand grabs mine, and our fingers entwine instantly. I smile as he stands up and comes closer to me. He looks terrible but gorgeous at the same time. His hair is a mess, and he hasn't shaved in a while, but I don't care. He takes my face in his hand, and his thumb runs over my cheek. "Thank God." His voice cracks as he bends forward and kisses my forehead. When he pulls back, his eyes shine with unshed tears, and I'm confused.

I try to sit up, but he shakes his head no and puts his free hand on my shoulder to stop me. "No. Stay still." He doesn't let my other hand go as he waits for me to process. I notice I am in a hospital room. "Stay still, baby. I will be right back." He lets my hand go, and I try to keep hold of it, but I'm so weak I can barely lift my arm. "Stay awake." His voice is hoarse as he looks over my face. "Please." He kisses my lips softly again before leaving me to figure out what is going on.

Seconds tick by, and he's right back in with a nurse. "Well, hello. You finally decided to join us again." She smiles at me as she starts to take my vitals.

"What?" I'm hoarse, and my lips hurt. My mouth is so dry that I can't even lick my lips.

"Let's take a look at you first, then we can explain." She listens to my heart and looks into my eyes. I'm so confused.

"I'm going to go get your mom," Ethan says and leaves me with the nurse again. My mom?

The nurse takes my pulse and pushes some buttons on the machines next to me as I watch. "I'm thirsty." The words are so rough as I cough.

"I've paged the doctor. He will be right in. We can determine what you can have from there." She smiles at me again as she continues, leaving me in suspense.

My head is pounding, and I move to reach up, but she stops me. "Just lay still for a few more minutes, okay?" She isn't as friendly as Nancy was. Before I can speak to ask, my parents come barreling through the door at a full run.

"Miranda!" Mom is at my side, crying in two seconds.

"Mom?" My voice is barely a squeak, and my throat feels raw. "How? When did you get here?" She looks surprised at my question.

"I haven't told her anything yet." The nurse explains, and Mom takes my hand as Dad touches my leg.

"Dad." I need answers. "What is going on?" My eyes search their red, puffy eyes as they exchange glances.

"Miranda, sweetie, we need you to take it easy. You had a small issue, and you are in ICU." Mom looks to the nurse, then back to me. "You have major bruising on your brain. It is causing problems." She continues to explain, and I am sure I look as shocked as I feel.

"Bruising?" I don't understand.

"Honey, you have been asleep for six days." Mom rubs my arm.

"Six days?" I glance at the nurse. "Am I okay?" The nurse's smile doesn't reach her eyes, and that throws me into another round of panic.

"Now that you are awake, we will be able to help you get better. You gave us all a scare. You will have some recovering to do, but you woke up, and that's step one. The doctor will be able to explain more." The nurse steps away to answer her phone and then tells us she will be back.

"Mom. Was I really out six days?" She only nods at me. "What happened?" I feel her hand tighten on mine, and I'm scared. "Mom?" I feel tears filling my eyes.

"Honey, it's okay. Shh." She is teary-eyed, too, and that makes it worse.

"Am I okay?" I ask again, and I feel a hand on my shoulder. I know immediately that it is Ethan. I didn't even see him come back. I'm so confused.

"Someone tell me what is going on!" I'm terrified.

Ethan's fingers tighten on my shoulder as he speaks. "You were at the office and were in a heated discussion with Jason and me. Things got a little out of hand, and you just passed out."

I hear Ethan's words, but I'm still lost. "I remember… you…you were being a jerk, and I yelled." I look around again and hear the machine beeping faster.

"Just stay calm. Please. We can talk it out later. Yes, I was completely wrong, and I'm sorry. Please, just don't get upset." His fingers brush down my face, and I'm not sure if I should be angry or happy that he is here.

Emma comes running in around the bed and screeches, stopping any discussion I want to have. "You wait until I'm in the bathroom to wake up!" She pushes Ethan out of the way and hugs me, kissing me hard on the cheek. "Damn you! You scared me half to death!" She hugs me again as tears run down her face.

"Sorry." I have no idea what else to say. When she finally

lets me go, she turns to Ethan, and he holds her as she cries into his shoulder. What is going on here? I'm so lost. Sensing my panic, Ethan's hand is back on my shoulder as he holds Emma.

"Miranda. Just rest. We will tell you everything in time." Mom is sitting on the edge of my bed now, rubbing her fingers across mine. They are all hovering so closely that it only tenses me more. I thought I was okay? I remember feeling dizzy and then this.

After what seems like forever, the doctor comes in and kicks everyone out. He gives me an exam and explains what happened. There is now slight swelling and bruising on my brain. It did not show on the last tests I had before discharge, so no one had any idea. They had kept me comfortable, so I had the time to heal, but my body had to wake up on its own.

"Are you in any pain?" He asks as he tests my vision and motions.

"No. I mean, I have a little headache, but that has been constant since the accident. You all told me that was normal from the concussion."

"It was. However, I am sure it was more than a little headache." He looks down his nose at me, and I flinch.

"Maybe it was worse at times, but I didn't think it was anything to worry about." I can't look him in the eye; he knows I'm lying. Damn.

Finally, he's done and says I can start with ice chips and then water. "Once we know that will stay down, you can move on to juices and Jello. I want soft foods and lots of liquid and rest. We will take it day by day. And Miranda, if anything hurts more than a small dull ache, we need to know." He is very stern as he waits for my acknowledgment.

"Ok, I am going to let your family back in, but only a few at a time, and I want quiet and rest. Hear me, young lady?" He smiles, and I smile back.

"Understood." I agree.

"I mean it, pain, aches, bright light sensitivity, anything."

"I will. Promise."

"Alright." He leaves me alone and goes to talk to my family as the nurse gives me ice chips and more instructions.

My parents are the first to come back in, and immediately, Mom is fussing over me and feeding me ice chips. Dad just stands at my bed and holds my fingers on my broken arm. He doesn't say much, but then he never does. I don't need him to. I can see his worry, and I know he cares.

"We were so worried. All these days, we just prayed that you would be okay." Mom brushes the hair from my face, which is becoming a new habit of hers.

"I woke up a few times, I think. I could hear voices, but I could never figure out what was going on. Well, until I started moving my fingers earlier, and you all wanted me to do it more. I knew something was wrong." Raising my arms, I wiggle them to make sure.

"We remember when you did that. It was yesterday morning when you first moved. We were so hopeful." Quickly, she swipes a tear away from her cheek.

"I'm sorry, Mom. I should not have gone back to work. And then arguing with Ethan and Jason." I look down at the covers.

"Open." Mom feeds me more ice. "Well, Ethan has not left your side. He's been here the entire time. He only left to change clothes and shower twice. And that was in record time. You know he really cares about you." Mom looks hopeful.

"Really? All six days?"

"Yes. He sat right here and held your hand. He would squeeze your hand, and then the other, and kept asking you to wake up. We all did. He was completely shattered when we arrived." Mom wipes my chin off from the water and takes a deep breath as if it's hard to think about.

"So many people have been here. We haven't let them all in, though." She gives me a wink and then smiles as if I should understand. "I will tell you all about that later. Right now, I think I should let your sister and some other people back in here." She smiles at me and touches her cheek to wipe away another stray tear.

"I love you, Mom. You too, Dad." They both kiss me and say the same, then slip out of the small room.

For the next little while, there is a steady stream of people in and out. Emma and Sophia, Joe and Tristen, Mom and Dad, my aunt and uncle who came up last night, but mostly Mom and Emma. Finally, Ethan comes in, and Mom leaves us alone.

"Hi." His voice is deep as he stands back from me, avoiding eye contact.

"Hi," I answer, but he doesn't say anything more or even budge from the spot where he stands just inside the curtain. "Please sit." I finally ask so he will relax. I can feel his tension from across the room. Slowly, he moves over to the chair and sits with his hands in his lap, and his head hung. He really does look like a hot mess, but damn, it makes me want to hold him.

"Mom told me you stayed this whole time I've been out." I can't see it, but I hear his deep breath and long exhale.

"I am so sorry, Miranda. All this is my fault. I cannot even begin to tell you how sorry I am." He stumbles through his words, his voice full of guilt. His entire being is sad, something I have never heard before. Without thinking, I reach over and take his hand.

"No, this time, it's my fault. I was having bad headaches and ignored them. I went back to work way too soon, and I'm paying for it." Now I feel guilty.

"But I put you in this mess to begin with." He runs his fingers across my knuckles, and I feel that familiar tingle from his touch. I know I should be angry at him, but I just can't bring myself to, not now.

"You really stayed six days here with me?" I squeeze his hand, and he looks up, his beautiful green eyes shining.

"I was not leaving until you woke up." He looks back down at our hands, and I feel his grip tighten.

Six days. I can't even imagine their fear.

"Tell me what happened? I only remember arguing with you. And I'm sorry for that."

Surprise flashes in his eyes as he moves forward in his chair. "No. You should not be sorry at all. I am. I'm embarrassed that I let all that happen in the first place." He pauses and looks at me for a minute before continuing. "I can't... God, I'm sorry. I can tell you later." His head hangs, and I am sure I hear him sniffle.

"No, please, tell me now. I want to hear you talk." For some reason, his voice seems to be soothing my terrified soul.

"Miranda." He says my name so sweetly that I almost whimper.

"Please." This time, he nods and squeezes my hand.

"You had just finished yelling at me. Do you remember that part? You were pretty mad." I nod, so he continues. "Then you got quiet, and I literally watched the color drain from your face as your eyes lost focus. Jason yelled your name, but I was able to grab you before you hit the floor. I called your name, but you didn't answer me. You were just shaking so much. I took off my jacket and laid it on you before carrying you to Paul's office to wait for the ambulance. You woke up once, said you were cold, and then opened your eyes when we got outside, but you never spoke again. That's it. You didn't move in the ambulance or here. I thought…I thought you were gone." His voice wavers slightly before he clears his throat. "Until you moved your fingers yesterday." He slowly turns my hand over and touches my fingers with his other hand, but he doesn't let me go.

"I remember the blanket. It smelled like you. And yes, I remember being so cold." Leaning my head back, I remember the smell. His smell. Rugged, outdoorsy, yet somewhat sweet.

"It was my suit jacket," he answers as if reading my thoughts.

"I remember looking up at you too. I saw your green eyes and knew you were there." My voice has softened as we smile at each other shyly.

"I knew you had me. I felt warm and safe."

"I did." He whispers back.

"Thank you for protecting me. Again."

He makes a sound and looks down away from me. I have no idea what he is thinking as he shifts in his chair, but it makes me nervous. "Ethan?" It's more of a question, and he looks up, his eyes full of emotions I can't figure out.

"I wasn't leaving you." His lips brush over the back of my hand that he has raised to his lips.

"Ethan…" I start, but he cuts me off.

"Not then, and not now. I am not leaving. Not this time. You and I, we will talk this out." His voice is so deep as he waits, and I can't help but smile.

"What is there to talk out?" I ask because I want to make sure I understand what he is implying here.

"Us." He whispers.

"US?" I test the word as my heart races against my chest.

"Yes, us. I was wrong for not telling you the truth right away, but if I had, I wouldn't have fallen for you. And when I realized it, it was too late. I knew when you found out, you would hate me. Like you do now. I wanted to have just a few more hours with you. And then hours turned into days. I tried so many times, but you were so perfect, and I knew the moment I told you the truth, it would be over. I'm sorry, Miranda. You didn't deserve any of this." His words fall in a quick stream, and I hear his grief, which touches me deeply. Maybe I was wrong. Maybe he isn't the jerk I thought he was.

"I do not hate you." My fingers tighten around his.

"You don't?" He seems surprised.

"No. In fact, I am having a hard time even finding a reason to be mad at you anymore." I am finally being honest with myself. The man just sat here for six days begging me to wake up, and I didn't forget that I heard him call me baby.

"Really?" His face lights up, and he pulls my hand up to kiss it again.

"I'm not happy about it, and you have some major sucking up to do, but I forgive you." My voice has softened to a whisper.

"I will do all the sucking up you want." His smile is so innocent and sweet that I can't help returning it.

"Can I just add, though, you look a little rough. You might need a shower." I use my broken arm to fan under my nose, making him laugh.

"Six days of sleeping in a chair next to your bed will do that. And I have had two showers since then, thank you. Besides, you don't look so hot yourself. I mean, how long has it been since you showered?" He raises his eyebrows, making me laugh.

"Oh, about six days." We continue to laugh, and it feels good. I missed this.

"You know, you can go home and rest now. I'm up. And don't you have a job and a life to tend to? And what day is it?" I joke, trying to keep the mood light.

"No, I'm not leaving. There is no way you are kicking me out. And I do have a job. I have done it while I have been here. No other life things are more important than this. It is Sunday. Do I really look that bad?" He brushes his chin with his hand a few times, causing me to giggle.

"You can't possibly have no other life things to worry about. And don't mess up your job for me. Go to work to-morrow. Sunday? Really? I am glad I set the DVR." Tilting my head to the side, I admire him for a second. "You know, maybe you don't look that bad. A little rough, but I think it might make you a little sexier." A giggle escapes as shock registers on his face, but he recovers quickly.

"Well, thank God for DVRs, then. And no, Miranda, I have no one to answer to. That's how I like it. I own my companies, so if I want to take a week to sit with a beautiful woman, I will." He grins, and I can't help but laugh to cover my embarrassment.

"Are you sure you don't have concussion symptoms too? I mean, I'm hardly beautiful, especially in this state." I pick up the gown near my neck, shake it, and then hold up my broken arm in explanation, making him smile warmly.

"I think you are the most beautiful woman I have ever met. Your wit, your sassiness, your smile, your eyes, you are almost perfect." He gives me a shy smile as he looks at our hands again.

"Almost?" I ask in a whisper.

"You do have this problem with rather un-ladylike lan-guage. That is very distracting. Not to mention the hygiene problem." He scrunches his face and laughs. He's joking.

"Well, if someone wouldn't have been so late for a stupid meeting, then I wouldn't be here. I would be home enjoying a quiet Sunday alone and showered." I smile to show I am teasing, too.

"It was a very important meeting." He counters as he brings my hand to his lips.

"So important that you almost killed yourself?" I raise my eyebrows, waiting.

"Yes." He grins playfully. I like this side of him.

"What meeting could have been that important?" I am curious, and he grins at my fake outrage.

"The meeting was with a gentleman to buy his very large and very profitable company. And if someone would have taken three more seconds before going through the intersection, I would have made said meeting." He laughs but then adds more seriously, "But then, I wouldn't have met you. So, no, I guess that meeting wasn't as important as what fate had in store for me." Again, I am the one shocked into silence.

"Sorry, I kept you from him and buying his very large company," I whisper.

"You didn't. I still bought it." He leans in and kisses my hand, his eyes shining bright with humor.

"What company was it? Jerks R' Us?" Giving him an overly exaggerated smile.

"Actually, it was Assholes R Us, their parent company." He tries to stay serious.

"Oh, I thought you already owned that one." This time, I bite back my smile.

"No, you are thinking of I am an Asshole. Totally different company."

At this point, I can't keep a straight face and bust out laughing. He laughs, too, and that makes me laugh harder.

"On that subject, I was hoping I could purchase Please Forgive Me Inc. if it is available." He stops laughing and holds my hand up to kiss my knuckles again.

"You can't purchase that. It's not for sale." His smile fades. "However, I Forgive You Inc. is available for a highly discounted price." His face lights up.

"You do? I mean, how much? Can I write a check? Or is it strictly a cash option only?" He is all smiles.

I'm not sure if he is serious, but I play along. "No money for this transaction. Just a real apology and a promise to never lie to me again. Okay?" He starts to talk, but I interrupt him. "Oh, and an agreement that I don't want your money. Just pay for what is expected and do not offer me more. I'm not in this for money or to be paid off, and I am not going to sue you or smear your name. No money, no argument." I am hopeful as he tilts his head in thought.

"Your terms are tough. I feel a negotiation might be in order and have a counteroffer." I roll my eyes in anticipation of what this will be.

"Okay, I'm listening."

He clears his throat and sits up straighter in the chair. "Hear me out. I pay for all the expected expenses, medical, lost wages, and anything that the insurance company does not cover. Then I pay your rent, utilities, and insurance for this month along…"

I start to interrupt him, but he holds his hand up, and I close my mouth. "…along with all the taxes, license, fees, insurance, and anything extra to replace your car. Then, you have one dinner with me at a real restaurant." He waits as I open my mouth and then stop to reevaluate.

"Counter counteroffer. Yes, to all the above and beyond what the insurance doesn't pay for on expenses on the car. No on the rent and bills." I wait for his answer.

"You need to recover, and we don't know how long you will be out of work. I will cover the bills this month only. Just to help you get on your feet and recover." He raises his eyebrows at me in return.

Inhaling deeply, I try to figure out how to win.

"Rent only." I offer.

"No. All of it." He crosses his arms.

"Wait, isn't this my deal, with my terms for you to get Forgiveness Inc.?" I cross my arms and see his jaw tighten. He's thinking, which makes me grin.

Someone knocks and is coming in, which makes us both look up. It's Emma and Jason. "Hey, you two, sorry to interrupt, but you have another visitor." Emma smiles.

"Jason, please come in. You arrived just in time for negotiations." I glare at Ethan, who throws his hands up, which makes Emma laugh.

"If you are negotiating with her, you might as well give up now. You will never win." Emma laughs harder.

"I'm starting to see that," Ethan grumbles.

"You are both welcome to stay." I give Ethan a wink, and he exhales loudly as they both sit.

"Pardon me while I finish my treaty," Ethan tells Jason.

"By all means, please continue. What are we negotiating?" Jason asks me.

"He's trying to acquire Forgiveness Inc., and he is not having any luck in swaying my terms." I offer, making Emma giggle. She knows my games; we have played them many times.

"Are you for real?" She looks at Ethan, then back at me as he looks down shyly before clearing his throat to recover.

"I'm trying to help her, and she's stubborn." He's pouting!

"You're pouting?" I crack up laughing, but Jason steps in.

"Okay, no name-calling or fighting; we are in the ICU. Let's hear these terms." He's trying not to laugh.

"My offer is to pay all the expenses above and beyond the insurance company, including all the additional expenses to purchase a new car. Also, rent, insurance, and utilities for this month only, and she has dinner with me at a nice restaurant. I pay." His voice is deep and stern as he explains.

"Wait, you just added on 'the you pay' part! That was not in the original draft." I squeak out in surprise.

"I just added it." He gives me a knowing grin, and I glance at Jason, who shrugs.

"Okay, I think that sounds fair," Emma announces.

"Not fair, but fine. Rent for just one month, and I pay for myself at dinner." I re-cross my arms.

"Not budging on the utilities and bills. I pay them. All of them." He's back to his hard attitude.

"Miranda, can I put in my expertise here?" Jason asks.

"Sure," I grumble.

"I think he has a fair counteroffer. You might be here for a while, and we don't want you to get overwhelmed." Jason glances at Emma, who has her hand over her mouth to keep from laughing. Of course, she would find this funny.

Jason does make a valid point. The insurance companies take forever, and I could take the extra and pay down my student loans. "Okay, my last counter counter counteroffer. I take your deal, as it stands for one month…"

"DEAL." He interrupts me.

"Really? I wasn't finished. Are you used to getting your way all the time?" I ask.

"Yes, every time." He's serious.

"Boy, you are gonna have to learn to lose that really quickly with this one." Emma is laughing hard now.

"I accept your deal as it stands for one, and I mean just ONE month on the rent and utilities. The items before are all okay, and I also accept the dinner, but I pay for it. And before you answer, this is my last offer. Forgiveness Inc. is off the table after that." I give him a dazzling smile.

I watch his mouth open and close twice. Jason and Emma are laughing so hard they can't breathe.

"Oh wait, I have one more addendum to add, you go home and shower and shave right after we shake." I smile even bigger, and the two of them are about to fall out of their chairs.

He just sits there with his mouth open. "How bad do you want Forgiveness Inc.?" I raise my eyebrows, and he literally huffs.

"Fine. Deal." I hold out my hand, and he shakes it. The look on his face is priceless, and I can't help but join in the laughter. "Now see, that wasn't so hard. Congratulations on your new acquisition of Forgiveness Inc." I tease him, and he shakes his head, but his grin gives him away.

"Miranda, I think I need to hire you. That right there was the best negotiation I have ever seen. This big animal never gives in to counteroffers, ever." Jason laughs.

"That's nothing. You should have seen her growing up.

It was painful. I always said she would be a badass lawyer," Emma states while winking at me.

"Well, congratulations on your new Forgiveness Inc." Jason shakes Mr. Grumpy's hand.

"Thank you." He growls out.

Ethan reaches over and takes my hand. "You drive a hard bargain, but thank you for forgiving me. That is what is most important." He kisses my hand as his eyes find mine.

"Wait, part of the deal was you had to ask nicely first." I grin as he rolls his eyes this time. I love watching him squirm.

"Miranda, will you please forgive me for causing all this…mess and then arguing with you and putting you back in here. Please." He really tries.

"And for being an asshole," I add.

"Yes, and for being a giant asshole. And for barging into your office and calling you difficult, which you still are, and looking into your background when I should not have. I was wrong. And, well, for anything else that I should apologize for. I am truly sorry to have caused you pain and grief. Please, please forgive me." His apology went from grumpy to sincere and heartfelt. I squeeze his hand to show I understand.

"You are forgiven," I say softly. He exhales and drops his head onto the bed as we all laugh. "I'm glad that is settled. Now, if you will, Ethan, you need to go shower, shave, and burn those clothes. You look like hell. Part of the deal." Jason tries to keep a straight face but can't as I wave my hand under my nose.

"I will. Just not quite ready to go yet." He has both of his hands on my one and brings it up to brush his lips over my fingers. My body shivers at his gentle touch. He's gorgeous all the way to his core. His black hair is a mess, and the days of beard growth make him look rugged and sexy as hell. Although the stubble on his face does look so soft and inviting, I just want to reach out and feel it.

His lips brush over my knuckles again, and this time, I stretch my fingers out to touch him. My mouth is dry, and I lick my lips, thinking how much I want to crawl out of this bed and into his warm, waiting arms just to feel him and touch him. I swallow down my desire and just smile back as he squeezes my hand, knowing there are others in the room.

Focusing back on our visitors, I change the subject away from him. "Emma, have you met Jason?" I'm trying to distract myself from Ethan.

"Yes, we met the first day, well, evening, when she arrived. I followed the ambulance with Paul and April." Jason gives Ethan a quick look before continuing. "To make sure you were okay."

I notice how uncomfortable Jason looks as he moves in his chair. "Actually, I stayed here until your family arrived to make sure he was okay as well. He was pretty upset." Jason nods at Ethan, who also shifts slightly in his chair. Something more happened, but I am not in any place to question the two of them. I just hope it was civil.

"That was very kind of you."

"I was worried. For you both."

"He's been by here every day," Emma adds as she looks at Jason.

"I have. I just needed to check on you both. I am really happy you are awake. And you look great. I mean, great for being out of it for six days." Our eyes meet, and he gives me a shy smile.

"I appreciate that. Thank you." I am touched by Jason's words and that he checked on Ethan too. I want to tell him how much that means to me, but with how unsure his words were, I am certain it was due to Ethan.

Emma laughs out before covering her mouth. "Upset? When I got here, he was a little more than upset. The poor man was downright distraught. They were running tests and wouldn't tell him anything, and he was frantic." Emma reaches over and pats Ethan's shoulder, and he nods, but his eyes come back to me.

Without warning, I let out a huge yawn. "Sorry," I announce, embarrassed.

"You know, I think I will take you up on that addendum. I am going to go home and clean up; give you time with some other friends." Ethan glances at Jason, then stands and stretches, his wrinkled shirt creeping up to reveal his taut stomach and a dark patch of hair that my eyes follow to his waistband. Without thinking, I lick my lips and then quickly look away. Dear God, I hope no one saw that, especially him.

"I will be back in a few hours." Ethan bends down and kisses my forehead.

"Okay, you really don't have to rush back. You can sleep at home." I try not to sound disappointed that he's leaving, but I am. I don't want him to go. It's a big change from how I felt a few…oh, well, six days ago.

"Not part of the negotiation. You can't get rid of me now. I own Forgiveness Inc., and I will be back to check on its progress shortly. Do you want anything on my way back?"

He pulls on his suit jacket, and again, I watch for that flash of skin.

"Uh, no, I'm good. Thank you."

Ethan shakes Jason's hand and hugs Emma before turning back to me and smiling as he runs his finger up the sole of my exposed foot. "Be back soon." He winks and walks out the door, leaving me almost breathless.

As soon as he's past the curtain, Emma is on the side of the bed, in his seat, looking at me expectantly. "So? Are you two dating now?" She is almost giddy with excitement.

"What?! NO! Emma! I barely know him, and honestly, I'm not sure I even like the man at all anyway." She always embarrasses me.

"Sure. Uh-huh. I have been sitting here for the last 20 minutes of this drool fest. Neither of you have taken your eyes off each other. It's sad, really." She reaches over and pretends to wipe my chin off.

"EMMA!" Swatting her hand away, I want to punch her, but not here. I will get even later.

"Fine, if you aren't head over heels in love, then explain what it is to me. And while you are at it, what was all that negotiation nonsense then?" She looks down her nose at me, and I know she won't go without real answers.

"Yes, I like him, but head over heels, I am not. I forgave him. That was what it was. I had to find a way to make him understand that I couldn't be bought. That man and his money drive me crazy. I don't want it, but I figured if we negotiated a deal, then maybe he would stay within his boundaries." Emma's not buying it, but that's all she's getting for now.

"If you say so. BUT in my expert opinion, you are. And that battle of wits was a lot more than forgiveness. I am happy you worked it out, even if it was weird." With a pat on my arm, that is her sign that she has said her peace, and she thinks she's right. She's not, but I'm too tired to argue with her.

"Actually, I think it was a great way to talk to him. Sometimes, I wonder how he makes it through normal life. It's all calculations, numbers, and end results with him. Don't get me wrong, he's a hell of a guy but hardheaded as a rock." Jason laughs freely.

Emma's jaw drops open as she turns to Jason. "So is she! I mean, trying to get her to do something she doesn't want to do, you might as well forget it. It's ridiculous to win with her. I noticed he's as bad as she is, too. The man stayed here the entire time she was out. He wouldn't go home to rest or even leave to eat. We had to force him from this room twice, and even then, I think he must have literally flown home and back." Emma is overly dramatic, and it's hilarious.

"Yeah, when I was here, I told him the same thing. I know he felt responsible for her, and he told me he wasn't leaving her side until she was okay. I tried to talk some sense into him, but he was having no part of it. I didn't know that he wasn't eating, though. That makes sense why he looks so rough." Jason has leaned back in his chair and is rubbing his hand over his face.

"My mom had to make him eat. She threatened to shove a protein bar and a banana down his throat. He did, but only for her. She tends to scare people." Emma turns in her chair to face me.

"He sat and slept in this chair, barely leaving it, just held your hand and talked to you and begged you to wake up."

"He's stubborn. We all agree on that. When he has his mindset, he goes after it and doesn't stop until he's got it. You should see him in business negotiations. He's a bear. Scares the hell out of people, and he always gets his way." Jason glances at me.

"Devoted is the word I'd use," Emma adds.

"You both know I'm sitting right here, right? Stubborn is not the word for what he is; more like impossible. And he is responsible for most of this, so he should feel bad." I'm still a little angry, and I know it shows in my voice.

"Miranda, I'm sorry I couldn't control him in the office. I tried, but he was determined to get you to accept it. I still can't believe he tried to give you a check." With a laugh, Jason shakes his head, showing his disapproval.

"Yeah, well, I'm sorry I couldn't control myself either. It was very unprofessional, but I just wanted to punch him in the face. I was so mad at him." A groan escapes me as I adjust in the bed.

"I was there, remember. I wasn't sure who was going to win, but it wasn't going to be pretty. You two were furious, and I was waiting for daggers. Unfortunately, you passed out before it was finished." Jason is teasing.

"Alright, as much as I love bashing Ethan, can I ask you a serious question? And I want an honest answer."

"Of course." Jason's tone changes as he sits up straight and leans against the bed.

"Was he originally trying to pay me off to shut me up?

To me, that was how the letter read." I brace for the answer as Jason exhales loudly.

"No, it was not. Honestly, we originally talked about offering a large settlement if you tried to sue, but I advised him to wait it out. Miranda, I know you personally and knew you wouldn't sue, but as soon as he found out you worked for a law office, he freaked." Jason looks around before continuing.

"I am going to tell you this as a friend, but it goes no further. Understand?" He leans forward more, and I find myself doing the same as Emma, and I agree.

"Okay, as my friend, and since you know the implications of client-attorney conversations, I am trusting you with this. When he first called me, he wanted the whole thing sealed up. He didn't want his name in anything and was willing to pay you an outrageous amount of money to keep quiet, and as his lawyer, I was for it. Understand he is a man who does very high-end business, and we have to protect his image. I drafted letters and started to get things in order, but that Friday night, he called me back and told me he had changed his mind. He had spent time with you, and something changed. I was against it at first, but he told me he wanted to do the right thing and take care of you. He wanted to take full responsibility. He wanted to do right by you. I drafted that letter to you, but neither of us expected you to be so…stubborn." Jason looked relieved at letting that cat free.

"It didn't surprise me at all that he had changed his mind after spending time with you. For the record, I tried to talk him out of the whole deal and just let the insurance company handle it. Clearly, he did not listen. He never does. In fact, I don't know why he even employs me or the firm. He does his own thing the majority of the time." Rubbing his hands over his face, I can see that Ethan irritates him, too.

"Anyway, I guess he decided to pursue you even against my advice. And for the record, I did not know about the check. The envelope was a last-minute addition that he asked me to add. I figured it was some kind of personal note. Miranda, I'm sorry he's so stubborn and didn't listen, and now you are here once again." Jason is frustrated.

"It's totally not your fault at all. And have I mentioned how much I just want to throat-punch him every time he starts in about money? He has no clue how to accept the fact that I do not want a dime from him. I explain it, think he gets it, and then he starts in again. He's working towards a seriously fat lip. Although, like I told Emma, I don't want to mess up his pretty face." We both giggle as Emma agrees.

"Miranda. I know he is a pretty face, but uh…." Jason looks around again, and when he speaks, he's quieter. "… please be careful with him. He tends to love 'em and leave 'em, if you know what I mean. He's a great guy. Don't get me wrong. He's a total gentleman and will treat you like a queen, but in the four years I have known him personally, he has not stuck with anyone for more than a few weeks. I do not want to see him hurt you."

"Well, that clears that up. Thank you for telling me. All of it. I appreciate you being truthful." I lean my head back and close my eyes. That was more info than I was expecting and a lot to take in. Now, I have an entirely new perspective to look at.

"Look, I should go and let you rest. I really am glad you are awake. I was worried to death about you." Jason stands and comes over to hug me. He kisses my temple and then whispers in my ear. "I still care about you and can see why he adores you. Seeing you like this drives me crazy. Whatever you decide to do, just please be careful." I kiss his cheek in return and hear him sigh. Our eyes meet as he pulls away, and he pauses close to me, too close. And as he looks down at my lips, mine instinctively part, but instead of kissing me, he blinks and stands up.

"I'll come to see you tomorrow after work if that's okay." He says as he clears his throat.

"Yes, please do." I get a smile as he says goodnight to Emma on his way out. Jeez, what is wrong with me! I must have hit my head way too hard.

"Two hot guys after my little sister. What is this world coming to?" Emma's mouth is hanging open, but I can see her sarcasm in full swing.

"Stop," I warn.

"No, girl, you better decide on one before it gets U.G.L.Y." She glances at the door.

"Emma, I have no idea what is going on. I've known Jason for years. We kissed once. Once, a long time ago, and that was it. He has never made a move or said a word all this time until today."

"Sometimes it takes nearly losing someone to make you notice them. The other one, I haven't quite figured out yet." Emma laughs freely, and I feel her move next to me. "Pick the dangerous one, though. He's rich." Emma punches my arm softly.

"Money isn't everything." I open one eye and look at her.

"No, but the way he carries on for you…I mean, come on, six days, Rana? Six. The man sat here begging you to wake up. He held your hand, kissed you, and even promised you a trip around the world if you opened your eyes. Don't pretend he doesn't adore you. Mom and I almost couldn't take it. He was heartbroken every night you didn't wake up. I think he might have even cried." She whispers the last part, but I catch it and open my eyes.

"Really?"

"Really. Mom had to force him to eat. She even made him eat donuts, which I don't think he liked, but he did it. I kept him supplied with coffee, and for the record, he does like Kit-Kats. We got him to eat quite a few of them. He told us they were his guilty pleasure." More important info to note.

"I will remember that. Emma, how can he care so much? We barely know each other. He's so sweet, and he makes my heart flutter, and honestly, he is gorgeous too." I can't help but groan as I stare at the ceiling.

"I know, and those eyes!" She makes a moaning sound, which causes us to laugh loudly.

"What are we giggling about in here?" Mom comes in at that moment, and I hate that I will lose this secret conversation with Emma now.

"Miranda has two hotties after her, and we are debating on who is better."

"Emma!" I yell at my sister as Mom sits in the chair next to me.

"Well, Ethan hasn't left your side this whole time. The man is very stubborn, just like you. Did Emma tell you I had to make the man eat? Then we had to push him from the room to go home and shower. Although, I see you did that pretty quickly." Mom gives me a look before continuing. "Now, Jason is handsome and very polite. He has stopped by every day to see you, but I don't think anyone can hold a candle to Ethan." Mom pats my leg.

"Okay, Mom, who is hotter?" Emma teases as I groan.

"Oh, I've always had a thing for dark hair." My mom's cheeks actually turn pink, and I want to gag.

"This is so wrong, you two." I cannot believe we are having this conversation!

"Rana, we are living through you. I mean, what are the chances that a tall, gorgeous hunk of a man will literally crash into my life and fall for me? You have to admit, it's pretty awesome."

"Emma has a point." Mom agrees.

"Alright, I admit he's pretty damn gorgeous, but he's a little out of my league, don't you think?" The look on Emma's face stops me.

"Seriously? No way! No. You are young and pretty and have a great career going for you. You are super smart and funny. Miranda, you have a heart the size of Texas. What's not to love about you?" Emma is now leaning over my bed, giving me her best dreamy eyes. I still do not feel it.

"Thank you, but he's bound to get bored of my plainness."

"But those eyes…" My mom adds in, making everyone laugh at her gestures.

The nurse comes in with meds and food, interrupting us, and I am thankful. "Well, it seems like there's a party in here. What are we laughing about?" She asks as she sets down the cup and gives me a few pills to take.

"Trying to decide which of the two hotties Miranda should date." Emma pipes up.

"Ooo, that tall, sexy drink of a man isn't your boyfriend already?" She seems shocked. "All the ladies on the floor have been checking him out. Someone told me he is a billionaire or something like that."

I'm the one shocked now. And then a little edgy that all the women have been checking him out. Not that I wouldn't if he were here with someone else. He is a looker. "No, he is not my boyfriend. He's a very nice guy who…"

Emma interrupts me. "And he has it bad for her."

"He doesn't have it bad for me. And I don't know or care what he's worth, but from what I hear, he is a player." I glare at Emma, wanting her to stop making a big deal over it.

"Miranda, if a man sits by your bedside for a week and won't leave, he has the hots for you. And if I had something that sexy after me, I'd scoop his hot little butt up and take him home." The nurse's comment makes me blush as everyone laughs.

"Okay, I get it. Maybe he does." A groan escapes as I try to find a way to stop being the center of attention.

"How do you feel about him?" The nurse asks me while she works to change up the fluids.

"He irritates me to no end, but he is a sweetheart. Honestly, I don't know if I want a relationship, especially with a rich guy who throws money and caution out the window. I just want a simple, down-to-earth, fun, go out and not care what people think kind of guy. You know, the one all your friends are jealous of because he's perfect for you. That's what I want.

"Miranda, close your eyes and tell me the first things you think about Ethan." Emma giggles.

"Emma."

"Do it."

"Fine." Closing my eyes, I picture him, and immediately, a smile crosses my face. "He makes me smile."

"And?" She pushes me.

"His touch is soft and makes me feel calm and safe. When I look at him, I want to crawl into his lap and be held in his arms." An exhale escapes as I think of the way he looks at me, making my face warm.

"And from what I saw today, he's pretty ripped under that shirt." Giggling, I open my eyes back to see my sister grinning from ear to ear.

"I noticed you checking him out when he stood up." Emma's giggle makes my cheeks burn darker.

"Was it that obvious?" I panic.

"Um, Miranda, I almost held out a tissue for you to wipe your chin."

Immediately, I put my hands over my face. God, he probably noticed, too, and thinks I'm a weirdo.

"Seriously, though, think about what you just said. If you think he's that great, irritating stubbornness aside, don't you think you should give him a chance?"

Of course, Emma is right. She is always right when it comes to romance. I suck in this department.

"Honey, I'd let him eat crackers in my bed any day." The nurse comments, cracking us all up.

"I get it. I'll play along and see how it goes, but I'm not promising anything. Now, I'm going to eat this delicious meal of Jello and apple juice, and then I want you all to go eat a nice meal somewhere besides the cafeteria. Then go rest. There is no need for everyone to be here now. I'm awake and fine." I wave them off.

"Miranda, if you don't eat him up, I will," Emma says as she hugs me.

"Em, Joe would die if he heard that!" I'm surprised at her.

"What he doesn't know won't hurt him. Besides, a sugar daddy boyfriend wouldn't be so bad." She pretends to fan herself, and I swat her shoulder and laugh.

"Go home. I love you!" I say as she kisses my cheek again.

"Not a chance. You just woke up. We aren't leaving your side. We will let you rest, but we won't be far. I love you too." Emma hugs me tightly, and then they leave me to have some peace.

Chapter 13

⁕

Since Emma was kind enough to charge my phone, I decide to do a little stalking of my own. I've been sleeping for six days, and I really don't want too again. Unlocking my phone, I see 78 messages, and my voicemail box is full. I will deal with it all later. I am on a mission right now. Opening Facebook, I type in Ethan Bradley. Immediately I see his green eyes staring at me in his cover photo, and I click on the picture, but his account is locked. Damn. Well, I can see he lives in Chicago, which I kind of figured out. He's the CEO of Bradley Publishing, and we have no friends in common. That's not helpful. I hover over the friend request but decide against it for now. Next is Google.

I am not in it for pictures this time, although there are tons of them. I only want info, so I only click on the articles. I learn he went to the University of California, Berkeley, and has a master's degree in business. Wow, impressive. He owns an apartment in Chicago, an apartment in New York, and a beach house in the Keys. I read about the companies he has acquired and those he has invested in and notice he does a lot with animal charities. "Aww," I say out loud as I read about a local shelter he supports.

I'm so engrossed in what I am reading that I don't notice that Ethan has returned and is standing beside me. "I could have told you anything you wanted to know," his voice makes me jump and drop the phone.

"HOLY HELL!" I almost scream as I grab my chest, which makes him laugh as he picks up my phone.

"Jesus, Ethan, it is not nice to sneak up on people!" I snap. My heart is racing as I try to calm down. The machines will be going crazy!

"I did not sneak up; I walked in, and you were so into what you were reading that you did not see me. I have been standing here reading over your shoulder for at least two minutes." He hands me back my phone and I know I am beet red.

"So, did you read anything interesting?" He sits down in the chair and raises that damn eyebrow in question. I start to yell at him again, but he looks incredible. He is freshly shaven, the circles under his eyes are gone, and he smells good enough to eat. I glance down and he's wearing jeans and a dark blue sweater, and he looks hot. I follow his body back up to his face, and he's grinning.

"Like what you see?" Crap! I have been caught.

"You look very nice." My voice squeaks.

"Thank you." He looks at my phone again.

"You didn't answer me. Anything good in there?" I am so embarrassed that I have to clear my throat to talk.

"Actually, there was. I'm also a little impressed." I answer softly and look down at my hands to avoid his gaze and further embarrassment.

"I'm not sure if I am offended or flattered." He is teasing me.

"Flattered. I do my homework on my business partners." I try to stay serious, but after I glance up at him, I can't wipe the smile off my face.

"I see. So, what impressed you?" He has now leaned back and is crossing his arms, waiting for my answer. He looks so relaxed and in control. It's not fair.

"That you do so much with animals. You try to be this badass, but you're a softy. I bet you have a whole house full of kittens, don't you?" My schoolgirl giggling has started again.

"All that I have and all that I've accomplished, and you are impressed by the kittens?" He seems surprised.

"Yes, Ethan, I'm not impressed by money and fame or what you own, I'm not that superficial." I am a little peeved for some reason.

He studies me for a minute before he speaks. "Most women like the flash of status and money." He's serious!

"I'm not most women. In fact, I was googling you to find out more about you as a person. I could care less what kind of car you drive." I try, but I can't stop my eyes from rolling. Here we go with money again.

"Audi." He answers quickly.

"What?"

"You asked what car I drove. An Audi R8. Or I did."

"Oh." That surprises me. I was expecting a Jag or BMW.

"You have no idea what that is, do you?" He's laughing at me!

"I do, thank you very much. I know cars, even though I am a girl." My glare makes him hold up his hands and laugh.

"Soooo, how many kittens do you have?" I ask again, giggling this time.

"None. I'm not home enough to have pets, but yes, I like cats, dogs, and horses."

"Men with pets are sexy."

Ethan shakes his head at my comment before that sexy smile spreads over his face. "So I should go get a dog?"

"Nope, I don't know if that would help you, you might need a few." He pretends to be hurt as he puts his hand on his heart.

"So now I'm an ass and ugly? Wow, I'm hopeless." When he leans forward, I hit him in the arm, causing him to laugh.

"I never said you were ugly. You are an ass, though." This is nice to tease him, but I am curious again. "Can I ask you something?" I ask seriously.

"Of course, anything. I would rather you ask me than google the answer." He raises his eyebrow.

"Haha. I'll get all the facts quicker."

"Incorrectly." He counters with a glint to those green eyes. He's right, but it's easier than 50 questions.

"Alright, serious question, have you ever had an accident like this before?" I feel stupid after I ask, but he answers me right away.

"No. Why would you ask me that?" He leans over the bed to look at me, but I just fidget with my fingers.

"I don't know. I just wondered."

"You have to have a reason." I look up and meet his eyes, which are challenging me.

"I just wondered if you were reckless all the time or if this was just an accident. I don't know, I just, I want to know the real you." I feel completely stupid.

"No, Miranda, I am not reckless, and this was my first major accident. Whatever you read earlier, do not judge me by it. Give me a chance. I want you to know the real me, and I want to know you, too. So please, ask me if you want to know something."

His words are so sincere, and I breathe a sigh of relief. "Alright."

"Okay. My turn." He says smoothly as he sits back and relaxes a bit. "Only fair." He adds, and I nod in agreement. "Why did you not take the bar to become a lawyer?" His question completely throws me, and I have to blink several times to compose myself.

"What?" I try to stall since I do not want to answer him. How did he even know that?

"You told me that you didn't go back to finish school. That was not true. You did finish; you just never took the bar exam." His eyes are on me, waiting, and I know hiding anything is wrong, but it's so personal.

"I'm waiting." His arms cross over his chest, and I'm a little taken aback. I'm not even sure how to answer him, but like him, it's only fair to give him the correct information. Even though he clearly searched my past and info.

"When I left home and moved up here, I fully intended to take it after I was settled. But then, with all the stuff that went on, things just…there were just things I needed to do more. And I found my job, so that was it." His eyes darken, but I see compassion in them, so I tell him the entire truth.

"I couldn't afford to." His face softens, but I can't look at him for long. It's not something I wanted to share. I always feel weak when I admit that. Instead of making it a big deal, though, he reaches out for my hand, and his words surprise me.

"You should take it. You would make one hell of a lawyer. I would hire you in a nanosecond." The warmth from his hand brings that familiar comfort, and suddenly, my mouth is running away. I just want to tell him everything.

"I had a bad go when I got here. And after the mess, it took me a lot longer to get back on my feet."

"You followed a boy who tore your heart out and left you stranded in the big city all alone, but your determination to come out on top kept you here. Am I close?" I watch in shock as he lifts my hand and kisses it. I want to argue, but I can see he already knows.

"Your Mom told me." He admits and I pull my hand away and swat at him as his sweet laugh echoes in the room.

"Here, I was going to pour my heart out, and you are mocking me!"

"I would never mock you. I just find it funny that as strong-willed as you are, you let some little boy tear you down."

"Love makes you do stupid things," I say shyly, but he kisses my hand again, making me look back up at him.

"Never let a silly boy tell you what to do ever again."

"I won't." We exchange an understanding look, and then, with a sexy wink, he sits back in his chair but keeps my hand in his, which lies on the side of the bed. We end up talking for a while until I start to fight to keep my eyes open.

"Rest." He whispers as he brushes the hair behind my ear.

"Why don't you go home and get a good night's sleep? I sent everyone else away to rest, and you should do the same." I try to be stern, but his silly grin disarms me.

"Are you kidding me? You think because you woke up you can send me away? You ordered me away once, not going to happen again." His smile is shy, but his eyes tell me he's not going to be swayed. I'm too tired to argue with him anyway.

"Make yourself comfortable, and don't snore." I enjoy teasing him, and it's hard not to smile when he looks at me like that. Without a word, he stands, still holding my hand, and I notice a bit of uncertainty on his face as he looks over me.

"Miranda, would it be alright if I kissed you?" His question is the sweetest thing ever.

Goosebumps immediately cover me as I tug his hand, bringing him closer with that sexy grin on his face. Everything else stops the minute our lips touch. No noise, no motion, just his lips against mine. He kisses me gently at first, savoring me as I do him. He tastes so good and smells even better. His scent is intoxicating. My hand slowly slides up the arm that is supporting his weight causing him to lean into me more. Deepening the kiss, he pushes me back against the pillow, and a moan escapes me. It feels so right, his mouth on mine. His free hand touches my cheek causing electricity to tingle where his fingertips brush over my skin.

Our tongues explore each other, and a need I don't understand builds in my chest. I have never wanted anyone as bad as I want him right now. My hand moves into his hair, pulling him closer, holding him to me. There is a deep grumble in his throat which ignites my body with desire, I need him closer.

My hand leaves his hair and runs down and around the back of his neck; a moan escapes him, and it drives me on. The fingers of my casted hand trace down his neck, over his collar, and onto his chest. I feel his strong, solid chest through his shirt and remember the view of his taut stomach from yesterday, which only turns me on more.

"Miranda." He groans out my name as my hand reaches the bottom of his sweater. He breaks the kiss and I bite at his bottom lip to keep him near me. My blood is thumping in my ears, and warm desire has pooled deep in my belly, causing me to whimper at the loss of his mouth.

As if knowing, he brushes his lips over mine again, and his nose rubs against mine. "We really shouldn't do this here." He whispers against my lips.

"You started it." I tease.

"I just wanted a simple kiss." He brushes his lips against mine once more.

"Nothing with you is simple," I mutter as I try to get him to kiss me again.

"Touché." A chuckle vibrates his chest as my hand still lays against it.

"Don't go," I whisper as he pulls back a little more.

"I don't plan to." His fingers brush down my bare arm, and a shiver runs through me from head to toe. "Get some rest. I want to get you out of this place as soon as possible."

He growls, and I shiver again. I can't even force myself to respond, he has me ten kinds of twisted. My lips tingle from our kiss and my body is still vibrating from his touch. What is happening to me?

His fingers brush down my cheek and onto my neck as his eyes stay locked on mine. Instinctively, my head tilts back, and I close my eyes as his fingers gently slide down to my collarbone. I swallow hard to keep myself from moaning. His touch is so hot it almost burns against my heated skin.

"Your skin is so soft." He whispers as he lifts himself away, leaving me craving more. The loss causes me to moan in frustration as I look up at him. His eyes are now the deepest green, and I know I could get lost in them if I let myself.

A noise comes from his throat that is part groan, part growl and it makes me shiver. "I am going to go over there and crash into that recliner, but before I go, do you need anything?" He is almost panting as he accentuates the word need and I notice the glimmer of humor in them.

"No, nothing that I can think of." I smile sweetly as my eyes skim down his body, drinking him in. He knows what I am doing, and his own desire is written all over his face. With one more sexy grin, he leans forward and kisses me on the forehead.

"Goodnight, Miranda." His voice is barely a whisper as his fingers move gently over my cheek, and I lean against his hand.

"I changed my mind. Will you please kiss me again?" Glancing up through my lashes, I see the corners of his mouth turn up as he leans down to me, pausing a half a breath before he leans forward and lets his lips lay against mine. They are so soft as they brush over mine, pausing before he does it again. His mouth is lifted slightly away from mine as a smile forms on his lips. I can hear his deep breaths as he waits briefly before speaking.

"Miranda, as much as I want to keep kissing you, I am afraid that I would not be able to stop myself from taking you right here." His voice is so deep and full of need that I whimper. I can't help myself, and instantly, my hand is on the back of his neck, pulling him down to my lips as I pour my own desire into the kiss. His mouth fits perfectly on mine, and after a few glorious moments, he finally pulls away from me with a grumble.

"You." He chuckles and I glance up into those gorgeous green eyes. I don't know what he's done to me, but I don't want him to go. When he steps back, our eyes stay locked, but I exhale the breath I am holding. He doesn't say a word, but I watch, drinking in the way his body moves as he walks. He walks over, turns off the light, and then settles into the chair.

After a few minutes of staring at him, I am just too tired to watch him anymore and I close my eyes as I whisper goodnight to him. "Sweet dreams, baby." I hear him whisper back as I drift off to dream.

The nurse messing with my IVs wakes me, but she puts her finger up to her lips to keep me quiet as she points to the recliner where Ethan is sound asleep. I can't help the face-splitting grin I have as I notice how sweet and peaceful he looks.

The nurse takes my vitals and gives me a dose of medicine before we make the quietest bathroom break ever. Once back, she tucks me in and winks as we both glance at Ethan. He hasn't moved a muscle the entire time. He must be exhausted, and I feel terrible that he's stayed here another night.

I glance at the clock, and it is only 5 am, but of course, I'm awake now. I tilt my head and move myself up a bit in the bed so I can just watch him sleep. His dark hair is a mess, his beautifully sculpted lips are slightly parted, and his arms are crossed over his chest under the blanket. I watch as his chest slowly rises and falls with each deep breath. He is absolutely stunning for a man.

As I watch him, I remember that little patch of exposed skin on his stomach yesterday. Oh, what I wouldn't give to see more of him or all of him. I lick my lips and smile. I don't think I have ever seen a man so beautiful, and it's not just his looks that make me like him; it's his huge heart that he is now wearing on his sleeve. My mind races with all the possibilities that being with him could bring. He makes me happy in a way I haven't experienced in a long time. These last few years have been so hard, but the thought of a relationship with him doesn't scare me as much as I expect.

Just as I start to think that I want to try, the words that Jason said yesterday start to filter through my thoughts and doubt creeps in. *He's so perfect, and I'm so average; how long would it be before he gets bored with me and moves on? Would it be once I am out of this mess and back on my feet? Is this all because he wants to take care of me, then when I don't need it, will he leave?* My heart aches at the thought. I've only known him a few short days and I already like him way too much.

I can't fall for him. I just need to ride this out with as little emotion as possible and protect myself. I take a few deep breaths to calm the tears that are now forming behind my eyelids. It's too much. I need to pace this and protect myself. When I open my eyes, I see he's watching me. His morning smile is breathtaking, and my fears suddenly melt away.

"Good morning." His voice is as silky as his hair.

"Morning." I almost croak out. He sits up, and the blanket falls as he stretches, revealing his tight white t-shirt against his chiseled chest. My mouth goes dry as my eyes rake over him, but I quickly look away.

"How are you feeling this morning?" He stands and comes to sit on the edge of the bed next to me; his closeness makes my body heat up.

"Good. I've been up and moving already. I'm not as sore as I was yesterday." I try for casualness, but he reaches up and brushes my hair back behind my ear, and I can't help but lean into his touch. My breath catches, and he notices, giving me a grin that would melt my clothes off if I had any on. I suddenly feel shy about my appearance. I must look awful.

"What?" He asks as he traces his finger down my cheek. I shake my head, but he gives me a sideways glance with that one questioning eyebrow.

"Tell me." He almost breathes out and I'm done for.

"I must look horrible." I scrunch my eyes closed but immediately feel his breath on my lips.

"Not to me." He kisses me gently, then sits back, leaving me wanting more.

"I think you need your eyes checked along with that head of yours." I groan, but he just laughs at me. The doubt I have from earlier still hangs on slightly in the background.

"What is bothering you? And don't say nothing because I can see it in your face." He takes my hand and holds it.

"Nothing. Really." I try and he gives me that I know you are lying to me look.

"You are a terrible liar, Miranda."

"I'm just being a girl," I say, and then I feel incredibly stupid.

"Well, I hope you are a girl, or I might have some interesting questions." He's trying to be silly, which makes me laugh. I like it when he's like this.

"Miranda, what is bothering you?" He tries a serious approach.

"It's stupid."

"Nothing you feel is stupid. Ever. Tell me."

I want to argue that point, but instead, I roll my eyes. It's my best defense right now. "No, it's nothing really."

He leans down to kiss me again but pauses so close to me. "Tell me." I feel his warm breath on my lips, and I try to close the space, but he backs up a bit. "Tell me." He whispers.

"It's just me being silly."

He moves a little bit closer now, and I'm aching for his lips. "No more kisses unless you do." I try to lean up to him, and he pulls back again; it's so frustrating.

"That's not fair," I whine. *What is he doing to me?* Damnit. "Kiss me, and I will tell you." I pout, but he only brushes his lips against mine.

"No, tell me first." He's teasing me and enjoying it!

"No." I can't help but smile.

"You won't win this one." He teases me more by blowing out against my lips.

"Okay, then, I guess that means you won't get any more kisses either." Laying my back on the bed, he looks a bit shocked. I don't think he expected that, but I can play this game too.

His grin grows as he waits.

I won't break, even though my body is fighting me with every fiber of its being.

"Stubborn woman." He growls.

"Even more stubborn, man." I counter with a little sass.

He shakes his head and starts to sit up but then leans down and kisses me quickly, leaving me giggling.

"I win." I grin.

"You test my willpower to the fullest. " His green eyes shine with delight.

"I try."

"That you do. Okay, cough it up; what is bothering you?" He isn't going to let it go.

"Uh, it's really silly, Ethan, just let it go." I try.

"Nope, we had a deal, one kiss, you spill it." He looks at me sternly, and I laugh, which makes him laugh.

"Fine. Don't laugh at me." I glare at him.

"I wouldn't dare think of it. Go ahead." He tries to hold back his smile, but it's not working. I shake my head and, this time, close my eyes to tell him.

"I am just worried...I mean, I'm concerned a bit. I am so

average, and you are…well, not…and it worries me that you will lose interest in me when I'm back on my feet. I mean…I am nothing special, and you…you are you. We are on two different levels." The words all tumble out in a rush, making no sense, and I need to clarify.

"Ethan, you are way out of my league." I finally finish in a huff, which makes me feel flushed and silly.

He doesn't speak for a few minutes, so I open my eyes, and I am not sure what I am expecting, but he is just looking at me. The longer he waits, the more restless I feel.

"I see your point." He finally says without a smile, and my heart stops. Panic sweeps through me as time stands still, waiting for him to finally tell me I'm not enough.

"However, may I make a few of my own points?" I nod, severely on edge.

"Miranda, I see you in a different way than you see your-self." He starts to speak slowly. "To me, you are not average at all. You are sassy and feisty, and you give me a tough go at every turn. You don't lay back and take what I want to give you; you fight me, and that drives me crazy. You keep me guessing at what is going to come out of that mouth of yours every time you open it. You are most definitely in a different league, one so far above my own it makes me dizzy to think of it. If anything, you will tire of me and my childish ways, leaving me heartbroken and lost." He's honest and sincere and, oh my God, way too serious.

"You are so full of shit that your eyes should be brown." I laugh, and he finally grins back.

"Miranda, I am serious. You are beautiful. So incredibly

beautiful. I think you have a fire within you that will eventually tear me down to a pile of ashes. Add in your honest soul and sassy mouth, and I can't help but be attracted to you more than I can even bear to admit."

Wow. I blink as his words register, and warmth runs through me. I wasn't expecting that. "I think you're pretty hot, too," I say softly, and just like that, the seriousness is gone, and he's laughing with me.

"Like I said, you will be running for the hills when you can get out of this place." He leans down and kisses me quickly, but before he can move away, I grab his arms and pull him down to me.

"Guess I better not heal too quickly then," I say against his lips as he crashes into me.

We melt into one another, gently kissing, touching, and exploring one another. It feels different this time, calmer, more tender. It's not as intense as before, but definitely different. Maybe it's me that has changed, knowing how he feels. It doesn't matter why, only that it is amazing, and I want more. I feel his hands on my face and let him kiss me while I enjoy his lips, his tongue, and his touch.

We are interrupted by a knock on the glass door, and Ethan slowly pulls away, staring into my eyes as he goes. I can't bring myself to look away from his eyes as they hold so much mystery while they stay locked on mine.

"Sorry to intrude." Jason clears his throat, and I pull my attention away from Ethan, who barely looks in Jason's direction; he's still focused on me.

"Good morning." I am embarrassed to be caught, especially by him. I give him a shy smile, and he barely returns it.

"I wanted to stop by on the way to the office and see you." He glances at Ethan, who finally stands and walks over to shake his hand in greeting.

"Ethan." Jason shakes his hand.

"Jason." Ethan nods and I feel the tension in the air between them. Shit.

"Well, you seem to be doing much better today." Jason is clearly uncomfortable as he turns to me.

"I am, thank you. I feel a hundred times better, and I might even get to move to a regular room later today." I try to give him a bright smile, and finally, I see him relax as he moves to my bedside.

"Please sit." I nod to the chair next to the bed; he hesitates but finally does.

"I'm so glad to hear that things are going well. Sounds like you will be out of here in no time. You are going to take it easy this time, correct?" He glances at Ethan, who I think sits a little taller. I want to groan and roll my eyes as I watch these two.

"I'm going to grab some coffee. Can I get either of you anything?" Ethan asks as he puts his shoes on, breaking the tension. As he stands, I watch him slide his sweater over his head and down his chest, covering that skintight t-shirt and that amazing chest. I almost moan as he runs his fingers through his hair and gives me a wink. God, he knows just what to do to get me flustered. Finally, he steps over to me and plants a kiss on my forehead, pausing long enough for effect.

"I'll be right back." His eyes glance down at my lips before turning to Jason. "Keep an eye on her for me." He emphasizes the word me as he walks out, and I sit there stunned.

"I see you two have moved past the disagreements. Guess that means I won't be fielding a harassment charge from you and Lester after all." He sounds a little bitter, and I feel a bit bad.

"No, you will not. Ethan has been very nice to me and..." I shrug my shoulders, not knowing what to say to him, as I feel so awkward and uncomfortable. Looking down at my hands, I am wondering what to do.

"I told you he was a good guy and would treat you right." Jason sounds almost cold and doesn't look directly at me as he speaks

"Jason, I'm sorry. I really did not mean for this to happen." Now, he is the one who looks uncomfortable.

"No, you didn't do anything at all, I am the one that is sorry. I should just go." He stands to leave, but I am torn and don't want him to go yet.

"No, please don't. It's nice to see you. Please stay." I mean it. He is my friend, and I don't want him to leave like this. Jason looks down at me for a second, then glances at the doorway before speaking.

"I just didn't know you would be so affectionate with him so quickly. Miranda, please be careful, I care about you, and I don't want to see him hurt you."

"I appreciate that, and trust me, I will be. I don't even know where this is going or what I want. I am attracted to him, and he makes me laugh; that's all I know right now. I promise to be careful. I'm not ready to be laying my heart on the line." Jason seems surprised.

"You are so levelheaded; I guess I just didn't see that coming so fast." He straightens the blanket on the edge of the bed.

"I am, and very cautious too. I'm not throwing myself at him, trust me." I smile sweetly and get a grin in return.

"I was just looking forward to that catch-up dinner." He messes with the blanket again.

"There is nothing saying we can't still go. He's not my boyfriend, and he will not be telling me what I can or cannot do." I am being honest. I will not be letting anyone tell me what to do, not ever again.

"He is my client, and if he's involved with you, I need to just stay on the sidelines." Jason stands with a smile and turns to leave, but I suddenly feel sad.

"Jason." I don't know what to say to him, but he bends down and kisses me on the cheek.

"Guess I should have moved a little faster." He whispers.

"You should have." I take his hand to cushion the blow, even though I know it won't.

"I have to get to work. Take care of yourself, and please call me if you need anything. Okay?" He pulls his hand free and turns to go.

"I will. Promise." My answer makes him smile over his shoulder, and he gives me a small wave, and then he is gone.

Leaning my head back, I start to talk to the ceiling. "Why? Months, years, and nothing. Then, two men in a matter of days. This sucks." I say out loud. I don't want to lose either of them. I am sad that Jason finally admitted something, and I'm messing around with someone else. Dammit. I felt like either way, I am going to hurt someone. I just hope it isn't me getting crushed in the end.

Ethan returns with coffee while I am on the phone with Mom, so he settles back in the recliner while I talk. I give her an update on everything, and she informs me that they will all be back up after breakfast, which I agree is perfect, but I add that they are not going to sit around here all day.

"Jason, leave already?" Ethan's smirk is clear over his coffee cup.

"He did. Just came by before work. And speaking of work, it's Tuesday, that's where you should be. I am sure after missing so many days, you have stuff to do."

"I have nothing urgent that my staff can't handle." He takes another drink of his coffee and scrolls through something on his phone.

"Really, I'm fine. Go home, shower, go to work, buy something, make something, do whatever it is that you do." I try to keep my voice light and playful.

"Are you trying to kick me out?" His smirk spreads.

"No, just think you should be out there doing your thing, not sitting in here staring at me all day."

"I like staring at you." He smirks again, this time looking up from his phone.

"I'm sure you do. However, you have to go to work sometime." I try to sound stern.

"No, I really don't. I own it. I can do as I please." He is going to be difficult.

The man seems to have an answer for everything, and it is driving me crazy. Of course, I don't want him to go, but he has a life to live. He glances up at me from his phone as the silence stretches, that grin growing across his face. Ugh.

"You know, eventually, I will kick you out." I sit up from the bed, crossing my legs to be able to watch him.

"Mmm-hmm." His eyes stay on his phone, but his smile is hard to hide over that coffee cup.

"Ethan James Bradley, I demand that you go to work." He looks up in surprise at my use of his full name.

"No." He looks back at his phone.

"I will physically throw you out." I try hard to be serious and not laugh.

"A little thing like you, you wouldn't get me far." He is laughing at me now.

"Ethan, seriously, you can't sit here for however many more days I'm in here."

"Yes, I can."

"No, you can't."

"Miranda, you fail to realize I can do anything I want, anytime I want to do it." He is maddening! I need to figure out this man's weakness and get my way.

"Are you getting sick of seeing this ugly mug of mine?" He finally sets down his phone and crosses his legs as he leans back.

"No, but I feel bad that you are living in this ICU room, and it's not fair to you." I try to reason with him.

"I have been home, and I have worked. Now, I need to tend to you."

"Tend to me? I have nurses for that." I squeak out.

"Not the way I meant it." He throws that sexy half grin at me, and before I can argue more, the nurse arrives with breakfast, effectively ending the conversation.

After I have eaten, and he has made sure I have what I need, he finally excuses himself for breakfast and a quick run home once my family arrives. I tell him to take his time, but he gives me a quick kiss and that killer wink.

"Not a chance, baby." He whispers softly so only I can hear.

The day goes by quickly with visitors, and at four, the nurses finally come in to get me ready to move. Emma packs up my few belongings while I send Ethan a text with the new room number. He had sent me a text earlier that he was going to go into the office for a few hours and he'd be back up after, which made me happy, and I told him so.

Before long, I am settled into a new room, and my whole family can be with me at once. It is loud and there is lots of laughter, just the way I like it. The kids are back and have brought me flowers and a little angel to watch over me. I might have to carry it around with me, although I think my other guardian angel might be a little more successful in watching over me.

After dinner and lots of visitors, I am finally alone and stretch out to watch TV. After flipping channels for a while, messing with my phone, and pacing around my room, I am restless and stir-crazy. I miss having Ethan here, but I had told myself earlier that I wasn't going to call him to come back. He needs to take care of himself for a while.

After a few phone calls to friends, I notice that I have a new text from Ethan, and I instantly feel better.

Finishing up some business, then I will be there.

Take your time. You DO NOT have to come back. STAY HOME AND SLEEP.

I will be there in about an hour. Your shouting will not keep me away.

As much as I want him to rest, I miss him, but I will not tell him that. I am trying to keep myself from falling too hard and acknowledging I have feelings for him out loud will only make it more difficult. I am working on a comeback, but my normal, witty self has taken a leave of absence today.

Don't let me keep you from your business. I am just lying around with nowhere to go.

He doesn't answer, so I go back to the TV.

Time passes, and I glance at my phone. Two hours have gone by, and I am starting to get antsy again. I want to go for a walk around the halls, so I call the nurse, and we ended up making two rounds around the halls, and I feel better.

After that, she decides I am well enough for an assisted shower. Washing all the crud and aches of the last week off is amazing. It is weird how the little things, like brushing your teeth, can make you feel so much better.

When I am done, and back in bed, another wave of disappointment hits me. Ethan is still not back, and after glancing at my phone one more time, I have no missed calls or texts, so I decide to text him.

Guess you got tied up. I'm headed to bed. Go home and sleep. Goodnight.

I also send texts to Mom and Emma to say goodnight. It is 10 now, and I am exhausted, so I roll over and try to sleep, but it is no use. I just lay here and stare out the window.

My phone vibrates, and I jump to get it. It is Ethan, finally.

Be there soon.

It's late. Go home and rest.

No. See you in 5.

Ethan, go home. I'm tired.

So am I.

It's after 10, they won't let you in.

Yes, they will. Thought you were going to sleep.

You are impossible.

Yes, I am.

I roll my eyes and start to answer just as he walks in.

"Hello, beautiful." He walks right up to my bed and lays down two gift bags.

"What is this?" I motion at the bags as I sit up.

"Gifts." Without missing a beat, he kisses my forehead and takes off his suit jacket, laying it over the back of the chair.

"Why?" I am a little excited to see what is in them.

"Because I can." He sits next to me and rolls up his dress shirt sleeves. "Open them." He gives me a bright smile.

"You don't need to buy me things."

"I know, but I wanted to. Now open them." His smile is so bright it's ridiculous, and I can feel his excitement. I look at the bags, and before I can choose, he picks up the smaller one and hands it to me. I pull out the tissue and gently pull out a pair of silky blue PJs, a pair of light blue panties to match, and some fuzzy blue socks.

"Emma told me what size, so they should fit. I thought you might like something a little more fashionable than itchy hospital gowns." His grin is infectious, and I can't quit smiling.

"Thank you, they are perfect." Pulling out the tissue from the second bag, there is a large black box. It is too heavy for another pair of PJs. And when I pull off the top of the box, my mouth falls open. Inside is a brand-new touch screen Laptop.

Before I can say anything, he pulls more out of the bag. "There is a detachable keyboard, digital pen, and a red leather case. Your favorite color is red, right? It has everything you need software-wise, plus a bunch of other stuff that I will let you figure out." I sit there a little overwhelmed.

"I can't..."

"You can. It's to give you something to do while you

are here. You mentioned to Emma earlier about bringing up some crossword puzzles or magazines for you and I thought this would be easier. It has all that stuff on it. You can play games, read, whatever you like." His excitement is just too much.

Turning it over in my hands, it is super nice, but so expensive.

"Ethan, it's so much." I don't want to argue, but it is.

"No, it's not. Please take it." He touches my arm, sending chills along my skin. "It's just a get-well gift." He explains, waiting expectantly.

"Flowers and balloons are get-well gifts. The pajamas are even great, but this is expensive." I brush my hand across the leather case. It is pretty, but I can't take this. It is too much.

"Just a gift, Miranda." He answers, knowing the worry in my mind.

"It's a crazy expensive gift. You are over the top." I sigh and try to decide what to do.

"Not expensive. If it makes you smile, it's worth it. Please take it, don't argue with me." I really like it, but it is so over the top. But he is trying, and it would keep me busy. I could even do a little work. Maybe I could just use it for a while.

"ONLY because I am stuck in here will I accept this." I offer, and immediately he is grinning from ear to ear. He suddenly pulls me into a hug before planting a kiss on my forehead.

Before I even have a chance to mess with it, though, he is collecting it all up and putting it on my table out of the way.

"I can help you get it all set up in the morning. You need

to get back into that bed and go to sleep; it's late. I see you were able to take a shower." He tugs on my slightly damp hair.

"I did, and it was amazing. I think I might put those pajamas on now, though." They look so comfortable.

"Want help?" He wiggles his eyebrows and I act shocked as he puts his hands up in surrender.

"How about I step on the other side of the curtain, and you let me know if you need help." He is so sweet I almost can't take it as I watch him take out the items and lay them on the bed for me before closing the curtain.

"No peeking!" I call out and hear him chuckle from the other side of the room.

Picking up the top, I stop at the tag. Of course, they are real silk. I can't imagine anything less from him. Untying my gown, I slip the top on, and it fits perfectly, and is so soft. Better than anything I have ever had. Quickly, I lay back and pull on the panties and then the pants and absolutely love them.

"Okay, I'm done," I announce, and when he comes around the curtain, he whistles when he sees me.

"Stop." He makes me feel shy as he looks over me.

"Blue is definitely my favorite color." He comments as his eyes travel down my body, making me squirm.

"Thank you. They are so cozy and soft." Running my hand down the pants leg, he reaches out and follows my path but continues down to my feet.

"You missed the socks." His finger runs up the bottom of my foot, making me jump 4 inches off the bed.

His focus is on the socks, not the ticklishness, which I am thankful for. Slowly, he takes the socks off the bed and gently slides each one on, making a show of the whole thing. Once he is done, he comes to sit on the bed next to me.

"I'm glad they fit and that you like them."

"I do, very much. Thank you." I blush as he takes my hand and rubs the back of my knuckles.

"We need to get you in bed. It's late, and you need rest." He stands up, pulls the covers over me, and tucks me in. Then he kisses my forehead and sits with me, holding my hand.

"Thank you for my gifts." I feel shy and blush thinking about him shopping for these for me.

"You are welcome. Now close your eyes and get some rest."

"You go home and rest. Really."

"Maybe after you fall asleep." He leans in and kisses my forehead again, and I close my eyes.

"Ethan?" I whisper.

"Yes." I can hear the smile in his voice.

"Will you kiss me goodnight?" He doesn't answer, but the bed shifts and his lips touch mine. They press gently, just for a second, before he pulls back, but he doesn't immediately move away. I feel his nose rub against mine before he kisses the tip of my nose.

"Goodnight, sweet Miranda." He whispers.

"Goodnight, Ethan," I answer, completely happy he's here again. His lips brush mine again before he sits up, but he doesn't move off the bed. Instead, he holds my hand until I fall asleep.

Chapter 14

Three days have passed without much excitement. Friends and a few co-workers have stopped by since I woke up, and even Jason has stopped in for short visits every day before work. I think it is because Ethan isn't here yet. My family finally went home yesterday, but only after Ethan promised them that he would take care of me. It was a fight, but I didn't want them to hold up their lives anymore.

Finally, it is Friday, and I get to go home today. No work, though—I am off for at least two more weeks, making it an entire month that I will be out of work. I am a little relieved that I agreed to let Ethan help with the bills. Now, I won't have to worry.

Ethan has come by around lunchtime every day and has stayed until I fall asleep every night. He has been so sweet and attentive, and it has been wonderful to just sit around and talk. Learning more about him and his life has been wonderful. And even though I am trying not to, I am falling hard for him.

I thought spending countless hours together would be

hard and that we would run out of things to talk about, but it has been fun. And just as I thought, he is a big softy. If I bat my eyes enough, I get my way every single time.

Yesterday, he brought me another pair of silk pajamas, along with a box of Chocolopolis chocolates. The man is a sweetheart but so damn extravagant. I explained that a simple bag of Dove would have been fine by me, and his response was, "Only the best for his girl."

I pick one up now and wonder, what "his girl" means? We have yet to really talk about it. He can be so aggravating sometimes. He doesn't listen, he spends too much on me, and he is so hardheaded. I don't know if I want to be attached, but I know I want to be with him.

Speaking of being a pain in the backside, I realize it is already lunchtime, and I haven't heard from him yet today. He did tell me he had early morning meetings, but he also knows I am going home today. I should probably call him and let him know I will be released after lunch to give him time.

I pick up the phone and suddenly worry about going home alone. Before I can think too much, though, he picks up his phone on the second ring.

"Miranda." He is all business.

"Good morning. I know you are busy, but I wanted to let you know that they are releasing me today after lunch." I pause, wondering how to ask if he can take me home. He mentioned doing it yesterday, but we never confirmed it.

"That's wonderful news," He answers.

Why am I nervous? "I was wondering if you might be able to take me home. If not, it's no big deal, I can call a friend." I feel like a kid.

"I'm in the middle of a meeting, but as soon as I am done, I will be up there to get you. Please send a text when you are ready." He is clearly preoccupied, and I don't want to keep him.

"Okay, thank you."

"You are welcome. I need to go. See you soon." He hangs up with no goodbye, no chance to say okay, or even thank you. Hmm, the first taste of business Ethan at work.

After my calls to my family and a few friends, I get to take a shower and put on the fresh clothes that Emma had dropped off before leaving. I finish up just as the nurse comes in to take out my IV and give me instructions for going home. Typing out another quick text to Ethan, I let him know I will be breaking out soon as I wait for my prescriptions.

Another text to Ethan, and still no answer, so I try to call him and end up leaving a message. "Hey, it's Miranda. I know you said to text, but you haven't answered either one I sent, so I'm calling. I'm ready whenever you can get here. Thanks."

Again, I wait. And again, no answer. The nurse offers to call a ride for me, but I decline and call him again. And like before, it goes straight to voicemail. "Me again. Hey, I am going to call someone to pick me up. I know you're busy, so just call me later. Thanks." I am a little frustrated, not just with him, but with myself, for not setting up something yesterday.

I have triple-checked that I have everything, and still no Ethan, so I decide to call Nicole to pick me up. Just as I start to dial though, my phone rings and it is finally Ethan.

"Hello," I answer timidly.

"I hope you have not called anyone else to pick you up. I will be there in one minute."

"No, you are just in time, but really, if you are busy, I can—"

"I will be there." He cuts me off, and before I can say more, he walks into the room, and my mouth drops open as I take him in.

A dark-gray fitted suit highlights every part of his body, from his perfectly combed hair down to his black polished shoes. The light green shirt makes his eyes almost glow against his freshly shaven face. He has loosened his tie just enough to break up the perfection, and all he is missing is that gorgeous smile of his. All I can do is stand there and stare at him. He looks so freaking magnificent.

Silently, he steps up to me, and I am speechless. He takes the phone from my hand, hangs it up, and kisses me on the lips like it is the most natural thing to do.

"Hi, beautiful." His whispers only make him yummier.

"Hi," is all I manage to force out as I continue to take him in, that sexy grin finally appearing on his face.

"See something you like?" He holds out his arms, and it breaks the spell.

"Nope." I grin, but he pulls me into a hug, wrapping his arms around me as my face lays against his chest.

"Ready to go home?" He kisses my forehead like he always does, which I am beginning to love.

"I am. Just have to call the nurse." He plants a kiss on top of my head this time, and I relax into his warm embrace.

"You have to let me go for that," I add, but instead, he

leans over and pushes the button hanging on my bed, then returns to hold me tightly.

He feels so good, and I slide my arms under his jacket and nuzzle my face against him, getting a rumble from his chest in response. This is the first time I have been able to just stand in his arms, on my own. I can feel his muscles under my hands on his back, but what gets to me the most is his warmth and the way I feel protected. Inhaling his scent, which is spicy and woodsy, I feel myself relax into him more.

"I love the way you smell," I say out loud, causing him to chuckle.

"I'm glad to hear that." His exhale is deep and long as his arms tighten around me. A smile spreads across my face, and I feel the same way.

When the nurse comes in with the wheelchair, I give his chest a kiss and pull myself out of his arms.

"You have everything packed up?" Ethan asks, and I nod.

"Okay, then I will take this and the flowers. You take your small plant, and I will meet you downstairs." He picks my duffle bag up off the bed, kisses my forehead, and nods to the nurse as he walks out, leaving me in a dizzying wave of happiness.

It is a typical dreary Chicago afternoon, but I am in a great mood as I take in the fresh air.

"Which car is his?" the nurse asks.

Crap, I didn't even think to ask him. "Um, I don't know, he just got a new one." I try to cover my embarrassment as I look around, but there are so many cars waiting that I am not sure. That is until I see the sleek silver sports car pulling up, and I know it is him. It is just flashy enough.

He jumps out and comes around to my side, helping me into the car before closing the door and thanking the nurse. Suddenly, I am nervous as I watch him go around the front of the car.

"All set?" Ethan asks as he pulls away from the curb, not noticing my fidgeting hands.

"Yes. Very ready to go home." He glances over at me but doesn't say much as I check out his car. It is sleek, and the dark gray interior smells brand new. I notice how the seat wraps around me, reminding me of a racecar but with much more class. Running my hand over the panel near the door handle, I glance over at Ethan to see he is smiling from ear to ear.

"This is an Audi R8." His quiet laugh doesn't hide the fact that he is teasing me.

"R8 Spyder, I know, it's beautiful." I continue to admire it.

"Wait..." He is stunned.

"Told you, I like cars." I shrug as he recovers.

"I didn't think I would find another so soon, but my car guy came through." He is proud of it, as he should be; it is beautiful.

"It fits you." I grin.

"I think so, too, but I sense you might mean it differently than I do." There is a questioning tone to his statement, and I am sure I do mean it differently.

"It's strong, beautiful, and sexy as hell," I admit, and he laughs loudly, but I continue. "It demands attention and gets it. It's classy but screams expensive, so yes, I think it fits you well." I turn in my seat to smile at him, but he shakes his head silently.

"You really think I'm flashy?" I am sure I hear hurt in his voice.

"No. Well, sometimes you are quick to flash your money. And well, there is no denying you demand attention. Ethan, I meant it in a playful way, and I also meant the sexy and strong part, too." I reach over and touch his leg. He glances at me quickly, but he isn't smiling.

"Seriously, you are too much sometimes, but I wouldn't change you, well, not most of you." I run my hand up his leg, making him shift in his seat.

"Do you want to make me crash this car too?" He snaps at me, surprising me. Quickly, I pull my hand back as hurt spreads through my chest.

"Wow. I'm sorry, I was trying to be playful." I turn in my seat and wrap my arms around myself as I look out the window, a little deflated. What has gotten into him that day?

After a few minutes of silence, I realized that I have not told him exactly where I lived. "I'm on West Adams at Ark-adia Tower," I mumble.

"I remember," he answers smoothly, but nothing else. I go back to my window and watch as it starts to rain. Perfect, now my mood matches the weather.

"You can park in the garage, in my space," I mumble as he gets close to my building. He silently pulls up to the gate, and I give him the code, then point him to my space. I only have one and no car, so he might as well use it.

He parks, and I go to get out, but he stops me. "Wait," he says a bit softer before getting out and walking around to my side. I wait, as instructed, until he opens the door and offers me his hand, which I think about not taking, but I do. And when I stand up, he pulls me to him and kisses me gentle and sweet as he holds me close.

"I should not have snapped at you. I'm sorry. I just wanted to get you home in one piece." His eyes search mine for understanding. "And you know just what buttons to push." He adds before kissing me again.

"I'm sorry, too. It really is a great car. I like it, just like I like you," I say against his lips, and this time, his kiss gets a little more force.

"Let's get you upstairs." He lets me go and grabs the flowers and my duffle out of the back as I find my keys in my purse. When we get to the elevator, I push the button and then watch him out of the corner of my eye as he stands next to me. He doesn't say anything, just stands there, which doesn't help my mood.

Slowly, we walk down the hall to my apartment, still in silence, but I notice he is walking closer, almost protectively.

"Mine is 610," I mumble, pausing outside my door as his hand lays on my lower back.

"Are you all right?" he asks from next to me, his voice lighter than I expected.

"Yep." I shoot him a quick smile before pushing the door open and see Kasey come running to me.

"Hey, Kase, how's my baby?" He stands up, wanting me to pick him up, so I set the plant down on the island and pick him up. He proceeds to rub all over my face while purring loudly, and I let him.

Ethan closes the door behind us and comes to stand next to me. I am a little nervous about his quietness.

"Welcome to my home. This is Kasey, my bestest buddy in the whole world." I kiss him on the head and sweet-talked him as Ethan reaches over and scratches under his chin. Kasey is purring like crazy at all the attention.

"You can set the flowers on the counter." I offer, and after setting my bag down on the couch, he walks around to look out the windows. He is too quiet.

"Nice place," he says, looking back at me.

"Thank you. It's kind of small, but I love it. Since it's just me and Kasey, it fits us perfectly." Moving into the kitchen, I let Kasey down before going to the fridge.

"Can I get you something to drink? Emma said she went shopping, but I'm not sure what there is." I open the fridge and review the contents. "There's milk, OJ, bottled water, and Sprite." I glanced back at him and notice he is now smiling at me.

"Water would be perfect." He strolls back over to the kitchen, and he seems more at ease now.

"Or I could make coffee?" I offer, but he takes the bottle of water from me, tilts his head back, and takes a long drink. His exposed neck makes my mouth dry. And now all I can think about is planting tiny kisses all over his exposed skin. Even if he is acting weird.

"Thank you," he replies as he puts the bottle down and pulls me into his arms, holding me close to him. We are quiet, but it isn't awkward at all. In fact, it is sweet.

"Do you want to stay for a bit? We could watch a movie or order a pizza or something? I mean, if you don't already have plans." I am suddenly so shy, and I'm not sure if it is him or the fact that I haven't invited a guy over to my place in a long time.

"I would very much like to stay here with you. I'm not much of a TV watcher, but anything with you would make me happy. As far as food, we could go out or stay in." His voice is so deep, and the possibility of staying in holds so much more than pizza and TV. My cheeks heat at the direction of my thoughts.

Ethan reaches up and brushes his fingertips over the top of my cheek. "Your blush gives your thoughts away every time. Want to tell me what you are thinking, or should I guess?" His grin makes my heart leap.

"No, I think I will keep this all to myself." My eyes lower as my body heats from his gaze, but he tilts my chin up to look at me.

"Guessing it is." He almost growls as he lets me go, and a tiny whimper escapes my lips.

He slides his suit jacket off and lays it over the island chair, then loosens his tie the rest of the way before pulling me back to him. Sliding his hand into my hair, he bends forward, and his mouth is quickly on mine, kissing me so gently that I think my knees are going to give out. He has one hand in my hair, the other is on my waist, holding me to him as he deepens the kiss.

Without thinking, my hands move up his biceps, feeling his muscles tense, and a deep moan escapes his throat as my fingers move to touch his face. His other hand travels down my lower back to my ass, where he pulls me closer to him, making me gasp for air. The hand in my hair pulls back slightly, and as we break the kiss, it leaves me panting against him.

When I open my eyes and glance up at him, he gives me that sexy grin and kisses my nose.

"I have been wanting to do that for days." His silky voice is so deep and smooth it makes me shiver.

"Really?" I breathe out, my entire body reeling from that kiss.

"Yes. I have been waiting to run my hands all over this exquisite body of yours." His lips brush over mine again before he runs his nose over my cheek to my ear.

"Was it all you expected?" My grin is playful, but my lungs are having a hard time keeping up.

"And more." He whispers before his lips find mine again, and this time he slides both hands down my lower back to my ass and bends, picking me up to him. I squeal in surprise as he sits me on the counter and continues to kiss me, his hands holding my face.

"I think I might have figured out why you were blushing, and I just might be thinking the same thing," he whispers against my lips as he pulls away. His finger lightly brushes down my cheek to my neck and stops right at the collar of my sweatshirt. I can't breathe as the thought of his touch over my bare skin comes to mind.

"And what might that be?" My voice is husky and full of need. He doesn't answer, just leans in, brushing his lips across my cheek, over my ear, and down my neck, stopping at the place where his finger was. His tongue brushes across my neck, causing me to tilt my head back for him. He kisses my favorite spot behind my ear, and my back arches as I moan again.

"Hmmm, I think I just found a favorite spot." He kisses me there again, letting his tongue dance over my skin, and I moan louder, which makes him continue to give it attention and make me squirm. He has me so turned on that I think I am going to explode.

My head is back, and I feel his hand run up under my sweatshirt along my spine, his fingers barely brushing my skin. I pant as he continues to kiss along my collar. His other hand slides up the outside of my thigh and around to my ass to pull me closer to him. My hands move into his hair, and I wrap my legs around his waist, causing him to moan against my neck.

My body arches into him as his hand moves from my ass and up under my sweatshirt on my other side. His hands are so soft on my skin. It feels incredible being touched by him. My anticipation grows as his hands continue to slide over my body. I ache with need as his mouth comes to mine, and I take him hungrily. Tugging on his hair, I move my lips down onto his neck as my legs squeeze him and his hard erection pushes against me.

Needing more, my hands raked down his back to his waist, where I pull on his shirt to untuck it. He shivers against me as my fingers move around to the front to work on the buttons. I frantically fumble with the buttons, needing to feel his skin as his mouth captures my moans. He finally takes his hands from my sides to help me.

Once the buttons are undone, I push the shirt over his shoulders and down his arms, leaving me free to run my hands over his chest. He groans against my mouth as my hands explore him. He is solid and strong, just as I expected to find him. His smooth, soft skin feels amazing under my fingertips, and I need more. Brushing across his stomach, he shivers as he bites at my lower lip, his groans getting louder. My hand move down his sides to his waistband and around to the front, feeling the hair and remembering that perfect patch of skin. Excitement fills me as I touch it.

My fingers find his belt buckle, but he pushes against me as I try to undo it. Breaking our kiss, he holds my head with his hands to look into my eyes.

"Miranda, I want you so very badly right now, but only if you want to do this. I can wait." His voice is so deep and needy as he waits for my response.

"Ethan?" I give him a shy smile.

"Yes?" He groans as his heavy breathing matches mine.

"I have never wanted anyone as much as I want you right now."

He doesn't wait another second as his mouth is back on mine while his hands run up the outside of my thighs, which are still holding him tightly.

He pulls his lips off mine, and my heart is about to beat out of my chest as he gently pulls my sweatshirt over my head, careful of my arm. Once it is free, he stares into my eyes and I see how dark his have become.

"You are absolutely beautiful," he says as he touches my shoulders before he looks down at me. This gives me a chance to look at him, and my breath catches. My eyes take in his broad shoulders and chest, which is chiseled to perfection, along with his strong arms that have held me close and protected me.

Reaching out and touching his chest causes him to moan as his body shivers yet again under my fingers.

"So are you," I whisper as he pulls me back to him and kisses me hard while his hand moves from my waist, up my side, and over the edge of my bra. His fingertips graze along the top of the lace, and I push up into him, needing more. When his hand closes over my breast, I throw my head back, disconnecting our lips. It doesn't stop him; it just allows his tongue to roam over to my ear, down my neck, and stop to tease the spot that drives me crazy; damn, he's so good with that mouth.

Slowly, he pushes me back so he can kiss down my chest to the edge of the material that is straining to contain my breasts. And when he licks over my nipple, I almost come off the counter. His hum tells me how much he is enjoying this, too.

Gently, he pulls down the lace, and his mouth closes over my hardened nipple. His tongue runs soft circles over my skin, and I am barely holding it together as I call out in pleasure. I am so close to falling apart at his touch. I want him. All of him.

The fire building inside me is too much. I needed him. My hands quickly find his waistband and undo the buckle, but before I can get very far, he pulls his body back away from me.

"Not yet," he whispers against my breast, making me groan in frustration. Ignoring my protests, he moves to the other breast, doing the same, and the fabric pushes my heaving chest to him. I am on the edge of bliss as his mouth works on my nipple, one hand on my breast and the other on my ass, holding me close to him as he continues to drive me crazy. All I can do was run my hands over his back, his arms, and his chest, feeling every inch of his bare skin. As my fingers run through his hair, I pull slightly, causing him to moan, which makes me pull slightly harder.

Suddenly, he stops and grins up at me with deep, dark, emerald eyes and a devilish grin. I need him. I need something, anything. I am about to scream for more. And without a word, he stands, lifting me up as I wrap my legs around his waist and my arms around his neck and he carries me down the small hallway to my bedroom.

Gently, he lays me down on the bed and kneels to pull off my shoes, then slowly runs his hands up my still-covered legs, around to my hips, and up to my waistband, making me arch my back at his touch. As he looks up my body from his kneeling position, it only fuels my fire. He is the most gorgeous man I have ever laid eyes on.

His eyes are now dark green pools of desire, and I am sure he can now see the need all over my face as well. That grin returns as he pulls at my waistband, causing me to lift my hips for him to remove my pants. Except he stops just short of exposing me and looks up at me again, this time with concern on his beautiful face.

"Are you sure?" he asks softly, and I want to scream yes but choose to keep my response at a whisper to match his. Holding my breath, I watch him peel my leggings down, leaving me in my panties and bra. His hands skim up my bare legs, barely touching me before skirting around the edges of my panties. Leaning forward, he places tiny kisses on my belly. I feel his grin against my skin as he holds my hips and continues kissing right below my belly button. I want him so badly that I am now panting and can't help but whimper.

"Ethan, please..." I beg as he continues those barely there tiny kisses across the tops of my thighs before running his nose along the outside of my panties.

"You smell delicious," he growls, causing me to make noises I didn't even know I could make. Finding my breath is getting more difficult, and I will literally combust at any moment just from the sound of his voice.

Gently, he pulls my legs slightly apart, and I feel his lips on my thighs as he moves up, and his tongue brushes along the seam of my panties. I call out in pleasure the moment he pushes my panties aside, and his hot mouth is on me.

It only takes a few strokes of his tongue to make me scream out my release hard and loud. I'm barely through it, and he doesn't stop for a second. Instead, he increases his movements, and in no time, I am at the edge again. My body is so hot that I am positive that I am going to pass out as he pushes me over the line more intensely than before. This time, he stops, letting me come down slightly before planting a few more kisses on my thighs and sliding up my body, his mouth kissing a path to my lips.

When he reaches my mouth, he kisses me hard, and I taste myself on his lips. It is erotic and only increases my need for him. As he kisses me deeply, his fingers find their way to where his lips just left, and I'm struggling to breath as he pushes into my sensitive flesh. My body is on fire, and I start to move my hips against him and within seconds I fall off the edge, calling out his name as pleasure overtakes me.

He takes his mouth off mine and stares down at me, his eyes shining and that gorgeous smile spread wide on his face.

"You are an exquisite creature, Miranda, and I'm going to make you scream my name again and again. Are you ready?" His voice is tight with need and I'm like putty below him. I can only breathe out what I consider an acceptable version of the word yes, which he accepts as he slides off me.

I watch as he unbuttons his suit pants, and they easily fall to the ground. His boxer briefs are strained tight against his solid erection, and I can't help but hold my breath in anticipation. Slowly, he bends and slides those lucky pants down his legs. As he stands up, my eyes widen as I take him in. And I do mean all of him.

My mouth dries at the sight of his naked body. He's absolutely gorgeous. And when my eyes make it back to his face, he is grinning, with that damn eyebrow raised in question. Then, with a wink, he reaches down and pulls something from his pants pocket. Oh, thank God he is prepared. And now, I can't sit still.

He is taking his time, though, making me wait, and it is almost too much to take. Finally, he climbs on the edge of the bed and pulls me to him, lying down over me to look into my eyes.

"I'm going to go very slowly. Tell me if you want me to stop," he whispers as his eyes search mine.

"I will." It is barely a word as I breathe out and arch up to him. His eyes find mine, and he slowly enters me as I call out in pleasure. Holding his arms for support, he slowly pulls out and pushes back in a little further each time, letting me adjust to him. Inch by inch, I take him, and he continues until he is fully in, pausing for me to get used to him.

"You are so tight," he says between gritted teeth as his nose runs along my neck. My entire body is on edge, waiting for him to move again. Finally, he pulls part of the way out and starts in again, building a rhythm, a little faster and a little deeper with every few thrusts. My body starts tightening, and instantly, I am so close. And if knowing, he angles himself and hits me deeper.

I can't.... "OH MY GOD, ETHAN!" I scream and explode around him, falling into tiny pieces, but he keeps up his pace, not letting me relax. I can only hold onto him, letting him take me to a new place.

"That's what I want," he growls as he quickens his pace again. It feels incredible, almost magical, and I close my eyes to focus on all the sensations flowing over me.

He plasters his mouth on mine and kisses me hard, pushing deep into me, and soon, I feel the pressure building again. No way. I am stunned at what he is doing to me. He is now slamming into me, pushing me towards another release.

"Come on, Miranda, one more time." His words rip through me like electricity, and I explode, calling out his name as I try to hold on to my sanity.

He only pauses for a brief moment, and then he changes pace, and everything gets tighter as his own climax builds.

I am sure he is going to tear me in two, but it is so amazing that I don't care. He thrusts into me hard and calls out my name as he finds his release. Even the aftershocks make me shudder. He collapses, his weight anchoring me down as pleasure and exhaustion flow over me.

After a minute, Ethan kisses me gently and whispers in my ear, "That was so much more than amazing. Better than my wildest dreams. Better than my best fantasy." He nuzzles the side of my face, and I hum out my agreement before he moves off me and heads for the bathroom. I watch his toned ass walk away from me and smile in appreciation. I have never experienced so much pleasure...my brain can't even form thoughts. My eyes close as my body relaxes, and I doze off in complete contentment, waiting for him to return.

When I wake later, the room is dark and quiet. The covers have been tucked gently around me, and I still feel the bliss from earlier. I roll over, but Ethan is not next to me. Sitting up, I look around for him but quickly realize he's not here. My heart sinks, thinking that he left after all that. Slowly, I get up, find my robe, and wander into the living room, still naked and dazed. And there he sits on my couch, in just his pants, with my cat. Relief washes over me.

"I see you have stolen my cat's affection." I walk around the couch and sit next to Ethan.

"He gave it freely." He leans over and kisses my cheek without a bit of hesitation. "How are you feeling?" His grin just keeps getting sexier.

"Sore, but wonderful." I grin back up at him, slightly embarrassed by the thoughts still in my head.

"Well, I'm both happy and sad to hear that." Taking my arm, he gently tugs me over to him.

"Why would you be sad?" My curiosity is now piqued.

"Because I might want round two later." He gives me the biggest shit-eating grin ever, which makes me laugh out loud.

Crawling over, I surprise him when I settle into his lap.

"No one said I was that sore." I bite back my shy smile as he wraps me in his arms.

"In that case...." With his finger on my chin, he tilts my head up and kisses me softly as I straddle him before he pulls me forward to fully fill the space against him.

"Hmmm, maybe later should be now," he says against my lips and pulls my braid slightly to tilt my head back more for access to my neck. He licks and bites along my shoulder, and I am already panting at the thought of him inside me. How can this man turn me on so quickly?

My hands glide up along his arms and pull his face up to mine so I can kiss him. His hands are on my thighs, moving over my ass, and then he pulls my hips closer to him. My center rubs across his tight suit pants, and a moan escapes him. I grin against his lips as I realize how hard he is below me.

"You taste so sweet," he growls against my lips.

"So do you." I want all his kisses.

Running my hands over his bare chest, he exhales in pleasure as his head falls back onto the couch, giving me a full view of his torso. Good Lord, this man is ripped. I can't wait any longer to have more of him.

Lifting myself up, my fingers work to unbuckle his pants as he pulls on the belt of my robe, causing it to fall open. His hands are instantly on my skin as he kisses my neck. I can feel his grin spread on my neck as I reach between my legs and feel him.

This isn't enough, so I pull back from him and stand. I need to remove the material between us. Pulling off his pants, I am on a mission now, which causes him to chuckle deeply as I tug them and his boxers down his muscular legs and off his feet clumsily. As my eyes travel up from his bare feet, I stop when I get to his solid erection. I have to contemplate whether to drop to my knees or climb back on his lap. After a second though, he makes my decision easy as he grabs my arms and pulls me back to him.

Straddling him again, he returns to my chest with his hands and his mouth. I scoot all the way forward so that my soft, wet flesh is on him, and he pauses to moan out loudly. Slowly, I begin to grind against him for friction as he sucks and nips at my breasts. The action makes me quicken my pace as he moans louder. His hands move down to my ass, holding me to him as he releases my nipple, and his head falls back.

Ethan's eyes are closed tightly, and his fingers are digging into my hips as he moans and makes noises while I slide against him. It's so good. His noises just drive me on.

"Slow down," he moans, but that just makes me move faster.

"Miranda…" He groans out my name, and I can't help myself. Lifting up, I lean forward to kiss him, and he takes my mouth hard. Kissing him back harder, we both moan in unison before he pulls me up higher so he can get to my breasts. Pulling away, I slide down his chest, his arms holding me tight to him. Our earlier tryst, and being turned on full tilt, has me soaked, and I feel him slide along my wet center. Gliding along his shaft a few more times, I can feel him thrusting against my stomach on each downstroke.

He skin is so smooth and soft, but he's rock hard and ready. I lift myself up with the intention of kissing him, but he pulls me back down by my hips, and he slides into me. I call out as he fills me so full, just skin on skin. His fingers dig into my hips, and he groans out loudly while holding me still as the sensations overtake us. Then suddenly, he pulls me off him.

"NO." He growls before picking me up off him, and I immediately whimper at the loss. He stands me on my feet, finds his pants on the floor, and grabs another condom out of his pocket. He tears it open with force, rolls it on, then pulls me back to him as he sits.

Slowly lowering myself down onto him, I rise and fall a few times to adjust, finally sliding all the way down as we both call out in pleasure. His fingers encircled my hips as I start to pick up speed, but he leans me backward and grabs hold of my breast with his lips, sending me into a new level of ecstasy. I ride hard and fast, enjoying every inch of him as he sucks on each of my nipples. Leaning my head back, I start to tighten, and he thrusts up into me, making me scream out his name as I release hard around him.

With barely a moment to catch my breath, Ethan takes over and pushes into me harder, pounding through my release, which drags out, making me beg him for more. Finally, he pushes in deep, giving me all of him. My name spills from his lips, and it has never sounded sweeter. Falling against his damp chest, he holds me tightly, both of us panting for breath.

"Miranda, you are incredible," he whispers in my hair before planting a few kisses on the top of my head and gently sliding me off onto the couch. His finger runs over my cheek before he gets up and leaves me there. It takes me a moment to compose myself before retying my robe and lying back against the couch to recover. Damn, he's amazing. And so good. I can't help but smile.

When Ethan comes around the corner and sees me, he smiles, but I giggle.

"What's so funny?" He asks as he sits next to me.

"That I'm so exhausted. All of this...activity has worn me out," I giggle again.

"Hey, I was just fine relaxing here with you all evening, but then you came on to me. Twice if I remember correctly," he teases as he pulls me back over into his lap sideways.

"Are you complaining?" I wiggle my eyebrows.

"Absolutely not. In fact, I'm hoping you do it again." Gently, he brushes his nose against mine, and my insides warm.

"I just might." My giggles continue, and this time, he laughs with me as he wraps his arms around my waist loosely and lays his head back against the couch to watch me.

"I will admit, it was a nice change from my usual. Normally it's a quick fuck with me doing all the work." He chuckles, then immediately closes his eyes as if in pain.

What? Did he really just say that to me? Am I just a quick fuck to him? I tense, and he senses it as he opens his eyes. He must see the look on my face because his arms tighten on me.

"I mean, it's usually just quick releases and being done with the girl...wait...I didn't mean that...I just..." Quickly, I move off his lap and back onto the couch, my heart a little wounded.

"Miranda, I didn't mean to say that out loud." He flinches, knowing that just made it worse. "I mean at all." He reaches for my hand, but I move to get up off the couch.

"Miranda, please, I didn't mean it like that. I would never compare..." I jump off the couch, effectively cutting him off as I grab my robe and head to the bathroom. I'm not sure why, but I have to get away from this conversation.

I hear him get off the couch and call after me, so I hurry into the bathroom and shut the door. He just talked to me like I was another girl on a list. Just a quick fill to a need. Am I? Shit, was that all he wanted? No, I will not cry. I won't. He doesn't get that. I pace the small bathroom, trying to calm my shaking body. I will not let him ruin this. I will not be another notch. I won't.

There is a soft knock at the door, but I don't respond. I can't at the moment.

"Miranda, I didn't mean it that way. Please, come out of there." He sounds mad. Why was he mad at me? This is so not my fault. Rubbing my face in frustration, I am trying to figure out what to say to him, when I hear his voice again.

"Miranda, please," he asks, softer and sweeter. "Come on, please."

"Ethan, leave me be," I whimper out, on the verge of tears. The door creaks slightly, and I can only imagine he is leaning against it on the other side.

"Please come out here and talk to me." You know what, two could play this game. I am not letting him do this to me. I straighten myself up, smooth my hair, and open the door. I was right; he is standing in the doorway in just his boxers with both arms on the doorframe above his shoulders, staring at me.

"Miranda..." He looks down into my eyes, but I quickly look away and duck under his arm to head to the kitchen.

"I'm good," I call back, not turning around.

"Miranda, I didn't mean it like that," he says from behind me, but I hold my ground.

"It's okay, I get it. No worries, I got what I wanted, too. Just a good screw." I hope it sounds as cold as I mean it to. My insides are still shaking with hurt, but I will not cry and let him win.

Filing up a glass of water, I take a long drink and watch as he gives me a look, I'm guessing trying to either figure me out, or try to come up with something to smooth this over. He won't.

"I'm going to throw some clothes on, then order some pizza. You are welcome to stay and eat." I smile as I walk around the other side of the island and back down into my room, avoiding walking too close to him. I shut the door, hoping he respects my privacy.

I hear him say fuck a few times, and I grin to myself. Serves him right. He should be pissed at himself. Keep playing it cool, I remind myself. I can do this; just think of him as the opponent in court.

I am looking for fresh clothes when he knocks on the door.

"Miranda." I can hear him exhale loudly after my name.

"I'll be out in a minute, just finding some clothes." I try to keep my voice even.

"I don't want to fight with you. Will you please just talk to me? I didn't mean to hurt you." I can tell he is against the door again, and it makes me wonder how many times he has to do that with a woman?

"Miranda..." He tries again as I look down at my fresh purple lacy bra and panties and grin at my next thoughts. Fire with fire, baby.

"You can come in. I'm just looking for clothes." I turn so I am facing the closet as he opens the door and walks in.

"Miranda, please, I didn't mean..." He stops, and I glance over my shoulder to see that he is staring right at me. Good.

"Ethan, it's okay, really." He just continues to stare at me for another few moments, his eyes roaming my body, but still without saying a word. I turn back around and pull out a t-shirt, holding it up to gauge if it would fit over my cast.

I hear him clear his throat, but I choose not to look back.

"I was going to suggest we go out for dinner, but..." His words are strained, and I want to give myself an air punch or high five for the payback.

"I might feel like doing something normal. Nothing fancy, as I don't want to put in too much effort." I smiled sweetly over my shoulder, hoping he catches my tone and meaning.

His face registers that he, in fact, does, and he closes his eyes and exhales. "I deserve that," he mumbles. I don't respond, but he moves over to me, takes my hand, and spins me around.

"You are anything but normal, Miranda. You are so much more to me than that, and I truly am an asshole who needs to ask to be forgiven yet again. I'm serious, Miranda; you are special to me." When I glance up at his pleading eyes, he looks so helpless. I want to be mad at him, to argue, to stand my ground, but I can't. Those eyes do me in almost immediately.

"Damnit, Ethan, you are a fucking mess. Look, I know you have been with a lot of women, who I'm sure normally throw themselves at you, but I don't want to know about it, and I sure don't want to hear about it. I already have a hard time dealing with most of this. I don't need it in my face. So, if you even think about saying something like that again, I will punch you so hard in the face that you will forget my name. I will then leave your ass on the doorstep and move on. Got it?" My temper flares unexpectedly, and he studies me for a few moments before pulling me into his arms.

"I would expect nothing less." With a kiss to the top of my head, my anger wanes. "And for the record, there is no comparison." He holds me tight, and after a few moments, I can't help but relax into him and exhale my anger. The man is infuriating.

Knowing he is forgiven, Ethan pulls me back in for a

kiss on the nose, then turns me back to the closet, where he reaches in and pulls out a light blue sweater. "This and slacks will be perfect and warm." He hands it to me before leaning down to kiss my shoulder, then back up to my cheek, and across to gently kiss my lips.

"Get dressed so we can go to dinner before I can't help myself anymore." He growls in my ear, then runs his finger down the strap of my bra and over across the top of the lace cup, making me shiver. Gently, he tilts my head up to look into his eyes, which are soft and reassuring.

"Please, come onto me anytime," he whispers against my lips, making me grin. "You are absolutely amazing, and what you do with that mouth and body of yours..." He groans, brushing his lips against mine again before continuing, "... but that's nothing compared to what you do to my heart." He kisses me once more before pulling away, leaving me standing there in shock.

"You better get dressed before I go for round three." He lightly smacks my ass and leaves the room, glancing back with a full megawatt smile as he goes.

Once he is gone, I can exhale my frustration and try to rein in the mirage of emotions I have going on. What am I going to do with him? He makes me angry one second, then melts me into the floor the next. He is going to be the death of me.

After pulling on a pair of slacks, I get dressed before throwing on some makeup and brushing out the braid so my hair falls in soft waves over my shoulder. I add a little jewelry and am impressed with the outcome.

Ethan is waiting in the kitchen, dressed back in his suit and looking cool and put together like nothing out of the ordinary has happened. I wonder how many times he has done that. I start to say something but then noticed he is on the phone, so I save it. Besides, I really don't want to know.

When I come around the island, he gives me a huge grin when our eyes meet before holding up a finger to tell me to hold on. He agrees with whoever is on the phone and then hangs up and turns to me.

"Wow, you look stunning in blue. I like this too." His fingers brush down my hair before leaning in to kiss me. "I hope you are hungry." His face moves to my hair, where he inhales deeply and leaves a kiss.

"I am. Very." My answering grin makes him shake his head.

"I meant for food." He winks.

"So did I." I try to say without giggling as he pulls me out the door.

Ethan slides his hand into mine, and I lean against his arm as we ride down in the elevator. I guess I really am not upset anymore. He is so sweet and affectionate that it's hard to be mad at him for long.

"So, where are we going?" I push against his shoulder with mine, and he pushes back playfully.

"A little place, I know. I hope you like Italian." He leaves a kiss on the top of my head as the doors open.

"I do," I answer as I follow him out, hand in hand.

The little place is truly a little place, and it is off the beaten path. We walk in arm in arm, and the hostess is quick to welcome us.

"Mr. Bradley, what a pleasure. Your normal space, sir?" He nods, and without another word, we follow her to a small booth in the back, where I slide into the seat, and Ethan sits across from me. The hostess gives Ethan a smile and pauses for a moment before walking away.

"Do you come here often?" I am curious.

"I do, yes." He never gives much away, and I want to ask more questions, but I don't have the energy to process anything more. Besides, I want to have a nice dinner.

"Great, what do you recommend?" I ask brightly, and he glances up from the menu at me.

"Everything. You won't find a bad dish here. I personally like the seafood risotto with bacon and chives."

I crinkle my nose, making him laugh.

"I don't like seafood," I answer, and by the look of shock on his face, you would think I just said I hated puppies.

"You are serious? You do not eat seafood?" He is clearly stunned.

"Nope. I only like fried shrimp."

He laughs at me this time. "So then, chicken?"

"Oh, I eat all the other meats." My comment causes him to cough as he covers his mouth, suppressing his laugh.

"You are a strange woman." With a shake of his head, Ethan closes his menu and waits for me to decide. I could say the same for him. Very strange indeed.

We enjoy a delicious dinner and talk about my plans for the week. I don't really have much in the way of things to do, just lots of rest, maybe a little shopping, and catching up on some reading. We talk about the books I like to read, and we find that we like some of the same authors. He also tells me about some of the new authors that I should check out.

We do plenty of talking but even more, laughing, and I realize I am having a great time with him. I wondered if it might be strange to be out in public with him, but it is not at all. And to my surprise, we keep finding things we have in common.

"My ribs are sore from laughing, and I'm so full you might have to roll me out of here." Laying down my fork, I lean back in the booth and rub my tummy.

"I am glad you enjoyed your dinner." Ethan reaches across the table and takes the fingers of my casted hand.

"I did. And the company," I add with a shy smile.

"I agree." Raising his wine glass, I do the same and toast with my Sprite.

"Can I ask what you plan to do about a car?" Ethan asks as we take the elevator back up to my apartment.

"I haven't even decided."

"I would be happy to take you to find a new one." He pulls me to his side.

"I would appreciate that." I lean into him, and his arm gets tighter around me as I inhale his amazing scent and yawn.

"Tired?" His voice has turned warm and smooth. I love the way it comforts me.

"Very. Someone has thoroughly used me and worn me out." His chuckle vibrates in his chest, and I close my eyes for a moment. It feels so right to be cuddled into him, and I am glad I let him take me to dinner. This is amazing.

Once in the apartment, I take my meds, change, and get ready for bed as Ethan patiently waits out in the kitchen to give me privacy. I am beyond exhausted. My body is spent, and I need to sleep.

When I return to the kitchen, he is sitting at the island, drinking a glass of water.

"All set?" he asks as his eyes trail down my body.

"Yes. You are more than welcome to stay; my bed is big enough for two." I walk over, and he turns so I can lay my head against his chest as he wraps me in his arms.

"I had an amazing evening. Thank you," I whisper.

"As did I. Thank you. As much as I would love to stay, I think you need to rest, so I should probably go." Standing up, he tilts my head up to look at him. "Can I see you tomorrow?" His question is hopeful and sweet.

"I would really like that."

"Me too. Call me if you need anything at all." He hugs me once, pulls on his jacket, and then pulls me back into a deep kiss before I walk him to the door.

As I stand there watching him leave, he turns around and blows me a kiss before turning the corner and getting into the elevator. I think I might like him a bit more than I want to admit, flaws and all. I turn around, lock the door, and head to bed with Kasey at my feet. We curl up and crash hard, enjoying the feel of home.

Chapter 15

The ringing of my phone wakes me up, and I struggle to find it through the sleepiness in my eyes. Glancing at the clock, it is 10:30 a.m. Holy hell, I must have been exhausted. I see that it is Mom, and she is relieved that I am okay since I did not answer earlier. We talk for a while, and I tell her about going out with Ethan last night, which makes her very happy. Then she proceeds to tell me what a great man he is and that I should snag him up immediately.

Once I hang up, I notice I have missed texts, mostly from friends, and two missed calls from Emma. I send her a quick text letting her know I just got out of bed and will call her later, followed by answering a few people before reading all four of Ethan's texts.

Morning, Beautiful. Hope you are feeling better.

Hope you are okay. I have not heard from you.

Miranda, are you ignoring me?

I am getting concerned. Please answer me.

The last one was just 10 minutes ago, so I text him back.

Just woke up, sorry. I was exhausted.

It takes him a few minutes to respond, so I stretch out and check Facebook while I wait.

Thank God, I was getting ready to come over there and check on you.

I'm fine, just tired. I slept straight through the night and morning, apparently.

You needed to rest.

Yes, I did. Some crazy man had his way with me and kept me out late last night.

Are you complaining?

Nope.

Maybe he will do it again.

I hope so. Okay, gotta go eat and take meds.

Enjoy. Call me when you are done.

Okay.

After breakfast, I decide to take a shower, and I feel better after what I consider to be a successful shower by keeping the cast dry. I have no idea what I want to do today yet, but I start by crashing on the couch and turning on the TV to lay around and relax.

Two mind-numbing hours of flipping channels has made me restless. I am ready for lunch and bored out of my mind, so I decide to walk over to the little restaurant across the street to get out for a bit.

Once I have my sandwich and Gatorade, I opt to sit by the front window of the restaurant since it is sunny, and with the calm wind, it is a beautiful day. I am not paying attention to the world around me as I eat and scroll through Facebook until a familiar voice makes me jump.

"Glad to see you out and about." I look up to see Jason and I can't resist smiling.

"Hey you, what are you doing in my section of the world?"

"I was out meeting a client a few buildings down and remembered you talking about this place, so I stopped by to grab a sandwich." Jason looks around before turning back to me. I am sure he is looking for Ethan.

"Working on a Saturday? That is not right." I add with a smile, ignoring his unspoken question.

"Demanding client." He winks back.

"Go get your sandwich and join me. I'm just hanging out enjoying the sun." I offer, and he agrees. We talk for over an hour, just catching up on life and my progress. He is happy to hear I am on the mend, and I am happy to hear he is doing so well in life.

"So, any big plans for the next two weeks?" Jason asks as he finishes his chips.

"I don't know. I plan on going home for Thanksgiving, but I haven't decided when or how since travel might be tough."

"You might be in luck. I'm driving home also, and you are more than welcome to ride along with me." He offers with a bright smile.

"I just might take you up on that, thank you. Let me talk to Emma and see what the plans are, and I will let you know." He was very sweet for offering.

"Perfect." He nods, and we chat for another half hour before he has to leave.

Checking my phone, I see it is after 1, so I head back to my apartment to rest and figure out my evening. The fresh air has worn me out so fast today that I just want to crash for a bit. As soon as I am in the door, though, my phone buzzes, and I see a text from Ethan. Shit, I forgot to call him.

'Forget about me?'

'Nope. Just hanging around and then went out for lunch. Back home now.'

'Was it good?'

'Yes. Always is.'

'With Jason?'

'What?'

'You had lunch with Jason.'

'I ran into Jason, yes, and he sat with me and ate his sandwich. How did you know?'

'I had a meeting with him near your building.'

I drove by and saw you together.'

'You should have stopped and had lunch with us.'

And then there is silence from him. He is so frustrating! I wait ten minutes and send him another message.

'Are you mad at me for having lunch with my friend?'

'I don't share well.'

Oh, hell no! I will not do this through text. I dial his number, and he picks up on the second ring.

"Miranda."

"What the hell? I have a life and friends that I am allowed to hang out with. I can have lunch with whoever, whenever I please. Jason and I have known each other since college, and we are FRIENDS. He stopped for a sandwich, saw me, and I asked him to join me. You have no right to be mad." I am way louder than I want to be, but he has no right to be angry.

"I don't want you seeing him." I roll my eyes and try not to explode at his response.

"He is my friend."

"He is my lawyer."

"And we don't talk about you."

"I would hope not."

"This is crazy. I'm not a child, Ethan, and you are not my keeper. Goodbye." Pushing end, I hang up on him. I am not doing this again.

The phone rings, and I see it is him. "What?" I snap.

"Do not hang up on me." He is calm, but I hear the edge in his voice, which only fuels my anger, and without a second's hesitation, I hang up again. I can't deal with him right now. I will not be told what to do!

My phone rings once, and I send it directly to voicemail. It rings again and again, and each time, it goes to voicemail. By the fourth time, I answered just to make him leave me alone.

"Seriously? What part of me hanging up on you do you not understand? I do not want to talk to you." I hang up again, and this time I turn the phone off. Fuck him.

So much for my relaxing afternoon; now I am mad and stomp into the kitchen for some coffee. *That man is…ugh!* Tapping my foot, waiting for the damn coffee pot to finish, I pull out the cup the second it is ready. I am about to take a sip when there is a knock on the door. Damnit.

Looking through the security hole, I see Ethan. Fucking great. I pull open the door with more force than necessary, and he just stands there looking at me.

"Come in." I turn around and walk back to my cup on the counter, leaving the door open for him. "Do you want a cup?" I grumble as I hold up the cup in explanation.

"Please." He grumbles back as I get out another cup, slam a pod into the machine, and make him one. When it is finished, I slide it over to him as he sits at the island without a sound.

We are both silent as we watch each other over our cups. I am glaring, and he is just watching me. We are testing each other, I think, so I just lean back against the counter and wait until, finally, I cannot take it anymore.

"Are you going to say anything?" I ask with a little venom in my voice.

"You are maddening," he grumbles in response.

"Yeah, well, you are an asshole." I counter.

"We have already established that." He grins as he takes a drink, and I want to throw my cup at him. He will not grin and stop me from being mad! Except he does. UGH!

"I don't like being told what to do," I say softer since I really don't want to wear myself out with a fight.

"I don't like to share." He is still watching me over his cup.

"First, it's not sharing if it's just my friend. Second, I have the right to hang out with people. Third, you can't insist on no sharing if you are not my boyfriend." My hands go straight to my hips as I wait for his response.

"First, he's not just a friend; he clearly wants you. Second, he is my lawyer, and I don't like crossing business with pleasure. And you are most definitely a pleasure. Third, do you want me to be?" He gives me that huge, gorgeous grin that makes his eyes shine, and I am done for.

"First, I am well aware of said fact, but he has never made a move in years of knowing each other, so why start now. Second, I know that he is, and so are you. And third...I'm not sure." He immediately looks like I have slapped him.

"Is it me or men in general?" He takes another sip from his cup.

"You." I regret the words immediately after seeing the look on his face.

"I see. Well, again, this is a first." He looks down at his cup, and now I need to make him understand.

"Look, Ethan, I do like you a lot. I really do, but you frustrate me. We have fun together, but I'm…you are so far out of my league in all things. I'm trying to keep my head on straight with you while trying to keep my heart from getting broken again. I just want you to stick around longer than it takes me to heal."

Slowly, the corners of his mouth turn up, and that sexy half-grin takes over. "What?" I am a little ruffled by his smile.

"You silly woman. I will never tire of you. I've told you this more than once. You frustrate me also but in a positive way. And yes, I am used to getting my way the first time, every time, but somehow, you keep that from happening constantly. You push my buttons, all of them, and you challenge me on everything." He stands and walks to me. "And I like it." He bends down and pauses at my lips. I am still mad at him, and he knows it.

"May I kiss you?"

"No. Yes. No."

"Which is it?"

"Ugh, I don't like you."

"I think you do." He moves to me, and his lips push slightly against mine. I don't fight him, so he moves more, kissing me soft and gentle, just the way I like, before pulling back from me. Moving back to lean against the island opposite me, he watches and waits.

"I see." I uncross my arms.

"Do you?" He reaches over and takes my hand. "I like

that everything is a negotiation with you. It keeps me on my toes. Baby, I just want to be with you, only you." He tugs on my hand, trying to get me to come to him, but I resist.

"I have just one request." He smiles, and I can't wait for this.

"What's that?" I grumble.

"No sleeping with the enemy."

I can't stop the laugh that bursts out of me. "Jason is hardly the enemy, and I do not sleep around anyway. In fact, you are the first in almost a year." My face burns as I look at the floor.

"A year?" He tugs harder, and this time, I walk to him.

"Yes," I whisper.

"I want to be the only one." He growls as he wraps his arms around me.

"Same to you."

"I'm sure that can be arranged. I will just need to call the other women and tell them it's off." I try to pull away in mock outrage as he laughs and holds me to him.

"I'm kidding." He kisses the top of my head, and I relax back into his arms.

"So, if you are not my girlfriend, what should I call you?" he asks.

"Miranda."

He laughs hard at my answer. "And how will you introduce me to your friends?"

"Ethan."

"Oh, of course." He holds me tighter. "Okay, now that it's settled, I have a surprise." He releases me and walks back to the door, going out into the hallway and returning with a huge white box. More gifts, yay. I groan internally. *We really need to talk about this.*

He tries to hand it to me, but I give him a hard look. "I thought I made myself clear on throwing money at me." My hands are on my hips in protest, which makes him pause.

"Fair. However, I have tickets to the theater tonight, and I was wondering if you would like to join me."

"This is more than tickets." I glare at him.

"Woman, let me finish. It starts at 8, and I know that's not much time, but I would have asked you sooner if you had called me back earlier." He teases. "I would like you to join me, and yes, the box accompanies the tickets." He offers the box again, and this time, I take it.

It is heavier than I expect. Putting it on the counter, I open it, and there, lying in tissue, is a beautiful blue beaded dress. My surprise is clear when I look back up at him.

"I knew you didn't have much to fit over the cast, so I bought you this. I hope you like it and that you will go." He is a madman. I lift it out, and it is long, strapless, and fitted. Glancing down at my not-perfect body, I worry it is not going to fit.

"There are also undergarments and matching shoes." Gently, he moves the tissue in the box, revealing beautiful blue heels.

"Ethan, this is way too much." Holding up the dress again, it really is pretty. "It's beautiful, though." My admission makes him smile.

"Go get ready, and I will run down and grab my clothes

from the car. Is it okay if I get ready here?" He is asking? I'm shocked.

"Of course. I have already had a shower, so it won't take me long." Ethan pulls me into a kiss and then trots out the door as I shake my head. How did that even happen? Ugh, I am still frustrated at him.

In my bedroom, I pull out the contents of the box, and sure enough, there is a push-up corset bra. I check the tag, and of course, it's in my size and blue lace panties. What is with this man and buying panties? It's odd but sweet. The beautiful rhinestone heels match the dress, and although they are a little higher than I am used to, they fit, and I love them. I struggle with the bra but finally get it on before heading to the bathroom for makeup and to curl my hair into waves.

Now, the dress. I look at it lying on the bed and pray it fits. I sit and put the heels on first, then step into the dress and slide it up, holding my breath and crossing my fingers as I pull up the zipper on the side. I exhale, and it fits perfectly. When I turn to the mirror, holy wow, it is just tight enough to show off my curves and chest, but it looks like it was made for me. I almost cry as I spin around. I feel incredible. It is perfect.

Carefully, I put on my diamond dangle earrings and matching necklace; they are the only real diamonds I own. Then I dig through my closet for my small black clutch. One more coat of my lipstick, and I am good to go.

As I enter the kitchen, Ethan is standing in a black tux, looking like he just walked off a page of a magazine. Our eyes meet, and my mouth waters. He is breathtaking. I can't take my eyes off him. He is on the phone but hangs up immediately when he sees me.

"Miranda, you look stunning." He doesn't break eye contact as he walks to me.

"As do you." I smile shyly.

He takes my hand and spins me around. "I changed my mind; we are staying in." His growl causes goosebumps to cover my arms.

"No way, you already mentioned the theater, and I'm wearing this thing out." I hit his arm with my clutch.

"Only if I get to take it off you later." He groans against my ear, causing me to shiver.

"Deal." Like I would argue that stipulation. I am looking forward to that almost as much as wearing it out! The thought of him peeling it off me already has my knees weak.

Before we leave, he pulls a heavy black shawl out of another bag and drapes it around my shoulders. It is lined and warm but beaded like the dress. "Thank you. Thank you for all of this. It's an amazing dress."

"It's my pleasure." His eyes shine with something more than happiness, and although I am not sure what it is, I take his arm and walk with him to the elevator.

"You do look absolutely beautiful, Miranda." He tucks me under his arm as we ride in silence, and my heart might like him just a touch more in that instant.

At the lobby, he leads me to the front door instead of the parking garage, and I glance up, confused, as he gives me that sexy grin. My confusion is quickly extinguished when I notice the limo waiting just outside the front door. All I can do is shake my head as I take his hand and slide in without a word. No reason to argue tonight.

"What are we seeing?" I am more excited than I expected to be.

"*Cosi Fan Tutte*," Ethan answers, and it sounds so sensual coming off his lips.

"I have no idea what that is, but it sounds amazing."

"It's an opera by Mozart that is in Italian. It means, 'Thus Do All,' and is about two officers in the military who have a friend that wants to test the fidelity of their fiancées, who are sisters, while they are away at war." He explains to me. "You will enjoy it."

"I am sure I will." *Hell, in this dress, I would enjoy just about anything.*

On the way, Ethan informs me that it is opening night, which makes it even more exciting to me. When we arrive, I wait for Ethan to step out and take his offered hand to help me out before he wraps his arm around my waist. The flashes are crazy as soon as we start to walk, and I hear someone yell his name. He puts his hand up in acknowledgment but doesn't stop or say anything, just pulls me closer as we head inside.

It is a beautiful place, and we are just a few rows back from the orchestra pit and stage, which increases my excitement even more. I think I am going to vibrate away as soft music comes over us. As we enter our row, Ethan shakes a few hands of men that he must know and introduces me to them as they introduce their lady friends to us. Only one is married, and two are introduced as girlfriends, but one is definitely way too young for the guy and is clearly arm candy. I just smile politely and let Ethan talk. It is not my business.

Finally, the lights dim, and we take our seats. I am drumming with anticipation as I have never been to an opera before, only regular theater. I am immediately in awe as the actors start to sing. Ethan reaches over and pushes my mouth shut, making me blush as he takes my hand. Even though it is in Italian, I understand it, and he was right; it is beautiful, and the love story is easy to follow.

At intermission, Ethan kisses my cheek and whispers in my ear, "You haven't stopped grinning."

He is right, I haven't. "It's so good," I admit, and he squeezes my hand and winks. We stand so he can talk to the others, and one of the men asks me if I am enjoying it.

"I am. It's absolutely amazing." I can't wipe the silly grin off my face.

The man then turns to Ethan and says, "Must be her first time." I don't know if I should take offense or not, but his tone makes me think I should.

"Actually, yes, this is my first time seeing this production." I smile sweetly, holding back all the comments I really want to make.

"I am glad you like it." Ethan smiles warmly at me, completely ignoring the man's comment.

One of the other men says something that I do not hear, and Ethan answers. "Ms. Michaels is an up-and-coming lawyer at Lester and Associates." His hand wraps around my waist, and he pulls me closer possessively. I glance at him from the corner of my eye, but he just smiles. He knows that is not true.

"We use that firm, and I can say I have not heard your name before." Mr. Fancy Pants says. I wish I could remember his name so I could put him in his place, but I choose to play nice.

"I work mostly under Paul Lester..." I have barely started speaking when the man speaks over me.

"Aww, so just a lowly assistant, very good." The man cuts me off with a laugh and then turns away from me to talk to someone else. What?

My body tenses, and I open my mouth to speak, but Ethan senses my outrage and beats me to it.

"Actually, Miranda works with Paul and is a damn good lawyer. I have seen her in action, and I would watch yourself if you ever end up on the opposing side; she will kick your ass." He speaks a little louder than necessary, and the man turns back to him, his eyes a little large.

"Well, I will have to keep that in mind. If Ethan says you are good, I will make sure to only have you on my side of the table." He winks at me and turns back to his conversation with the other man and I want to gag.

Ethan keeps a hold of me but raises my hand to kiss it, knowing I am pissed. The other gentleman, who is married, speaks up.

"Don't let Rich get to you, he's an asshole." The man chuckles as his wife swats his arm.

"I know a few of those myself." I look at Ethan, who visibly flinches, and the man's wife laughs.

"Mary, don't laugh; she's mean." Ethan takes a step away

from me, and I give him a look

"Oh, I'm glad to hear that; someone needs to keep you in line." Mary laughs harder.

"I like her," I admit to Ethan. I do. She is feisty.

"Mary, don't give her any ideas." Ethan lets my waist go but keeps a hand on my back as Mary and I talk while the boys banter about work. She is a sweet lady, and I could talk to her all night. When the lights dim, she reaches into her bag and hands me her card.

"Call me, and we can do lunch." She offers, and I thank her before Ethan takes my hand back to guide me to my seat. Once we sit, he leans over and kisses my cheek.

"Good lady to befriend." He whispers in my ear, and I can't help but let my smile spread.

The rest of the opera is even more amazing. When it is over, I stand and clap hard, my body a mess of emotions. I didn't realize how tense I was. Ethan reaches over and wipes away the tear running down my face, and I look over with a smile, but keep clapping as the actors bow until my hands hurt.

"That was...wow." There are no other words to say. I just keep clapping in awe.

After saying our goodbyes to the others, we walk arm in arm to the front. "Thank you, Ethan. This was incredible." Hugging his arm, he lays his other hand over mine, which sits on his arm.

"Successful real first date?" He leans into me as he asks.

"Well, technically, dinner last night was our first date, so successful second date." I give him a wink. "You know, I could get used to this," I add, and he gives me his bright, all-teeth smile.

"Me too." Pulling out of my embrace to let me go through the door first, he then slides his arm around my waist and pulls me back to his side as we wait for the limo.

The entire ride back, we talk about the performance and how much I like Mary and her husband, Alan. He informs me that Mary has connections to people all over as she was a teacher and a senator's wife. He tells me that he has known Alan for a very long time, he was friends with Ethan's father, and Ethan thinks of him as another father figure. I love how his face transforms as he talks about him.

Ethan also apologizes for Richard, but I am not really bothered by him anymore. He was clearly an asshole. "Do you bring a lot of different women to these kinds of things?" I think my question takes him off guard as he pauses before answering.

"I have, yes." He looks away from my eyes and down to our joined hands. "Why?"

"I just heard the young girl say that I must be the flavor of the week." Along with some other things that I am not willing to admit.

"I was hoping you hadn't." He seems mad now.

"I assume that is why Richard was so frigid with me."

"He doesn't have much room to talk; at least the girls that hang off my arm are around my own age."

I am sure my expression is visible because he closes his eyes and exhales. Instead of being mad, though, I have to laugh at him.

"You aren't good with this whole TMI thing, are you?"

"No, apparently not."

"It's okay, I know you, um, get around and like your women. I get that." Do I? I shudder at the thought of being another girl on the long list.

"Do I have that bad of a reputation?" He asks, but he knows he does. I can tell by the way his jaw clenches.

"Yep." I know it, too.

He takes my hand and turns to me, his face open and raw. "That's why you don't want to be with me, isn't it?" His question throws me off this time. I am trying to think of what to say, but he looks hurt at my pause.

"Honestly, it's a small part of it, yes." I want to be honest with him.

"Ouch." He sits back in his seat and exhales loudly.

"Ethan..." I start, but he doesn't look back at me. "...look at your life and then look at mine. I'm far from a model. I don't hang in your same circles, and I don't have money. And I surely don't know how to act with people that do. I don't want to be known as the next flavor of the week. I want to be someone's happily ever after. From what I know, that isn't you, or the way you what to be. I understand that, and it means I don't want to get too attached. I thought I had forever once, and it failed miserably, so forgive me if I'm cautious." I am a little harsher than I mean to be.

"Miserably?" His voice softens.

"Yes, very miserably." My own sigh is heavy. I don't want to ruin this night with my sad story or with this discussion between us.

"He missed out," he whispers, still not looking at me.

"I think so too. Ethan, just be with me, enjoy our time together, and if it lasts a while, great. And if it doesn't, then that's alright, too. I will be happy that I knew you and thankful for the fun we had. Okay?"

This time, he turns back to me, and even in the darkness of the car, I can feel him studying me. "I enjoy every minute with you, even when you are difficult." A small chuckle comes through the space between us.

"I am that, I agree, but so are you." Gently, I punch him in the arm, and in return, he carefully pulls me up into his lap so I am sitting sideways, his hands around my waist.

"Miranda, I don't want you to be a flavor of the week either. I really like you." He emphasizes the word "really" before his hand pulls my face to him. He gives me a deep kiss that goes on for a long time, but it is just a deep, sweet kiss that shows he cares. It's not passionate and wild like before.

The driver announces that we are back at my place, and he releases me to get out. "I think we should probably eat before we go upstairs because once I get you out of that dress, I am not leaving." He leans down and growls into my ear so no one else around us can hear.

"I agree." And that is all it takes to have me following him to his car.

"Maybe next week, we can get you a new car," he says casually as he backs out of my parking space.

"Then where will you park?" I say a little snarkily.

"Don't you have two spaces?" He asks like it's no big deal.

"No. Just me, no need for two. Family and friends just

park in the visitor lot." I shoot him a glance, and he is smiling. Silly man.

"Since I can't drive for a while, I'm really not in a hurry," I answer absentmindedly as I try to figure out where we are going. This is not somewhere I have been before.

"I know where to take you."

"Take me?" I ask, unsure of what he means.

"For your car. My guy can find you whatever you want with whatever options you choose. I am assuming you want another Camaro, but we can get it fully loaded this time. Or if you want something else, we can do that also." Ethan sounds like it is a done deal.

"Oh, okay, but I'm not even sure what I want yet." He looks at me out of the corner of his eye.

"On the car," I clarify and leave it at that.

We pull up outside a pub of some kind, and I am a little surprised at his choice. "Don't you think we are a little over-dressed for a bar?" I ask as he helps me from the car.

"They have great food, and I know the owner. Not many places to eat at almost midnight." He chuckles as he takes my arm to guide me into the pub.

There are only a few people sitting around, and Ethan waves to the bartender. "Hey, Ethan!" the man calls to us.

"Joe, I would like you to meet Miranda. Miranda, this is Joe." Ethan introduces me as we get to the bar.

"Nice to meet you, young lady." Joe smiles at me, then gives Ethan a look with a raised eyebrow. There is clearly a question there, and now I am curious. I add it to my mental notes to ask about later.

"Hello. Nice to meet you as well." I nod back to Joe.

"Joe, can you wrestle us up a couple of burgers and fries, please? And a beer for me and a Sprite for the lady."

"Actually, I will have a Goose Island Matilda if you have it, please." I smile shyly as Ethan gives me a double-take.

"One beer is not going to hurt me, and I guess you come here often, too?" I try to be playful as we sit at a table.

"More than I like to admit." He winks at me.

"Why did Joe seem so surprised to see us?" I can't wait for later, I want to know why Joe gave him that look.

Ethan actually looks embarrassed at my question, so I lean forward with my head cradled on my hands to hear this. He shifts in his seat and glances away.

"Go on." I smile, and he laughs uncomfortably before answering.

"Surprised to see you. I only come here all the time, but it's always alone. This is my secret place." He clears his throat and loosens his tie.

This is priceless; no way can I let this go. "Oh, so you don't bring all your girls here?" I grin.

"No, I do not." He gives me a look, but I don't drop it. He is way too easy to tease.

"No wonder he is surprised." I sit back against the seat to watch him squirm.

"We need to eat." He answers, and it is meant to be the explanation, but he doesn't look at me, and I can't help myself from continuing on.

"And…you could have taken me anywhere." I love this uncomfortable side of him.

Joe brings drinks over, and Ethan looks relieved for the

distraction.

"Thank you, Joe," I say sweetly, and Joe's face lights up.

"You are most welcome. Burgers will be out in a minute. So where have you kids been tonight?" Joe looks at Ethan, then at me, but Ethan is quiet, so I answer with a laugh.

"He took me to see *Così fan tutte*." I give Ethan a smile, but he is still mute.

"Another one of those fancy things I don't understand." Joe's laugh is rough but sweet.

"Don't feel bad; I didn't know what it meant either, but it was lovely." I wink at Joe, and he gives a deep chuckle, but Ethan just takes a long drink of his beer, still not saying a word.

"I'll take a baseball game over that fufu stuff any day." Joe lets out a huff.

"Me too!" I answer a little louder than I anticipated.

"You a baseball fan?" He seems surprised.

"Absolutely!" I grin.

"Cubs or White Sox fan?" He eyes me with caution. And I am very aware that the side you chose makes a difference up here.

"I'm from St. Louis, so Cardinals all the way. I'm a huge fan."

"Well, as long as it's not the Sox, you are welcome here anytime." He glances at Ethan again, who is now leaning back, watching us with a smile on his face.

"Thank you. Congrats on your team, though; they kicked butt last year." I would much rather talk baseball all night since I understand that.

"You come in during the next series, and the beer is on

me. I like a little competition." He throws another wink at me again, which makes me laugh. I like him. Ethan has some cool friends.

"It will have to be Sprite or water until this comes off." I hold up my cast in explanation, and he nods.

"Don't be trying to steal my girl, Joe." Ethan finally speaks up, his voice playful.

"Don't think I will have to try too hard." He grins before walking away, leaving Ethan with his jaw hanging open.

"You like baseball, really?" I can't believe this fact surprises him.

"I do. Huge fan of baseball and hockey, Blues hockey, of course."

He shakes his head. "You really are out of my league." He takes another long drink of his beer as he watches me.

"You are not a sports guy, are you?"

"Nope. Never have been."

"Not even hockey?"

"No, never even been to a hockey game."

Now, I am the one who is shocked. "Oh, I have to take you to a hockey game. They are so much fun. We will fix that right now." I take my phone out of my clutch and do a search.

"What are you doing?" He leans over the table to look at my phone.

"Looking for tickets for the next game," I answer as I scrolled.

"Miranda, I'm not a..." I cut him off.

"They are playing the Blues on Thursday!" Ok, that was a

little too loud. "I'm taking you, so don't make plans." Laying down my phone, I pull my credit card out of my clutch, but he takes my phone from the table in front of me.

"No!" He is holding the phone away from me.

"Ethan!" I struggle to try and get it back over the table, but I am laughing too hard at his expression. "Come on, I went to your thing; now you go to mine!" I laugh as he shakes his head no.

"Joe, did you know this man has never been to a hockey game? Isn't that a sin or something?" I ask as Joe sets down our burgers.

"I think it might be." Joe agrees.

"The Blues are playing the Hawks on Thursday, and I'm trying to get tickets, but he's being a child." I stick my tongue out at Ethan, who still has my phone.

"I am not." Ethan tries not to laugh as Joe looks between the two of us.

"You have tickets?" Joe asks me.

"No, I am trying to buy them, but he took my phone. Not that it will stop me. I think it would be fantastic to take his stuffy ass out somewhere normal." Ethan's expression makes me laugh so hard I think I am going to wet myself.

"You come by here tomorrow after 5, and I will have a set for you." Joe throws a leathery smile at me.

"Really? That would be wonderful, Joe."

"Absolutely." Joe pats my arm.

"Wow, thanks for helping me out there, Joe!" Ethan yells after Joe as he heads back to the bar.

"Welcome!" Joe calls back, and I laugh harder.

Ethan gives me back my phone, and I put it away. "Aww, don't pout. You will enjoy it, promise." I pick up my burger and take a huge, un-ladylike bite, causing him to groan before picking up his own food.

"This is so good. So big and juicy." I say, wiping off my mouth with a wink. Ethan just watches me with a smirk. "No wonder you keep this place a secret." I bite into my burger again.

"Miranda, you surprise me at every turn. I am glad you like it." We eat dinner and I pick on Ethan some more. I am really enjoying the night. The theater was awesome, but this is more my style, even in my insanely beautiful dress.

After we finish, Ethan walks to the bar and hands Joe some money, and Joe nods in return.

"Joe, it was an absolute pleasure to meet you," I say, offering my hand for a shake.

"The pleasure is all mine. Come on by tomorrow, and I will have those tickets for you. Just promise me some pictures of this guy at the game."

"Deal!" I playfully punch Ethan in the arm as he grumbles

"Here I thought I found a nice, classy lady, but no, I get a beer-drinking, sports-watching, car-loving girl who calls me out on my shit and is very non-princess-like." Ethan pulls me to him, and I can't help but give him a huge smile as he presses me to his chest in a hug

"I like her. She's good for you. Bring her around more often," Joe offers.

"No," Ethan laughs at Joe.

"Don't worry, Joe, I can bring myself." I wink back, and

Ethan pulls me out of the bar, waving at Joe as I go.

At the car, he goes to open the door but pulls me to him and kisses me instead. "You are so much more than I could have ever imagined you would be. One look in those beautiful eyes, and I knew you were special," he whispers as he kisses me again.

"It was fear," I giggle, and he starts to laugh.

"Thanks for ruining the moment." He kisses my nose, and I squeeze his sides under his jacket. He jumps, and my eyes light up in realization.

"You are ticklish!" My mouth drops open.

"No, I am not." He tries to be stern, but the twinkle in his eye gives him away.

I try to grab him again, but he twists away and runs around the car. We are both laughing so hard that I can hardly stand up.

"It's a good thing I'm in heels, or I would so test my theory!" I am crying with laughter now as he stands on the other side of the car, waiting to run, his expression playful.

"I'm getting in the car, and there is no touching while I'm driving!" He laughs out a warning as he points at me.

"Deal." I hold up my hands before opening my door and sliding in. Watching me nervously, he starts the car, and I giggle some more.

"I won't touch, promise." I grin at him and notice his face is carefree and alive with excitement. I have never seen him this way before. I buckle up and then turn to watch him, my hands in my lap, where I leave them the entire ride.

We just exchange glances and grins until he pulls into the

garage and parks.

"Are you coming up?" I try to be serious and not laugh.

"I promised that I was going to take you out of that dress, so yes." He is sexy as hell when he talks deep and slow like that. He knows he is trying to disarm me, and it is working, but I will get ahold of him, and he knows it by my evil grin.

In the elevator, I slip off my shoes and bend to pick them up as we get to my floor, giving him a sly grin as I stand back up.

"I don't think so." He chuckles with his hands held out so I can't get close as he backs down the hallway.

"You know I am stronger, and you are injured, so you need to behave." He tries to deter me.

"I feel fine." I smile.

"Open the door, Miranda." His eyes are wide, and he is about two feet back from me.

"I will get you." I threaten with a giggle.

"No, you will not," he counters with a chuckle. I don't know who will win, but I have a good chance if I plan correctly. I open the door and stroll in, laying my purse on the counter and removing my shawl. He watches me closely as he unloads his pockets and removes his own shoes and jacket. This dress is not going to let me move too fast, so I have to strike at the perfect moment.

He doesn't take his eyes off me as I slide into the kitchen, turning my back to him. I hear him take a step onto the tile, and I turn, launching myself at him, but he is quick and grabs hold of me just in time to stop me.

"I don't think so." He laughs freely as he holds my arms

down, and I struggle to get away.

Before I can process it, his mouth crashes onto mine, and suddenly, I don't want to play anymore; I want him. I try to pull free, but he has my hands, so I push him back to the wall and stand up on my toes to get more of him. He gets the point and lets me go. My hands go right into his hair as he fumbles with the dress zipper. Finally, it falls to the floor as he pulls away to look at me.

His eyes take in every detail on the way down and then back up, and I just stand there, waiting as his eyes come back up to mine. Without a word, he grabs me, flips us around so I am against the wall now, and picks me up as I wrap my legs around him. His mouth leaves mine and travels down my neck, leaving burning kisses against my skin.

"I love the way you smell." I groan as I pull on the back of his shirt, trying to touch more of him. He leans back, and his mouth travels down to my chest, where I am pushed up and out with this bra, and he is all over me.

His fingers follow the line of my panties, pulling them out of the way and touching me in all the right places. I moan out in pleasure as he continues to assault my breasts.

"So wet." His voice is deep and almost vibrates against my skin.

"For you." I fight to stay upright as sensation starts to overcome me. He doesn't let me fall over the edge. Instead, he sets me down, spins me around, unbuckles my bra, and throws it to the floor behind us. Biting at my shoulder, his hands run up my sides and back around to my breasts as he leans into my back.

I am a panting mess as he plants kisses down my back,

his hands on my hips, pushing me into the wall. He is hard against me, kissing my shoulder before his foot pushes my legs apart, and his hand travels around and under my panties, teasing me.

"Oh God, Ethan, please," I beg as he rubs along my most sensitive parts. I want him now. "Please," I whimper as my body starts to tighten against his fingers.

"Come for me," he whispers, and I do, and it is so hard my knees almost buckle.

"Good girl." He is still at my back, kissing my neck as his fingers slowly swirl around inside of me.

"Ethan..." His name is a plea for more, for him. Finally, he releases me and turns me to him. His eyes are deep emerald green, and he stares into me for a minute before his mouth is back on mine, his hands running up my sides, one into my hair and the other around to my ass, pulling me to him.

It is my turn to tease him. My hands glide over his back and around to his front, to his stomach, to that little patch of hair, and then down to his cloth-covered length, making him groan into my mouth. My fingers pull at his button, releasing his pants, before sliding my hand into his boxers to feel him. Soft and solid. His chest rumbles as he calls out when my fingers wrap around him.

"Miranda...." His voice is strained as I squeeze, pulling him up and down. His head is thrown back in pleasure, his neck exposed, and I stretch up to kiss along the front of his throat. He mutters something as he pulls away, reaches into his pants pocket, and pulls out a condom. Putting it in his teeth, he rips it open, takes himself out, and rolls it on before picking me up and growling out, "Hold on." Lifting me up, he slides into me in one swift move, and I call out as he fills me.

"So fucking tight." His teeth are clenched, and he is breathing heavily as he presses me against the wall. He thrusts up a few times slowly, but I already know this is not going to be gentle.

"Ready?" He looks into my eyes, and I nod. He pushes all the way in, and I think I am going to scream. I am so full, but it feels so good. Not giving me any warning, he starts to pound into me, making me cry out with each thrust. My fingers dig into his arms, which I think makes him go faster.

He gets deeper each time, and suddenly, I scream out my release, but he continues to push me into the wall over and over. Just when I think I can't take anymore, he finishes with a loud groan, his fingers digging into my hips as he pushes the last of his release into me. My head falls against his chest, and he relaxes into me as we both come down from the incredible high.

"Wow," I mumble, causing him to chuckle.

"Uh-huh." His nose runs along my cheek and into my hair.

"I'm going to set you down," he says softly as he lifts me off him, and I stand shakily on my own. With a gentle kiss, he pulls back, kicks off his pants, and heads to the bathroom, leaving me standing there in a daze, in my panties that he didn't even remove.

When he returns, I walk past him for my turn. "That was mind-blowing," I giggle as he grabs me and presses his lips hard against mine."I have to agree." With a smack to my ass, he lets me go past.

Standing in the bathroom looking at myself in the mirror, I look...happy. Happier than I have been in a long time. He does that to me. I don't want to overthink it, so I wash off my makeup and go in search of jammies. Then I head back into the living room to find the man who has completely turned my world upside down.

Ethan is sitting on the couch in just his boxers and his white T-shirt with Kasey. I sit down at the other end from him, but he immediately crawls over to me, leaning us back onto the arm of the couch.

"I am becoming quite addicted to you." He growls as he pulls at my bottom lip with his teeth.

"I'm okay with that," I reply, matching his grin.

"Good. I don't think there's any stopping me now that I've had you." He kisses my nose and then lays his head on my chest, so I wrap my arm around his shoulder and my free leg around his.

"Can I just stay like this?" he asks sleepily.

"Fine with me." I agree as I close my eyes, feeling him kiss my bare skin above my shirt with the side of his mouth. We lay there for a long time as he runs his hand up and down the back of my thigh, soothing me into a sweet sleep.

I am pulled awake as Ethan picks me up off the couch. "Shh, just moving you to bed," he says softly, and I curl into him, feeling his strong chest against my face. He's so warm. I nuzzle closer, feeling so safe in his arms, his sweet scent surrounding me. He lays me down, covers me up, and kisses my forehead.

"Goodnight, sweet Miranda," he whispers, and I feel him

move away.

"Stay, please," I whisper without even opening my eyes.

He takes my hand and kisses the back of it instead of answering me.

"Sleep now, and I will see you tomorrow." His voice is softer this time.

"Please," I ask again. I feel him pause next to me as he holds my hand for a minute longer, but he sets it down and brushes the hair from my face before he's gone. I fall back to sleep, a little disappointed that he doesn't stay.

Chapter 16

When I pull myself from my fantastic dreams, it's 8 a.m. and another sunny day. Stretching, I feel the soreness from last night's activity, and it makes me happy. The man is amazingly talented and knows exactly how to make me scream. I lay there, thinking about his beautiful green eyes and the sexy, shy grin I've come to adore. He's incredible.

After a while, I decide to get up and make myself breakfast before I sit at the counter to read the day's happenings on my new computer. I start with Facebook and respond to a few "get well" posts on my wall before getting up for another cup of coffee.

When I sit back down and start scrolling, I almost spit my coffee across the counter. I see a post from Shannon. It's a share of a picture, and there I am with Ethan outside the theater. The article reads: Publishing Mogul Ethan Bradley and His Next Beauty at the Premier of Cosi Fan Tutte at the Civic Theater. Her post reads: Her name is Miranda Michaels, and she has tagged @TMZ. I click on the picture, and it takes me to their site, where there are more pictures of celebrities and famous people from opening night. Wow, I missed some pretty cool people, but I don't go any further. I just go back to her post and comment my thanks.

Closing Facebook; I don't want to get wrapped up in that and move over to the real news. After a few articles, I can't help but go back to the picture, clicking on it to download the photo to my computer. I do look good in that dress and make a mental note to thank Ethan again, for everything.

I leave the computer, clean up my dishes, take my meds, and open the blinds to let in the light. I love the floor-to-ceiling windows in the living room, but being only on the 6th floor, I have to close them at night, or people can see in.

I look around my apartment at all the flowers. Emma cleared out a lot of the ones that had died, but I still need to take care of a few more; it's a sad sight. I pull over the kitchen trash can, carry the vases to the counter, and pull out the dead flowers. When I'm finished, the vases are bare, so I combine what's still alive into one vase from four, and it looks better. I still have the two new bouquets and the five plants, but I miss the fresh flowers. Deciding to replace some of them, I plan to head down to the little market on the corner to see what they have.

After a shower, I throw on a pair of jeans, a sweater, and my tall flat boots. My soft brown hair dries into waves over my shoulder, and I'm starting to really like it this way—it hides the still-bare spot from the stitches. At least that doesn't look so angry anymore. I transfer everything back from my clutch to my purse and pick up my phone to see a missed call from Ethan and a text from Emma.

Saw the picture on Facebook. Wow. You look great, and he is smoking hot. Was the show good? How are things with you two? Call me, I'm dying here for info!'

Thank you. Ethan bought the dress to surprise me since I had nothing fancy to wear over this stupid cast. Nothing more to report, Em. We're just dating, nothing serious, so slow your roll.

He's rich.

Don't care. Money doesn't interest me.

I know, just think it's cool that a millionaire likes my little sister.

I don't look at it that way. He's just a guy who is incredibly frustrating at times.

Have you slept with him?

Emma! I'm done with this conversation. I'm fine, thanks!

YOU DID! Was he good? Is he as big as the tabloids say?

EMMA LYNN! Not sharing that info ;-)

Emma is so nosy! I call Ethan back as I get out of the elevator, and he answers on the second ring as usual.

"Morning, beautiful." I can't help the grin that splits my face.

"Morning," I say brightly.

"What are you up to today?" I can hear his smile through the phone, and it makes me feel like I'm floating.

"I'm headed down to the little market on the corner, then maybe a little retail therapy."

"Want company?" He sounds hopeful, and it makes my smile bigger.

"You want to go clothes shopping?"

"I don't mind," he answers quickly.

"Okay. I'll be at the market in a few minutes, and then I'll head straight back." I'm surprised at how excited I am to see him again today.

"I'll take a quick shower and be there in 45 minutes. Meet me out front."

He isn't wasting any time, either.

"Sounds great. See you then. Bye."

He actually says goodbye this time before hanging up. I'm digging this new thing we have going.

After picking up two bouquets of fresh flowers, I head back up to my apartment. Quickly, I throw them in water and freshen up before going down to the lobby to get my mail. Not much in there, so I stick the bills in my purse and throw the junk in the recycle bin. I glance out the window— still not here—so I walk over to the building bulletin board and read the ads. It's been 60 minutes, so I go outside and sit on the wall. He seems to have a problem with time.

Finally, I see his car pull into the circle, and I don't wait for him to get out before I open the door and hop in.

"You're late," I announce, but his sweet smile disarms me.

"Phone calls and problems. Only by 20 minutes."

He leans over, and the minute our lips touch, the frustration evaporates.

"Twenty-seven, but who's counting," I whisper, causing him to shake his head at me.

"So where are we headed?" He changes the subject with a smile.

"Shopping. I guess Michigan Ave., the mall."

He cringes. "You want to go to the mall?"

"What's wrong with that? Too normal for you?" I turn to look at him, and his frown makes me giggle.

"A little."

"It's good for you." I lean my head back and watch the people pass by as he drives.

We shop at a few clothing stores, a home furnishings store, and two shoe stores, and he never complains once. We laugh and have an amazing time just being together on a normal day in a normal mall, which is exactly what I want. I even talk him into having lunch in the food court and getting an ice cream cone on the way out.

"Normal isn't so bad, is it?" I ask, and he pulls me under his arm as we walk to the car.

"No, it hasn't been too bad. The sandwich was good, the ice cream even better, but spending the day with you—it was worth the crowds and crazy people." The top of my head receives his kiss, which is now my favorite thing he does, well, almost.

"Thank you for coming with me and carrying my bags," I add as we walk.

"I did enjoy watching you try on clothes, but I wish you would've let me buy some of them for you."

"Ethan, let's not discuss this again. I don't want you to buy me everything. Besides, I didn't want most of those things anyway. I purchased what I wanted." Leaning into him and nuzzling his chest should help my cause.

"I appreciate that, but I just want to buy you nice things. I enjoy it."

Rolling my eyes, I groan. "I gave in on the one pair of shoes." Only because I wasn't going to spend that much, and he was so insistent.

"They looked good on you. You needed them."

All I can do is shake my head.

As we get back to the car, he loads everything into the trunk while I climb in and relax into the seat.

"Are you alright?" Ethan asks as he starts the car.

"Yes, just very tired. Shopping wore me out." I smile at him to show I'm fine, and he brushes his fingers down my cheek.

"I really enjoyed today. Thank you," I tell him, then kiss his fingertips as they brush over my lips, and I see the grin on his lips grow larger.

"Miranda, every day could be this good if you let it." His eyes shine, but he doesn't say anything else. He just pulls out into traffic, leaving me to decipher his meaning. Instead of asking, I choose to study his profile and leave the thinking for later. My eyes trace over his straight nose, strong jaw, and cheekbones. I can even see his beautiful green eyes from here. He's solid and strong, but I'm lucky to know his softer side—where he's gentle and sweet. I notice how the corner of his lip turns up slightly and how his long lashes fan over his cheeks when he blinks. I see the flare of his nose as he breathes in and how his lips part slightly as he exhales. I notice the stubble starting to show on his jaw and how his hair is slightly longer on the sides, brushing over the top of his ear.

"Are you enjoying yourself?" Ethan grins as he speaks, not taking his eyes off the road.

"Just enjoying the view." I can't help the stupid grin I have.

"What exactly are you enjoying?" He takes a quick glance at me at the stoplight.

"All of it."

"All of it?" He glances at me again, and I laugh.

"All of you."

He just shakes his head, but he's smiling shyly, which makes me giggle as I go back to watching him.

"Don't forget we need to see Joe for my tickets." I yawn.

"Would you like to go by there now or head home to rest first?" He's stopped at a light and can fully look over at me this time.

"Pub first, then rest." I yawn again. I'm so tired that I lean back in the seat and stretch out, letting my body rest.

When we pull up outside the pub, Ethan parks and turns to me. "Let me run in and grab them for you. You stay here." Ethan takes my hand and kisses it.

"No, I want to go in and say thank you." Ethan starts to argue but then agrees and comes to open the door for me.

We visit with Joe for a few minutes, and as promised, he gives me two tickets to Thursday's game, and to my surprise, they are right on the ice.

"Joe, these are at the glass! How did you do this? Wow, thank you!" I jump up and down as Ethan laughs at me, making me feel a little silly, so I compose myself.

"Sorry." I blush and look around at all the people watching me.

"Don't be." Ethan takes my hand and squeezes it—our sign of comfort. "I like seeing you excited," he whispers as he pulls me into a hug, tucking me into his chest and holding me close. I never thought he would be so affectionate.

"Okay, let's get you home to rest." Ethan lets me go and straightens his posture. I've realized he's not used to being mushy in public, and it makes him uncomfortable, but he does it anyway.

"I'm too excited to rest now! Thank you so much, Joe. I owe you." I run to the edge of the bar and surprise him with a kiss on the cheek and a hug.

"You are most welcome," Joe chuckles, and Ethan grins at our exchange.

"You hang on to this one, or someone's going to steal her away," Joe says as he shakes Ethan's hand.

"I plan to. Thanks again, Joe." They exchange a nod of understanding before Ethan takes my hand, and we walk out to the car.

"I guess this means I have a date this Thursday with a beautiful young woman at a hockey game." Ethan grins.

"Really? What a coincidence. I'm going to a hockey

game on Thursday, too." I pretend to be surprised. "Only, I haven't decided who to take yet."

"I hope it'll be me," Ethan picks me up and spins me around, and I laugh uncontrollably in his arms.

He lets me slide down his front before taking my face in his hands and kissing me.

"I like this, Ethan," I admit against his lips, and I feel him grin before he kisses me quickly again.

"I'm very happy to hear that." He spins me around once more and then walks me to my side of the car.

Chapter 17

Once we're inside the apartment, Ethan drops the bags in my bedroom, and when he returns to the kitchen, he wraps me in a warm hug.

"I propose we head to bed so I can have my way with you. Then you take a nap, and later, we go out for a nice dinner," he says, pressing tiny kisses to my neck.

"Or," I tease, running my nails lightly over his scalp, "I could have my way with you."

He shivers, a low hum vibrating against my neck. I smile at his reaction and do it again, enjoying the way his grip tightens on my shoulders.

Slipping out of his embrace, I slide his jacket down his arms and let it fall to the floor. I join it, kneeling at his feet, my hands finding the waistband of his jeans. Slowly, I unbutton them, untuck his shirt, and trail kisses along the exposed skin at the top of his boxers. The softness surprises me—it's even better than I imagined.

His fingers thread through my hair as I lower his jeans, sliding them down his thighs. I kiss the skin I reveal, listening to the way his breathing deepens. Tapping his leg gently, he lifts his foot so I can remove his shoes, then he steps out of his jeans entirely. My hands glide up the backs of his legs, and I revel in the little sounds he makes.

When I reach the top of his thighs, I press a kiss against the fabric of his boxers, feeling the tension beneath. He's already straining, and the thought makes me grin. Taking my time, I ease the waistband of his boxers down, revealing him completely. As soon as he's free, I let my tongue glide over him, savoring the way he groans.

His hand tangles in my hair, his other steadying himself against the counter. I look up at him, seeing his head thrown back, and I increase the rhythm, drawing out more of those deep, throaty sounds. His grip on my hair tightens as I work both my hands and mouth in perfect coordination.

"Good Lord, Miranda," he breathes, his voice tight with restraint.

His hips begin to move in time with me, his control slipping. When I glance up again, his eyes are blazing. Before I can think, he pulls me up by my arms, his strength catching me off guard.

"Enough," he growls, capturing my mouth with a searing kiss. His hands are everywhere—gripping, tugging, peeling away my sweater. The heat of his touch ignites every inch of my skin.

In one fluid motion, he strips me of my jeans and panties. Then, with a strength that always surprises me, he lifts me onto the kitchen counter. I'm now at his level, my hands finding his arms, sliding into his hair, pulling him closer.

"I like it up here," I whisper against his lips. "I can see into your eyes."

His response is a deeper kiss, his hands moving over me, exploring, claiming. A gasp escapes me as his lips trail down to my chest.

"I like it too," he murmurs against my skin. "I don't have to bend down as far for these." He chuckles, and I laugh, though the sound is cut short by the sensations building within me.

"I'm not short," I manage to say, breathless. "You're just—oh—really tall."

His touch turns deliberate, his fingers sliding between my legs, making me gasp. "So ready," he growls, his lips brushing mine. "Stay right here."

I watch him stride out of the room, my heart pounding as he disappears into the bedroom. When he returns, he tosses a condom onto the counter, tearing open another and rolling it on with practiced ease. His eyes lock on mine as he steps between my legs.

Wrapping my arms around his neck, I hold on as he slowly presses into me. A low moan escapes his lips as he begins to move, each stroke deeper and more intense than the last. His hand cups my lower back, holding me in place, while his other hand tangles in my hair.

"So good," he whispers against my ear. "Come for me, baby."

His words send me spiraling over the edge, my body tightening around him. He doesn't stop, his movements pulling me higher and pushing me further, over and over, until

I find release again Clutching him with trembling hands, he is moaning as he keeps up his. Then a final deep thrust sends him over the edge, his body shuddering against mine as he whispers my name.

We stay there, holding each other as the tension ebbs away. When I finally pull back, I find his eyes closed, his expression blissful. Those green eyes open, meeting mine with an intensity that makes my breath catch. He brushes a hand over my cheek, leans in for a gentle kiss, and then slips away to the bathroom.

Spent, I slide off the counter and head to the bedroom. Pulling on a robe, I meet him as he steps out. His gaze roams over me, and a mischievous grin spreads across his face.

"Who said I was done with you?" he murmurs, pulling me close and kissing my neck.

The robe falls away as his hands find my skin again. And as he looks at me, his expression filled with desire, I realize how completely at ease I feel in his arms.

I thought I was resting, but my wandering hand has other ideas. I reach down and stroke him gently, eliciting a muttered word followed by a deep moan.

"Go, before I keep you here all night," he teases, pressing a lingering kiss to my lips before pulling back. Reluctantly, I release him, and he disappears down the hall.

Smiling at myself in the mirror, I finally notice it—the spark in my eyes that I thought was lost. Pure happiness. It's there, clear as day. If the days ahead are anything like today, I'll gladly take it. Ethan has become everything I didn't realize I needed, and my heart flutters at the thought of him. A grin spreads across my face as I exhale my content and go to find him.

He's in the living room, on the phone, standing near the window in just his jeans and bare feet. The sight is enough to make me pause. Quietly, I tiptoe into the kitchen, start a pot of coffee, and begin tidying up. But I can't help glancing his way. He's completely still, listening intently to whoever's on the other end of the line. After a moment, he glances over at me, gives a small nod, and steps outside, closing the door behind him.

I shrug and return to my chores, putting away clothes and sipping coffee. I leave his cup on the counter and head to the living room, curling up on the couch with a throw blanket. The TV flickers in the background as I idly flip through channels. Glancing at the clock, I realize it's already six. I wonder if dinner is still on the table, figuratively speaking. Before I know it, my eyes grow heavy, and I drift off.

A soft kiss stirs me awake. Ethan is kneeling beside the couch, his green eyes twinkling.

"Hey, sleepyhead. Ready to wake up and grab some dinner?" His grin is infectious.

Stretching, I rub the sleep from my eyes. "Sorry, you were gone so long."

"Business," he says simply, pulling me to my feet. My robe falls open slightly, and he glances down before I hastily pull it closed, my cheeks flushing. He chuckles, planting a quick kiss on my nose.

"Come with me," he says, leading me down the hall to the bedroom.

When I step inside, my breath catches. Draped across the bed is the beautiful violet dress I had tried on at the mall but decided against buying.

"Ethan..." I turn to face him, a mix of surprise and confusion in my expression. He shifts nervously, scratching the back of his neck.

"I know you said no, but you looked amazing in it," he admits, his voice soft. "I bought it while you were trying on the other dress."

I can't help but smile. "I should be mad," I tease, "but I loved it, so I'll let it slide. This time." Stepping forward, I wrap my arms around him, resting my head against his chest. "Thank you. But seriously, Ethan, I don't need things. I just need you."

He pulls back slightly, his eyes warm. "Well, since you're not mad..." He walks to the door and reveals the matching black and purple fuzzy jacket hanging there. "It's cold out, so I had to get this, too."

Laughing, I shake my head. "You're too much."

He shrugs, an unapologetic smile on his face. "I just want to take care of you."

Before I can argue further, he steps closer and unties the belt of my robe. The fabric slips from my shoulders, pooling on the floor. His gaze is intense, but his touch is gentle as he lowers me onto the bed.

"I thought we were going out," I murmur as he kneels at the foot of the bed, his hands sliding along my thighs.

"We are," he says with a wicked grin, "after I'm done with you."

His lips trace a path over my skin, and I shudder at the sensation. He's deliberate, every movement a promise, and I can't help but lose myself in the moment.

Later, when we're both spent, he collapses beside me with a contented sigh. His arm wraps around my waist, his head resting on my chest.

"I'm not going to inflate your ego," I say breathlessly, "but I think that was the best I've ever had."

He chuckles, the vibration warm against my skin. "I told you I'd make you scream my name."

"And you did. At least three times," I admit, a blush creeping up my cheeks.

He leans up and kisses my belly softly. "It's never sounded better."

As he leaves to clean up, I stay on the bed, letting the events of the evening wash over me. I've never felt this way before—so complete, so seen. It's overwhelming in the best way possible.

Ethan returns, his mischievous smile making me laugh. "With a sight like this," he says, crawling onto the bed, "I'm not sure I want to go out."

His kisses trail from my belly to my lips, and I shiver at the tenderness in his touch.

"Mind-blowing," I whisper. "You've turned my brain to mush."

"Well," he says with a smirk, "I could revive you."

His hand drifts downward, but I cross my legs, stopping him with a laugh. "No, please. I need to recover. You're insatiable."

"And you love it," he teases, his grin widening as he pulls me into his arms.

I laugh, leaning into him, already feeling the pull of sleep again. Happiness like this—it's everything I didn't know I needed.

"Sorry, not sorry. I just can't seem to get enough of you," Ethan murmurs, nuzzling into my neck. I lean my head against his, relaxing into him.

"I can see that, and I'm definitely not complaining. You can do that again after dinner if you like." My voice takes on a playful purr as his hand grazes up my stomach, brushing against my already sensitive nipple. My body betrays me again, and he takes full advantage, nipping gently at my earlobe. A shiver runs down my spine.

"Ethan," I protest weakly, "you can't possibly be ready to go again."

He grins against my ear, catching my hand and guiding it to his hardening length. "You. All you," he whispers.

I squeeze him gently, and he moans, the sound reverberating against my neck as he nuzzles me.

"Ethan," I groan, "I'm hungry and sore. But I promise, after dinner, I'm going to make you scream my name." My voice carries a playful growl.

"Promise?" he teases, gently biting my shoulder.

Before I can answer, his hand glides down my body, brushing between my legs. The sudden jolt of pleasure makes me arch into his touch.

"Ethan," I gasp, torn between wanting to stop him and wanting more. My body decides for me, and he takes it as an invitation. His fingers slide into me, and I gasp again, the mixture of soreness and pleasure sending sparks through me.

"I think you're ready now," he murmurs before capturing my lips in a deep kiss. He rolls over me, his weight a comforting pressure as he parts my legs and slides against me. My body trembles, a mix of anticipation and desire.

He pauses, his green eyes locking with mine, his expression searching. Without a word, he begins to ease into me, slowly, deliberately. I close my eyes, overwhelmed by the sensation as he fills me completely. His quiet groan of pleasure spurs me on, and I tighten my legs around him, urging him deeper.

Suddenly, he pulls back, rolling off me to grab a condom from the nightstand. I watch him, my chest rising and falling as he quickly prepares himself. When he returns, he's gentler, his movements slow and careful. He knows I'm sore, and his tenderness only deepens the moment.

It doesn't take long before the wave crashes over me, leaving me breathless. He waits for me to finish before moving again, his rhythm deep and steady. Each stroke builds the intensity until I'm tumbling into another climax, gripping his shoulders as I cry out his name.

Ethan follows, his own release overtaking him as he collapses onto me, holding me close. For a long moment, the only sounds are our breathing and the soft beat of our hearts. He kisses me gently before rolling away and heading to the bathroom without a word.

I lay there, spent, the aftermath of our passion leaving me in a haze. After a moment, I manage to pull myself off the bed and drag my feet to the bathroom door. When it opens, Ethan's face is tense.

"Are you all right?" I ask softly.

He leans down to kiss me, but when he tries to move past, I stop him with a hand on his arm. "Shower with me," I say, more a statement than a question.

He hesitates, his gaze searching mine, before pulling me into the bathroom with a childlike grin as I squeal in delight.

Under the warm spray of water, he washes my hair with careful attention, his hands gentle yet thorough. Then he moves to wash the rest of me, his touch reverent as though memorizing every inch of my body. I return the favor, exploring the details of him—the tiny scar below his right pec, the three freckles on his lower back. I commit it all to memory, marveling at how perfect he is.

When we're both clean, I turn off the water, and we wrap ourselves in towels, heading back to the bedroom. But something feels off. His silence lingers, and my worry grows.

"Ethan, are you sure you're alright?" I stand in front of him, searching his eyes for answers.

"Of course," he replies, though his tone isn't entirely convincing. "Just a little worn out. Some little minx won't stop seducing me." His grin is playful, but there's something in his expression that holds me back from teasing him further.

"Well, if you weren't so damn hot, maybe she would," I quip, smacking his backside as I move to retrieve my underwear.

"I'll try to be less hot," he says, smirking.

"No, don't do that. I like you just the way you are," I reply over my shoulder, earning a deep laugh from him.

"So," I begin, turning back to face him, "are we still going out, or should we grab something quick? It's getting late, and I know you have to work tomorrow."

He studies me intently, his silence stretching the moment until I grow uneasy. "You know, I'm going to break my own rule," he says finally, "but why don't you pack an overnight bag? We can grab dinner somewhere and head back to my place."

I blink at him, surprised. "What rule would that be?"

"Just grab a sweater and jeans for tonight," he says, avoiding the question as he pulls out the clothes he bought earlier.

"What rule?" I press, hands on my hips. He meets my gaze for a long moment before rolling his eyes.

"I don't do sleepovers," he admits, turning away as he pulls on his jeans.

I raise an eyebrow. "And why is that?"

"Because I don't," he says, his tone firm.

"That's not a reason," I counter, waiting.

"Just leave it," he warns, but I can't help myself.

"Not if you want me to go with you," I say, trying to keep my voice steady. Ethan's behavior feels bigger than he's letting on, and I need to understand what's going on.

"Then don't go!" he snaps, slipping on his shirt and tossing his dirty clothes into the bag before storming past me into the kitchen.

I stand there, stunned. Did he just yell at me?

"Are you serious right now?" I stomp into the kitchen, my voice rising as I follow him.

"Yes, I am," he replies, his tone sharp as he glares at me. I glare right back.

"If you don't want me to go, then why did you ask me to?" I demand, throwing my arms in the air.

"I *do* want you to go, but I don't want to tell you my reasons," he says through clenched teeth, his frustration palpable.

He's so infuriating. I slap my forehead in exasperation but immediately regret it. "Oww!" I wince, pressing my fingers against my still-sore injury as tears spring to my eyes.

"Miranda?" Ethan's tone softens instantly. He's at my side in a heartbeat, concern etched on his face.

"I'm fine," I say, though my voice wavers as I try to blink back the tears. "I just hit my sore spot."

He reaches out, gently tilting my chin so he can look into my eyes. "Your head's still that sore?"

"Yes," I admit, my voice cracking, though I try to sound nonchalant. "But I'm fine."

"Are you sure?" His voice is tender now, the anger from earlier melting away as he studies me. His sweetness tugs at my resolve, and I sigh.

"I am. And Ethan, I'm sorry. I want to go with you if you still want me to. If you don't want to tell me your reasons, I'll drop it."

He exhales a deep sigh, his shoulders relaxing as he pulls me into his arms. "When I spend the night with a woman, they get too attached too quickly," he says, his voice low.

I bite back a laugh. He's serious. "Really? Well, don't worry—I won't be begging for a ring or anything. I'm not looking to get *that* attached." I shrug playfully against his chest, and he chuckles softly, though I can't tell if it's genuine.

"Okay, settled then," I say, stepping back. "I'll pack, and then we'll eat."

I gather clothes, pajamas, and the other essentials from my room, along with my meds and chargers. After filling Kasey's food bowl, I'm ready to go. Ethan helps me into my jacket without another word, grabs our bags, and we head out.

We stop at my favorite Chinese restaurant for dinner, but Ethan's unusually quiet throughout the meal. His silence makes me worry I've done something wrong. I'm also nervous—I haven't stayed over at a man's place in years. What if I do something embarrassing?

"Hey." Ethan's voice pulls me out of my thoughts. His hand rests gently on my leg. "You okay over there?"

"Yeah, sorry," I lie, offering a small smile. "Just daydreaming."

"Want to share?" His lips twitch into a small smile, and I laugh nervously.

"Nope." I answer and we exchange a smile.

We drive the rest of the way in silence, my nerves bubbling over as he pulls into an underground parking garage beneath a towering building. Ethan grabs our bags, takes my hand, and gives it a reassuring squeeze. His smile, though, looks forced.

We ride the elevator up after he punches in a code, and I glance at him questioningly.

"Penthouse," he explains, answering my unspoken question.

"Oh." Of course. My stomach flips as the elevator climbs

higher. The doors slide open to reveal a spacious entryway, and Ethan unlocks the door, gesturing for me to go in first.

I hold my breath as I step into the dark room. Lights flicker on, and I exhale in awe. It's massive. Still, part of me wonders if there's a hidden red room somewhere. I've seen *Wolves at the Door* and *Fifty Shades.* Anything's possible.

"Welcome to my home," Ethan says behind me. He steps up and guides me into the living room. The floor-to-ceiling windows on two walls steal my attention. The couch could seat ten people, and the open kitchen looks large enough to host a small banquet. My entire apartment could fit here. Twice.

"It's so big," I murmur, still taking it all in.

Ethan laughs deeply. "Not the first time I've heard that."

I shake my head, swatting at his arm. "I bet it's not."

He grins, his mood lightening as he gives me a tour. The living room, the sleek kitchen, two spare bedrooms, and a den full of books—I'm enchanted by it all. Finally, we reach the master bedroom. My jaw drops.

The bedroom is as luxurious as the rest of the apartment. A massive bed dominates one side, while a fireplace and plush chairs sit on the other. More floor-to-ceiling windows line the wall, offering a breathtaking view.

I walk to the windows, my fingers brushing the glass. "How many floors up are we?"

"Twenty-eighth," he answers, stepping beside me. "I own the entire floor."

"Impressive," I whisper, shivering as the cold air seeps through the glass. Ethan presses a button on a remote, and the windows begin to slide open. The cold air rushes in, and I step back, wrapping my arms around myself.

"Beautiful, isn't it?" he says as he steps closer, his hand resting lightly on my back.

"It is." I nod, but the chill becomes too much. He closes the windows with another press of the remote.

He gestures toward the bed. "Are you tired, or do you want to watch TV or something?"

His voice carries a hint of nervousness that makes him even more endearing. For all his confidence, he's worried about me being here. It's adorable.

"Ethan, this place is amazing," I say with a smile, hoping to ease his nerves.

"I thought so when I bought it," he says, shrugging. "I've been meaning to add some color to the walls, but I haven't gotten around to it."

"It's perfect," I say sincerely. "A little big for one person, but perfect."

He takes two steps toward me, wrapping me in his arms. This hug feels different—more intimate. I mirror his actions, holding him close as he exhales deeply and kisses the top of my head.

"How about a glass of wine before bed?" he asks, pulling back to look at me. "I have to go to the office tomorrow, but you can stay here, or I can drop you off at home before I go."

He's trying to sound casual, but I can hear the hope in his voice. Warmth floods me, and I smile. "I'd love to stay."

Ethan is the CEO and co-owner of the family business, alongside his mother and two sisters. From what I gather, his sisters and mother don't involve themselves much in the day-to-day operations; they just reap the benefits of ownership. Ethan doesn't seem to mind it at all. In fact, he speaks highly of them. I also learn that he's the sole owner of six other companies, though he's bought and sold many more over the years. By the time he finishes explaining, my head is spinning.

"You're a busy man," I remark, sipping my wine.

"I am," he agrees, taking a long sip from his glass.

"Doesn't all that keep you from enjoying life?" I ask, genuinely curious. How can someone running an empire still have time to savor life's pleasures?

"Sometimes," he admits, "but I try to make time for myself. I have teams that handle the day-to-day operations at each company. They run everything efficiently, so I mostly just oversee."

He finishes his wine, staring into the empty glass. His expression grows pensive, and I can't help but wonder what's on his mind.

"Do you ever get tired of all that money and power?" I ask, my tone serious.

His deep laugh surprises me. "No. I'll never want for anything, and my family is taken care of in every possible way. When I decide to have children, their children will be taken care of, too. That's how my family has always done things. I've just expanded on it."

His tone holds a trace of something—sadness, maybe, or deep thought. I can't quite place it.

"Too much money makes you stop appreciating things,"

I say, standing and stretching. Ethan tilts his head, studying me before chuckling softly.

"What's so funny?" I ask, narrowing my eyes.

"You. Money makes the world go around," he replies, his chuckle deepening.

"No, angular momentum makes the world go around," I counter with a grin. "Other than that, love is what keeps it turning. And don't you know—money is the root of all evil." I wink at him, drawing another laugh.

"Miranda, you're the first woman I've met who thinks like that. Most care only about how much I can spend on them."

I shrug. "You've been hanging around the wrong women. Not all of us want money. I'd rather be happy and poor than rich and lonely."

He falls silent, his gaze lingering on me for several long seconds. "You'd rather be poor?" His confusion makes me laugh.

"I don't *choose* to be poor, no. But given the choice between money or love and happiness, I'll pick happiness every time."

"Money makes me happy," he counters, his tone playful but firm.

"Then you're missing out on the little things money can't buy," I say, taking his empty glass and walking into the kitchen.

He follows me, clearly intrigued. "Like what? What could money possibly not buy?"

I turn to face him, trying to find the right words. "How

about you think about that, and we'll talk later," I say, too tired for a full debate.

"Just give me one example," he presses, taking my hand and gently pulling me back around.

"A kiss," I answer without hesitation.

He laughs. "I can buy a kiss. If I throw in dinner, I get at least that."

"No," I say, smiling, "a real kiss. One from the heart."

Standing on my tiptoes, I touch his cheek and press my lips to his, letting the kiss convey everything I mean. When I pull back, his slight grin tells me he understands.

"Like that," I say softly. "It didn't cost you anything. I gave it freely."

He looks stunned, and I feel a giddy rush as I turn and walk toward the bedroom.

"You've got it all figured out, don't you? True love? Happily ever after?" he calls after me.

"Ethan, I lost faith in happily ever after years ago," I reply without turning back. "But I do believe in true love. It's not for everyone, though—it takes work, dedication, and trust."

I grab my pajamas and head into the bathroom to clean up. When I'm done, Ethan takes his turn while I crawl into bed. It's as comfortable as I imagined, and I snuggle in, waiting.

When he emerges, he pauses at the far side of the bed, smiling down at me. "Just make yourself comfortable on my side," he teases.

"Had to," I say, holding up my cast in explanation. He nods in understanding.

"Fair enough. Be right there." He grabs the remote from the table and climbs into bed. Pressing a button, he turns off the lights, letting the moonlight stream in through the windows.

"Wow," I murmur. "It's like the moon is your own nightlight from up here."

"If it's too bright, I can fix it," he offers.

"The moon?" I ask, feigning surprise.

He chuckles and presses another button, activating a mesh curtain that dims the light. "Better?"

"That's perfect," I say, wanting to see a little of the moonlight. He sets the remote aside and pulls me closer, his arm wrapping securely around my waist. His warm breath brushes my shoulder as he curls behind me.

"I haven't shared a bed for actual sleeping in a long time," he murmurs, kissing my shoulder. "Please don't push me out."

"I'll try," I tease, relaxing into his warmth. His fingers twine with mine, and I exhale deeply, the moment perfect as I drift off to sleep.

Chapter 18

I wake up in a panic when I open my eyes. I don't know where I am, and I'm confused. Then I feel Ethan behind me. As I stir, he wakes up.

"You alright?" He asks sleepily.

"Sorry, just confused for a minute."

He pulls me back toward him. "Don't go anywhere," he murmurs against my neck.

"I'm not." I turn around in his arms to face him, and the moonlight is bright enough to see his face.

His eyes are closed, and I study his features until he opens them. His grin spreads as his sleepy eyes sparkle in the low light.

"Why are you staring at me?" His voice is soft, deep, and silky.

"Because I can."

His eyelashes flutter. "You know it's still dark out, right? Go back to sleep." He pulls me closer.

"So bossy," I giggle.

"Uh-huh. Sleep."

I lean over and gently kiss his lips. They're so soft while he's half-asleep. He grins, and I tuck back into his arms, falling asleep again.

When I wake again, it's bright, and I'm still tangled in Ethan's arms, but now he's awake, watching me.

"Good morning." I can't help but smile at his goofy grin. I can tell he's only been awake for a little while by the sleepy look in his eyes.

"I see you're watching me now."

"I can't help myself." He pulls me into a gentle kiss. "How did you sleep?" He nuzzles my neck, and it's quickly becoming my favorite thing he does.

"Actually great. I thought sleeping in the same bed would be difficult, but it was very nice." My admission makes me blush.

"I must agree with you, and waking up next to you is even nicer." He growls, pulling me against him as he kisses me gently.

The kiss deepens as his hand slides down to my hips, pulling me closer. I feel his erection pressing into me, and I grin. Definitely a perk of waking up together.

We have slow, gentle morning sex, after which we lie there in comfortable silence while our bodies recover.

"I have to go to work." Ethan quietly says from next to me.

I roll over and curl into his side. "Wish you didn't."

"I won't be gone long. You can stay here." He tucks my hair behind my ear.

"I just might have to do that. This bed is fantastic." I giggle and pull the covers up to my chin.

He leans over, kisses my forehead, and without another word, he walks naked to the shower.

After his shower, he gets dressed in his tailored black suit and flips through the ties in his closet. I get up, walk over to him, and watch as he sifts through his collection. I reach around and grab a light green tie with black lines.

"This one." He takes it and holds it up as I pull one of his white shirts off the hanger and slip it on. He looks at me with surprise as I sashay into the bathroom to freshen up.

When I'm done, I come out into the bedroom, but he's not there. I follow the smell of coffee into the kitchen, where Ethan sets a cup down on the counter for me.

"There's food in the fridge and pantry, or there are menus in this drawer for places that deliver." He takes out a notepad, writes down a few things, and turns it around to me. "Here's the code for the elevator, my direct office number, and my assistant Lisa's desk." He takes a key out of his pocket and places it on the notepad. "This is the key to the front door, in case you decide to leave."

When he looks up, I see the same uncertainty from last night reappear.

"This should be all you need. You're welcome to go anywhere or use anything that's here. The only place off-limits is my office, and it's locked. If you need anything, just call me."

I'm a little overwhelmed by all this information, but I know I can figure it out.

"I appreciate that. I brought my computer, so I plan on lying in that bed of yours, opening the blinds, basking in the sunshine, and maybe scrolling through Facebook. I can cook myself something, so I won't be leaving." Smiling back at him, he finally relaxes.

"I'll call you when I'm leaving the office so you know when to expect me back." He's all business this morning, and I tell him so.

"And you look super-hot in this suit," I add as I pull his tie, making him lean down to give me a kiss.

"And you look even hotter in my shirt and panties. Good thing I have an important meeting, or I'd have you on this counter." He growls, pulling me around and caging me against the cabinet.

"I'll be here when you get home." I raise my eyebrows, causing him to chuckle.

"I have to go." He kisses me deeper this time, and I run my hand along the waistband of his pants.

"Miranda…" He sucks in a breath, then pulls away. "I have to go." He kisses me hard and walks toward the door.

Leaning against the counter, I sip my coffee, which is delicious, and watch him go. When he reaches the door, he turns around, and I grin over my cup as he shakes his head and then walks out. This is kind of nice.

I make myself some scrambled eggs and toast before crawling back into his bed. I figure out the blinds and open them all the way before flipping through my phone and reading some texts. Then I decide to mess with Ethan. I snap a picture of myself in his bed, his shirt unbuttoned just enough. My hair is a mess, but it's a good shot. I text it to him with a message:

Your bed is so lonely without you.

It doesn't take long for a response.

I think I miss my bed more than ever.

I snap another picture, this time with the shirt unbuttoned a little more, showing more of my chest.

I'm in a very important meeting.

I send one more shot of my breasts, the sheet just covering my nipple.

Now I have a raging hard-on in this important meeting.

You're welcome.

I laugh and decide to browse Facebook for a while. Before long, I'm up wandering around the apartment. I watch some TV and make another cup of coffee, but time seems to crawl. It's only been two hours, and I'm bored.

I lie on the couch, call my mom, Emma, and Shannon, and tell them all about this massive apartment. After another hour, I can't take it anymore. I need something to do. I head to his library and look over some of his books—most are boring—but I do find a few that look interesting. I'm deciding which one to start when I get a text from Ethan.

What are you up to?

Checking out your library.

I can see that.

What?

I have video surveillance of the apartment.

Oh really? This could be fun. I sit in the chair, throwing my legs over the other side.

And what have you seen?

The phone rings, making me jump. It's Ethan, which makes me laugh out loud.

"I see you sitting in my favorite chair," his voice is deep and husky.

"It is a very comfortable chair." I glance around and spot the camera in the corner. I open my legs, swing them around, then unbutton the shirt so it's hanging open.

"Don't tease me," he growls, but I can't help myself and unbutton the shirt the rest of the way, pulling it to the sides.

"See what you're missing?" I lean back, close my eyes, and run my hand down my side. I hear his heavy breathing but no response.

"You're in a boring meeting, and I'm all alone here. I guess I'll just have to take care of myself." I slide my hand down to the edge of my panties, waiting for his reaction, but all I hear is more breathing, and it makes me grin.

"I never knew you had such a naughty side," he says, but it's not over the phone, which makes me jump. I open my eyes, and there he is, standing right in front of me, that amazing grin on his face.

"Hi," I whisper, suddenly feeling shy.

"Hi." He drops his phone on the table beside me and pulls me up from the chair into a deep kiss. I let my phone fall to the chair and wrap my arms around him.

"I thought you were going to call when you were on your way back," I say between kisses.

"I was, but then I checked in on you and couldn't help myself. Besides, that raging hard-on is back." He kisses me hard, and I slide my hand down to feel him. His pants are tight, and I giggle as he sweeps me up into his arms.

He carries me to the bedroom and suddenly drops me onto the bed. "I've been thinking about this bed all morning." He starts making quick work of his suit, shedding his clothes onto the chair, and I watch in fascination as layer after layer is removed to reveal his muscular body. Once he's down to his briefs, he nearly jumps onto the bed, pulling me along as he rolls over, placing me on top of him.

"It is a pretty fabulous bed," I agree, sitting up. He runs his hands over my bare chest, his fingers tracing a line down to my bent legs.

"It's not the bed I want. It's what's in it," he growls, pulling me back down for a kiss.

"Pillows?" I tease, my giggle quickly turning into a soft moan as I feel his arousal against me.

"You," he groans as I start moving against him, the friction instantly sending sparks through me. His head falls back against the pillows as I continue, and he closes his eyes.

"Those pictures this morning… I couldn't concentrate at all. All I could think about was your beautiful breasts in my mouth." His hands move up to my chest, pulling me down as he licks and sucks on my nipples until I'm gasping for breath.

When I can't take it anymore, I pull away and stand to slide off my panties, watching as his eyes darken with desire. I go to shrug off his shirt, but he stops me.

"Leave it on," he nearly begs, and his voice sends a thrill through me. I adjust the shirt so it hangs open, exposing just enough to keep his eyes locked on me. I'm panting now, aching for him.

I crawl back up the bed, pulling off his briefs and then sliding over him until he grabs my arms and pulls me into another kiss, his hands tangled in my hair. I grind against him, teasing him with every movement.

"Miranda..." His voice is strained, and I know he's barely holding back.

I shift forward just enough to brush him against my entrance, and he tenses beneath me. "Don't tease me," he growls.

"Who said I was teasing?" I reply, locking eyes with him as I lower myself slowly, taking him in inch by inch. His hands grip my waist, and his eyes close tightly as I settle over him, adjusting to his fullness. His control is slipping, and I can feel it. I rock my hips slightly, eliciting a deep moan from him.

"God, you feel so good." His mouth is slack, and his back is arched. I know I can't last much longer.

I sit up and start to move, but his hands grip my waist, holding me still. "Let me finish, please," I beg, arching my back for more friction.

Without a word, he loosens his grip, allowing me to move. Skin against skin, it's overwhelming, the sensations building quickly. I ride him, grinding until I'm on the edge of release. It hits me hard, and I scream out his name as I fall apart around him. He holds me tightly as I come down, shuddering against him.

But he isn't done. He pulls me up and then down again, controlling the rhythm now, thrusting into me with force. Each time he slams into me, he groans, and I can feel him building toward his own release.

"Shit! Miranda!" He cries out as his body tenses, and he spills into me, hot and hard. The sensation pushes me over the edge again, and I scream his name as I ride out another wave of pleasure.

For a moment, we both lie there, panting, our bodies still trembling from the intensity. Then, suddenly, he rolls me off him and stands up, his expression panicked.

"Fuck! Goddamn it, Miranda." His voice is filled with frustration, and I realize what happened. No condom. The realization crashes into me, and I feel a cold wave of panic.

"I'm sorry," I whisper, scrambling off the bed and running to the bathroom. Tears blur my vision as I turn on the water, desperate to scrub the reality away. How could I be so reckless?

I sit in the tub, crying uncontrollably as the water runs over me. Thoughts race through my head—*what if I get pregnant? What if...*

"Miranda." Ethan's voice is soft, full of concern.

"I'm sorry, I'm so, so sorry." I continue crying, unable to stop.

"Please don't cry," he says, his voice breaking through the panic. "It was my fault too."

The water scalds my skin, but I don't care. Suddenly, Ethan reaches in and turns it off. He pulls the stopper from the drain, kneels beside the tub, and takes my hand. I still can't look at him.

Gently, he wraps me in a towel and pulls me close, holding me as I sob into his chest.

"Shhh, don't cry," he whispers, his hand stroking my hair. He dries me off and leads me back to bed, where he pulls me into his arms.

"I should never have..." I start to apologize, but he presses his finger to my lips.

"Miranda, stop." His voice is gentle but firm. "That was incredible. I've never had sex like that before. You felt like velvet pulling me in, and I couldn't stop. I think I finally know what true ecstasy feels like."

His words soothe me, and the tightness in my chest starts to ease. "It was pretty incredible," I agree, my voice barely above a whisper.

We lie there in silence for a few minutes before I gather the courage to ask, "Ethan, I mean, you've been with a lot of women... Are you..."

"Yes, Miranda. I get checked regularly, and I'm clean." His reassurance calms me.

"I never have sex without protection—until now." He traces my bottom lip with his thumb, his eyes serious.

"I'm not on birth control," I admit, swallowing hard. "I haven't been with anyone in a really long time."

He's quiet for a while, and I can tell he is thinking. "We just need to be very careful going forward. And we'll monitor your… situation." His words hang in the air, but I don't dare ask what he means.

"I'll get on birth control right away," I offer.

"That's probably a good idea," he agrees.

"So," I say, trying to lighten the mood, "do you think we could have more mind-blowing sex later? Because I cannot get enough of you."

He grins, his lips brushing over mine. "With protection, of course."

"Of course." I reach down and stroke him, and to my surprise, he's already hard again.

"How can you be ready again so soon?" I ask, laughing softly. But I'm ready too.

"It's you. I've never wanted anyone this much."

He kisses me, rolling me onto my back, and I open for him, eager and wanting. He lays against me, and the heat between us is electric.

"We just had this conversation," he murmurs against my lips, trying to be stern, but I can see the playfulness in his eyes.

"We did, but you feel so good," I moan, and he pushes into me before pulling back out again.

"That's all you're getting." He grins and reaches for a condom, rolling it on quickly before thrusting into me hard. There's no time to adjust; he's moving fast, each thrust deep and powerful. My body responds instantly, and I'm moaning as I ride out another orgasm. He follows, groaning my name in my ear as he reaches his release.

Later, after a trip to the bathroom, Ethan pulls me back to his side with a deep exhale.

"I think we made a mistake," he says playfully.

"Didn't we just hash this out?"

He shakes his head. "Not that. I mean, now that I've had you bare, I want you like that every time."

I look into his eyes, my heart skipping a beat. "I know what you mean," I whisper. "But we can't."

"No, we can't," he agrees, but there's something in his voice that makes me wonder if he wishes otherwise.

After spending the rest of the day in bed, talking, laughing, and making love, we finally order takeout pasta for dinner. As we clean up the dishes, Ethan takes my hand, spinning me around to face him.

"I think you should stay again tonight," he says, his lips brushing my neck.

"I have to feed Kasey and get more clothes," I reply, but I'm already nodding in agreement. I want to be here with him.

"Get some clothes on, and I'll take you home. But you're coming back."

"OKAY," I laugh, only wearing his shirt, which has been my uniform all day. As I walk past him, he smacks my bare ass, making me giggle.

That evening, we curl up on the huge sofa for a movie, but I find myself watching him more than the screen. I can't get over how different he is now that I know him and how much I enjoy his affection.

I catch him watching me, too, and when I giggle, he moves closer, laying his head on my shoulder.

Yeah, I know I'm falling for him—and harder than I ever expected.

Chapter 19

The morning light meets me as I open my eyes. I absolutely love it. As I stretch, I wince at how sore I am, but I crawl out of bed, slip on clothes, and go in search of Ethan, who I hear talking loudly in the other room.

As I round the corner to the kitchen, I can hear him clearly, and I can tell it is business. I pause and wait, not sure if I should interrupt him or go back to bed? My stomach growls, and I need coffee, so I have my answer. I almost tiptoe in, but he looks up just as I walk in, and his eyes light up his entire face. He is already dressed and ready for work, and like yesterday, looks incredible in his chosen suit and tie. I move around him and make a cup of coffee as he plants a kiss on my forehead. He has a cup in front of him, so I make myself one, and go to the fridge to pull out the eggs and cheese.

I try to make as little noise as possible while I make an omelet, so I don't disturb his conversation, which is most definitely work-related. When it's finished, I plate it and set it in front of Ethan. He looks up in surprise, and then mouths thank you. I wink at him as I turn back to make my own. While it is cooking, I lay two pieces of toast on his plate and two on mine and get out the butter and jelly. I love that he likes strawberry jelly, too.

He continues to talk while I sit next to him, and he takes a forkful and makes a sound. "Wow, this is delicious." He says, then apologizes to the person on the phone, explaining that he is eating an omelet. It makes me proud, and he finishes his conversation.

"I hope I did not wake you, but I needed to take care of some business early. I need to go into the office this morning, but I can have a driver take you to the doctor, and maybe we can meet up after for lunch. I have a full afternoon, so I won't be able to stay out long, but we will be able to spend a little time together. I can't go all day without you." He seems shy at the admission as he looks down and eats the last two bites of his breakfast. "This was great, thank you. I usually just have coffee and a bagel or something."

"You are welcome. I woke up hungry from all our activity yesterday and thought you might need a little more than coffee." I finish up my food and stand to clean up.

"I am always hungry for you." He pulls me over in between his legs. "I would have had you this morning, but you mumbled you were sore." He laughs at me.

"I am, but I am sure I will be fine before you get back." I give him a sly grin this time before moving over to put the dishes away. Admitting my desires is new and strange, but I like it.

"Good. So, are you okay with a driver today? You can call me when you are done, and we can meet up if you would like to."

"That sounds wonderful. I would like Charlie, if that's okay, I feel comfortable with him." I turn, and Ethan cocks his head to the side in question,

"The guy you and Jason hired to drive me to work," I explain, and I watch as the lightbulb goes off.

"Alright, I will call Jason and get his number." Ethan starts packing his pockets with his keys and wallet.

"Actually, I have it. He gave it to me to call when I was ready to leave, I think the second day." I feel silly as he pauses.

"Go ahead and call him and just have him put it on my account. If he's not available, he can send someone else." And just like that, he's fixed it.

We give our heated goodbyes, and he comes back for more, twice, before finally breaking free and heading to the elevator. I head to the bathroom for a quick bath and to get dressed, then I call Charlie, and he's available, which makes me happy.

I am done and back in the car at 11:15, and after a quick call to Ethan, he informs me he is finishing up a meeting and to meet him outside the office. It's strange that I miss him so much, and it's only been a few hours. I have no idea how that is possible.

While I wait for Ethan, I call Emma, I need someone to talk to. I know she is at work, but thankfully she answers.

"Hey, stranger!" She sounds excited to hear from me.

"Hey! How are you?" I ask.

"I'm good, and I see you are spending a lot of time with Ethan." Her smile is clear, even over the phone.

"I am. How do you know?" I'm curious since I haven't really told her much.

"Miranda, you are in the gossip columns, and you have been seen all over town together, from the theater to shopping and dinners. They say he might be smitten with you." She giggles and is surprised I don't know.

"Really? I knew about the one that Shannon shared, but I haven't seen any others. You know I don't read those things." I don't. I hate gossip.

"You should. You are a hot topic on TMZ." I hear her soft exhale, which makes me even more curious.

"I will look later." And before I can do it, she calls me out.

"Stop rolling your eyes at me. So…tell me, how is it?" She is waiting for the juicy details.

"It's wonderful, actually. I'm not sure what I was so worried about; he is amazing. And I mean that in every sense of the word. Em, he's nothing like I expected him to be. He's so gentle and kind and sweet. And he takes great care of me. I've spent the last two nights at his place, he's so freaking incredible." I feel silly telling my sister this stuff, but she has always been the romantic one.

"That's wonderful, Rana! I'm so glad he makes you happy. It's nice to hear it and to see you smile. And wow, I can see the way you two adore each other in all those pictures.

"Emma, I think I'm falling for him. I swore to myself I wouldn't, but I am, and the whole mess scares me.

She's quiet for a minute. "Why?" She finally asks.

"He's a playboy and likes his women, so I'm afraid when I heal, he's going to drop me." Saying it out loud makes me sound silly, but I am nervous about the entire thing.

"I think you are letting your past scare you. People can change Miranda, especially when they have someone to change for. You have always brought out the best in people, so maybe that is what he needed. And besides, we never know how long a relationship is going to last, so just enjoy it."

She's right, of course. "I know, and you are right. I just don't want to jinx myself. He keeps telling me he isn't going anywhere; it's just hard to believe it." Putting my head back against the seat, I close my eyes and take a deep breath.

"You won't jinx it. I'm pretty sure he is falling for you, too. That man is a grinning fool in those pictures; take a look for yourself. By the way, when are you coming home for Thanksgiving? I need to plan. And how are you getting here? I know you can't drive yet, so train or plane?"

I haven't even thought too much about it, and it is next week, so I guess I should decide. "Yes, I am coming home, just not sure when or how. Jason had mentioned going home and offered me a ride, but I am not sure that's a good idea now. So maybe I should just buy a plane ticket." I need to figure it out sooner rather than later.

"Is Ethan coming with you?" I hear the hope in her voice.

"I never asked. I didn't know if I would be ready for the whole take him home for the holidays." She makes a noise that is part excitement, part she wants to slap me in the head. I know her too well, but it's not worth the discussion.

"Just keep me posted so I know if I should deep clean the house." She laughs.

"Alright, I will figure it out today and let you know when I'm leaving." Just as I say it, Ethan opens the door and slides in the car. He gently kisses my cheek and waits for me to finish my call.

"Em, I have to go, but I will call you later. Love you." We say goodbye and I hang up, as I hear Ethan tell Charlie where to take us for lunch.

"What do you have to figure out, and where are you going?" He takes my hand, curious as always.

"Thanksgiving. I have to figure out how I'm getting home since I can't drive and when I want to go."

He pulls me over to him. "When are you leaving, and for how long?" He asks as he holds me to him like we haven't seen each other in days. It kind of feels that way too.

"I usually go home for just a few days, but since I'm off, I thought maybe a week. I could probably leave Sunday or Monday and come home over the following weekend; just depends on when I can get a flight on short notice." I watch his face for a minute as I can see he's thinking.

"A week is a long time to be without you." His voice is soft.

"Maybe I won't go for an entire week then. Maybe just a few days." I blush at the craziness between us. As I watch him, suddenly, I don't want to be away from him either. Just as I start to say so, his face lights up, and I can see the idea forming in his brain.

"Planes are faster, but a boyfriend's car is more fun." He gives me his silly grin.

"I can't drive." I detour the statement he made. Is he wanting to come with me, or is it the boyfriend thing that sets me sideways?

"Good point. However, said car would come with a driver." He leans in close to me, rubbing his nose to mine.

"Would said driver be available on short notice? And he has to be really good-looking." I giggle, knowing that Charlie just heard me.

"He just happens to be available, and of course, he is very attractive, only the best for my girl."

I can't help but laugh at him. "You want to come home with me? Really? Didn't you get enough of the crazy at the hospital last week?"

"Never enough of you. They are not crazy; I like them. And only if you want me to go." His smile is full of hope as he waits.

"What about your family?" I have to ask since I know nothing about them and their traditions.

"Trust me, they won't mind." Do I want to make this leap? It's a big step and will make it harder to recover once we cross the going away together line. I can't say no to him, though, especially when his beautiful eyes are almost pleading with me.

"Ethan, would you like to go home with me for Thanksgiving? IF your family is okay with it, though, I don't want them to dislike me before I even meet them."

He grins from ear to ear and digs out his phone from his pocket. "I will call Mom now." His grin is so big I'm afraid he's going to hurt himself.

"You don't have to do that now!" He dials anyway and I sit silently beside him as I process the last two minutes.

"Hi, Mom." I don't hear her, but he smiles and waits.

Then he nods and takes my hand, giving it a squeeze.

"I am well...Yes...Her name is Miranda...She is a lawyer." He lets out a chuckle, and it's adorable watching him talk to her, even though I can only hear his side, which makes me crazy. "No, she's different. Mom, I like her a lot." His words warm me, and I feel shy as his eyes are once again on me.

"Actually, she has invited me to Thanksgiving in St. Louis with her family." He pauses again, and then I watch as a tiny blush crosses the tops of his cheeks. "She made me ask you first." He bites at his lip shyly, and I want to laugh, but I don't dare make a sound.

"Hold on." He puts the phone on mute. "Mom wants to know if we can come for dinner tonight. She wants to meet you." My jaw falls open, but I don't answer. "Are you available?" He coaxes me for an answer.

"Yes, I would be happy to go." I'm freaking out inside, though. He kisses me and then goes back to his conversation as I notice we have stopped outside a restaurant. He agrees with her a few times and then hangs up.

"All set. She meets you tonight and I am free to go with you for Thanksgiving."

I blink a few times, processing. "Why does that sound like a job interview?"

He laughs at my statement. "My Mom is great, she will like you, don't worry. She has been wanting me to come over for weeks, and I haven't, so this is just an excuse." He pulls me over to kiss me before moving to get out of the car. "Come, let's eat, I have to get back soon." And just like that, he made it all happen, I think.

We enjoy a great lunch and talk about how Thanksgiving is at my sister's and what he should expect.

"Do you really think your mom will like me?" I ask and he seems surprised at my question.

"I know she will adore you. Besides, you are not some money-hungry twit." His wink stops me, and I am frown at his use of word.

"Twit?" I repeat it. He clarifies and continues to eat. "Has she met a lot of your twits before?" I laugh at his expression.

"A few, but mostly, she just sees the pictures and hears the rumors in her social circles. She tells me all the time I need to slow down and that women are not underwear. She wishes I would settle down, but everyone knows I'm not one to have a steady girlfriend." He quickly looks up at me with a worried look, realizing what he said. The man is hopeless.

"Would you like help with that hole you are digging?" I watch him struggle.

"Maybe you should hold the shovel." He swallows hard, waiting to see if I am going to react.

"Ethan, you are a mess." I laugh, and he relaxes.

"I'm going to have to kiss up some more, aren't I?" He groans.

"No, it just makes me uncomfortable when you talk about all the women you have been with."

"I can completely understand that. For the record, you are the only one that matters to me now, and I'm hoping that will be for a very long time." He gives me that shy grin, and I melt.

"I hope so too," I whisper to myself, but by the look on

his face, he heard me.

We finish our lunch, and Charlie takes us back to Ethan's office. I'm ten kinds of nervous thinking about meeting his mom. "What should I wear tonight?"

"Miranda, just be you. It will be fine." He takes my hand and kisses the back, then the palm.

"I hope so."

"It will be. She will adore you, trust me." I get a long, deep kiss goodbye and after telling me what time he will pick me up, he leaves me in the car. I watch him go inside and then ask Charlie to take me home.

After I have flipped through my closet numerous times, I still have no clue what to wear, and it's making me freak out more. I don't have a thing to wear that fits over this stupid ass cast that looks good. I have work attire and everyday attire, nothing in between. I throw a few outfits on the bed, pull out some boots, and then cry with Kasey in my lap, purring as I sit on the floor.

"Oh Kasey, what am I doing? I am a confident, strong woman. I can do this." I decide on a purple sweater dress since it stretches and will fit over my cast. I find my tall black, heeled boots and black leggings, lay them on the bed, and look through my jewelry.

I try on the dress, and I'm frustrated; it feels off. Maybe I should just go buy something; I have time. I pace around my room thinking and decide I need help, and I know just who to call. I dial Nicole, my in-town bestie, and thankfully, she answers.

"Miranda! Girl, I was just thinking about you. How are

you feeling?" I think of the long list of feelings I have right now before answering the standard.

"I'm doing well." There is a pause.

"That is not an, I'm doing well when you are doing well. Girl, what is wrong?"

"I need fashion help and advice."

"You came to the right place. Wait, you never need help; you always look fabulous. This is more than fashion; spill it."

"I'm sort of dating the gazillionaire Ethan Bradley." I pause, waiting for all the questions.

"Hello, I know that already. I saw the post on your Facebook the other day. Plus, you know I have totally been following the celeb sites to see what's up." She acts like it's no big deal.

"How does everyone know that but me?" I stomp in frustration. I really need to look that up.

"You don't read them, we do, gotta stay in the know. He's hot, by the way."

"I know, and that's my problem."

"Your problem is he is hot? You might need to go back to that ER." She laughs at me as I grumble.

"No, not him being hot. That's fine. My problem is he is all suits and designer clothes, and I'm all jeans and t-shirts and..." I am not getting my point out.

"Miranda, what is your real problem here?" She gets me without me having to explain.

"I'm meeting his mother tonight, and I'm freaking out. This stupid cast is making life difficult." Immediately, I start to cry in frustration.

"Miranda, don't cry, sweetie. What are you freaking out? And wow, mom already?"

"I know! I said that, too, but it's a long story, and I just need help. Are you busy?" Exhaling, I try to calm my nerves, but it's not working.

"Meet me at the boutique, and we will get you straightened out. I will be there in 10. Love you, girl." She hangs up, and I am relieved. Throwing my clothes back on, I grab my purse, rub Kasey, and head back down to Charlie, who I had asked to wait for me. I tell him where to go and relax back in the seat.

"Are you okay, Ms. Miranda?" Charlie asks me as I get out at Nicole's shop.

"Just stressed about meeting Ethan's mom."

He pats my shoulder. "The woman would be crazy not to like you." He winks and tells me to call when I'm ready; he's going to find a spot to park. That earns him a hug before I run into the store to find Nicole waiting.

Forty-five minutes later, Nicole has transformed me into a work of art. I stand there in a wine-colored cap-sleeve dress that zips up the back, making it easy to slide over the cast and fits perfectly on my body. It has a large gold buckle and is pulled in at the waist, with a low but modest front neckline that she has paired with long gold jewelry and black booties. She has even given my makeup and hair a do-over. My hair lays over my shoulder in soft waves, and my eyes and lips are lined in a wine color.

"Damn girl," Nicole says as she spins me.

"I must agree. Thank you so much. This is perfect."

She makes a sound and runs into the back, coming out with a black wrap jacket. "It has large open sleeves, so it will slide on easily." She claps her hands together once it's on. "Perfect!" She exclaims, and I hug her tightly.

"Lifesaver!" I look at myself again and know this is what I need. "I don't even care what it costs; it's amazing." I hand her my credit card and she rings me up while I put my other clothes and shoes in bags.

"Nicole, I owe you so big," I say as I sign.

"Just make sure I'm in the wedding." She winks.

"Deal." With a few tight hugs and some well wishes, she waits with me as I call Charlie for a pickup.

"You have a driver?" She is in shock as I hang up with him.

"Only while I can't drive."

"Oh, the life of the rich and famous." She bats her eyes.

"You know me, I don't care about the money."

"And that is why everyone loves you." She hugs me one more time tightly before letting me go to Charlie, who makes me blush when he whistles at me in approval.

We arrive at Ethan's apartment with about 20 minutes to spare, so I thank Charlie as I take my bags and run them up, thankful that I remembered to bring the elevator code. I drop everything in the living room and run back downstairs with 5 minutes left as I catch my breath.

I see Ethan's car pull up right on time, and as he comes around to open my door, he stops when he sees me. His eyes travel from head to toe at least twice.

"I didn't think you could get any more beautiful. I was

so wrong." He pulls me gently to him, spinning me around before pulling me to his chest. "And you smell like heaven, too." He kisses me again as his hand slides down my back.

"Thank you." I am suddenly embarrassed at his attention. I think because my nerves have me in knots.

"You are quiet tonight." Ethan reaches over and takes my hand, pulling me from the million thoughts in my head.

"Nervous," I answer truthfully.

"No reason to be nervous." He squeezes my hand, which we both know is my comfort.

"Does she know who I am? I mean, how we met? I need to know what to say to her or what not to say. And oh, what should I talk about?" I hear the panic in my own voice as he glances over at me.

"Miranda, deep breathes. Yes, my sisters included, know that we had an accident, and I met you. They also know it was my fault."

"Oh, okay." I'm happy he told them. "As far as what to talk about, just be you. I promise you, she is going to adore you, just like I do." He raises my hand and kisses my knuckles, all of them, and I relax.

The drive takes about 40 minutes, and as we turn into the neighborhood, the houses get bigger, making my stomach turn. I am intimidated already. Ethan pulls into a long driveway that we follow back aways until a house comes into sight behind the trees, and I almost gasp. It's huge and beautiful and huge.

Ethan parks in the circle drive that runs by the front door and tells me to wait, which this time I do. He knows I sometime have an issue waiting for him to open my door. I can do this, no need to be so nervous. As Ethan helps me out of the car, I stand tall, put my shoulders back, and set myself straight, but before I can take a step, Ethan grabs my hand and pulls me close to him.

"I have one question before we go up. Can I introduce you as my girlfriend?" He's serious, and it's so sweet.

"Yes, I think at this point, you can."

He gives me a huge face-splitting grin and kisses the hand he is holding before leaning in to kiss me gently.

"I'm so glad to hear that I have finally won you over." His arm is around my waist as we walk up the steps together.

"That you have, Mr. Bradley." I giggle, and he pulls me in tighter.

Before we reach the door, it opens, and a tall, beautiful woman with dark hair gives us a smile that could light up downtown. It has to be his mom. I can see the resemblance immediately.

"Mom, this is my girlfriend Miranda Michaels. Miranda, this is my mother, Eloise. " I go to move to her, but Ethan holds me still. I don't question it, but instead greet her properly.

"Mrs. Bradley, it is such a pleasure to meet you."

"Oh, Darling, it is wonderful to finally meet you, I have heard all about you. Please come in." I glance at Ethan, and he grins devilishly. We walk through the door, and in front of us stands a grand staircase with a beautiful chandelier hanging above it. I can't help but look up as Ethan guides me to the right into a sitting room, where a younger version of Eloise stands and comes to Ethan, wrapping him in a hug.

"Ethan." She gives him a kiss on the cheek. "And you must be Miranda!" She pulls me into a tight hug, squeezing the air out of my lungs.

"Easy, Isabell, she's still tender." Ethan is a little stern with her as I breathe in deeply to replace the air in my lungs. She has the bearhug thing down.

"Miranda, this is my youngest sister, Isabell. Isabell, Miranda." I smile politely at his introduction.

"It's wonderful to meet you."

"You too!" She smiles at me and then at Ethan before punching him in the arm. "She's beautiful." Isabell loudly whispers as she passes him on the way back to the couch, and I hear it.

"I know. " He calls after her, and I feel myself turn pink.

"Children, behave." Eloise chastises them and I want to laugh but bite my lip as Ethan pulls off my wrap and his jacket and takes them to a coat rack.

"Please sit." Eloise offers, and I sit on the couch and watch as Ethan stands next to me, looking at his mom.

"Can I get you two a drink? Wine?" Isabell offers.

"I would love a glass, thank you." I glance at Ethan, hoping that is okay.

"I will take a bourbon and water on the rocks." He tells Isabell as she goes to the bar on the other side of the room, and he sits.

I lean in and whisper to him. "Bourbon?" I get a shy grin in return.

"Nerves." He answers and I laugh, as his mom glances at us and smiles.

"So Miranda, Ethan tells me you are a lawyer, although he didn't mention where or what kind of law you practice."

And here come the questions. "Actually, I am a paralegal right now as I still need to take the exam. I work for Lester and Associates in the corporate law division." I am in serious need of that drink now.

"That is wonderful; when do you expect to take the bar, dear?"

"Mother." Ethan gives a warning, but I touch his hand.

"I am hoping to take it early this coming year after I finish a few needed things.

"That is wonderful. Good luck."

"Thank you." There is a brief silence, and thankfully, Isabell brings the drinks. "Thank you." I smile up in appreciation before she sits in the chair close to Ethan with her glass.

"Ethan tells me that you two met at the accident. How are you recovering? I understand it was pretty bad last week." Eloise takes a sip of her wine and watches me closely and I'm getting the feeling she doesn't like me.

"I am actually doing very well now, but after a week in ICU, anything is an improvement." I chuckle but no one else laughs, so I continue to talk to cover my uncomfortableness.

"With all the stitches out, now I just need to get this silly cast off, and I will be much better." I hold up my arm and smile, but I just keep talking. "It helps that I have had such a great nurse." Flashing Ethan a smile makes him cough back a little shy smile, which makes his mother laugh, and I relax a fraction.

"I don't know about nurse, but I try." He takes a long drink and winks at me over the glass.

"He's such a hard ass. It's hard to think he could be gentle and kind," Isabell speaks up, making me smile.

"He followed me around the first day I was home making sure I took my medicine and that I was drinking enough water, even fluffed my pillows on my bed."

Everyone laughs, and Ethan looks mortified.

"So you can be a good guy?" Isabell chimes in.

"He is." My comment makes him light up.

"That's enough embarrassing me, please." He says to all of us.

"Oh, we are just getting started," Isabell says and punches his arm again. "I bet he is all sweet and sappy at home, isn't he? He tries to be all hard and mean around everyone else." We laugh at his expense.

"Actually, yes, he is. And I have found he is really fond of my cat. I catch them snuggling on my couch all the time." I think Isabell is going to wet herself; she is laughing so hard. Even Eloise is laughing, so I squeeze Ethan's hand to show I'm teasing and get a sweet smile in return.

"Well, if you kids are hungry, dinner is ready," Eloise announces, and we all stand as Ethan threads his arm through mine. After following Isabell into the dining room, I wait for Ethan to show me where to sit as a young woman comes out of the kitchen and places bowls of food on the table. Eloise fills everyone's glass, but when she gets to me, I pass on the wine and say I will just have water. I explain I am still on medicine and need to limit my intake. She smiles and then disappears into the kitchen to help with the food.

Ethan leans over and whispers in my ear. "Are you okay?"

I nod silently, afraid to talk. "She likes you." He adds, and I give him a sideways glance. I have my doubts.

"Be right back." He abruptly stands and goes into the kitchen, and I want to scream no, but he's too quick. I'm left with Isabell alone.

Isabell scoots closer and puts her elbows on the table, grinning as she leans in. Oh God, here we go.

"Okay, so how serious are you about my brother?"

I'm a little taken aback by her question. "Excuse me?"

"He hardly ever brings girls home, and when he does, it's fake anyway. I see the way he looks at you, and it's not something I'm used to seeing. I want to make sure you are in it for him and not his money because if you aren't, he will find out and drop you immediately, just like all the rest." I am completely caught off guard with her. Where did the sweet, bubbly girl go?

I clear my throat and try to stay calm. "Well, you will be happy to know that I don't want his money. Any of it. I have my own and support myself just fine. And for the record, I have told him as much at least a hundred times. I would rather have love and happiness than all the money in the world. As far as how serious I am, I did invite him to spend Thanksgiving with my family, so to me, that's pretty serious."

I hold my breath and watch as a smile forms, then widens across her face. I think I passed. "Good." She clears her throat, looks around, then leans in closer. "Did he really stay with you in the hospital?" She is whispering now.

"Yes. Originally, almost the entire time. Then he stayed

for six straight days while I was in ICU." My cheeks warm as I remember waking up with him by my side.

"He told us it was his fault and that he hit you. I would have been so pissed."

"Oh, I did not like him at all at first. Trust me, I wanted to be as far away from him as possible. He wrecked my car, broke my arm, gave me stitches, in the head no less, and a horrible headache that lasted for over a week." She laughs at my pause.

"How did you end up with him then?" I can hear the curiosity in her voice, and knowing Ethan, I imagine he didn't give up many details.

"I didn't really know what happened at the accident; I was out of it. I remember him holding my hand and talking to me, and I remember looking up and seeing brilliant green eyes. He kept telling me to hang on, that I would be okay. I was in and out after we got to the hospital, but I remember those eyes always being there and him holding my hand. I didn't even know who he was, other than Ethan, for days. When I found out he was the one that caused it, I wasn't too happy about it, but I guess his persuasiveness and six-plus days in ICU with him won out over my anger." I feel my cheeks pink thinking about those last few days.

"Aww. He's such an ass, I can't believe he stayed still for six days."

"He did. According to my sister, he slept in the chair and wouldn't even eat or go home because he did not want to leave my side. I thought it was guilt, but then I got to know him, and he's a pretty incredible guy."

"Our Ethan? He must have it bad for you; he's never stayed still for anything that long." She bats her eyes and giggles, making us both crack up just as Ethan and Eloise come out of the kitchen. Ethan eyes me, and I smile sweetly as he sits back beside me with a look of question on his face.

We enjoy a wonderful dinner and small talk. Isabell and I have bonded, and we talk about my dress and my friend Nicole's boutique. Ethan squeezes my knee a few times when his mom asks me a question, I think for support, since it's mostly about my family, what they do, and where I went to college. I try to limit the amount of detail because, for some reason, I am a little intimidated with their money and status.

Once we are done with dinner, I offer to help with the dishes, but Eloise tsk-tsk at me. "Just leave everything, and let's go have coffee." We stand and follow her back to the sitting room where coffee is waiting.

Eloise asks me more questions and I answer truthfully because I know I'm being quizzed, even though she is making it seem like small talk. I can understand her thinking, though; I'm just a random girl who is attached at the hip to her son; I'd be curious, too.

After coffee, Evan finally announces that it is time to go, and I am very thankful, as I am exhausted. He stands and helps me into my coat, brushing my hair off my face with the back of his hand before putting on his own. I love his sweet gestures. We walk hand in hand to the front door with our fingers laced tight; as his thumb brushes over mine,

"Miranda, it was so great to meet you." Isabell pulls me into a hug, making Ethan let go of me.

"You too. Please call me, and we will go shopping." I get a tighter hug from her as she agrees before pulling Ethan into an equally tight embrace.

"I like her, bring her back, and don't screw it up." She whispers loudly to him. I can't help the smile on my face as I hear her.

Eloise is another story. "It was wonderful to meet you, dear. " Eloise nods at me.

"It was wonderful to meet you as well, Mrs. Bradley. Thank you again for having me for dinner. It was delicious, and your home is beautiful."

"I hope that my son will bring you back again. Maybe during the day, when he can give you a proper tour of the grounds." She nods at Ethan.

"I would like that. Thank you." I look over at Ethan, who looks like he's about to run.

"I look forward to seeing you again then, and please, call me Eloise." She pulls me into a gentle hug, and I'm very relieved.

We say our final goodbyes and get into the car, where I relax back into the seat, exhausted.

"I think that went well." Ethan looks over at me when he gets in.

"I was worried your mom didn't like me all night, though I'm still not sure." I groan.

"She does, she's just cautious about me and a new woman; do not take it personally." He squeezes my knee.

"I won't." He glances at me again, but I close my eyes, I can't deal with him and his women right now.

The next thing I know he is lifting me out of the car. "Shh, I'm taking you up to bed." He whispers.

"Okay," I mutter as I snuggle into him. He's so warm and safe as his arms hold me close, and I inhale his delicious scent. The next thing I remember, he is kissing my forehead before I drift off to sleep.

Chapter 20

The next two days are great. We have playful mornings before he heads to work, and I spend my days running errands with Charlie. Ethan has graciously employed him for the entire week, which has been a blessing. I've been to the grocery store, shopped around, and had lunch with Nicole. I even managed to check out a car lot, although Ethan doesn't know about that yet. I'm pretty sure Charlie ratted me out because Ethan has brought up the car shopping at least three times this week.

This morning was my doctor's appointment, which went well. I should only have to wear the cast for another two to three weeks. Everything else has healed up nicely except for my bruised ribs, which might be sore for a while longer. After making a follow-up appointment for two weeks, I send an update to Ethan, then spend the rest of the afternoon at my apartment. I have a mailbox full of bills, a crabby cat, and a mountain of laundry to catch up on. Ethan said he'd pick me up around 5, and I'm so excited to take him to his first hockey game.

At exactly five minutes to 5, there's a knock at the door. It's Ethan. I greet him with a long kiss, which he eagerly returns.

"Hello there," I say, smiling.

"Hi," he replies with his sweet half-grin before kissing me again. I notice he's already changed into jeans and a gray sweater.

"You ready to go? I thought we could grab dinner before," he says as he lets me go, his eyes trailing down my body with heat. I know exactly what he's thinking, so I lick my lips, teasing him.

"We're leaving. There will be time for all that later."

"You sure? Those jeans..." He rubs his hands over my ass, and I giggle.

"Come on, we'll eat at the game. That's half the fun."

Charlie is waiting at the entrance, and I look at Ethan, surprised. He explains that if he decides to drink, he doesn't want to drive. Smart move. I'm glad to hear it.

We grab food and eat standing at a table before I take Ethan into the team shop to buy him a Blackhawks hat. He has to wear something from the enemy team, after all. He looks absolutely adorable in it, and I snap a few pictures as he rolls his eyes at me. He doesn't quite understand the excitement of being in a crowded arena with thousands of people screaming at the top of their lungs. I tell him he's in for a treat because I'll be screaming right along with them, but he just shakes his head.

When we get to our seats, I immediately get teased by some Hawks fans because of my Blues jersey, which I don't mind. Ethan doesn't know how to take their razzing and looks a little irritated, but once the game starts, he's awe-struck. He comments on how loud it is, which doesn't stop me from screaming and cheering with the other fans. I'm glad there are a few Blues fans sitting behind us, so I have some people to cheer with.

Before the second period ends, Ethan is really getting into it. He's cheering for the Hawks, buys us another round, and toasts to my team getting crushed. He's not his usual composed self-tonight—he's noisy, relaxed, and drinking. I'm loving it.

Throughout the game, he continues teasing me that my team is going to lose. We're behind by one goal midway through the third period, and he's relentless. I remind him that 24 hours ago, he didn't care about hockey, but he just grins and says he's converted and he's ready for me to lose.

Then, the Blues score. With only seconds left, we pull ahead and win. The guys behind me and I go wild while Ethan hangs his head in mock defeat. We keep celebrating as the fans clear out, and even though he's lost, Ethan is all smiles.

"Of course, your team would win. I'll never hear the end of this," Ethan says, holding my hand as we leave the arena.

"Nope, you definitely won't. But I am so glad you enjoyed it." I admit as I lean into his shoulder. I really was happy he was happy.

"Thank you for this evening. It was surprisingly fun and...what is your word? Mind-blowing." And as usual, he tucks me into his side to hold me close.

"It was," I agree, feeling a warmth spread through me as we fit together so perfectly. *For the first time, I let myself consider that maybe I want this to last—maybe for a very long time.* The thought would normally be unwelcomed, but I don't shy away from it this time. My heart is happy.

On the ride back to my place, we talk about how much fun we had and how relaxed Ethan feels. We agree we'll definitely do this again, maybe in St. Louis next time. Even Charlie chimes in on the conversation, and I don't mind at all.

As we get closer to my apartment, Ethan turns serious. "Are you coming home with me?" I can hear the hope in his voice.

"Do you want me to?" I already know the answer, but it's fun to rattle him.

"Of course." He admits as he brings my hand up to kiss my knuckles.

"Maybe I want to go home." I tease again.

"Fine, we'll go to your place then." And as if that is all that needs to be said, he pulls me into his lap and holds me to him.

"No, yours is more fun to wake up in," I admit with a grin, and he agrees, although he does comment that it would be fun anywhere, as long as I was there with him.

When we arrive at my place, I run up, grab my things, and meet him back at his car. He's leaning against it, looking so sexy that I nearly drool. When he glances up from his phone, my heart speeds up. I can hardly wait to get back to his place. He quickly grabs my bag, kisses me deeply, and practically pushes me into the car. I guess he has the same kind of plans.

The ride back is filled with teasing touches, lingering glances, and promises of what's waiting for us. By the time we park, I'm so turned on that I leap out of the car and can barely wait as he grabs our bags. We don't break our kiss as we wait for the elevator doors to open. He presses me against the wall, his hand in my hair, holding me to him as he punches in the code without even looking, and I wonder how many times he's done that. I shake off the thought—it doesn't matter.

Once we're inside, he drops my bag and picks me up, my legs wrapping around his waist. He carries me to the kitchen counter, and we waste no time. Off go our coats, then my shirt and bra. His mouth is on me, and I'm quickly becoming putty in his hands. I tug at his shirt, but he's not budging.

"Please, Ethan..." I moan, desperate.

"Patience. I'm not done here." He continues teasing me, sucking and biting my nipples until I cry out in pleasure.

Finally, he releases me and pushes me back onto the counter, pulling off my boots, then my pants, leaving me naked as he stands fully dressed.

"You are so beautiful," he says as he pulls off his shirt.

"So are you..." I barely manage to say before he's standing between my legs again, biting on my shoulder as I tug at his pants, letting them fall to the floor.

"Ethan, I need you now," I demand. He pulls me to the edge of the counter, and I feel him press against me. When I wrap my legs around him, he moans into my mouth. The heat of his skin making contact with mine, driving me wild with need. I reach down to stroke him, making him groan louder as my fingers tighten around him. He backs up slightly to let me touch him more, his head falling back as I tease him with long, tight strokes.

But suddenly, he pulls me close and lifts me off the counter. I expect him to carry me to the bedroom, but instead, he slides me down onto him—bare. My eyes widen in surprise as he looks at me, waiting for my approval. I can feel him just inside me. Before my mind can catch up to my body, I nod, letting him push deeper inside.

I cry out as he fills me, pausing only for a breath, then moving deeper. I've never felt so full. We fit together so perfectly. He starts to move, and the pleasure rushes through me, overwhelming my senses. I explode around him almost immediately, gripping him tighter as waves of pleasure crash through me.

He walks us to the wall and presses me against it, using the leverage to thrust even deeper. I hear him groan my name, which only turns me on more. His lips find mine, and we kiss hard as he continues, his skin moving against mine. It's almost too much to handle.

As he slows down, enjoying each thrust, I feel the heat building again. He's thrusting deeper, his mouth at my ear, and I can hear his ragged breathing, which matches my own. I'm on the edge again, but I don't want this to end.

I can't hold back any longer. As he pushes me over the edge, I call out, my body convulsing around him. He pauses for a moment, then continues thrusting, tightening, building, and I know he's close.

"Miranda?" It's a question I already know the answer to.

"Yes," I breathe out, and with that, he grips me tighter and spills his release deep inside me, groaning my name through clenched teeth.

When it's over, he rests his forehead against mine, both of us catching our breath, with no words needed. That was magical.

Finally, he speaks. "I... I shouldn't have... Miranda..." He trails off.

"I wanted it as much as you did. Don't, please," I say softly, my voice hoarse with emotion as the reality of what just happened starts to settle in.

Slowly, he lifts me off him, gently lowering me until I can find my footing. He brushes a strand of hair from my face, then leans in to kiss me softly. I offer him a small smile before excusing myself to the bathroom, my legs shaking as I walk away. *What the hell did I just do... again? I'm asking for trouble, but the truth is, I can't say no to him. I don't want to say no.*

After a quick clean-up, I step out to find him sitting on the edge of the bed, waiting for me. He stands as soon as I enter the room.

"Miranda..." He takes a few steps toward me and stops, just short of pulling me into his arms. There's a noticeable tension in the air, his face etched with concern. I know what he's thinking, and I can feel the heaviness between us, but I won't let this moment be ruined by doubt.

"It was amazing, and I am completely fine," I say, trying to reassure him. Standing on my tiptoes, I kiss him lightly, and after a moment, he wraps his arms around me and holds me close.

"I can't help myself when I'm with you. You make me do things I'd never normally do," he admits, his voice low, as if confessing a secret.

"I know the feeling." I look up at him and smile, whispering, "I completely understand." His eyes soften, but there's still a trace of tension as he guides me toward the bed.

Once we're under the covers, he pulls me tightly against him, his body curved around mine as if he's trying to keep me close, to keep me safe.

"Miranda, I want you... all of you," he whispers, his voice filled with something deeper, something that makes my heart race. His words resonate, and warmth floods my chest.

"Me too," I whisper back, the weight of those two words settling between us. I relax into him, feeling safe, wanted, and for the first time in a long while, certain. I close my eyes, letting the rhythm of his breathing lull me into comfort.

We lay there for what feels like hours, wrapped in each other's warmth. As I begin to drift off to sleep, I hear him murmur something, but I'm too far gone to make out the words. All I know is that, in this moment, everything feels right. I'm exactly where I want to be.

Chapter 21

Stretching, I feel Ethan stir beside me. I'm sore, but it's a good sore. Rolling over to face him, I see he's staring at me. "Good morning," I say shyly.

"It will be," he replies with a grin, pulling the covers over his head. I feel him slide down my body, taking my panties with him. The man is an animal, and I can't keep him off me.

"Ethan." My moans make him chuckle as I try to tug on his arm, hoping to bring him back up to me, but he continues kissing all over my middle.

"I'm not done here yet," he says, his voice deep and thick with desire. I immediately feel my body heat up. How can I be this close to him already? Everything he does makes me feel incredible.

When he finally reaches my chest, he stops to give each breast and nipple his full attention. His talented, glorious tongue explores me, and I moan as he nips gently at my skin. "Ethan, take me, now," I beg. I can't handle this teasing; I need him. I'm sure I sound like I'm whining, but he only chuckles.

"As you wish." He brushes his lips up my body until he reaches my mouth, kissing me deeply. Then, leaving me wanting more, he reaches over to the nightstand for a condom. He holds it up for me to see before rolling it on. Leaning down, he kisses me again, slowly lowering himself and sliding inside me.

He makes sweet, soft love to me, ensuring I've had my fill before finishing himself. Afterward, he nuzzles into my neck, just beathing into my skin, both of us holding on to the afterglow of our connection.

Soon, he rolls over and pulls me close, neither of us saying a word. I can feel his heartbeat and his breathing slow down. He's incredible.

My own heart is racing—not from the sex but from the feelings I have for him. I know I've crossed a line. I've fallen for him, and even though I didn't want to, I have. I'm terrified. His hold tightens around me, almost as if he knows my thoughts. The warmth of his kiss grounds me, makes me feel safe.

"Ethan, I think..." I start, but he cuts me off with another kiss.

"I need to get up and get ready for work," he says when he finally breaks away. "I don't want to get out of this bed, though." His hand brushes up my bare leg and onto my ass. "I might need to have you again before I go." His fingers squeeze, making me grumble.

"Haven't you had enough?" I ask, a little surprised.

"No." He pulls my leg up onto him so he can have better access. "Unless you want me to stop." He growls into my ear as his fingers brush over me, making my back arch. Damn, my body is sore, but I'm already thinking about him again.

"Again, already?" I ask, my hand finding him ready.

"Always, for you." He rolls onto his back, pulling me up with him. I sit up, running my hands over his chest. When I rock back and forth, he growls with appreciation. Then I lean down and kiss his chest, rubbing along his length as I do. I can feel him at my entrance, and start to push, until his hands grip my hips, holding me close.

"Enough." He stretches and pulls out another condom from the drawer, handing it to me. I tear it open with my teeth, my body screaming with both need and soreness, but my desire wins out.

I watch his face as pleasure washes over him. I'm in control, and the faster I move, the tighter his hands hold me. I'm building fast, and I tilt my head back, moaning, but he sits up and locks his mouth on mine as the waves of my release squeeze him. He doesn't wait for me to finish. He grabs me, pulls me down with him, and takes over, slamming up into me hard and fierce. I'm about to scream from the intensity when he calls out, thrusting into me, growling my name. I feel it deep inside me as my body explodes with him.

Collapsing on top of him in pure exhaustion, I think I'm about to pass out when I hear him call my name, but I can't move.

"Are you okay?" he laughs.

"Can't move," I breathe out, but he gently rolls me over and kisses me.

"Sleep. I'll be back." With that, he heads to the bathroom, and I hear the shower start before I drift off.

"Miranda." He kisses my lips softly.

"Hmm." I smile sleepily.

"I have to go to work. Are you okay?" There's humor in his voice.

"I think you broke me," I whisper. He lifts the sheets and kisses my tummy.

"You're still in one piece on the outside," he chuckles.

"Inside is completely a mess." I laugh with him, my eyes still closed.

"I'll fix that when I get home." He nuzzles into my neck as he sits next to me

"Oh." My eyes open quickly, and I glance up at him, my cheeks burning with embarrassment that I'm already thinking about the next time.

"You have all day to recover." He kisses me softly as I wrap my arms around his neck, kissing him back. The kiss deepens, and he pulls me up to sit in his lap, the sheet pooling around my waist.

"You keep kissing me like this, and I won't leave." He growls as he rubs his nose against mine.

"Okay." I kiss him again, deep and hungry.

"Mmm, I would love to stay and give you more, but I have to go to work." He pulls back, and I understand, smiling as I move back to the bed.

I lay down, watching him stand there, staring at me. "I'm going to be picturing this all day," he says, nodding at me.

"Oh, let me improve it." I pull the blanket down, revealing my chest, and giggle as I lower it to my belly.

"Miranda, stop, or I won't be able to walk." He warns, and I can visibly see his pants tightening.

"Making sure you have a great day." Batting my eyes, I try to be sweet and innocent.

"I'm going to be miserable," he groans, shifting his pants and shaking his head.

"Then hurry home," I tease, sliding my hand down between my legs and spreading them slightly. I watch him struggle to keep his composure.

"Woman, you might want to stop now," he growls, his voice rough and deep.

"I can't. Some sexy man has me turned on." I run my finger around my lower belly and then bring it to my lips to lick. Keeping his eyes locked on mine, he groans as I do it again, and I can see every inch of his solid erection straining against his pants. As my eyes travel over him, I spread my legs wider to tease him more.

He moves so fast that I barely have time to register what's happening. He grabs me, flips me over, and smacks my ass hard, making me flinch.

"You asked for it," he growls, holding me down as I hear his zipper. He pushes me up the bed and kneels behind me. I hear the rip of the foil, then feel his hands grip my hips as he pulls my ass up and slams into me. I cry out as he slams into me again. It's both sexy and painful, but I don't say a word. He's rough, thrusting hard, moving me up the bed, and pulling me back over and over. Finally, he grunts and slams his release into me.

"Fuck!" he yells, his voice raw.

I lie perfectly still as he finishes, trying to catch my breath and make sense of what just happened. He pulls out of me and slaps my ass again, harder this time, making me yelp.

"Punishment for that little show," he growls. I roll over, pulling the blankets up to cover myself, but his sexy grin makes me relax.

"Punishments are sexy," I tease, though he just shakes his head, heading for the bathroom.

When he returns, his expression has changed. "Are you alright?" He's stern, but I can see the concern in his eyes.

"Yes, I'm fine. Just sore." I smile, hoping to reassure him.

"Good. I didn't mean to hurt you. You just pushed me, and I couldn't handle it." I can tell it is his way of apologizing.

"Like I said, punishment sex is hot." My body is screaming for a break, but I just can't get enough of him, especially when he's so big and tough.

"You're a drug, Miranda, and I'm having trouble getting enough." His voice is flat, but his eyes continue to say so much.

"Then don't," I whisper, and he leans down to kiss my forehead.

"I'll see you after work. Let me know where you'll be." He lingers for a moment, then leaves before I can say anything more.

After Ethan leaves, I lay there, feeling a strange mixture of satisfaction and unease. His words linger in my mind—especially the part about me being a "drug" to him. He's right. There's something about him that pulls me in, that keeps me wanting more, even when I know I should probably slow down.

I get out of bed, stretch, and feel the soreness between my legs. It's a reminder of how intense our morning had been, and yet, a part of me feels...unsettled. I decide to send Ethan a quick text.

I'm sorry if I made you angry this morning. I was just playing. I didn't mean to upset you.

Shaking off my uneasy thoughts, I focus on the day ahead. I have some errands to run, and, of course, there's the surprise I want to do for Ethan.

I decided on a couple of great selfies of us and send them to be printed before heading to a small boutique down the road. I find a gorgeous, masculine photo frame that I know he will love. It's sleek—black and silver— and will look great on his desk.

While eating lunch at a nearby deli, my phone buzzes with a message from Ethan.

Nothing to be sorry about. I hope I did not hurt you.

No, I'm okay. I just didn't want you to be mad at me.

Not at all. In fact, I've been thinking about you all morning.

Really? Me too.

Once I make it through this boring afternoon, we can pick up where we left off.

Are you stuck in your big office all by yourself?

All alone.

I'll be waiting right here...

Tease.

Always.

Stay out of trouble, and I'll be back around 6.

XOXO.

I giggle to myself after I send the last message, feeling like a teenage girl. Something about Ethan makes me giddy in a way I haven't felt in years. I finish my sandwich, and after a bit of people-watching, I get an idea.

I want to surprise Ethan at his office with the framed picture. I know it's risky, as I've never been to his office before, but the idea of showing up with a sweet, thoughtful gift excites me.

I grab a cab and head to his office building, wondering if I should text him, but I decide against it. I want it to be a surprise. I'm a little nervous, but I tell myself it will be fine. He will be excited to see me, too.

As I walk into the lobby, I'm greeted by a polished-looking receptionist behind a large, modern desk. "Hi. I'm here to see Ethan Bradley," I say with a bright smile.

"Do you have an appointment?" She asks with a neutral expression.

"Uh, no," I stammer, realizing I hadn't thought that part through.

"I'm sorry, ma'am, but Mr. Bradley is a very busy man and only available by appointment," she says, her smile fading slightly.

"Well, I just wanted to drop off a gift," I say, holding up the gift bag with the framed picture, hoping that might soften her. But she only looks more irritated.

"You're welcome to leave it here, and we'll have it taken up," she replies, the sweet facade now completely gone.

Frustrated, I try again. "I'm Miranda Michaels, his girlfriend. I just wanted to surprise him."

Both the receptionist and the woman sitting next to her stare at me, and then—unbelievably—they laugh.

"I'm sorry, Miss, but you're most certainly not his girlfriend." The other woman pipes up with a look of disgust.

"I most certainly am," I say indignantly, pulling out the photo I had printed, hoping that would convince them.

But they barely glance at it. "Miss, you need to leave, or I'll have to call security," the other woman says flatly.

Fuming, I snap, "Call security then! Call his assistant, she knows who I am. Just ask her!"

The receptionist picks up the phone, presses a button, and in seconds, a security guard walks over.

"Are you kidding me?" I ask in disbelief as the guard approaches.

"Miss, I need to ask you to leave," he says, grabbing my arm.

"Don't touch me!" I snap, jerking away. "I'm trying to call Ethan right now!" I snap as I desperately try to dial his number on my phone.

As I struggle, I hear a familiar voice. "Miranda?" I turn to see Jason walking toward me, his face a mixture of concern and confusion.

"Take your hands off her immediately," Jason commands, his voice booming. The security guard releases me at once, and I step closer to Jason.

"What the hell is going on here?" He demands, looking between the receptionist and the guard.

"I was trying to surprise Ethan, but they wouldn't let me up. They called security on me," I explain quickly, still feeling a bit shaken.

Jason turns back to the receptionist, who looks nervous now. "Mr. Baker, she said she was his girlfriend. We were just following protocol," she stammers uncomfortably.

Jason doesn't buy it. "Miranda Michaels will accompany me to my meeting with Mr. Bradley," he says sternly. "And for the record, she is his girlfriend."

The receptionist's face goes pale as she nods apologetically. Jason signs us in and leads me to the elevators. "Thank you," I whisper, feeling a mix of embarrassment and relief.

Once in the elevator, Jason looks at me. "What happened?"

I sigh. "I just wanted to surprise him with a gift. They laughed at me when I told them I was his girlfriend. They refused to call his assistant. I should've known better."

Jason gives me a sympathetic look. "He's the CEO of a very large company. They don't just let anyone up here, even if you're his girlfriend. But they were out of line." He pauses, glancing at me. "Are you hurt?"

"No, I'm fine. Just humiliated," I mutter, rubbing my arm where the guard grabbed me.

"You shouldn't be. And it will be dealt with." His voice softens as he gives me a warm smile.

We arrive at the top floor, and he tells me to wait as he goes to speak to another women behind a desk. After just a moment, Jason comes back telling me that Ethan is in a meeting, and we can wait in the conference room. His smile is tight and doesn't reach his eyes, not like a few minutes ago in the elevator.

As I start to question him and his sudden change, I hear the large door open across the hallway and turn to see Ethan and my face warms at his handsomeness. And then I see her. A tall, beautiful redhead steps out next to him, and before I can even process what is happening, she kisses him. And he kisses her back. On. The. Lips.

My world stops. I can't move. I can't breathe. Jason grabs my arm and tries to pull me into the conference room, but I'm frozen as I watch her straighten Ethan's tie. He looks up and sees me. His smile instantly vanishes, and I watch the color drain from his face.

Jason is saying something, but I don't hear him. Everything around me fades as I watch the woman say something to him, then walk past, flashing me a smile as if she has no cares in the world.

The moment hits me like a brick wall, and my chest caves in. I feel myself being pulled away as the air in my lungs evaporates, but I can't move. Time rushes forward, and suddenly, Ethan is standing in front of me.

His eyes move from Jason to me and back to Jason. He's angry, but I'm still trying to process what just happened. My brain is stuck on the last 60 seconds.

"What the hell are you doing? Did you bring her here?" He snaps, his voice loud and sharp.

"Hell no!" Jason cuts in. "I found your security guard manhandling her in the lobby!" Jason is angry, and I instinctively rub my arm where the guard grabbed me.

Ethan looks at me with alarm on his face. "Are you alright? Are you hurt? What happened?" I can hear the concern, but I just stand there in shock, not able to answer him.

"He about ripped her arm off because your damn receptionist thinks every girl that walks into this building is a threat. So no, she's not ok!" Jason is yelling now, but I'm still stuck. All my words are gone as I look at Ethan's beautiful face.

All I can see is the red lipstick lining the edge of his lips, cheek, and along the top of his collar. Red like a warning light flashing in my brain. Red, like the blood that has drained from my shattered heart.

"Miranda," Ethan says softly, trying to reach for me, but I pull back. "That wasn't what you think it was. I can explain." He tries to reach me again, but I step back. I can't listen to him. All I can hear is the sound of my heart breaking. His white shirt is wrinkled and slightly untucked. Bile rises in my stomach as everything clicks into place.

Slowly, the gift bag falls from my grasp, and the glass from the frame shatters as it hits the floor making everyone jump. Jason looks at me, concern etched on his face. I can hear him call my name, but I can't respond.

Ethan bends to pickup the photo, dumping off the glass. I can see his clenched jaw, but all that matters is the lie that is screaming from the red marks on his face.

"I was a fool," I whisper, my voice barely audible. My heart is in my throat, but I am so much calmer than I should be. "A complete fool. I was never good enough, was I?"

"Miranda. Please. Please let me explain." He steps closer, but I choose to turn and walk into the elevator with Jason, who is holding the door with a look of murder on his face. I don't even look up as the doors close, still hearing Ethan's pleas from the other side. The sound of his hand slamming on the door makes me jump, but I don't speak. I can't.

The elevator moves, and I brace for the heartbreaking realization of what just happened. I wasn't enough. I would never be enough to keep him from his previous life.

Jason's soft voice comes from beside me, asking if I am ok. I lie and say I'm fine, but we both know I'm not. And I won't be for a very long time. I should have just left when they wouldn't let me in. Now I understand why. I wouldn't have believed me either. She was already here.

"He's the fool, Miranda. You are amazing and beautiful and so very sweet. You are all the things that a perfect woman should be. If he's too stupid to see that, then he really is an idiot."

Jason's words are sweet and all the things you want to hear, but I'm too numb to care. And I refuse to cry here.

When the elevator dings that we are on the main floor, I steady myself to walk out of here with my head held high, but instead, there stands Ethan. He's a mess, pure panic on his face.

"Miranda, baby, please. Talk to me." He tries, but I just walk around him and ignore him. "Please, baby, please. It wasn't what you think."

Ethan grabs my arm above my cast, and I wince in pain. "Let me go, Ethan." I cry out.

"Not until you listen to me. I need to explain." He tries to pull me closer, but I pull away.

"Stop. You are hurting me!" My yell is loud, and before I can even react, Jason moves from beside me and punches Ethan square in the jaw. Ethan falls backward onto his ass, and the security guard from earlier appears out of nowhere and tackles Jason as I stand there in shock.

Ethan immediately gets up and puts out a hand to help Jason up as he tells the guard to back up. "I deserved it." He nods at Jason before wiping away the blood on his split lip.

"I'm sorry I hurt you. Baby, please, just let me explain. I know what you are thinking, and I didn't screw her." His voice wavers, but it doesn't matter to me. The evidence is clear. And this is over.

"I don't need to hear anything. I'm going to get my stuff from your place, and you will leave me alone to do it in peace. I'm done. And you might want to wash off the lipstick before it stains." I walk away and know my shattered heart is not even beating anymore.

When the elevator opens on my floor, Ethan is there waiting. Wonderful.

"Miranda, don't leave me. Please. I know you hate me, but I only want you. It's only been you. I swear. Just let me explain. Please."

"Go away, Ethan." I push around him with my bags in tow, hoping he will just leave me alone. I am barely holding it together.

"I'm not letting you go, baby. I worked too hard to win you. I'm not losing you now. You are…" I spin around and cut him off.

"Stop! Don't win me back. Don't call me or send me presents. Don't interfere with my life anymore. I trusted you. I took a chance on you, and you broke my heart. You broke my heart Ethan. You did it. Just leave me alone." The tears break free, and I barely make it into my apartment before I slam the door and fall against the wall.

I am completely broken. More than I have ever been in my life. My soul is shattered.

Chapter 22

My alarm goes off at five, and I drag myself into the bedroom to get dressed. It is more difficult to function than I thought possible. I struggle to get my things together, put Kasey in the carrier, then stand in the kitchen, feeling completely lost while I wait for Nicole.

Last night, I booked a flight home for Thanksgiving. Alone. I need to get out of here. Especially after he stayed until all hours of the night and begged me through the door to listen. He tried to explain that he didn't do anything with her, but I just turned up some music, and then he continued with texts and phone calls.

When I open the door to leave, I see a gorgeous bunch of pink roses in a vase in front of it. I look at them for a few minutes before I pick up the card.

Please let me explain.
~ Ethan

Dropping the card back in the vase, I push it aside to pull out my suitcase, leaving the flowers in the hallway alone.

I struggle to the lobby, and thankfully, Nicole is already waiting and helps me with my luggage as I slide Kasey into the back seat. We don't talk much during the drive; she knows I'm upset, so she lets me be. I said everything I needed to last night.

Even at the gate, she only hugs me and tells me to call if I need anything. Then she's gone, leaving me to check my luggage and wait with Kasey to go home.

Once on board the plane, I find a seat next to a very nice man who doesn't mind Kasey at all, and I'm thankful. I don't want to fight with anyone today.

"You look like you've had a rough night," he says with a smile once I'm settled.

"You could say that," I groan.

"Bad breakup?" He asks. I nod.

"How could you tell?"

"Sadness isn't hard to miss," he says sweetly.

"Yeah, I'm sure I look like a hot mess," I mumble, looking out the window.

"Actually, it's the red ring of tears around your eyes that gives you away. You look lovely otherwise."

Did he just hit on me?

"Thank you. I caught my boyfriend with another woman at his office."

"Ouch." He flinches.

"I should have known," I grumble, and thankfully, he leaves it at that.

We take off, and I pray for safe passage like I always do, then close my eyes and hold on. I hear Kasey meow between my feet and reassure him that we will be home soon. Once we are safely up, I relax, and the guy starts talking again.

"So how should you have known? If you don't mind me asking, I would really like the answer to that as well since my girlfriend just dumped me for my friend," he explains, and even though I really don't feel like talking, for some reason, I answer.

"Sorry to hear that. However, I don't think my situation would help you," I mumble.

"You don't? What happened?"

I glance down at my hands. "He slept around a lot before I was with him, and I knew it, but I believed him when he said it was only me, and, well, I was wrong. I wasn't enough for him in the end, and he was caught with someone else." I feel pathetic admitting it out loud.

"Not good enough? That's kind of harsh to say about yourself."

If he only knew.

"Well, I'm feeling kind of low right now," I grumble.

"Understood. My girl had been cheating on me for at least four months. I found out when we installed a nanny cam for our dogs." I'm sure I look as surprised as I feel. "She wasn't that bright," he admits, which makes me smile. "I'm sorry your guy was a cheater too."

"Me too. I could have seen him being my forever." I swallow the tears that are on the verge of escaping.

"That's a double ouch." Exhaling, I fight not to cry again.

"I'm Preston, by the way." He holds out his hand.

"Miranda." I shake it.

"Nice to meet you, Miranda. Can I buy you a drink for your misery?" I agree, and we have a few cocktails and end up laughing about our misfortune. I tell him how I broke my arm and the entire debacle of my life, and by the time the flight is over, I feel a little better. He gives me his number and tells me to call if I want to see a movie or have dinner sometime. I tuck it into my wallet and hand him one of my cards in exchange.

At the luggage carousel, we run into each other again, and he helps me with my suitcase. His ride ends up being parked next to Emma's, so he helps me put my case in the trunk. Giving him a hug, I hold on a little longer than I should, but he made me feel a tiny bit better.

"Thank you for being such a nice guy to spend the morning with."

"Pleasure was all mine." He winks, then walks off to his ride.

When I turn back to Emma, she is staring at me.

"Spill it. That is not Ethan, and I'm pretty sure he was blushing."

"Em, I will explain it all on the drive. Please, let's go."

Once we are in the car, I explain the entire thing to her, including Preston, who was a stranger who talked too much.

"I'm so sorry, Miranda. That is awful. I liked him so much, too," she pouts.

"Hello, me too. Actually, I think I liked him more than a little. He made me feel so special." My voice cracks as I fight another round of tears. I miss him so much, and it is killing me that he should be here with me.

"He says he didn't sleep with her, though?" she asks more than states.

"That's what he says. I don't know. Doesn't matter. It was cheating just the same. You don't let some woman fondle you and kiss you all over when you have a girlfriend." I am angry now.

"True," she answers, but I can tell that word means more.

"What, Em? What?" I snap.

"I don't know. I just think maybe you should talk it out. I mean, he's rich and hot and likes you and—"

"Are you serious? He cheated on me. No, I'm done. Once a cheater, always a cheater. It's not going to happen to me again. I've had my fair share of those. And what does rich or hot have anything to do with it? I don't care if he was piss-poor and ugly—he crushed my heart." I cross my arms, letting her know I am mad and done with this conversation.

The rest of the ride is quiet after my outburst. I'm sore, tired, and just miserable by the time we get to her house. The only bright spot is when the kids run out to give me hugs and help with getting me and Kasey into the house. It makes me happy and cheers me up. I love these kids like they are my own.

The next few days are filled with holiday activities with the kids, visits with family, and lots of downtime. I received a text from Ethan asking why I didn't take the flowers inside, which I ignored. Then he texted a few more times, and I ignored those, too. That is until he threatened to break down my door if I didn't answer him because he was worried sick.

I struggle with him being worried, so I text him back

that I left and went home to St. Louis. He asked how long, and I just answered, "weeks." Jason has also texted me a few times to make sure I was okay, and I told him where I was so he wouldn't worry either. Unfortunately, he told me that Ethan was miserable and had canceled all his meetings for the entire week. It was wrong, but it felt good that he was suffering, too.

Thanksgiving Day has arrived, and although I am not great in any way, I feel a little better and am enjoying the day. My family is together. We have played games and laughed, so my mind is distracted and not focused solely on Ethan. Which is good because that is all I have thought about since I left.

After dinner, I decide to text Preston. I'm not sure why—maybe because he is going through the same heartache I am and can relate. And honestly, I could use someone else to talk to besides Emma, who keeps pushing me to talk to Ethan.

> *Hi. It's Miranda. I just wanted to wish you a Happy Thanksgiving.*

> *Hello! Thank you. I had a great Thanksgiving. And you?*

> *Very good. Feeling better and ready to get back home. I get to go back to work Monday.*

> *I dread going back, but life must go on.*

> *Yes, it must. Well, time for dessert. Talk to you again soon.*

> *I would like that.*

For the first time in a week, I feel a small smile on my face as I lay down my phone, only to look up and see Emma staring at me.

"What?"

"Who were you texting?" She picks up my phone to look.

"Preston. Wishing me a Happy Thanksgiving."

"Uh-huh. Don't you think it's a little soon to move on to the next guy?" Her question takes me a bit off guard.

"I'm not moving on, Emma. I don't want another man."

My phone lights up, and I ignore Emma's nagging, but my smile fades as the name appears on my screen.

"It's Ethan," I announce to Emma, and she stands there waiting, not finished with our earlier conversation.

My mom and Isabell wanted to wish you a Happy Thanksgiving. And I hope you are okay.

In my head, I can hear his voice as I read the words. I know he's hurting, but he did this. I don't want to answer him, but my fingers type anyway.

Tell them the same, please. Thank you.

He answers right away.

I miss you.

I don't answer him.

How long are you going to ignore me?

Forever, I think to myself as I refuse to answer him.

*Please, Miranda, just tell me you are okay. I
worry about you.*

Ugh, again, with the worry! I want him to just stop. Stop
texting, stop talking, stop everything!

I'm fine. Is that what you want?

Are you?

Putting down my phone, I turn back to Emma.

"Look, I miss Ethan like crazy, and being here has helped,
but I'm miserable. Preston is going through the same thing
and understands. He is just my friend. I'm not in any way
ready to move on. In fact, I would rather just not ever do any
of this again." I take a deep breath and fight back the tears
that have suddenly filled my eyes.

Emma pulls me up into a hug. "I understand. Your heart
will heal, just like it did before, and you will find someone
else to love." She holds me tight and then lets go when I pull
back.

"That's the problem—I don't want to love anyone else,"
I mumble. I know she hears me, but she chooses to pull me
out of my room for dessert, which sounds fabulous. More
sugar, less talking.

Once in bed for the night, I tuck in and pull out my
computer to read some emails. At least I got a great computer
out of the deal, then immediately feel horrible for thinking
that. I'd give the damn thing back if I could—not that I want
to, but I might. Ugh. I go back to emails to distract myself.

As I lay there, I decide to do a Google search on Ethan

again. This time, I am looking for something specific. I see that there isn't much that is new, but I do find some pictures of us. They are all from when we were out somewhere, and a few of these I didn't even know existed. Huh, those people are everywhere with their cameras. I click on some, saving them, even though I am not sure why. We look so happy, and we fit well together, which makes me sad all over again.

I go back to scrolling, looking for her—my original reason for the search, as I want to know more. It takes me a while, but I find her right there in all her red-headed glory. She's beautiful. Of course, she is. Why wouldn't she be stunning? They all are. And the thought only pushes the knife deeper into my heart. I find a few pictures of them, and, to my surprise, he doesn't look as happy as he does with me. He's stiff and uptight in the pictures, and that makes me feel a little bit better. Wait, why do I care? She can have his sorry ass! For some reason, that stings so badly that I don't want it to be true. The tears push against my eyes, but I fight them. I've made it six days without him, and the irony is not lost on me, but it still rips me apart to think of him. I miss him so much, but he did this. I close my eyes for a minute and imagine his arms around me, my safe place, and his head nuzzling against me. No! I can't do this! I don't need him!

Maybe I should stay here longer, or maybe even just move back home permanently. No, I didn't let Andrew stop me, and I will not let Ethan stop me either. I love my place and my job. I want to go back, and I will.

This is stupid. I shouldn't be torturing myself. I start to close the webpage, but something catches my eye a few articles down. "Publishing Tycoon Ethan Bradley Has a Messy Split with Current Fling in the Lobby of His Office Building." There is a grainy cell phone photo of Ethan holding my arm, another of Jason mid-swing, and then one of Ethan on his ass. I trace over him and remember it all in vivid color. I don't need the photos for that. I close the page as I don't want to read the article; it will only hurt.

I do feel terrible about the mess in the lobby. He doesn't need that kind of negative attention. Then I laugh out loud at my stupid self—of course he does. It serves his cheating ass right. Closing the computer, I lay it on the floor. I am done. As I roll over and hug the other pillow, I realize just how much I really miss him, and now it will be another night of crying myself to sleep.

Chapter 23

Morning comes, and I have barely slept, and it shows. I feel worse than I look, which is bad. I kept dreaming of Ethan—his sweet touch, boyish grin, and strong arms that always held me and made me feel safe and warm. How he stayed with me for six days, begging me to wake up, and then this. How could he do this to me, to us? It makes me cry harder, even though I knew he would eventually leave, but it hurts so damn bad—more than I have ever experienced. Those stupid pictures last night did this. I should have never looked him up.

There is a knock at the door, thankfully stopping my thoughts.

"Hey, you up?" It's Emma.

"I'm awake," I croak, and she opens the door and comes in.

"Are you okay?" She sits on the bed and looks me over.

"Yes and no." I move up against the headboard to face her, holding my knees to my chest for comfort.

"Rana, talk to me. What's wrong? You've been crying.

I thought you were feeling better? What happened?" She brushes my hair back from my face, and I almost crack again. Exhaling a shaky breath, I look up, and tears fill my eyes.

"I saw an article about Ethan last night online, about his messy breakup with his latest fling, which is me, of course, and it tore me up. There were pictures too, of him and... I miss him terribly, Em. I miss his silly smile and the way he fussed over me all the time. I miss more than his physical being. I miss the way he makes me feel. Emma, he stayed with me for six entire days, then almost every night after. How could he care so much and then just throw me to the side? Why can't I be enough for him?" I break into an unexpected and uncontrolled sob.

"Rana, I'm sure that's not why." Taking my hand, she squeezes it, but that only tears into me more.

"Then why? I was with him that morning—it was just us, he..." I cry harder.

"I wish I had answers for you, but I don't understand myself."

Neither do I, and that is what's so awful.

Pulling out my phone, I show her pictures from the game.

"Does this look like we weren't happy?" She takes the phone and flips through the photos.

"You both look very happy," she says softly.

"I thought so, too." I take it back and scroll to a picture. "I was at his office to give him this one. I printed it and put it in a beautiful frame. I thought my boyfriend would like a picture of his girlfriend on his desk." I can't help but cry more. Why is this so awful? I curl myself up more, but it doesn't help.

"Miranda," Emma tries to soothe me.

"Little did I know, he already had another woman on his desk." I'm a mess as tears flow everywhere.

"You love him, don't you?" Emma's question hits me hard.

"I might," I cry harder.

"That's why this hurts so much." She moves closer and holds me as I cry into her shoulder. It hurts so badly. I don't even think it hurt this bad before with Andrew. It's never felt like my heart was literally ripped from my chest. I can't breathe.

"I think you should talk to him, maybe when you get back." She's trying to calm me down.

"I don't know if I want to because I can't take him back, Em. I would always be wondering if he's cheating," Taking deep breaths, I try to calm myself down.

"I understand that." She rubs my back as I finish my sobs. "Think about it. It wouldn't hurt to talk to him," she says again.

"Emma, I don't need another problem child."

"No, you don't. You do need someone to love you and take care of you," she raises her eyebrows.

"I have you." I smile, which causes her to laugh.

"True."

"Let's go out and have some girl time, just you and me. Come on, get up and get dressed." Emma smiles.

"It's Black Friday. Are you crazy?" We laugh together.

"Yes," she admits. Actually, girl time and shopping sound great and will clear my mind.

The next morning, Emma helps me load my bags into the car, and I say my goodbyes to everyone.

"Hey, you know you can stay longer. You are always welcome here," Emma says as she gets in the car.

"I know, and I appreciate that, but I think going home will help. I'll miss you all so much, though."

"We'll miss you too, but it's just a few weeks until Christmas, and we will see you then, right?"

"Yes, I'll be down, and thankfully, by then, I'll be able to drive." I grin at the thought of having this stupid cast off.

Our drive back is quiet as I think about all the things I need to do.

"Miranda, are you sure you're alright? I mean, I can come up and stay with you if you want. Or I know Mom would in a heartbeat."

"I'm seriously fine. It's just been a long, eventful week. Nothing a night home in my bed won't cure." I know she knows I'm lying, but she doesn't press me. In fact, she just lets me sulk the entire ride.

We arrive at the airport, and thankfully, there is curbside check-in, so Emma is able to drag the bags up for me and then hugs me goodbye. With promises of lots of updates, I leave her at the drop-off and prepare myself for another new start at home.

Once through security, I grab a cup of coffee and find a seat by the window to start on the new book I purchased. I've just settled in when someone sits right beside me. I glance up, ready to be snippy, but see it's Preston and laugh.

"Well, hello," he says as he leans back in his seat.

"Hi. Funny meeting you here," I grin at seeing him.

"I can't believe we're on the same flight back. So, how was your holiday with the family?" He seems truly interested, and I feel better having a friend with me.

"It was great. I ate too much and had too much fun. The kids wore me out. How about you?" I turn to listen to him, putting my book aside.

"I had a nice time with my family, then hung out with friends and partied a little too hard." He laughs freely as he crosses his legs at the ankle. "I'm ready to go home and rest from my vacation," he adds.

"Me too," I agree.

When they call our flight for boarding, we laugh that we are even on the same boarding schedule. We find a couple of seats together and talk about our families and where we live back in Chicago, and I'm surprised that he doesn't live that far from me. Our flight goes way too fast, and I'm actually sad that we are parting ways.

We walk to the baggage claim together, and he helps me pull off my bags from the return while I hold Kasey.

"Do you have a ride? Or would you like to share a cab?" he asks me as he hauls off the second suitcase.

"I don't have a ride, and that would be wonderful."

He stacks our bags and pulls them along as we walk towards the pickup area to find a cab, but as we round the corner, I stop dead in my tracks, as there stands Charlie with a sign bearing my name.

"Damnit, Ethan," I say out loud.

"Who is Ethan, and why are we damming him?" Preston laughs.

"I don't need a cab." I nod towards Charlie, who is waving.

"Okay, that's cool, I can grab one."

"No, I mean, Charlie can take you home too." I smile.

"Are you sure? And who is Charlie?"

"He's my driver while I'm healing and can't drive. Come on."

Preston looks lost but follows anyway.

"Hi, Charlie," I smile warmly at him.

"Good morning, Ms. Michaels. Did you have a good flight?"

"I did, thank you. I assume Ethan sent you?" He seems sad for a moment before answering.

"Yes, ma'am."

I shake my head at Ethan's audacity, but then, did I really expect anything less?

"Charlie, this is my friend Preston. Ethan is not in the car, is he?" I ask quickly, knowing that would be a whole other issue to deal with, and I am not ready for that.

"No, ma'am, and hello, Preston." Charlie nods.

"Perfect. Preston doesn't live that far from me, so if it's okay, I would like to take him home first, please."

"Yes, ma'am. This way, sir."

"Charlie, please—it's Miranda." I give him a look, and he smiles sweetly as he agrees.

Charlie leads us to the car, and we get in while he loads our suitcases.

"A personal driver, you must be someone important," Preston laughs.

"I thought I was, but now, just back to regular everyday Miranda."

"Well, I think you are pretty special." I see the slight blush over Preston's cheeks, and it's sweet.

"Aww, thanks." I think we embarrass each other because we are quiet for a while.

When we do talk, we find we have so much in common, and I haven't laughed this much all week. He is so funny. Like ridiculously funny. I can't believe how much better I feel being around him. I don't want another relationship, but if I did, he would be good boyfriend material. I mentally kick myself for my thoughts. I'm seriously so screwed up in the head right now.

As we pull up in front of his apartment, he gets serious as he turns to me.

"Miranda, you are funny, sweet, and super pretty. I can't believe someone would let you go. Do you think I could maybe go out for dinner later tonight?" He gives me a huge, all-teeth smile that makes me laugh.

"I think I would like that. Why don't you call me later, and we'll figure something out? I think I need a nap and a hot shower."

"Deal." He tells Kasey goodbye, then shoots me the sweetest boyish grin before getting out of the car.

"See you later." I get a goofy wave as he goes, and I wave back like an idiot. I have no idea what I'm doing, but hey, at least I'm not crying. I watch him go into the apartment and then meet Charlie's eyes in the mirror. He looks concerned but quickly looks away, and I wonder why.

"So, Ms. Miranda, your place or Mr. Bradley's?" he asks quickly, and I have my answer for the look he gave me. He either doesn't know, or Ethan has convinced him otherwise.

"Charlie, Mr. Bradley, and I are no longer together. I'm not sure what he told you, but he cheated on me, and I don't play that game. I appreciate him sending you to pick me up, even though I have no idea how he found out when I was coming home. So, my apartment, please. Oh, and everything that was said in this car stays in this car. Please, no reporting back to him. This is my life, not his. He lost the right to know what was going on when he screwed around with that redhead in his office." I feel a little furious now.

"Sorry to have upset you, Ms. Miranda. That was not my intention." He doesn't glance in the mirror, and now I feel bad for him being stuck in the middle of this mess.

"No, Charlie, I'm sorry. I shouldn't have gotten mad, but he just doesn't get it at all." I sit back hard in the seat and cross my arms. I see Charlie nod, but that is the last we speak.

As I get out of the car, Charlie offers to help me with my bags, which I'm happy to accept. He takes the suitcases, and I take Kasey, and we ride up in silence. When we get to my door, he pulls the suitcase inside for me before he speaks.

"Well, if it helps, Mr. Bradley asked me to give you this upon my departure." He takes out an envelope from his jacket. "If my opinion matters at all, he misses you terribly. You might not think he cares, but by the look of him, I don't think he's eaten or slept much this week. When he gave this to me, he looked awful, but it's just an old man's two cents." I take the envelope from him and feel a pull on my heart.

"Thank you, Charlie. And your opinion always matters to me." I turn it over in my hands. *Ms. Miranda Michaels* is written on the front in Ethan's neat handwriting.

"If you need me at all, I am a call away. Mr. Bradley has taken care of my services through next week. He wanted to make sure you had a ride to work and any other errands that were needed. I would also personally be available for your dinner date tonight." He smiles sweetly, and I can't bear it, so I give him a tight hug that surprises him. Ethan might be on my shit list, but he gave me Charlie, and I adore him.

"I think I might take you up on that for tonight, and for the record, it is not a date—just friends." I smile, and Charlie winks at me.

"You might want to tell that young man that; he seems to be very fond of you."

"I'll make sure to mention it again. And thank you for this." I hold up the envelope.

"You're most welcome. Just give me a call with your pickup time."

"I will. See you later tonight." He nods and leaves me alone with my thoughts.

I let Kasey out first, then turn to see a huge bouquet of pink roses on the counter.

"What the hell? How did he get in here?" They are just like the ones I left to die in the hallway.

"Damnit, Ethan," I growl to myself as I pull out the card.

Welcome home.
~Ethan

Breathing deeply to keep myself calm, I try to understand his thinking. Why can't he leave me alone? Why can't he just understand that I need space? But then Charlie's words come back to me, and I know why. God, he is so frustrating!

I make myself a cup of coffee, pull off my boots, and settle on the couch to read his letter. I want to call him and yell at him for all of it, but I don't have the energy. Inside the envelope is a handwritten letter, and with a deep breath to calm myself, I start to read.

Miranda,

I am not good with words or trying to describe my feelings, so please understand this is new and difficult for me, but I want you to know how I feel. I need you to know what I feel. I know what I did was wrong, more than wrong. It was horrible. I am so very sorry and ashamed that I hurt and embarrassed you. My display of foolishness has been made very public, and my heart breaks knowing that I caused you so much pain. I can only hope being out of town eased the backlash on you. I know you do not want to hear from me, but there are things I need to say, and this may be my only chance. My hope is that you will read all of this and know that it came from my heart. As much as I want you, I do not deserve you. I know that now.

You have said many times that you were not in the same league as me, and you were right. You are so much more than me. You are in a league that most women only dream of, and men can never reach. You are more than anything I could have ever imagined in my best fantasy. You make people who do not even know you smile with your kindness and warm spirit, yet you can bring a man to his knees to beg for mercy. You have a fight and fire in you that I have never experienced before but that I want to experience every single day. You are independent to a point that drives me crazy, but that I enjoy more than anything. You are hardheaded and defiant but loving and caring that makes even the toughest man cry.

You deserve someone who can make your world as bright as you have made mine, and as much as I want that person to be me, I am afraid I have lost that chance and saying that out loud tears my heart out all over again. Seeing the pain on your face that day hurt me more than I thought possible but finding out I may have lost you forever will completely break me. I miss you more than words can describe, and I want you more than the air I breathe. More than anything else in this world. I also know that it is not my decision—it is yours. I know you do not want to talk to me, but I only ask to have the chance to say this all out loud to you. Five whole minutes to tell you this: Miranda Michaels, I love you.

~ Ethan

I read that last line over and over while tears fall down my face. *How can he love me after what he did?* I don't understand. Kasey crawls into my lap, and I hold him while I cry. I don't know what to do. I re-read the letter again, and this time, I can hear Ethan's voice in the words, and it makes everything worse. It's painful, and it makes me cry even harder. He made an unforgivable mistake, but his words touch me deeply, and now I'm so torn.

I reach for my phone. *Emma will know what to do. She always does.* My hands are shaking as I dial her number.

"Hey, I was just going to call you and make sure you made it," Emma answers cheerfully.

"Emma…" I croak through my tears.

"Miranda, what's wrong?" Her tone changes immediately.

"I'm okay physically, I just… I need you," I say, my voice breaking as the tears come harder.

"Rana, what happened?" Her sweet, soothing voice fills the phone, and I wish I could be back home with her right now.

"Ethan sent a driver to pick me up from the airport, and he gave him a letter to deliver to me. It's heart-wrenchingly sweet, and I don't know what to do." The words spill out, mixed with sobs.

"Oh, sweetie, it's okay. Read me the letter, and we'll figure this out."

It takes me ten minutes, with many more tears, to get through the letter. When I get to the end, I pause and softly read the last line again. Emma is quiet.

"Emma?" I ask, worried the line cut out.

"I'm here. That… wow."

"I know." I sob into the phone.

"That's pretty open and honest, and he loves you," Emma says, her voice soft and thoughtful.

"I know, and as much as I want it to be true, how can I go back to him? He kissed another woman and let her touch him in places that, just hours before, I had been. He admitted it to me, and I can't trust him." I wipe my face, but the tears keep coming.

"No, he would have to win your trust back, and for you, that's going to be really hard. My question is, how do you feel about him right this minute?" Emma asks carefully.

I let the question hang in the air as I think. "I miss him," I whisper.

"And?" Emma gently prompts, knowing there's more.

"I know I was falling for him, and his words touch me deeply, but the cheating is something I can't get past. You didn't see the way he kissed her. It wasn't a kiss on the cheek, and that red lipstick on his face, I can never unsee that." I choke on my words.

"Well, then you have your answer. If you don't think you can forgive him over time, then there's no chance," Emma says, her voice cracking, and it almost breaks me again.

"I don't know if I can," I whisper.

"I just want you to be happy, sis. I don't care who it is, where he comes from, or how much he makes. I just want to know that he loves you and takes care of you."

"I know." I take a deep breath to calm myself, wondering why I keep falling into these situations.

"Why don't you rest and maybe give him a call later. You don't have to see him in person; just let him say those things to you. If you still feel like you can't get past the kiss, then don't. But if his words touch you and give you hope, give him a second chance," Emma suggests, and I can hear the smile in her voice.

"You're always so smart. I love you. Thank you." Closing my eyes, I'm grateful to have her.

"Anytime. Call me later and check-in, okay? And keep me posted. I love you too." She says goodbye and hangs up.

I look at the phone, thinking maybe I should call Ethan. My finger hovers over the call button. I dial his number only to hang up before the first ring. I can't do it, not now. Everything is so raw and painful. I touch the letter beside me and trace over his handwritten words: *I love you*. No, I can't. I put the letter on the coffee table and lay down for a nap. I'm exhausted.

When I wake up three hours later, I'm stiff and feel like hell. I sit up, and Kasey meows at me, sitting on the letter. "What?" He meows again.

"You want me to call him too?" He meows once more, then leaps onto my lap and purrs.

"Thanks for the support." I rub behind his ears and get up for some ibuprofen and water. I ache all over.

The kitchen smells like the pink roses, and it pulls at my emotions. They are beautiful—and my favorite. I reach over and touch a petal, the softness making me tear up again. *Damn him.* Why couldn't some loser have hit me? I could have sued him and moved on. Why did it have to be the sweet, funny, sexy man who tore up more than my car?

I lean against the fridge, staring out the windows into the sunny sky. I just need to call him and get this over with. I look at the clock, it's 4:30 p.m. and realize I need to figure out dinner plans with Preston. *Damnit!* I yell, scaring Kasey as he runs from my feet. *Why does this suck so badly?*

I grab my phone and call on all my inner strength to dial Ethan's number. It rings once, twice, and again. On the fourth ring, I'm ready to pull the phone away when he answers.

"Miranda?" He breathes out in surprise.

I swallow the knot in my throat and will myself not to cry at the sound of his voice. "I read your letter," I whisper, trying not to give in, though I know he can tell I've been crying.

"You called," he whispers back, his voice strained and hoarse. Suddenly, I ache for him.

"I don't know why," I say softly, the ache growing into a burning pain in my chest.

"Please, I want to tell you all those things again. I meant

every word and more. Miranda, please give me another chance. I will beg on my knees. I will move mountains for you, whatever you want. I just want you. I am dying here without you." His words tumble out in a strained ramble, and I close my eyes to keep from falling apart.

"Ethan, I want to believe you, I do, but I can't see past that bright red lipstick on your face every time I think of you. The way you kissed her—I can't. You betrayed my trust, something I don't give freely." Now I'm crying again.

"I know. God, I can't even tell you how sorry I am. I will do anything—anything for you. Please." He is begging, and its torture.

"It doesn't work like that, Ethan. I could never trust you again." I'm sobbing now.

"I know, but I will earn it back. I know I can. I want you, only you. It has always only ever been you." His words are like daggers, sharp and hot.

"I can't risk it. My heart couldn't handle being cast aside again, as I would expect it to be with you. This is who you are."

"No! I can be what you need. Please, baby—Miranda, please—anything, I need you."

"Ethan, I'm sorry," I say, my voice trembling as I prepare to hang up, but I can't.

"I love you," he whispers, and my heart pounds hard against my chest. I hold the phone, crying, as I hear his soft breathing, the silence stretching between us.

"Miranda, let me prove it to you. I can be what you want. You are all I need, the only one I want, and I don't deserve you, but I'm just asking for a second chance. Please."

His words echo in me: *Just a second chance.*

"Ethan…" His name floats from my lips.

"Please," he whispers back.

"I can't do this—not now. I need to think. I can't forgive you. Not now."

"I understand." And then I hear his tears. "I will always love you."

I want to scream. "Just… just let me be for now. Goodbye." I pause, but he doesn't hang up.

"I will be here," he says softly, and the line goes dead.

"FUCK! FUCK! FUCK! DAMN IT!" I scream out. *I hate him.* He flipped this whole thing on me. Stomping into the bedroom, I scream again.

"How can he do this to me?" I yell at Kasey, who just meows at me. I want to throw something. I pick up a shoe just as the phone rings in my hand, startling me. I don't recognize the number.

"Hello?" I almost yell.

"Hi to you, too." Preston laughs.

"Sorry, hi," I say, trying to smile, but my heart aches.

"I was calling to see if you still wanted to do dinner tonight. Say 7?"

I don't need this right now. I want to go, but I look at myself in the mirror and close my eyes. Why did I even call Ethan? I do want to go, but I don't want another mess.

"Yep, sounds great. I can meet you there, wherever *there* is." I'm frustrated, but it's not Preston's fault.

"Great, I'll text you the place. I need to call and see if we can get in. Are you okay?"

"I am. Just dealing with some issues at home, and I'm a mess. Preston, I want to make sure you know that I'm not in the market for a new boyfriend. I'm an emotional mess, and I don't want to lead you on. If you want to cancel, I understand. I'm sorry."

He laughs, and I think maybe I've read the situation wrong. "Good, because I'm not looking for a girlfriend either. You women are crazy. I just thought you and I clicked pretty well, and it would be nice to hang out as friends if that's still okay."

I breathe a sigh of relief. "That would be perfect. I'll see you at 7. Thanks, Preston."

"You're welcome. See you then."

Falling onto the bed, I exhale loudly, thinking about my life. Just over a month ago, everything was simple, just me, my cat, and my uncomplicated world. Now, it feels like everything has spiraled out of control. I want to scream more, but instead, I just lie there, drained. Even though I feel like crap, I am going to get up, get dressed, and go out to dinner. I need to escape these emotions, if only for a little while.

Charlie drops me off at the restaurant that Preston picked, and I'm immediately charmed by the ambiance. Taking a deep breath, I head inside to find Preston waiting for me, his face splitting into a grin when he sees me.

"Wow, look at you," he says, pulling me into a hug, which surprises me.

"Thank you," I reply, feeling a little awkward as we stand there. Just then, the hostess arrives to tell us our table is ready, and I'm grateful to sit down and escape the weird moment.

We order dinner and wine, and before long, we're laughing and having a great time. By the time I finish my third glass of wine, my cheeks hurt from smiling so much.

"My cheeks hurt," I tell Preston as he finishes his own drink.

"Mine too. I don't think I've laughed this hard in years. I'm glad we did this," he says with a smile.

"Me too!" I lift my wine glass, and we toast to our new-found friendship.

Dinner goes wonderfully until I catch movement out of the corner of my eye. I glance over and see Jason waving at me from across the room. Great—just what I need. I wave back and watch as he approaches our table.

"Miranda, I'm happy to see you made it back safely," Jason says warmly. Without thinking, I stand up and hug him tightly. His familiar presence brings me comfort, but I'm sure Preston is watching us curiously.

"Jason, this is my friend Preston. Preston, this is Jason." I introduce them, feeling a bit flustered as they shake hands.

"Nice to meet you," Jason says, his eyes scanning my face as if searching for something.

"Are you okay?" Jason asks softly.

"Perfectly perfect," I reply with a giggle, though I'm sure my expression betrays me.

"He called me earlier and said you were pretty upset." Jason's concern lingers in his voice.

"Yeah, I was, but I don't want to discuss it now. He had his chance. I called him and explained that and told him to leave me alone." I glance at Preston, who is watching the exchange silently.

Jason nods, stepping back to give me space. "Okay, I just wanted to check on you. Please call me if you need anything. Preston, it was a pleasure to meet you," he says before giving me another hug. As he pulls away, he whispers in my ear, "Don't move too fast. Rebounds suck. Trust me." He kisses my cheek lightly before walking back to his date.

"Ex?" Preston asks, once Jason is out of earshot.

"No, just a friend from college, a fellow colleague, and my ex's lawyer," I say with a laugh at the absurdity of it all.

"I see. So, he came over to size up the competition?" Preston teases, raising his eyebrows playfully.

"I guess so," I say, rolling my eyes. Jason is always looking out for me, but part of me knows he's going to report back to Ethan.

We finish the rest of the meal, sharing dessert, though I'm not sure "sharing" is the right word, as Preston seems determined to hog most of the ice cream. When the bill comes, he grabs it before I can.

"No, let me, please," I protest.

"Nope, I asked you. You can get it next time," he says with a wink.

Next time? Oh, okay. "Deal," I agree, without giving too much thought to what "next time" means.

When we stand to leave, I sway a little, and Preston quickly steadies me. "I think four glasses of wine might have been a bit much."

"Maybe," I giggle as he wraps his arm around mine, leading me to the door.

"I don't want to go home yet. Let's get another drink

somewhere… barsy?" I suggest, my tongue fumbling the word.

Preston laughs. "Barsy? Like a bar?"

"Yeah, like a bar. I know the game's on," I reply with a grin.

"You like hockey?" he asks, sounding surprised.

"Love it. And I noticed you checking the score earlier. Blues game, not Hawks," I laugh.

"I know me too. Hello, I'm from St. Louis!" He nudges me playfully. "I know a great place where we can catch the rest of it if you're up for it."

"Hell, yes! Oh, let's take my car, though. I have a driver, and we don't have to worry about drinking and driving."

"We don't need one," he says, pointing to a bar right across the street.

"Oh, lead the way, my good man," I joke as we walk arm in arm. I'm not sure if he's holding me up or if I'm holding him up, but we're having fun, and for now, I don't care.

Once inside, we grab a couple of beers and settle in to watch the rest of the game. I'm definitely feeling the effects of all the alcohol, and I can tell Preston is, too.

"Miranda, I think you're drunk," he teases.

"I am, and I think you are, too."

"I must agree. Maybe mixing wine and beer wasn't such a great idea. You're a terrible influence on me," he says with a goofy grin, making me laugh.

"I am not! Okay, maybe I am… but I'm so much fun," I retort, still laughing.

"That you are. And very pretty, too," he adds, his smile turning a little shy.

"Thank you," I say, blushing at his compliment.

"What, I'm not fun and pretty, too?" He jokes, pretending to be hurt.

"You are tons of fun and very pretty," I tease back. "Wait—aren't men supposed to be handsome, not pretty? Well, you're pretty *and* handsome. Maybe a little sexy, too," I add with a playful growl.

Preston nearly spits out his beer, laughing. "Did you just growl at me?"

"I did." The laughter is too much, and I announce that I need to use the restroom, stumbling my way there.

As I wash my hands, I look at myself in the mirror, wondering what I'm doing. I'm tipsy, but I'm having a good time, something I desperately needed. I reapply some lipstick, fluff my hair, and head back to the table, determined to keep the night going.

"Feel better?" Preston asks when I return.

"Much."

"Fresh lipstick too, nice. I like that color," he says, wiggling his eyebrows.

"You know what this color is good for?" I ask, then blush at my own suggestive thoughts.

"Writing sweet goodbyes on bedroom mirrors the next morning?" He's the one blushing now.

"That's a good one. I like your idea better." And I do. I'll have to use that someday.

"Suggestion," he winks, making me laugh.

"You want me to write one on your mirror?" I pretend to be shocked. "I thought we were just friends. Wouldn't that be crossing a line?"

"Unless we're friends with benefits," he suggests, his tone turning a little more serious.

I can't help but smile. "I guess we would need to figure out what those benefits are."

He's not laughing anymore but instead giving me a sexy grin that sends shivers down my spine. "Stop, you're killing me," I joke, trying to break the tension. "Let's get your drunk self home."

We stand, and Preston reaches out to steady me as I wobble a bit. He seems unsure as he looks down, then back up to me. "Can I kiss you? Just as a friend, I mean," he asks as he stands close to me.

"Oh, definitely. I kiss my friends all the time," I reply with a grin.

Suddenly, his warm lips are on mine, and I kiss him back without thinking. When he pulls away, our lips brush again, lingering.

"That was nice," he admits softly.

"It was," I agree, feeling the weight of the moment. "You know, earlier, I was going to say this lipstick might look good on you, and I was right." I reach up and gently wipe the smudged lipstick from his lips with my thumb.

"Maybe we should test that theory again," he says with a grin, leaning in for another kiss.

I kiss him back, losing myself in the warmth of the moment. But as good as it feels, I know I have to stop. It's not right. I pull back reluctantly. "Next time. No alcohol involved. I don't do one-night stands."

Preston smiles, his eyes soft. "Somehow, I don't think there would ever be just one night with you."

His words make my heart race, but I push those thoughts aside, because it has nothing to do with him. "Let's get out of here," I say with a grin.

Preston and I make our way out of the bar, arm in arm, laughing about the night's events. The cool night air hits my face, making me realize just how tipsy I really am.

As the car pulls up, I pause, knowing that if I get in, the night is essentially over. I want to keep the fun going, but I know I need to go home and let everything settle in my mind.

"Let me take you home," I offer, gesturing to Charlie. "I have a driver. No drinking and driving issues."

Preston shakes his head with a small smile. "If I get in that car with you, I won't be able to keep my hands off you. It's probably best if we call it a night."

There's a playful glint in his eye, but I know he's right. A small part of me wants to kiss him again, but I also know this is moving faster than I should allow. We're both tipsy, and I don't want to make a decision I'll regret later.

I sigh, smiling softly. "Okay, maybe you're right. Next time, no alcohol."

"Next time," he agrees, taking my hand and kissing it gently before letting go. "But, Miranda… you are amazing, just so you know. It's been a long time since I've had this much fun with someone."

My cheeks flush at his words. "Thank you, Preston. I've had fun, too. Really."

He smiles, turning to walk away before stopping and looking back. "Text me when you get home, okay? That way I know you made it back safely."

"I will," I promise. "You, too."

I watch him disappear into the night, then climb into the backseat of the car, sighing as I lean back. My head is spinning from the alcohol, the laughter, and the emotions of the evening. I'm exhausted, but I feel lighter than I have in days.

Charlie glances at me in the rearview mirror. "Home, Ms. Miranda?"

"Yes, Charlie. Home, please."

We ride in silence for a while, and I let my thoughts drift to Ethan again. His letter, his pleas over the phone, it's all a whirlwind in my mind. I know I need to figure out what to do about him, but tonight, after the week I've had, I just want to focus on feeling good for once. Except my mind keeps going back to him.

He's so frustrating. My emotions are all over the place, and I don't know what to feel. Part of me wants to forgive him, to give him another chance. The other part of me is still too hurt, too angry to move past what he did. And the third part of me, the sensible part, wants me to run far away, knowing he will just hurt me all over again.

"Ms. Miranda." I hear my name, but I roll back over and sleep. "Miranda." This time, I open one eye and see that I'm laying on the seat of the car. Oh.

"Miranda? Ms. Michaels, we are home." It's Charlie. I start to sit up, and the car spins. Holy Hell.

"Just a minute. Sorry." I know immediately I am going to be sick, so I push open the door by my head and throw up right out the door. And when I think I'm done, I throw up again. Shit.

"Ms. Michaels, are you alright?" Charlie sounds concerned as he stands by the open door near my feet.

"No, I'm not. I'm sorry. Please stay there. I plead as I throw up again. Embarrassment washes over me as I hang out the door, puking outside my apartment. "I'm sorry. Too much to drink." I cry as it washes over me again. My head is spinning, and I can't focus on the right words.

"It's ok, we all have been there. Just lay still and let it pass." He assures me with a pat to my leg. The cool air feels good, so I just lay there, taking deep breaths and trying to decide on how to get myself upstairs. This was entirely my fault. I should have stayed home!

"Miranda." I freeze. "No." Not him. Please let this be a dream. As I start to cry again, nausea washes over me.

"Come on, let me help you," Ethan says softly, his strong hands pulling me across the seat and out into his chest.

"No, put me down. I don't need your help," I yell, but he only mutters something under his breath. And honestly, I'm too drunk to fight anyway.

"I don't want you here," I sob, and then the world tilts. "I'm going to be sick!" Gently, Ethan sets me down on the ledge just in time for me to throw up into the bushes. And I do, more than once. Over and over, I empty the alcohol that I consumed until I'm left dry, heaving, wishing the ground would swallow me whole.

"Come on." He gently pulls me to my feet and then lifts me up again.

"Why are you here?" I sob, my voice cracking.

"Shhh," he whispers, his breath brushing against my face as he cradles me to him.

"No, go home. Leave me. I don't want you here." I cry harder as I protest being carried into the building.

"I know," he says quietly. "Just let me take you up."

I'm too exhausted to fight anymore, too drained to protest. I lean into him, his warmth somehow comforting as his grip tightens around me. My head rests against his strong chest, and I can hear his heart racing. My tears begin to soak his shirt, the pain in my chest intensifying with every beat of his heart.

Before I can say anything else, the exhaustion overwhelms me, and I close my eyes, drifting off in the safety of his arms.

Chapter 24

I wake up with a pounding headache and a horrible taste in my mouth. *What the hell did I do?* I try to sit up, but the light makes me groan. *What time is it?* I rub my eyes and look at the clock. It's 11 a.m. I can't remember what happened. Ugh, I remember drinking, I remember... *Oh shit.*

Slowly, I glance at the bed next to me and exhale in relief when I see it's empty. I remember making out with Preston. *Oh God, what did I do?* Was he here? Did I...? I run my hands through my hair and groan as everything hurts.

When I move to get up, I realize I'm completely naked, which makes my heart race with panic. I remember throwing up, but nothing more. I tiptoe to the bedroom door and hear movement in the kitchen. *Shit!* All I can do is run into the bathroom, closing the door quietly behind me. I brush my teeth, wash off my smeared makeup, brush my teeth again, and then slip on my robe. I look at myself in the mirror and feel ashamed. I have to go out there and face whatever disaster I caused.

I close my eyes, running through all the things I could say, how I should make this right. I just need to apologize, tell him it was a mistake, and that I can't do this. I open the door and walk softly toward the kitchen, wrapping my robe tightly around me. *I can do this.* It was all the alcohol.

As I step into the doorway, he turns, and I freeze.

"*Ethan?*" I'm shocked.

"Morning," he says, barely looking at me.

"Wait, what the hell are you doing here?" I'm mad and confused. And well, mad.

"Cleaning up after your fun-filled night of vomiting."

Oh, dear God.

"How? Why?" I close my eyes and groan, trying to remember.

"As drunk as you were, I'm not surprised you don't remember anything," he says cautiously, waiting for me to move.

"How did you get here?" I ask, walking over to the glass of water he's set on the counter for me, along with two ibuprofen, which I desperately need.

"Thank you," I whisper, avoiding his gaze.

"Charlie called me a little after two in the morning to tell me you were passed out in the back of the car, and he couldn't figure out what to do with you. Then you woke up and vomited everywhere. I couldn't leave you like that."

He stands back, watching as I down the water and rest my head on the counter. "I don't remember anything."

"That might be a good thing," he mutters, clearing his throat uncomfortably. My heart sinks.

"What did I do?" I ask, feeling my cheeks burn with embarrassment.

"Do you want bullet points or the full story?" He's serious, and I immediately want to die.

Oh God. "I'm sorry," I stammer, unable to meet his eyes. "Whatever I said or did…"

"I deserved everything you said." His voice is hard, making me feel about an inch tall. I want to apologize, but since I don't remember what I said, it feels pointless.

"Why are you still here, then?" I ask, my voice soft.

"You know why." He's right. I do know why. He cares.

"Tell me what I did," I mumble, keeping my head down on the cool countertop. I hear him come closer, but I don't lift my head.

"From what I gather, you went out with a friend for dinner, then hit a bar and got very drunk. Charlie brought you home, but you were sick and couldn't get out of the car, so he called me for help. I got you upstairs, and… well, things got messy." His voice trails off as he turns back to his coffee.

"Messy, how?" I ask, my voice shaking.

"Miranda, it might be best if I just finish up and leave," he says, his tone heavy with sadness.

"What happened?" I demand, a wave of anger rising in me. He flinches slightly at the sharpness of my tone.

"Miranda…" His eyes meet mine briefly, then he looks away again.

"Ethan, just tell me," I say more gently, noticing the uncertainty in his face.

He sighs, setting down his coffee before turning to face me fully. "You were… well, you were really upset. You kept saying things and yelling at me. I tried to calm you down, but you were too far gone."

"What did I say?" I ask, my voice barely above a whisper, dreading the answer.

He hesitates before answering. "You said a lot of things about how much I hurt you. How you couldn't trust me anymore. You kept bringing up the kiss, and then you…" He trails off, rubbing the back of his neck awkwardly.

"Then I what?" I press, feeling a mix of dread and curiosity.

"You started crying, saying you hated me, but…" He looks down at the coffee cup in his hand. "You also said you still loved me."

My heart sinks. I don't remember any of it, but hearing it now makes me feel exposed and vulnerable. "Oh God," I whisper, tears prickling at my eyes.

"You were drunk, and you were hurting. I didn't come here to make things worse. I just wanted to make sure you were okay." Ethans voice is deep and quiet, and I notice how red his eyes are.

I blink back the tears and nod, not trusting myself to speak. There's a long pause before he finally adds, "I'll go now that you are awake and alright."

I want to say something, anything, but the words are stuck in my throat. Part of me wants him to leave so I can curl up in my shame and hide from this mess. But the other part of me—the part that still remembers the good times— wants him to stay, wants to figure out what's left of us, if anything.

"Ethan," I finally manage to say, "I don't know what to

do. I don't even know how to feel right now. I'm so angry at you."

He nods, his expression sober. "I get it. And I don't expect you to have all the answers right now. Just... know I meant what I said. And I hope one day you will forgive me."

His words hang in the air, and I feel the weight of them pressing down on me. I nod again, and this time, he steps back.

"I'll leave you to get some rest," he says gently. "Oh, and you might want to call Preston. He's called five times." Hurt flashes across his eyes and he exhales before he puts his cup in the sink and walks toward the door. I don't stop him, but he pauses briefly before opening it. He glances back at me one last time, his eyes filled with a mix of hope and sorrow, before stepping out and closing the door softly behind him.

The moment he's gone, I collapse back into the chair, burying my face in my hands. The emotions of last night and this morning swirl inside me, making me feel like I'm on the verge of breaking down.

I can't keep doing this.

I sit there in silence, letting the tears fall, until suddenly, I run out the door and down the hall and hear the elevator ding. "Ethan!" I yell, but as I get there, the doors close, and I fall to my knees. "Please," I mutter, but there is no one to hear me. He's gone, and my heart breaks all over again.

Laying on the couch, feeling so defeated, all I can do is cry.

Sunday comes, and I'm still on the couch, my whole life in pieces around me. I pushed Ethan away, and he left, just like I wanted, or at least I thought I did. But now, knowing I'm not in control anymore, I feel broken. This hurts so much more than before. The thought that I might have lost him for good is unbearable.

I force myself to move, dragging myself to the kitchen. Even water has lost its taste. My phone lights up with a text, so I glance at it, but don't answer. There are so many missed calls, texts, and voicemails, but I don't even care. I swipe to delete them all from the screen and set the phone back down, but it rings again. It's Jason. *Nope.* I send it to voicemail, but it rings again... and again. I keep sending it to voicemail.

I don't want to talk to anyone. I just want to lie on the couch and fall apart. So, that's what I do. I can't cry. I can't move. I just... exist. Kasey nudges me, trying to get me to pet him, but I can't muster the energy. My body sinks deeper into the couch until I eventually drift off to sleep.

The sound of the front door opening wakes me, but I don't move. Nothing matters. There are sounds, and footsteps, and then Jason appears in my line of sight.

"Miranda? Are you okay?" He shakes me gently, but I just look up at him blankly.

"Go away," I mumble, my voice barely there.

"No. Sit up," he demands, his voice firm.

I close my eyes, ignoring him. I hear him say something to someone, but I can't be bothered to look.

"Miranda, I need you to sit up," Jason says again, more insistent this time.

Reluctantly, I move, and my robe slips off my shoulders. Jason fixes it and helps me sit up. "What are you doing here?" I ask, though I don't really care.

"Miranda, it's Sunday. Everyone is worried sick. You haven't answered anyone for two days. Your sister called Ethan, who called me, and I've been calling you all weekend. When you didn't answer, I had to come see what was going on."

He shakes me again, his frustration clear.

"I just want to lay here," I cry out, but the tears don't come.

"Miranda," he says softly but sternly.

"All of you men are the same. Ethan, Preston, you, none of you want me," I squeak, my voice cracking.

"Is that what this is about? You think none of us want you?" Jason's voice softens before he chuckles. "Miranda, it's just the opposite, we *all* want you. And who's Preston?"

"A friend. You met him when we were at dinner," I mumble, barely caring to explain. "Doesn't matter."

Jason shakes his head, clearly frustrated. "Come on, get up. Let's get you dressed and get some food in you. We need to talk."

He helps me get dressed and then makes me a PB&J sandwich and a glass of milk, which I force myself to eat. I can barely sit up because I am so exhausted and emotionally drained. Jason watches me like a hawk, standing over me, his arms crossed. I can tell he's mad at me.

"I'm sorry if I worried you all," I finally admit after finishing the sandwich.

"Call your sister, and I'll call Ethan," Jason replies, his tone sharp, but I don't hear the anger I expected.

I want to argue, but I don't. I call Emma, and she's more than thrilled to hear I'm okay. Once I hang up, I watch Jason talk to Ethan on the phone.

"She's okay. Just upset, maybe a little dehydrated, and ignoring all of us asshole men," he says loud enough for me to hear.

"I am," I retort from the couch.

Jason says "yes" a few times into the phone, then walks over and hands it to me, but I shake my head no. "Take it and listen," he says firmly, so I reluctantly take the phone.

"Hi," I huff.

"You gave us all quite a scare." I hear Ethan's deep soft voice. The one he uses when he's concerned.

"Sorry," I say, though I'm not sure I mean it.

"Miranda, listen to me, please. I just want you to be happy. Whether it's with me, Jason, or whoever this Preston guy is. But mostly, I want it to be me." I can hear the faint smile in his voice, and despite myself, it makes me smile too. "Just be happy. At least one of us should be. I'm miserable without you, but I know I was wrong, and there's nothing I can do except ask for your forgiveness, again."

He pauses, taking a deep breath, but I cut in. "I know. I'm sorry I worried you. I'll try not to give everyone heart attacks in the future."

"I'm glad to hear that. I hope I'll be here to hold you to that," he says, his voice hopeful. I feel the urge to run to him, but I stay rooted to the spot.

"If you need anything, call me," he adds.

"Okay," I say softly. I hear him exhale, but neither of us says anything more.

"Goodbye, Miranda," he whispers, sadness lacing his voice. He doesn't hang up right away, so I wait.

"Miranda..." he whispers.

"I'm still here," I reply just as softly.

"I hope so," he says, his voice barely audible before he hangs up.

Jason takes the phone from me. "Are you alright?" he asks.

"I will be. Thank you for coming to check on me. I'm sorry to you, too," I feel a bit ashamed.

"Well, let's not do this again. We all worry about you. All of us." He gives me a chuckle while shaking his head.

"Why are you laughing?" I ask, curious.

"I finally get to see you naked, and I'm here as a friend, not a lover." He throws me a wink, and I groan.

"You could've had me, you know. I mean, before, not now."

"I know. My timing's horrible," He's still laughing.

"It is." I smile.

"You're just as hot naked as I imagined, though." Now he's the one who looks embarrassed.

"Jason!" We both laugh, and it feels good.

"I guess I better get out of here. Call me next time, don't drink yourself away."

"I wasn't drinking to get drunk; it just happened. I feel horrible about all of this. I need to apologize to another man now."

"Preston?" he asks, and I nod.

"Jason, I was all over him last night." My admission makes Jason chuckle.

"I told you rebounds were awful."

"I didn't sleep with him. It was just alcohol and misery, never a good combination," I mumble.

"Like I said, call me next time." He pulls me up into a hug.

"So, I can get drunk and be all over you?" I tease, laughing.

"I'd happily take one for the team." He laughs too.

"I'll remember that." I hug him tighter, grateful for his support.

Jason pulls back and looks at me seriously. "I think you and Ethan will be really happy together. He loves you, and I'm pretty sure you love him too. Take a few days to yourself, but don't leave the big guy hanging too long."

He kisses my cheek, and I close my eyes, feeling the warmth of his affection. He brushes his face against mine and pauses.

"Miranda, if you choose not to go back to him... call me first," he whispers.

"I will." I lean in and kiss his cheek but accidentally catch the corner of his lips. I feel nothing.

Jason's eyes lock with mine for a moment before he pulls away. "I should go," he announces.

"Yes, before I have to apologize again," I reply with a small smile.

He squeezes my shoulder. "See you around."

After he leaves, I close the door and feel a little better. Jason is a hell of a guy, and a few weeks ago, I might've been all over him. But now, my heart belongs to someone else.

I guess I should apologize to the other one now. I call Preston, but before I can even get a word out, he's the one apologizing. Once he's done, I explain my situation with Ethan, and he completely understands. He doesn't want the drama of a girlfriend anyway. We agree to stay just friends, though whether that will actually happen, I'm not sure.

We say goodbye, and I settle back onto the couch, trying to sort through my thoughts. My life feels like a mess, but maybe, just maybe, I can start putting the pieces back together.

Chapter 25

I'm excited to get back to life this morning and move on from the weekend's mess. Last night, I called Charlie, and he was more than happy to pick me up today. When I head downstairs at 6:55, I find him already waiting. I greet him warmly, apologizing for my drunken episode.

"Ms. Miranda, no apology is needed. We all have our nights. I'm just glad Mr. Bradley was there to help. I wouldn't have been much use." He is smiling warmly, and I hug him briefly, grateful for his understanding. He's one friend I don't want to lose.

As I slide into the car, there's a single pink rose waiting for me on the seat. *Ethan.* I hold up the rose and ask, "Charlie, did Ethan do this?"

Charlie grins into the mirror and winks but says nothing more. He doesn't need to. I know who it was.

Work is light today, thanks to April handling things while I was out. I'm happy to be back, and I can tell April is relieved to have me return. She looks frazzled, which makes me chuckle, remembering when I was in her shoes. Lunch is a small sandwich at my desk, and the day passes uneventfully.

At 5, Charlie picks me up, and again, there's a single pink rose on the seat. I glance at him, and he grins at me through the mirror. It makes me smile. I left the rose on my desk in the vase from this morning, but I take this one home and place it on my bedside table. The sweet gesture brings me comfort.

I try to watch a movie and have a quiet evening, but I miss Ethan. Sometimes, the ache is crushing, but strangely, I'm okay. Whether it's the roses or knowing how he feels, I'm managing. I decide to give it time, taking things one day at a time.

The next few days follow the same pattern: work, lunch, more work, home, dinner, and bed. Every morning and every evening, there's a rose in the car. A single pink rose. Ethan doesn't call, text, or show up. He just quietly lets me know he's there, which touches me more deeply than I expected. It makes things easier to handle.

By Friday, I've made some decisions, and after work, I break my routine, asking Charlie to take me by the little market near my place. When I get back in the car, I tell him where I want to go, and though he looks surprised, he nods as I make a phone call.

Of course, I tell Charlie my plan, and his excitement mirrors mine. We're both grinning as we stand in the lobby of Ethan's building. Charlie pushes the call button for Ethan's apartment, and when we hear his voice over the intercom, a shiver runs through me.

"Yes?" Ethan's voice sounds grouchy.

"Mr. Bradley, it's Charles. I have a delivery for you," Charlie says.

"Fine. I'll be down in a minute."

I smile and duck around the corner, hiding behind a large plant. I can't believe I'm doing this.

The elevator dings, and through the leaves, I catch a glimpse of Ethan as he steps out. He's in shorts and a t-shirt, clearly he just finished with a workout. I try not to focus on his body, instead holding my breath as Charlie hands him the single yellow rose I picked out. Ethan takes it, looking at Charlie in confusion.

"What's this?" Ethan asks.

Charlie smiles and replies, "Ms. Michaels would like to know if you're free for dinner."

I can barely hold back my giggle as I watch Ethan's face light up with recognition. His entire stance changes, He stands taller, his eyes searching the lobby, though he doesn't see me.

"She does? Of course! I can be ready in 15 minutes. Where? When?" Ethan is practically bouncing with excitement, which makes me grin behind my hand.

"Eight o'clock at The Signature Room at the 95th." Charlie is barely containing his own amusement.

Ethan grins, his eyes twinkling. "Please tell her I'll be there," he says, hugging Charlie before hurrying back into the elevator.

As the doors close, I lean back against the wall and let out the breath I am holding. *Thank God that went well.*

"I think that went perfectly," Charlie announces as he walks over to me.

"I hope so," I reply, smiling as he holds the door open for me.

We head back to my place so I can get ready. Charlie promises to be back in about an hour to pick me up, so I race upstairs, the excitement and nerves kicking in full force.

I put on light makeup and curl my hair, then take the purple dress Ethan bought for me off the door. It fits even better than it did when I first tried it on. I add my diamond dangle earrings, slip into my shoes, and take one last look in the mirror. The dress hugs my curves perfectly, and I feel… spectacular.

Glancing at the clock, I see it's time to go. I grab my coat and head downstairs, where Charlie is waiting, just as he promised.

"You look amazing, Ms. Miranda," Charlie announces as he helps me into the car.

"Thank you." I grin, feeling a little more confident.

"Mr. Bradley is going to be eating out of your hand tonight," he teases, winking at me.

I laugh, though my nerves start to kick in again as Charlie closes the door. It feels like a first date all over again, and I've rehearsed what I want to say a million times. I've prepared myself for both the best and worst outcomes tonight. Either way, I will have a path to move forward.

When we pull up outside the restaurant and I take a deep breath, steadying myself. Charlie wishes me luck as I step out. And I know I am going to need it.

The elevator ride up is torture. The other couples are cozy and talkative; sweet music fills the air, and I can feel the excitement building inside me. By the time the elevator doors open, I'm a bundle of nerves.

I follow the crowd to the hostess stand, but before I get there, I see him. Ethan is standing by the window, looking out at the view. As if knowing I'm there, he turns, and when our eyes meet, I freeze.

He's breathtaking. His black suit fits him perfectly, his crisp white shirt and light green tie pulling everything together. His black hair is neatly combed, and those familiar green eyes I've missed so much are locked on me.

He steps forward, visibly relaxing as his face lights up. He's in front of me in what feels like an instant.

"Hi," he whispers.

"Hi," I breathe, my heart racing in my chest.

"You are absolutely exquisite," he whispers again, his eyes roaming over me.

"So are you," I manage to say, my mouth dry and my heart pounding. I don't know what else to say as he stands there, staring into my eyes.

After a moment, I manage to speak again, though barely. "Let's go eat. I'm hungry."

Ethan nods, offering me his arm. I take it, feeling his solid bicep twitch beneath my fingers. He places his other hand on top of mine, holding it gently, and I smile up at him as we walk together.

The hostess leads us to a corner table overlooking the city. Ethan is slow to let go of my hand, but he finally does, pulling out my chair before sitting across from me. The menus are placed in front of us, but when I look up, Ethan hasn't taken his eyes off me.

"Miranda, I…" he starts, but I hold up my hand to stop him.

"Let's just enjoy this dinner and see where it goes," I say, giving him a reassuring smile.

He nods, returning my smile. My carefully planned speech can wait. For now, I just want to take things slow.

Even after I pick up the menu, I can feel Ethan's eyes still on me, and my cheeks flush. "Dinner. Pick something," I tease, holding back a giggle. He looks so... adorable.

"I don't want to look away," he whispers, and I can feel the warmth of his gaze. Reaching over, I touch his hand, causing his fingers to twitch beneath mine.

"Don't make me regret wasting my one huge favor by not eating." I joke, and his expression relaxes. He grins, a hint of relief visible on his face.

He glances at the menu, then closes it without saying a word. "What are you having?" I ask, trying to focus on my own choices.

"Haven't decided yet," he responds, but I can feel his eyes on me again, making me fidget. I don't know if it's his presence or how much I've missed him, but I can hardly sit still. I force myself to focus and make a decision just as the waiter arrives.

We order wine and food, but the moment the waiter leaves, Ethan resumes his quiet observation of me, like he's trying to memorize every detail.

"You're making me nervous," I laugh.

"I'm committing you to memory. You look incredible." Though his voice is deep, it's soft and sends shivers down my spine.

"Thank you for the compliment and the dress." It feels

strange to feel shy around him again, but the moment feels new and uncertain, like we're navigating uncharted waters.

"I'm just happy I finally get to see you in it," he replies, his voice full of warmth.

I can't help but let my emotions surface. "I've missed you," I admit, looking down at my water glass, trying to hold onto my composure.

"Me too," he whispers back, and the tension between us deepens. Desperate to keep things light, I change the subject.

"How's work?"

Ethan grins, the corners of his lips lifting. "Nothing too exciting. How was your week? I know you came back on Monday."

I tilt my head in surprise. "How do you know that?"

"Jason told me." The tops of his cheeks blush slightly in embarrassment.

His honesty makes me happy. "Don't worry, I asked about you too. He told me you were miserable. It actually helped." I confess, grinning wide enough to make my cheeks hurt.

"I was. More than I've ever been in my life." When he looks up, his eyes soften as they meet mine. There's a sadness in them that mirrors my own, but I am hopeful we can talk tonight.

I decide to break the somber mood. "Thank you for the roses. They made every drive to and from work a little sweeter." I admit, taking a sip of water, trying to cover my shyness. The atmosphere between us is so uncertain, so fragile.

"I wanted you to know I was thinking of you." Reaching across the table, he takes my hand. His touch is electric, and I feel my heart speed up. "I thought about you almost every minute of every day. I prayed you'd find happiness, even if it wasn't with me." His voice lowers, the pain unmistakable in his eyes. "But I still hope it's with me."

"Dinner first." I offer, trying to keep my own self from caving in. He gives me that familiar nod of his but keeps a firm hold of my hand, which I don't mind at all. I've missed this too.

The waiter returns with our wine and bread, and once our glasses are filled, Ethan raises his glass. "To the most beautiful dinner date I've ever had."

I smile and raise my glass in return. "I must agree, to the most beautiful date I've ever had, period."

He winks, and a warmth spreads through me as we toast, the tension easing.

We sit in silence for a moment, exchanging small glances and smiles. It's different now—not bad, just different. The pain and uncertainty hangs between us, but also something more. And I'm thankful when the waiter brings our salads, giving us something else to focus on.

"I would give anything to know what you're thinking right now," Ethan says tenderly, his voice uncertain.

"I was thinking about how nice this is, and how much I've missed your company. And Ethan, you don't have to give anything up. Just ask."

Our smiles mirror each other's as he responds, "I'm happy to hear that."

There's another brief silence before Ethan asks about my trip. We laugh as I recount my shopping adventures and how I had to buy a second suitcase to bring everything home. He tells me about his Thanksgiving with his mom, sisters, and family. He mentions how miserable he was, mostly because his mom and Isabell were so mad at him. I want to remind him that it was his fault, but I hold back. Tonight, I want to focus on the positive, on what we can build from here. Our conversation flows more easily, and it feels good to relax with him again.

When our dinner arrives, I decline another glass of wine and stick to water. Ethan follows suit.

"I don't want a repeat of Saturday night," I mutter.

He chuckles, a deep, genuine laugh. "Me either. I didn't know someone as small as you could hold so much." He visibly shudders, laughing as he remembers.

"Sorry about that," I say, staring down at my plate, but his laughter continues.

"I've been there before, trust me. Not fun. But I won't tease you anymore." He is clearly trying to stifle his laughter. His eyes sparkle with amusement, and before long, I'm laughing freely too.

This is what I wanted: just us, enjoying each other.

Our dinners are finished, and I feel ready to give my speech. I close my eyes for a moment to gather my thoughts, but Ethan interrupts with a question.

"Are you okay?" His concern is genuine, it's written all over his face.

"Yes, just enjoying this," I reply, opening my eyes to see his raised eyebrows.

"Dessert?" he asks.

"No, I'm stuffed. But feel free," I say, and he gives me that sexy grin. I know exactly what he means, and I shake my head with a smile, making him chuckle.

"Actually, I have some things to say now that dinner's over," I begin, and Ethan instantly looks uncomfortable. I reach over, taking his hand to reassure him. He looks down at our joined hands, then back up at me.

"It's different, you holding my hand for support," he says softly.

"Funny how that works," I tease, watching as his eyes close for a long blink. I can feel his nervousness, but I give his hand a gentle squeeze, feeling his thumb brush over mine. That small touch still feels amazing.

"I need to say some things, and I want you to listen first, ask questions second. This is important."

"I'm listening," he says, his other hand joining to hold mine. I'm not sure who needs the support more—him or me—but I'm ready.

"Alright, so here it is. Ethan, you turned my life upside down when you crashed into my world. Literally." I can see a glimmer of a smile on his lips, but I press on. "It wasn't just physical either. You wrapped yourself around my heart in just a matter of days, breaking down walls I didn't think anyone could. You made me rethink everything I had sworn off, and you made me feel safe. I started to feel things I swore I never wanted to feel again. It was amazing. It was almost perfect. Then... I saw how you kissed her."

He tries to speak, but I shake my head, signaling him to let me finish. He falls silent, his grip on my hand tightening.

"It tore me apart, Ethan. My heart shattered. I had always thought that maybe, one day, you'd tire of me, but I didn't think it would be so soon. I wasn't prepared for the soul-crushing heartache that came with it. I wanted to hate you, and I tried. I kept replaying that moment over and over, seeing you with that red lipstick on your face. It was all I could see when I thought of you."

I pause, watching as Ethan's eyes stay locked on mine, filled with pain and fear. He's squeezing my hand harder now.

"But then you told me you loved me, and I didn't believe you. I thought it was a trick to get me back. I mean, how could you love me already? But then... you came to rescue me again. You took care of me—again. I was so busy being angry that I didn't listen to what you were really saying. I only saw that after I was sick, you left me, and my heart broke all over again. I didn't understand how you could just leave."

Ethan's breathing becomes unsteady, and I see the conflict in his eyes. I continue, "What you don't know is that I ran after you that morning. I tried to catch you, but you were already gone. I missed the elevator by seconds, and I took it as a sign that you didn't want to fight for me. So, I let you go."

I pause again, feeling the weight of my words. His eyes are full of regret, a tear rolling down his cheek as he listens intently.

"But something you said stuck with me. It reminded me of something I once said to someone a long time ago. That's when I realized... I was the one not fighting. I was the one giving up, and I realized I had fallen in love with you too."

Ethan gasps softly, a tear escaping his other eye, and my throat tightens. "Ethan, it's going to take time for me to trust you again. But do you think, maybe... we could try this whole mess again? With me?"

Before I can blink, Ethan pulls me out of my chair and presses his lips to mine, kissing me with a passion that feels like it's been building up for weeks. It's a kiss filled with love, with need, with understanding, and I give it right back.

When he finally pulls away, his hands cradle my face, and his forehead rests against mine. "I love you, Miranda. And yes, in a heartbeat. I want nothing more than to be with you. Only you," he whispers, tears in his eyes as he smiles.

I glance over at the waiter, who has arrived with a dessert menu, and I stifle a laugh, asking him to bring the check over. It takes another moment for Ethan to let go of me, and I'm okay with that. I don't want to be far from him either.

Once we're seated again, he grabs my hand, bringing it to his lips to kiss each knuckle tenderly. "You... woman. I thought... I..." His voice falters, the emotions too much to contain.

"I know," I whisper.

Ethan's green eyes shimmer with tears, but there's something else in them now. A new look of hope, a look that tells me he understands. This is our moment.

The waiter returns with the check, but when Ethan tries to object, I stop him. "No. Part of our original deal, I pay."

I hand the waiter my card before Ethan can protest any further.

"So... now what?" Ethan asks, his voice thick with emotion.

"Now, we finish our date. Like a normal couple," I reply with a smile.

I watch as Ethan mouths the word "couple," almost as if he's testing it. His expression is soft, a mix of joy and disbelief.

"Yes, Ethan. A couple," I whisper, letting him know that I'm ready to take this journey with him, to rebuild the trust and to love him again.

We ride down in the elevator, hand in hand, and I notice Ethan has moved closer, pulling me gently against him. I don't mind; it feels natural. Like it's just supposed to be.

"Would you like to take a walk down the pier?" He asks, surprising me.

"I'd love to," I reply, leaning into him as he wraps his arm snugly around my waist.

"I've missed you so much," he whispers, resting his chin on top of my head.

"I missed you too. Just promise me you'll never do anything that stupid again," I speak softly, though there's an edge of seriousness in my voice.

"I promise. Never, ever again," he says, pressing a gentle kiss to my hair. I lean into him more as we exit the elevator, feeling his warmth against the cold night air.

We walk down the pier, hand in hand, with Ethan keeping me close by his side. The night air is brisk, but the warmth in my heart makes me barely notice the cold. Ethan's arm never leaves my waist, and it feels right to be here with him. I know it will take time to fully trust him again, but I feel confident in the decision I've made.

As we walk past a street performer playing guitar and singing, Ethan suddenly spins me around, pulling me into a spontaneous dance. His grin is infectious as he twirls me, and I laugh, feeling lighter than I have in a long time.

He surprises me further by softly singing along to the song, "Take me into your loving arms, kiss me under the light of a thousand stars." His voice is gentle, and the moment is so sweet that it takes my breath away.

As the song ends, Ethan dips me dramatically before pulling me back up, his lips hovering just inches from mine, waiting for permission. "I think I'm crazy in love with you," he whispers.

"I know I am," I whisper back, leaning in to close the gap and kiss him.

After the kiss, Ethan lets go of me just long enough to take out a few bills from his wallet and drop them into the performer's case. "Thanks, man!" the musician says with a smile. "Can I play you another one?"

"Please," I say, and he starts to play a new song, one I don't recognize, but it's beautiful.

Ethan pulls me close again, spinning me around as we dance under the stars. The cool night air swirls around us, but all I feel is the warmth of being with him. "I don't think I could be happier than I am right now," Ethan murmurs into my ear.

"I was thinking the same thing," I reply tenderly, resting my head against his chest as we sway to the music. Nothing else matters in this moment. It's just us, dancing together, wrapped in the music and the cool night.

When the song ends, Ethan tilts my face up to look at him, his eyes searching mine. He grins when he finds what he's looking for, then lifts me off my feet and spins me around, making me laugh with joy. As he sets me back down, he shakes the musician's hand and thanks him before we continue our walk down the pier, still holding hands.

"If this is what normal feels like, I think I want to do it every day," Ethan says, his smile never leaving his face.

"I agree," I reply with a laugh. "Except maybe when it's warmer out."

"Are you cold?" He pulls me closer and wraps his arms around me.

"A little," I admit.

"Let's get you home. Your nose is kind of pink," he teases, leaning down to press a warm kiss to the tip of my nose. He starts to let me go but pauses. "Could I drive you back?" he asks sweetly.

"I'd love that," I say, smiling up at him.

We walk to his car in a comfortable, quiet peacefulness. There's still a lot to work through, but this, right here, feels perfect. When we reach his car, he opens the door for me and gently tugs on my hand, making me look up at him.

"Miranda, thank you for giving me another chance." He kisses me gently, letting his lips lay on mine for a long moment. I don't mind, I've missed his kisses.

"I'm glad I did. Now take me home, I'm freezing," I laugh as he tucks me into the car and closes the door.

When we arrive at my apartment building, Ethan pulls into the parking garage and turns to me.

"Would it be okay if I walked you up?" he asks, taking this whole dating thing seriously, and I love it.

"I would expect nothing less," I reply.

We ride up in the elevator, and I lean against him as he wraps his arms around me, both of us exhaling at the same time. When we reach my door, Ethan takes both my hands and turns me to face him.

"I'm going to kiss you goodnight, then I'm going to go home. This night has been perfect, and I don't want to mess it up." He pulls me into a deep, tender kiss that makes tears sting my eyes.

When he finally pulls away, he stays close, our foreheads touching. "I love you, Miranda Michaels." His exhale is long and full of emotion.

"And I love you, Ethan Bradley," I reply, smiling as he brushes his lips over mine once more.

"Goodnight."

"Goodnight," I say, though I don't want him to go.

"Until tomorrow." He gives my hand a gentle squeeze before kissing my nose. He turns and walks back to the elevator, glancing back to wave before disappearing behind the closing doors.

I stand there for a moment, watching him go, then press my hand to my lips, which still tingle from his kiss.

Chapter 26

At 7 a.m., I wake up feeling the best I've felt in weeks. Rested. Happy. Content. It's early, but I wonder if Emma is awake. I send a quick text, and she replies right away. So, I call her, eager to share the news.

"Good morning," I say when she picks up.

"Whoa, you sound happy." Emma is still groggy like she just woke up.

"I am! I talked with Ethan last night and decided to give him a second chance."

"That's wonderful!" She exclaims, now fully awake.

"It is. Oh, Emma, we had the best night. We had dinner, walked the pier, danced, and he told me he loves me. And... I love him. It took me a week to figure it out, but I do. More than I've ever loved anyone."

I can feel my happiness spilling out as I recount every detail to her. It was magical and perfect.

"Oh, Rana, I'm so happy for you. Ethan's a great guy, and I'm glad you two worked things out."

"Me too. It's weird, but I think I want him to stick around for a while. Maybe for a long while."

"I don't think I've ever heard you this happy."

"I don't think I've ever been this happy. It's different now, Em. It feels right. I mean, it felt right before, but now... I don't know. Maybe the fear of losing him made me realize I didn't want to."

"I hope you never do."

"I'll fight to the death for him now, no questions asked." I laugh at the idea, but I know I would.

We talk about the things we said, how he kissed me goodnight and left because he didn't want to mess anything up. I even tell her about him singing to me. I want it to be like this every day. After talking her ear off, we say our good-byes, and I lie in bed, smiling at the ceiling.

A text pulls me out of my thoughts, and I see it's from Ethan.

Good morning, beautiful.

It is a very good morning.

How did you sleep?

Better than I have in a long time. How about you?

Wonderful. My bed just feels really big and lonely.

Is that an invitation?

A request.

Noted.

Breakfast?

Are you asking me to breakfast?

Inviting.

I accept. When?

Open the front door.

I leap out of bed in just my cami and shorts, run to the front door, and pull it open. There stands Ethan, looking amazing in jeans and a sweater, holding a bag that smells incredible and a bouquet of pink roses. My smile stretches from ear to ear.

"Come in, please," Moving out of the way, I invite him inside. He sets the bag on the counter and hands me the flowers.

"They're beautiful, thank you." I barely have the words out before he pulls me into a quick kiss.

"You're breathtakingly beautiful this morning," he growls, and I giggle.

"Flattery will get you everywhere," I tease, pulling away to put the flowers in water.

"Let's eat, then I want to take you somewhere." He goes about setting out breakfast sandwiches and little round hash browns which look delicious. Stealing one as I pass, I admit that they are.

"Very yummy," I inform him as I grab plates and napkins. "OJ, milk, or coffee?"

"OJ and coffee," he replies, winking, making my heart race. I can't stop smiling.

"You seem to be suffering from the same aliment I am." I tease as I point to my face before pouring the drinks.

"And what would that be?" He asks, raising an eyebrow.

"You can't wipe that silly grin off your face," I reply, mirroring his smile.

He laughs deeply. "I think it has something to do with you." He reaches out and turns his chair to face me.

"Me? And why would that be?" I ask, feigning surprise.

"Well..." He pulls me over, rubbing our noses together. "You make me happy. Happier than I ever imagined I could be. You make my face do this silly thing." He points to his grin.

"I feel the same way," I whisper as his lips find mine.

The kiss deepens, and I melt into his embrace, my safe place. My hands cradle his face as his grip tightens around my hips. My fingers move into his hair as he slides his hands up my back, pulling me closer to his warmth.

"Hmmm, you taste like orange juice," he growls, pulling away.

"You need to eat first. Then go put on a pair of jeans, layers under a sweater, something warm. No heels, but boots are fine," he adds, kissing my nose and giving me a playful smack to the backside as I sit down to eat.

"Where are we going?" I'm curious.

"Surprise."

"I need to know how dressed up to get," I say, nudging him playfully.

"You're perfect just the way you are." He shoots me a sexy grin and I shiver with anticipation of whatever he has planned.

"We're going to my mom's. I want to take you on a tour of the grounds, and I thought maybe we could take a ride."

"A ride?" I raise an eyebrow.

"On horses," he clarifies, and my smile widens.

"On real horses? I'd love that!" I clap my hands and head off to get ready without a second thought.

Ethan pulls the car around to the back of the house, and I'm speechless. The view is stunning, with endless green fields stretching out before us. There's a large garage attached to the house on the left and stables down on the right. The house itself looks even grander from this angle.

I'm so lost in the beauty of it all that I don't notice Ethan getting out and coming around to open my door. I jump when he does.

"Extra jumpy this morning?" He's teasing me.

"This place is huge! I had no idea there was so much space back here," I say, more to myself than to him.

He pulls me out of the car and into his arms, and we stand there for a moment, just taking in the scenery.

"You know, my mother's probably wondering why we haven't come inside yet. Bet you a dollar, she's at the door waiting," Ethan says with a grin.

"I bet you four more that you're wrong," I answer with a giggle.

"Never bet against a woman, especially a smart one. You'll always lose," Eloise says, appearing behind us.

Ethan chuckles and turns to her. "Hi, Mom."

"Hello to both of you." Her smile is bright and happy.

"I saw her on the porch a minute ago and then heard the footsteps," I add, giving Ethan a playful nudge.

"Good morning, Eloise," I say, smiling. I'm surprised when she pulls me into a warm hug. She's growing on me quickly.

"Well, I'll let you two explore. Enjoy the ride. Thankfully it is going to be warmer today, perfect for a tour." She pats Ethan's arm before heading back inside.

After a quick lesson, we set off on horseback, exploring the sprawling property. It's even larger than I thought, with winding trails and fields that stretch as far as the eye can see. It feels like we've left the city behind and entered a peaceful countryside. I didn't realize life could feel this good.

When we return, Ethan helps me off the horse. "What did you think?" He questions curiously.

"I think I'll use my favorite word—mind-blowing," I laugh.

He laughs along with me. "I'd have to agree. Let's head inside and warm up."

He gives me a tour of the house, which is enormous. I lose count of the bedrooms and bathrooms, and the indoor pool in the basement is a surprise. By the time we return to the sitting room to join Eloise, my mind is spinning from everything I've seen.

"Your home is incredible. Everything is so beautiful. And the land, wow, I didn't know anything this perfect could be so close to the city. I love it." I feel Ethan wrap his arm around my waist as we sit together.

"I'm so glad you like it. The kids don't appreciate it as much anymore," Eloise says, looking pointedly at Ethan, though I can tell she's teasing.

"Mom, I grew up here. It's not that I don't appreciate it, it's just home. I've seen it a million times." Ethan sounds like a little kid defending himself.

"It's perfect if you ask me," I chime in, grinning.

Eloise's smile grows bigger. "Ethan, you look so happy, and it's wonderful to see." I notice Ethan sit up a little taller at his mother's comment.

"I am happy. All thanks to Miranda," he says, winking at me, and now it's my turn to feel shy. Ethan gets up to grab us all drinks, leaving me alone with Eloise.

"Miranda," Eloise says, lowering her voice. "When Ethan told me what happened, I was so upset with him. I told him you were a good one and not to mess it up, but of course, he managed to do that anyway. That boy!" She shakes her head affectionately. "He was a miserable mess these past two weeks. I've never seen him so down. Do you know he actually moped around. When he called me last night and told me you'd taken him back, I cannot tell you how relieved I was."

Eloise glances toward the kitchen and then back at me. *Oh great,* I think, *here comes another lecture.*

"Dear, I'll be honest. At first, I worried you might be interested in him for reasons other than love. But I was wrong, and for that, I am sorry. I can see how happy you make him. You've put the sparkle back in his eyes," she says warmly. "I just wanted you to know that." She straightens up just as Ethan returns to the room with the drinks.

"Know what?" he asks, looking suspicious.

"Nothing, dear," Eloise says with a huge smile which causes him to laugh.

"Girl talk," I say with a wink, and Eloise actually giggles. It's a sound I never expected from such a proper lady.

"Then I don't want to know," Ethan replies, handing me a glass. We settle back onto the sofa, and he holds my hand while I lean into him, contently.

Eloise announces that lunch is ready and sends Ethan to fetch Isabell, giving me a chance to respond to her earlier comment. "Just so you know, I don't want his money. I never did. He's just Ethan to me. My boyfriend, with the incredibly bright green eyes, who makes me laugh, smile, and occasionally want to punch him in the nose. That's all I care about. I have no desire for money. I'm a simple girl, and I'm happy just as I am."

Eloise laughs freely. "Miranda, I think I like you even more now. You don't sugarcoat anything, do you?"

"No, ma'am," I answer with confidence.

"Good," she replies, still chuckling. "Keep that son of mine in line. He's too much like his father sometimes. Some days, I want to smack the Bradley right out of him, so I understand how you feel." She laughs heartily and motions for me to sit.

We enjoy a light lunch of chicken salad sandwiches, fresh greens, and tangy lemon-shaved ice for dessert. Eloise shares more about the Bradley Estate, and Ethan fills in what it was like growing up here. By the time we're done, I'm stuffed, and my face hurts from laughing at the banter between Ethan and Isabell.

I learn that Ethan is eight years older than Isabell, making her just three years younger than me, which explains why we get along so well. Isabell is majoring in art and hopes to work with famous paintings or become an art professor at a university. Eloise rolls her eyes at this but doesn't say anything, so I sense it's a bit of a sore subject. Ethan, on the other hand, was a bookworm in college and graduated at the top of his class, which doesn't surprise me at all. The stories flow easily as the conversation goes on.

Eventually, Ethan stands and offers his hand to me. "I think I need to get my girlfriend out of here before you ladies completely ruin her opinion of me with all these stories."

"Maybe I'm not ready to leave," I tease, not wanting the fun to end.

"We have somewhere else to go today." And with the sparkle in his eyes, I can't wait to see what it is.

"We do?" I ask, surprised.

"We do," he confirms, pulling me from my seat with a playful grin.

"Eloise, today was amazing. Thank you so much for having us over for lunch, the stories, and of course, the horseback riding." She pulls me into a warm hug.

"Miranda, you are welcome here anytime. I think a girls' tea and lunch is in order, and I'll tell you all the juicy stories," she says with a twinkle in her eye, making Ethan groan beside me.

"You tell me when, and I'll be here." I am very excited about the invitation and Eloise laughs, clearly enjoying herself.

"I think we need to have a talk about appropriateness, Mother," Ethan grumbles, though I can tell he's teasing.

We say our goodbyes, and Eloise promises to call me next week. I wave again before getting into the car, and as soon as Ethan sits down, I can't contain my excitement.

"Today was incredible! I love your mom. I love your sister. I love the horses," I blurt out. "And... I love you," I add softly.

"I am so happy to hear that." When he looks at me, I can see how much he loves me too.

"I don't think today could get any better." Letting out a deep exhale, I relax into the seat. I meant it, today was wonderful. One of the best days of my life. There is still a bit of uneasiness in my soul with what happened, but I think with time, we will heal.

Ethan drives us back into the city, but when we pass my place, I glance at him, curious. "Where are we going?" I ask dreamily as I watch the city lights flicker by.

"There's something I haven't wanted to do in years, but for some reason, I can't wait now." Excitement is bubbling in his voice, which only piques my interest more.

"I'm intrigued," I reply, turning in my seat to face him, but he refuses to tell me more.

After a while, he pulls into a parking lot full of Christmas trees. "I haven't had a tree in years," he admits. "I never wanted to celebrate Christmas at home, but now I do—with you. You mentioned to Mom earlier how much you love Christmas, so... here we are." His face beams with joy as he gets out of the car, and I don't wait, I jump out to meet him. My own heart swelling with joy at his sweet gesture.

We walk through the lot hand in hand, searching for the

perfect tree. It's normal and sweet. Something I have always loved to do, and now, I get to do it with him. And once we find the one, which is a tad big, Ethan arranges for delivery later that night and hurries me back to the car.

"It's freezing!" I laugh as I climb in.

He chuckles, rubbing his hands together. "You're right, it's gotten colder out. Now we need ornaments and decorations. Any ideas?" He looks to me for direction.

"Kris Kringle Haus! It's the best!" I exclaim, feeling like an overly excited kid. He laughs at me and then drives us to one of the most festive stores in the city. This is going to be so much fun!

We spend over two hours browsing and picking out ornaments, lights, and decorations. By the time we're done, we have two carts overflowing with everything needed to make his place feel like Christmas. As we head to the checkout though, I suddenly remember something else that is very important.

"Wait! We need one more thing!" I exclaim as I give him a quick kiss.

"Miranda, I have no idea where we're going to put all this, but okay. I'll wait in line," he says with a shake of his head.

I dart through the store, finding exactly what I was looking for, and when I return, Ethan raises an eyebrow.

"Did you find it?"

"I did," I say, hiding it behind my back.

He reaches out for it, but I shake my head. "Nope. I'm buying this. It's a surprise," I grin.

He chuckles, shaking his head, then turns to pay for the mountain of decorations. I nearly faint when I see the total, but he doesn't bat an eye. After I check out and ask the cashier to keep my surprise hidden, we push our carts out to the car.

It takes two tries to fit everything in, but we finally manage, and as we pull away, Ethan says, "I think we've got enough holiday cheer in this car to last the entire season."

I nod in agreement, clutching the small package and the nutcracker Ethan insisted we buy. "I'm calling him Harvey by the way," I announce proudly.

Ethan laughs. "Harvey it is."

When we arrive at his place, it takes three trips to get all the decorations upstairs. By the time we're done, we're both laughing like fools. We barely have time to collapse on the couch before the tree guys arrive to set up the tree, which causes another round of excitement. It is so big! But I love it, and the absolute look of joy on his face as he watches is incredible.

After only 20 minutes, the guys have moved and adjusted the tree ten times to get it just right. Finally, we all agree it's perfect, and then Ethan tips them well and sees them out. I adore that he appreciates their hard work lugging this beast up here. It does look fabulous in here, just like he thought.

As he returns to the couch, I look up at the beautiful tree. "It's perfect," I say with a contented sigh.

Ethan pulls me onto his lap. "No. Now it's perfect," he whispers, wrapping me in his arms. This is what I've missed the most.

I snuggle into him, feeling the warmth of the moment. We talk about dinner and how we'll decorate the tree, laughing and teasing each other. Everything feels just right.

~ 427 ~

Chapter 27

"Done!" Ethan calls out as he hangs the last ornament on the tree.

"Not quite," I reply, grinning mischievously. I head to the kitchen and grab the small box I've hidden, along with a sharpie. After writing our names and the date on the back of a beautiful ornament that reads *Our First Christmas*, I re-box it and bring it back to him.

"Here. For you," I announce before handing him the little box. He looks at me curiously before opening it.

"Take it out and turn it over," I encourage him. When he does, a huge smile spreads across his face.

"Does this mean you plan on sticking around for more than one?" His tone is playful but hopeful.

"I'm kinda hoping to," I admit softly.

"I love it." He kisses me gently, then walks over and hangs it right in the front of the tree.

"Now it's done," I declare. He turns back, lifts me off my feet, and swings me around, making me laugh.

We order Chinese for dinner and then cuddle on the couch, the only light coming from the twinkling tree.

"It's only December 2nd, and this is already the best Christmas I've had in my adult life," Ethan whispers as he strokes my hair.

"Just wait until there are presents under the tree," I tease.

"Presents?" He lifts his head, looking at me with surprise.

"Yes, presents! You know, gift-giving?" I giggle, shaking my head. "You haven't had a tree with presents under it as an adult, have you?" I ask, realizing it almost immediately by the way he is looking at me.

"No, I haven't. I've never had that need," he admits casually.

Need? How is that a need? You've never bought gifts for a girlfriend and put them under the tree?" I'm floored.

"I've had girlfriends, and yes, I've bought them gifts. But usually, it's jewelry, and I just have the store wrap them. I give them when we're together, not under a tree," he shrugs as if this is completely normal.

I stare at him in shock. That's not right. "Well, that's not how it's going to work this year."

"Women love expensive jewelry. No one has ever complained before." He brushes my comment off like it's just natural. Nope. Not with me. I decide right there he's going to get the full experience this year. Presents, traditions, the whole thing.

"I don't," I answer him, making him sit up straight.

"You don't want me to buy you jewelry?" He asks, confused.

"No. I want gifts from the heart. Things I like or need, but not expensive ones. That's not what Christmas is about.

My family's tradition is to give something you need, something you want, something to read, and something to wear. It's simple, but meaningful."

He smirks. "So... a car, a trip to Italy, a mortgage contract, and a diamond ring?" He teases, trying not to laugh.

"NO!" I slap him playfully, and he wraps his arms around me, pulling me into his lap. "I mean simple things. For me, it would be something like... a new keychain, a watch, a good book, and fuzzy socks!"

"That's very... simple," he says, studying me.

"It's what fits me," I reply, nudging him again.

"You really don't want expensive things, do you?" He intertwines our fingers and holds them up to look at them.

"Nope. I've told you before, I want love, happiness, and maybe a happily ever after." I don't know what we will be, but I'm kind of hopeful now.

"You believe in that now?" He's surprised.

"I might," I whisper, watching as his eyes soften and shine with emotion. He lifts my hand and kisses it.

"So, what about you? What do you need, want, read, and wear?" Moving off his lap to see him, I change the subject to something not related to my future self.

He tilts his head thoughtfully. "You, you, you, and you."

"Ethan!" I laugh. "You can't read or wear me."

"I can. I read your expressions all the time, and I love wearing you right here." He gestures to his waist, and I push him playfully.

"Try again. I can't be one of those four options!" I scold, still laughing.

"Hmm... Miranda, I don't want or need anything. I read all day long, and I have too many clothes already," he says honestly.

"This is going to be harder than I thought," I mutter, shaking my head.

"I'll be happy with whatever is under that tree if it comes from you. Hell, you could wrap an orange, and I'd love it," he says, pulling me back onto his lap.

"An orange, huh? I can afford a whole bag of those!" I joke, snuggling into him.

"I do love oranges." He nuzzles into my neck. "But I love you more."

"I was wondering something..." I begin, trailing off as his lips find my neck.

"Hmm?" he hums, his hand finding its way to my waist. "If I..."

He pulls me closer, his hands sliding under my sweater, and I lose my train of thought completely. "What were you wondering?" He teases as his lips brush against my skin.

"Oh yeah..." I moan as his hand trails down my back. "If I..."

He pulls me up, so I'm straddling him, his hands running over me. My sweater comes off, and his lips return to my neck, making me shudder. "What were you saying?" he murmurs.

I push him back onto the couch and pull off my t-shirt. "Take me to bed," I whisper, leaning down to kiss him hard, and I feel his smile against my lips.

"My bed?" he asks, his voice full of amusement.

"Yes," I reply with a laugh.

"I think I can manage that." He scoops me up in his arms, and I plant kisses along his neck as he carries me to his bedroom.

When we reach the bed, he drops me onto the mattress, making me screech with laughter. He quickly pulls off my socks and jeans, leaving me in just my bra and panties.

"Up and in," he says, his voice deep and smooth.

I crawl up the bed and under the covers, watching as he empties his pockets onto the side table. Then, with a smile, he pulls off his clothes and tosses them aside. Instead of joining me, though, Ethan walks across the room, lights the fireplace, and then strolls back over, looking ten kinds of sexy. I hold up the blanket for him to crawl in, and he immediately wraps me in his arms, pulling me close to his chest. He speaks softly, so softly that I almost miss it.

"I never thought I would be here with you again."

I don't have the words to respond, so I kiss his chest gently.

"Thank you," he whispers, lifting my chin so I'm looking into his eyes. "I don't know what I did to deserve you in the first place, or why I was shown mercy for a second time, but nothing—and I mean nothing—will ever break me from you again."

"Good," I say with a playful wink. "Because I need my man."

His eyes shine with emotion. "I think that's the sexiest thing you've ever said to me."

"Well, I mean it. You're mine. No one else gets you." I

feel my heart swell at my admission. He is my mine, and no one is getting him from me again.

"I am yours. Always. Forever. I won't mess this up again."

"You probably will," I tease, "but if you keep loving me and being honest, we'll work it out."

"Thank you, Miranda," he murmurs before leaning in close, his breath warm at my ear. "Now, I'm going to explore you, love you, and learn you all over again."

"I welcome it," I whisper, wrapping my arms around him. I kiss the tip of his nose, gazing into his eyes. He's mine—no doubt about it. And then all thoughts evaporate as he does just what he promised.

As we lay tangled together in the dark, his head resting against my chest, he speaks softly as his arm tightens around me. "Stay the night with me."

"Okay," I answer, feeling his grin against me.

"Stay with me tomorrow," he adds.

"Okay," I reply, smiling.

"Stay with me next week and the week after that."

"One week at a time," I tease, pretending to think it over. "I might not like you that long."

He looks up at me, his hair tousled, wearing that irresistible grin. "Deal." He answers as he starts kissing my chest and then pulls me up and out of bed with him. "Let's go shower, and then I'm going to make love to you again. And then maybe again. And if you're lucky, I might let you out of this bed tomorrow."

I laugh as he chases me across the room and into the shower, my heart full of love and laughter.

Chapter 28

Before I know it, the week has passed in a blur of craziness. Work has been super busy for both of us. I've been handling new cases, and Ethan has been working on a major book series deal with a popular author he refuses to tell me about. Most nights, we get home late, but we always make time to curl up together on the couch, checking in on each other and making sure everything is good. I haven't had a chance to shop for a car yet, but Ethan graciously hired Charlie for the entire month, and he's been driving me whenever I need him. Charlie and I have become good friends, and I've grown fond of our chats during the drives to and from work.

Evenings are spent either at my place to take care of Kasey or meeting Ethan at a restaurant for dinner before heading back to his place. Despite the stress of work, Ethan's been so loving and carefree, and our time together has been nothing short of amazing. Every night, I fall asleep next to him, and every morning, I wake up in his arms. It's been a beautiful dream, and I never want it to end.

Today is Friday, and I have a doctor's appointment where

I'm hoping for some progress on my arm. I send Ethan a quick text on the way, so he knows where I am. He wishes me luck and tells me he has an important meeting this afternoon, and to text him when I'm done. I lean back in the seat, thinking about how wonderful he is and how much things have changed in just a week. The trust I thought he had lost is slowly rebuilding, with his constant texts and calls telling me where he is and what he's doing. He's trying hard, and it means everything to me.

At my appointment, I'm shocked when the doctor says he's going to remove my cast today. I want to jump for joy as it feels so good to be free. My arm is stiff, and it looks and smells terrible, but at least I'm free! The nurse soaks my arm and cleans away some of the mess before giving me instructions for home care, and then I'm out the door.

Charlie picks me up, and we celebrate with coffee and chocolate—my treat. I ask him to take me Christmas shopping afterward. On the way, I call Mom and Emma to share the news about my newly liberated arm and send them pictures. They're both thrilled for me. Next, I text Ethan to tell him I'm done and plan to stop by my house for a bit, but I leave out the part about my arm, so I can surprise him later. He's always adorable when surprised.

After picking up the custom jersey I ordered with Ethan's last name on the back, I browse through a few shops before deciding on two frames for a couple of photos of us that I'll give him for his place. Shopping for him is hard, he's the guy who has everything. But I figure I still have time to find something special, so I don't stress about it too much.

Once home, I add the photos to the frames and wrap the gifts. I start some laundry and feed Kasey, who seems annoyed that I haven't been around as much. It's funny that I haven't been at my place a lot lately, and, aside from Kasey, I don't miss it as much as I thought I would.

As I'm folding towels, an idea pops into my head, and my heart races with excitement. I open the bottom drawer of my desk and pull out an old, dusty box. I haven't opened it in years. The pages inside are dog-eared, and the top sheet has yellowed with age. Smiling at the memories, I decide it's perfect. I wrap it up in pretty paper with a fancy bow and add it to my growing pile of gifts.

Ethan calls while I'm folding the last of the laundry, and I giggle when I hear the new ringtone I put on for him.

"Hey, beautiful," he greets me, his voice making my heart flutter.

"Hi," I reply, already smiling.

"Where are you?" His smooth voice is so sexy.

"I'm standing in my bedroom putting laundry away. It's so exciting," I joke.

"That does sound thrilling. I'm finishing up here and heading home. Do you want to meet for dinner, or should I pick you up?"

I glance at the clock and it's almost 6:30, still early enough for dinner out. "I've got some fresh clothes and a few things I want to bring to your place, so why don't you pick me up, and we can load everything in the car?"

"I'm glad you decided to stay a few more days," he says, his happiness clear in his voice.

"I still like you this week, so yes, I'm staying a little longer," I tease. "Although Kasey might be turning on me. His fuzzy butt's been snippy since I got home."

"Can't have that. Why don't I pick up some dinner and meet you there? We can eat and keep Kasey company."

"Sounds perfect. See you soon."

"Yes, you will."

Ethan brings in pizza, and as soon as he sets it down, I wrap my arms around his neck, pulling him close for a kiss. My fingers trace the sides of his face, feeling him fully for the first time with my right hand, now free of the cast. I wait, anticipating the moment when he realizes the difference.

He closes his eyes, lost in the kiss, and then they flash open in surprise. He pulls my arm up, tugging back my sleeve.

"Your cast is gone!" He exclaims in shock.

"It is! Surprise!" I giggle as he runs his fingers gently up and down my newly freed arm.

"It's still sensitive," I warn him.

"I bet," he murmurs, bringing my right hand to his lips. He kisses the back of it, then turns it over to kiss my palm and each finger. "I can't wait to use it again...later," I whisper with a grin.

"Me either," he growls playfully, pulling me into a big hug and spinning me around. His joy matches mine, and it feels unbelievable.

After he has thoroughly admired my arm and showered me with more kisses, we sit down and dig into the pizza, sharing stories about our days. As usual, some of the corporate talk goes right over my head, and I tell him so, but he just teases me more. I don't mind because he's adorable when he's in his element.

"You know," he begins, stroking Kasey who's purring contentedly in his lap, "you could bring him with you. He could stay as long as he wanted."

I pause, surprised. "You want me to bring my cat?"

"Yeah," he says, looking a little sheepish. "That way you wouldn't have to come by here every day. Or... ever. For Kasey's sake, I mean."

I glance up at him, and he's got that mischievous look on his face. Sweet but slightly guilty. Wait a minute... Is he asking what I think he's asking?

"Wait. Either you want my cat, or that was a very subtle attempt at asking me to move in with you." I raise an eyebrow, trying to gauge his response.

"What? No," he says, but I can see the corners of his mouth twitch as he tries not to smile. And he's blushing!

I study him, curious about what's going through his head, but before I can speak, he starts talking again.

"What would you say if I *was* asking? Hypothetically, of course," he adds, still avoiding my gaze as he pets Kasey.

"Hypothetically?" I tease, turning to face him. "Well, I'd have to weigh the pros and cons."

"Of course." His voice deepening, and his eyes shine with delight as he sneaks a glance at me. "What would those be, exactly?"

I tap my finger against my lips, pretending to think hard. "Pro: I'd be closer to work. Con: I wouldn't have my own space. Pro: I love waking up with you in that fabulous bed. Con: What would I do with all my stuff? Con: I don't know if I could afford half of your mortgage payment. Pro:…"

He interrupts with a serious tone, "Miranda?"

"Yes?" I answer, feeling a flutter of nerves.

He leans in, his breath warm against my ear. "Move in with me."

I pull back, eyes wide. "I thought this was hypothetical?" I say, my voice shaky.

"Please," he adds softly, his sincerity tugging at my heart.

I open my mouth to respond, but the weight of what he's asking leaves me speechless. This is a huge step. I'm practically living with him already, but still... it's fast. My mind races through all the logistics - my apartment, my furniture, everything I would need to figure out to make that happen.

Sensing my hesitation, he reaches up and gently places a finger against my lips. "There's no need for pros and cons," he says. "What's mine is yours. You bring whatever you want and make it our place. If you need your own space, we'll turn one of the extra bedrooms into whatever you want. I just want you there. We can work out the rest as we go."

He kisses my hands, his smile so warm and reassuring that I can't help but exhale some of my nervousness. I know he's already thought this through, and it's a big step. Am I even ready for that kind of commitment? He still has a past that I need to deal with internally. Before I can think any further though, he pulls me to his lips and brushes them with a soft kiss.

"You make it sound so easy," I breathe.

"It is easy," he says with a shrug, kissing my hands again. "You pack up your stuff, we bring it over, and we live together. That's it."

"What about my furniture? And my apartment? I still have four months left on my lease."

"We'll bring what you want, pay off the lease, and you're done."

"You really have this all figured out, don't you?" Exhaling hard, I feel the last of my doubts melting away.

"I do," he says, never breaking eye contact.

"Well... I guess it's worked out then," I say softly, my heart racing.

He pauses, a stunned look on his face. "Is that a yes?"

"Yes," I whisper, as his face lights up. He pulls me into his lap and kisses me deeply, holding me tightly. I can feel his heart pounding against mine, and in that moment, I know this is the right decision. I love him even more now than I did a minute ago.

"I love you," he murmurs against my lips.

"And I love you," I whisper back, knowing that this next step in our relationship is only the beginning of something even more beautiful.

Ethan holds me tighter as he sees the tears well up in my eyes. "Hey, hey... don't cry," he whispers, brushing my cheek softly with his thumb. "I didn't mean to upset you. I just want this to be our home. Yours and mine. Whatever you bring into it will make it perfect."

I nod, wiping my eyes quickly, feeling a little silly for getting emotional. "I know. It's just... overwhelming. I've never done this, and I don't want to... I don't know, change things with us too much, I guess."

He tilts my chin up so our eyes meet. "Miranda, you're not changing anything, you're just making it better. My house felt empty until you started being a part of it. Now it's starting to feel like home. I want you there. I want your things there. Your desk, your clothes, even your pink panties in the washer. All of it."

I can't help but laugh through the last of my tears. "You had to bring up the pink panties again, didn't you?"

He chuckles, pulling me into a hug. "Absolutely."

I rest my head on his chest, listening to the steady rhythm of his heartbeat, feeling the warmth of his arms around me. "I'll figure it out," I say, my voice soft. "I just need a little time."

"Take all the time you need," he says, kissing the top of my head. "We're not rushing anything. We've got forever."

Forever. The word sticks with me, settling in my heart. It feels like the right thing, like the future I've always wanted but was too afraid to dream about. Now here he is building it back. Maybe I can dream about it after all.

Ethan pulls back just enough to look down at me. "Let's get what you need tonight and go home. We can figure out all the packing and things later this week. Right now, I just want to take you home and put you in our bed and have a sweet sexy celebration." He pats my leg, so I move off his lap, before he pulls me up to stand with him.

Ethan takes the basket of fresh clothes and the bags I have packed, while I grab the cat carrier and the presents off my desk.

"What are those?" Ethan reaches over to touch the wrapped packages.

"Presents for my boyfriend." My wink makes his smile spread from ear to ear and he quietly follows me out of the apartment. For being a big shot CEO, it doesn't take much to make him act like a small child. I feel special getting to see this side of him. And that warms my soul.

After all the touching and promises in the car ride here, the minute we are in the door, he is reaching for me to make good on his promise of bending me over the counter and having his way with me. As much as I want him, I'm not giving in so easy. He needs to work for it. And with a split-second decision, I take off running for the living room in an attempt to get away.

In an instant, he's chasing after me, and laughter fills the room as we run through the house. In that moment, everything feels perfect—the love, the lightness, the joy of being together. It's a future I never expected but one I'm so thankful for.

And as Ethan catches up to me, spinning me around and kissing me deeply, I know that whatever happens next, we'll figure it out together.

Ethan holds me close, as we come down from the bliss, his fingers running circles on my back. "You know, it's moments like this that make me realize how lucky I am," he whispers. I pull back from his chest just enough to look up at him.

"Lucky?"

"Yes, lucky. Because I know you love me for me, not for

anything else. And that's rare. I wouldn't trade that for anything. I know moving in is a big step, and you are nervous, but I am 100% sure, I want you here."

His words calm my heart, making me feel a sense of belonging that's deeper than I ever expected. I take a deep breath and plant a kiss to his chest. "I do love you, Ethan. So much. And I want this too, all of it, but it's going to take me a little time to adjust."

"Take all the time you need," he reassures me, kissing my forehead. "But just so you know, my closet is your closet. My house is your house. And if your hair in the drains is the price I have to pay to have you here, I'm fine with that."

As I lay against him, his arm wrapped around me, I realize how much my life has changed in such a short time. But in the best possible way. I'm home—not just in this house, but with him.

And that's all I've ever wanted.

Chapter 29

Monday flies by, and I decide to head to the apartment and start packing after work. Ethan has planned to meet me there after his meetings, but I want to get started first. I bring a few paper boxes with me for my smaller things, although I'm still unsure of what to do with my furniture and a lot of my other stuff.

I start by packing up my dresser drawers into the boxes, figuring I can carry some of the hanging clothes over a few trips. As I'm going through my closet, making a donation pile, Ethan arrives and laughs at the state of my room.

"It looks like your closet threw up," he says with a grin.

I roll my eyes. "Stuff on the bed goes with me. The stuff in that pile gets donated, and those boxes are my dresser contents. I'm still working on the closet."

"Where can I help?" he asks as he takes off his coat.

"I think I'll just take a load and come back tomorrow. I can empty the boxes and reuse them."

I explain my plan, but he's having no part of it.

"Why don't I get some moving boxes delivered tomorrow? You can pack it up this week, and I'll have movers bring everything over next weekend. We can put your furniture and anything else you want to keep but don't need in storage. That way, you won't have to rush or lose any of your stuff."

He pulls me up from the bed and holds me close.

"I like that idea. That way, I don't have to get rid of anything in case I decide I don't like you anymore," I tease, laughing.

Ethan grins down at me. "I am going to keep you forever," he growls, and somehow, I know he's serious. And I'm not terrified of that.

"You aren't arguing," he adds.

"About?"

"Me keeping you forever."

"I'm deciding. Like I said, one day at a time."

"Week," he corrects.

"What?"

"You said one week at a time," he reminds me.

"You did convince me to move in, so I think you're a little ahead of the game. Maybe one month at a time."

"I'll take that. Now, what can I carry out of here so we can go get dinner? I'm starving. And I want to eat too," he adds with a suggestive tone that makes me groan.

"Easy, big guy, it's early."

"Never too early for you. Which reminds me, I have early morning meetings tomorrow, so be prepared to wake up at dawn."

"No."

"Oh, yes."

Nipping at my neck, he almost convinces me to give in, but I decide to walk away instead. I have work to do and he's not distracting me this time! And thankfully I am able to at least sort all my clothes before he drags me off to dinner.

We're in the middle of a conversation about the hockey game as we leave the restaurant, so I don't notice the man until it's too late. Suddenly, a camera is in my face, and Ethan immediately steps in front of me, blocking the man from getting any closer.

"Mr. Bradley, who's the new girl? Is it serious?" The camera flashes again, and I squint from the brightness. Where did he even come from?

"Step back and don't mess with her," Ethan growls, his voice hard and protective, but the guy just stands there, snapping more photos of us.

Ethan immediately tucks me behind him, and I touch his back, letting him know I'm okay. At least I think I am ok. I mean there is a man practically shoving a camera in our faces.

"I said step back," Ethan repeats, his anger rising as he shields me.

"Just trying to get a picture of your new lady friend," the man says, unfazed by the warning.

"I'm not new!" I manage to say, but Ethan's having none of it and holds me firmly behind him, making me feel small as he seems to grow two more feet taller, towering over the guy.

"I'm not joking. Go back to your car and leave her alone."

The guy snaps another photo, and immediately Ethan grabs his shirt, making me jump.

"Walk away," Ethan growls again, and this time, the man seems to listen. He raises his hands in surrender, and Ethan lets him go.

"Alright! I'm going," the man mutters as he turns and trots down the street, not looking back. But I'm still trying to process what just happened.

"Damn, sleazeballs," Ethan mutters as he turns back to me, checking to make sure I'm okay. But all I can do is smile at him.

"Are you okay?" he asks, concern lacing his voice.

"Perfect."

"Why are you grinning at me?"

"No reason."

"You always have a reason."

"Nope." He's so hot when he's fired up.

"Don't let them bother you. It's not often I have to deal with them face to face, but when I do…"

"Hey, I'm fine," I reassure him, laying my hand on his arm. I watch him close his eyes and exhale, trying to calm himself down.

"That's probably a con of being with me, if you're still keeping track. You're going to be in the spotlight sometimes, which means jackasses with cameras invading your space."

"I'm cool with it. Let's go get some ice cream and cool off, Hulk."

"Not funny."

"Super funny," I tease, taking his hand and leading him away from the restaurant entrance. A few people have their phones out, and I'm sure he would be loving that too, so I don't mention it.

We grab some ice cream from a nearby creamery and sit at the picnic tables outside.

"Are you sure you are okay?" he asks, watching me closely.

"I'm fine."

"It's okay if you're not."

"Ethan, even if I wasn't, you had me. I'm fine. Really."

I take another bite of my chocolate ice cream, and he watches me intently.

"I did have you. I will always have you."

"I know." I offer him a bite from my spoon, which he takes before pulling me across the table for a kiss.

"Are you okay?" I ask in return, teasing him with another bite of ice cream.

"I am," he says, smiling.

"Are you sure?" I could make it better if you need me too."

"Here?" His eyebrow quirks up in question, making me giggle.

"Not right here, but when we get home," I offer.

"Deal. Eat fast."

We laugh together, the earlier tension forgotten, as we enjoy the rest of our night of ice cream and laugher. Sans photographers.

Ethan was good on his word and had movers take out the furniture and clean the room at his place while we were at work. I was planning on coming home and crashing, but now I stand in this big open room, contemplating what I want to do with it.

Ethan passes the doorway and stops, stepping in to where I stand. "I thought we were going to bed?"

"I was. I mean, we are. I just... thank you for getting this cleaned out today." I grab his shirt, pulling him close for a brief kiss before letting him go.

"You're welcome. I told you I would."

"I know, but it was so fast."

"I have people for everything. Nothing is too fast for them. Or for you. I promised you a place, and now you have it. We can go shop for furniture whenever you're ready."

"I love you." The words still feel new like I'm testing them out, but when I say it, his entire face lights up.

"I love you too, Miranda, more than anything. And I mean it—anything you want. The world is yours."

"No," I correct him softly, "you're mine. The rest of the stuff is just material crap."

He grins. "Well, my crap would like to go to bed when you're done in here."

"I hope you aren't planning on sleeping," I tease with a playful smile.

"Look who's needy now," he counters.

"Always with you."

"I know the feeling. Leave this. We can work on it later. Right now, I just want you."

"Oh, I want you too."

Without hesitation, he pulls me out of the room, and I laugh all the way down the hall as he pulls off my clothes, leaving them in a trail down to the bedroom. And he doesn't ever disappoint in that department!

"I have a question," I ask, tracing circles through the hair on his stomach.

"No, I'm going to sleep. You've had enough." His deep chuckle vibrates under my face where it rests on his chest.

"Haha, seriously. I have a question."

"Alright, what is your question?" He props himself up slightly, resting his arm behind his head so he can look at me.

"Have you ever lived with a girl before?"

"No."

"Ever?"

"No, I've had... wait, this sounds like a loaded question. Are you going to use my answer against me later?"

"Stop," I nudge him, trying to stay serious. "I'm being honest. I want to know, and I won't hold it against you."

He lets a small smile play at the corners of his mouth before pulling me up beside him so I'm face to face with him.

"Right after college, I had a girl stay with me for a few months, but she never officially moved in. She was one of the few women I ever cared deeply for."

"Did you love her?"

"I thought I did. I wanted her to move in, but she had other plans."

"She broke your heart, didn't she?" I ask softly.

"No... well, at the time, it felt like she did, but she wasn't the one who really broke me."

"Oh? I knew there was one," I tease gently, trying to read his expression.

"Two," he corrects, surprising me.

"Two?" I shift, turning my body fully toward him, my head on the pillow to wait for his explanation.

"Yes, two."

"And?"

"The first one made me chase her until I was completely head over heels. Then she left me for my best friend. I never thought I'd love anyone like that again. I didn't want to. Like you, I avoided serious relationships, swearing I'd never give anyone that part of me again."

"And the second?" I ask, hoping he'll continue, and to my surprise, he does.

"Oh, the second," he says softly. "She's a story all her own. She stole my heart before I even realized what was happening. I never stood a chance. One look from her, and I was done for. I knew, from the moment I held her hand, she was going to destroy me."

"Did she?"

"Yep. Completely." His finger traces a slow pattern on my chest, right over my heart.

"Did you love her?"

"More than life itself," he answers, his gaze locking with mine.

"She made me feel things I didn't even know were possible. The world was brighter with her in it. I wanted to be with her every second, just to see her smile. She made my heart feel whole. I didn't know life could be that perfect, just by having her in it. Her laugh made everything right. And every time I look in her eyes, I know I never want to let her go again."

His thumb brushes over my cheek, and suddenly, I realize he's not talking about someone else. He's talking about me.

"How did she break you?" I whisper, even though I already know the answer.

"She didn't," he says, his voice soft. "I did. I screwed up. She left me, and I shattered into a thousand tiny pieces. I thought my life would end with that broken heart."

"But you recovered," I say gently, my heart full.

"Only because she came back and loved me," he says, holding my gaze.

"She did?"

"She did, and I hope she always will."

"She will," I whisper, my voice catching in my throat.

"I hope she stays forever," he adds quietly, his forehead pressing lightly against mine.

"She might want to," I whisper back.

"That would make me the happiest man alive."

"Me too," I say softly.

"Now that you know all my secrets," he murmurs, his lips brushing mine gently, "let's go to bed so I can dream about you all night."

"You don't have to dream about me," I say, smiling. "I'm right here."

His arms tighten around me as he whispers, "I know. And I'll forever be grateful that you are."

"Goodnight, beautiful," he whispers, his voice filled with warmth.

"Goodnight," I reply, planting a soft kiss on his chest before drifting off into a peaceful sleep.

Chapter 30

I wake to the smell of bacon and an empty bed. The sheets are still warm, so he hasn't been gone long. Smiling, I slip out of bed, find his button-down on the floor, and pull it on. It smells like him as I wrap it around me. I have no idea how this all happened, but no matter the outcome, I'm happy. Truly and completely happy.

Walking down the hallway, I laugh at the trail of clothes we left behind. I hope we never have surprise company—just the thought makes me giggle. Which also makes me wonder how many close friends he has who would just drop by. I'll have to ask him about that.

As I enter the kitchen, I see Ethan cooking, with Kasey perched on the counter, watching him intently. The cat knows better, but clearly, Ethan doesn't mind because he's talking to him like he's a child. It's so adorable I want to squeal. Kasey's morning meow gives me away as I try to sneak in. Ethan smiles but doesn't turn around, so I slide up behind him and wrap my arms around his chest.

"Good morning," I say, planting a few kisses on his back.

"Good morning," he responds, one arm reaching back to pat my side. Then he pauses, turns around, and smirks. "You enjoy wearing my clothes?"

"I do. Is there a problem?"

"Not in the least," he says, leaning over to peer down at my legs. "Yes, I have panties on," I answer his unspoken question.

"We need to make a rule against that."

"Well, you could have torn them off me this morning."

"You were sleeping too soundly. Besides, I want..." He stops mid-sentence, staring at me for a moment before shaking his head and turning back to the skillet of bacon.

"You want what? You can't start a sentence like that and leave me hanging." I swipe a piece of bacon, then hop up on the counter next to Kasey, who gets a head rub from me. Grabbing the bowl of eggs, I start whisking them as Ethan watches me, clearly lost in thought.

"I really enjoyed our talk last night," he says quietly, focusing on the bacon again.

"Me too. I like learning things about you."

"I did too, but I mean... I... wow." He looks at Kasey and shakes his head, clearly struggling to find the right words. It's endearing and, honestly, a little sexy—he's never like this.

"Spill it, Bradley," I say, turning his face to me.

"I can't."

"Why not?"

"I'm... you... Jesus, Miranda." He huffs, looking flustered.

"Jesus, me? What did I do?"

"Everything. I'm like a teenage boy with you."

"And? Is that bad?"

"No, it's not bad, but I'm finding myself..."

"Speechless?" I tease, enjoying this vulnerable side of him.

"That too." He laughs softly, then looks away.

"Okay, seriously, what's going on with you this morning? Are you okay?"

"Yes. That's the problem. I am so okay. It's kind of... sickening."

"I'm lost."

"You. You're...perfect, and I'm freaking out a little this morning."

"Okay, let me take over the bacon, and you talk to me."

"No. I'm making you breakfast, so sit and be... perfect." He waves the spatula at me, clearly feeling a little unbalanced this morning.

"First, I'm not perfect. Second, why are you freaking out? What happened between last night and now?"

"Nothing. I mean, everything. I just... why is this so hard?" He takes a deep breath, turning back to face me with a determined look on his face. This should be good.

"Last night, I told you I'd love you forever, and I meant that."

"I know. So did I."

"And I said a lot of other things that I wasn't ready to say."

"Like?"

"Like... I don't really want to discuss it again."

"Ethan, we've already discussed it once."

"Yeah, but I told you I didn't want you to ever leave."

"Do you want me to leave?"

"NO! God, no. Please, never leave me again." He sets down the spatula and steps between my legs, taking my hands in his.

"I want to be with you. I want every morning and every night with you, and that scares the crap out of me. I never thought...I just...damnit. Miranda, I love you more than my own life, and that has never happened before. I don't know why I can't say everything that's in my heart, but trust me, I meant what I said. I never want you to go anywhere. I want you here, with me... kind of forever."

"Kind of?"

"Yes. Kind of." He's so serious, so intense.

"Well, let's take it one step at a time. But I kind of want you that way too." His visible relief warms me, and I pull him into a long, deep kiss before rubbing our noses together.

"We have all the time in the world to talk about things. Right now, your bacon is burning."

"Don't care."

"I do. I'm hungry."

"Oh, then let me serve you, my queen."

"That's more like it." We share another kiss, laughing off the conversation, but his words stick with me. I'm not sure I'm ready to go down that road yet, but I know one thing—I'm happy, and for now, that's enough.

After breakfast, I call my mom and Emma to let them know that my permanent residence is officially moving to Ethan's. Emma is ecstatic, already making plans to come see the place. Mom, on the other hand, is a little more hesitant, worrying that we're moving too fast. But after I assure her that I'm happy and tell her how much I love Ethan, she eases up, saying she just wants what's best for me. She also makes sure that we're still coming home for Christmas, which I haven't even discussed with Ethan yet. I promise to call her later in the week after figuring out how his family handles the holidays.

Ethan and I spend the day shopping for a big comfy chair and a small table for my new office. They'll be delivered next week, which makes me excited to finally make the space feel like my own.

After, we head home to get ready for a dinner meeting with some of his clients.

"Damn." Ethan pauses mid-tie as I step out of the bathroom. His eyes roam over me appreciatively.

"I'm not sure if…"

"Oh, I'm sure. Don't even think about taking it off. Wow." He motions for me to spin, and though I'm a little self-conscious about the dress's low back and neckline, I twirl for him.

"I'm 100% sure," he says, pulling me toward him before I can argue.

"We don't have time," I protest as he wraps me in his arms.

"I know, but you look incredible."

"Thank you and thank you for the dress. But you really need to stop buying me things."

"I won't. Now, get your shoes, and let's get out of here."

He playfully taps my backside, returning to finish tying his tie.

"Well, for the record, you look good enough to eat yourself. I might have to fight to keep my hands off you tonight," I tease, buckling my shoes.

"Never fight that." He chuckles, taking my arm to help me up, and we leave arm in arm.

The dinner meeting is with three executives from Ethan's company and two young authors whose books are about to be published. One of the authors, Julie, is a delight, and we hit it off immediately. We end up chatting through most of the dinner, sharing laughs about her book series, and avoiding the dry business talk.

What isn't so enjoyable is the attention from Adam, one of Ethan's senior editors. He's polite enough, but I notice his eyes lingering on me far too often, making me regret my choice of outfit. Ethan, ever in tune with me, senses my discomfort and gently squeezes my hand as he finishes his conversation.

"Everything alright?" he asks softly.

"Yes," I lie.

"Liar," he whispers.

"Later." My eyes briefly flick to Adam, and I can tell he knows exactly what's going on. "I'm good," I say quietly, assuring him I am in fact ok, although I do shift in my seat.

"Ignore him," Ethan murmurs near my ear, his breath sending a flutter over my cheek.

"I'm trying," I whisper, my eyes dropping to our hands.

"Do I need to pull out his eyes? Because I will." His voice is a low growl, making me giggle despite myself.

"Stop," I warn, shaking my head, and he chuckles.

"So, Miranda, how did you two meet?" Adam suddenly chimes in, his eyes still fixed on me as he sips his drink.

"I was in a car accident, and Ethan came to my rescue." I keep my answer simple, not really wanting to engage with him.

"Oh, that's right. You were the one who kept him out of the office for two weeks." Adam chuckles, but the tone isn't friendly.

"She didn't keep me. I stayed because I didn't want to leave her side," Ethan replies, his voice cool but firm.

"Aww, that's so sweet," Julie adds with a smile.

"It was. He stayed with me for days while I was unconscious." I would tell her the entire story if we were somewhere else. I exchange a look with Ethan that sends warmth rushing to my cheeks.

"For the record, we'd known each other before that," Ethan clarifies, lifting my hand to his lips. For a moment, I forget we're in a room full of people. It's moments like this that make me fall deeper in love with him. He's so incredible.

"And weren't you the one who caused that scene in the lobby with the lawyer?" Adam's tone turns sharp. I don't know what his problem is, but I flinch, and Ethan's grip tightens on my hand.

"Adam, that's enough," Ethan warns, his voice low.

"I was just asking. I mean, this girl came out of nowhere, and now she's here at our meeting. Just wondering who she is. We barely know her." Adam's gaze is pointed and invasive as he waits for my answer.

"What would you like to know?" I shoot back before Ethan can respond, startling both Adam and Ethan. "My bra size is 36C, since your eyes haven't left them all night," I snap.

"Miranda," Ethan warns softly, but I ignore him.

"No, really. If he wants to know, let's clear the air. What else, Adam? Want to know my favorite color or where I work?" My tone is sharp, and I realize I'm standing up, with everyone's eyes on me.

"Sit down," Ethan says firmly, his tone controlled but clearly angry.

"I'm sorry," I mutter, sitting back down, and Adam laughs smugly.

"Adam, I invited her here, and you will show her respect," Ethan says calmly, though his anger simmers just beneath the surface.

"I apologize," Adam responds, raising his glass in mock sincerity, though he's anything but sorry.

I drain my wine in response, and when Ethan's hand slides onto my leg, I shift away, still irritated.

After dinner, we say our goodbyes, and I give warm hugs to Julie and the other guests. When it comes to Adam, I completely ignore him, walking right past his outstretched hand.

"Miranda," he calls, offering his hand.

"No, thank you," I reply curtly, making my way toward the door. Ethan exchanges a few words with Adam and quickly catches up to me. Smart enough not to say a word until we're out of the restaurant, he lets me simmer in silence while we wait for the valet to bring his car.

Ethan's hand rests on my back, right above my waist, and under normal circumstances, I'd welcome his warmth. But right now, the cold from the evening air isn't the only thing freezing me out.

"Are you still mad at me?" he asks softly.

"Yes."

"I just wanted to keep it professional," he explains.

"You did."

"I plan to talk with him on Monday."

"Great. Happy to hear that. In the meantime, maybe you should let me be mad." I step away from him, opening my own door before getting in and slamming it shut.

Ethan follows suit, getting into the car without saying a word, which only fuels my frustration. The silence between us thickens as he pulls away from the curb. After just eight minutes of stewing, I've had enough.

"So, you were just fine with him staring at my chest all night?" I snap.

"No," he answers, his jaw tight.

"Then you could've said something."

"I did."

"No, you didn't."

"I told him to be respectful. He understood."

"That was idiotic."

"What did you want me to do? Punch him in the mouth?"

"Yes."

"Would that make you happy?" he asks, his tone hardening.

"Yes!" I bark back.

Before I can even process what's happening, Ethan whips the car into a U-turn right in the middle of the road and races back toward the restaurant.

"What are you doing?" I yell, gripping the edge of my seat.

"Doing as you wish," he replies calmly.

"ETHAN! You're going to wreck!"

"I can handle it," he says, sliding to a stop outside the restaurant. He goes to get out of the car, but I grab his arm.

"Are you crazy?" Now, I can't help but laugh at the absurdity of it all.

"Yes, I am. Now, if you'll excuse me, I have a man to punch for staring at my woman." He pulls away, but I scramble out of the car, running in heels to get in front of him.

"Ethan, stop."

"No, I'm here to do as you wish," he answers with a wild grin.

My laugh is uncontrollable as I try to hold him back. "I'm sorry! I take it back."

"Oh, no takebacks," he laughs, holding me up as I wobble in my heels.

"You're nuts."

"I am." He grins, not denying it.

"Get back in the car," I say, leaning into him and kissing his chest. I tug his hand to turn him back toward the car.

"I didn't finish my mission," he teases.

"It's fine, really."

"You sure? He's still in there."

"No! In the car," I insist, barely holding back my laughter.

"Okay." He starts to get in but then notices a group of people standing on the curb, eyeing the scene.

"Are you looking at my girl?" he yells at them, and they scatter like scared pigeons.

I burst into laughter. "Ethan, in the car!" I command, pointing to the vehicle.

Finally, he listens, getting back in with a satisfied grin.

"Next time, he's all mine," he says as we pull away.

"No, next time I'm punching him myself," I say with a smirk.

His grin widens as he glances over at me. "Are you still mad at me?"

"Maybe. You frustrate me. And then you make me laugh, and I can't be mad at you."

"I thought this was settled?"

"It was, but then I started thinking."

"Oh, and can I ask what the reason is now?" I can hear the humor in his voice, which only makes me want to punch him too.

"I'm a woman, I hold onto things."

"I can see that. Tell me what it is so I can fix it."

"I know what his problem was, I know why he was asking me all those questions about where I came from."

"Ok, fill me in. I'm lost."

"I've seen the pictures of your other girlfriends. They were flashy and let everything hang out on display. I'm not like that."

"I like how you are."

"I know, but see, he only sees me as some poor girl that found herself a sugar daddy."

"For fuck's sake, do not say sugar daddy."

"I don't want your money, Ethan. They all think I do. He thinks I am just another one of your, what was the word? Twits. That's why he didn't care if anyone knew he was staring at me. He thinks I'm just another flavor of the month." My words sink in as his head hangs in understanding.

"Miranda, I am going to get out of this car, we are going to go upstairs, and I am going to strip you out of that dress. I don't care what anyone else thinks. I love you. I want you here with me. At meetings, at events, at home, wherever I am. I asked you to move in with me, that counts for something. Right?" His eyes are focused on mine, and he's right. It doesn't matter.

"You are right. I'm sorry. I overreacted. I just don't like being looked at that way. I'm not a gold digger."

"I will never let it happen again. However, people are going to look when you look this amazing in this dress. I've been looking down it all night." He tugs the front of my coat so that I lean over to him.

"Never let anyone make you feel less than who you are."

"I'm trying," I grumble.

"Try harder. And so we are clear, I don't want any other flavors but yours. They can stare all they like, but you are always coming home with me. Now, if you are finished, who's screaming tonight?" He sweeps me up into his arms and walks me into the building, before pressing the button.

Once inside, he sets me down but pins me against the wall as he unbuttons my coat. "You are my flavor. My girl. Mine. They can speculate all they want, but I know where you belong."

"Where is that?" My breath is hitched, and my heart is racing.

"Around me." He lifts me, settles me at his waist, and kisses me deeply. That's all I need to know. And I let him take me inside, where I do scream out his name. Multiple times.

Chapter 31

The next morning, we meet the movers at my apartment to clean out my things. I'm going to miss this place, but I don't regret my decision at all. It's strange to think this chapter of my life is over, but I'm excited about the new one that's just beginning.

"You seem sad," Ethan says, coming to stand beside me at the windows.

"Not really. I mean, maybe a little. This was my first real place, and I built myself up from nothing here."

"You never have to worry about anything again, Miranda. I'll make sure of that."

"Speaking of which," I say, turning to him, "we never discussed the issue of bills. Before you argue, I know I won't be able to afford half of your apartment, but I can handle the groceries and other expenses."

"No."

"No?" I arch my brow. "Yes. I'm going to help."

"You help enough just by being there, cooking, and doing all the little things I need."

"Ethan," I protest.

"Miranda. I have more than enough."

"That doesn't matter."

"Fine, we'll discuss it over dinner tonight. Grab the bag off the counter, and we'll follow the movers home."

"I'm not letting this go."

"I don't expect you to," he says with a smile, giving me a quick kiss before we leave. Home. It feels strange to consider somewhere else home. But I'm beginning to feel like anywhere he's at, I will be happy.

After sorting boxes into rooms, I'm standing in the hallway staring at Nicole's text, and the pending link on my phone. I could tell by just the header to the article, I wasn't going to like it.

Ethan Bradley and Girlfriend Miranda Michaels Have a Heated Argument in Downtown Chicago. Of course, there are photos showing what looks like me yelling at Ethan outside the restaurant last night. Damnit. And they know my name now.

"What is it?" Ethan's voice comes from down the hall as he walks in barefoot.

"Nothing," I answer, but the irritation is clear in my voice.

"Not nothing," he replies, looking over the half-open boxes in my office. "What happened? Did something break?"

"No." Grumbling, I toss him my phone. He glances at the screen, then shrugs.

"We weren't fighting. However, you were mad at me in that first one." His finger taps the screen as he shows me the photo he's referring to.

"Ethan…"

"Miranda, this is part of my life. I don't let it bother me, and neither should you."

"My family and friends have seen this," I reply, exasperated.

He pauses at my comment, then takes my hand, leading me to the couch. "Sit," he says, disappearing into the kitchen and returning with two glasses of wine. "Drink."

"Ethan, wine isn't going to help. People are going to think I'm a horrible person."

"No, they'll think I'm the horrible person." He's so calm. How can he be calm!

"I don't want them to think that either."

He takes a long sip of wine and leans back. "I deal with this stuff weekly. You'll get used to it. It doesn't last long before they find someone else to focus on."

As I take a sip of wine, Ethan hands me his phone. There's another picture of us, this time with the moving truck outside my apartment and a shot of me wiping my eyes.

"Oh fantastic! They are making it look like we're breaking up!" Now I'm really frustrated!

"Scroll up," he says with a smirk.

I scroll and find another article showing me hugging Jason after running into him while shopping. The picture makes it look much more intimate than it was, which sets off streams of anger through me.

"I'm not cheating on you!" I blurt out.

"I know you're not. Keep scrolling," he says, still smiling.

I scroll further and find a shot of Ethan and me standing by his car, my hand in his, followed by a picture of us kissing passionately. The headline? *Amid Cheating Rumors, Ethan Bradley Moves Girlfriend In.* So much for not telling friends yet—now the world knows.

"How do they know this already?" I am flabbergasted at the amount of back and forth these magazines have going on. Like hours apart we are on, then off. It makes me wonder how celebrities deal with it. No wonder we think they are all in horrible relationships.

"They're everywhere. And they don't miss a chance to create another scandal. That sells copies. I know." His eyes are smiling, even if he's not, as he shrugs like it's no big deal. It is a big deal!

"This must be awful for you."

"I'm used to it."

"They follow you around?" I am bewildered.

"They follow us around now. You're part of me. The question is, are you okay?"

"I'm frustrated. At least my parents know, but this whole thing with Jason—I swear, Ethan, it's nothing. We're just friends."

"Miranda, I know. I'm not worried. Would you like me to issue a statement? It might stop some of the rumors."

"You can do that?" I ask surprised. Wow, issuing statements about his personal life with me. It's odd. And weird.

"I can do anything. I have a whole PR team. Sometimes, it's better to get ahead of these things before they spiral out of control."

My heart races at the thought, but Ethan's calm demeanor keeps me grounded. "No, let's just let it pass."

"Okay, but let me know if you change your mind. I can have something out in an hour." He pulls me into a swift kiss on the lips, then the nose, then leaves me to finish my box organizing while I process this new reality of statements and paparazzi.

Later, after I've moved boxes around for the tenth time, we order takeout and then curl up on the couch under a blanket. I notice a few more presents under the tree, and I'm reminded that I do still need to finish my shopping for him.

"Christmas is next week, and I still have no idea what to get you," I say, resting my head on his chest.

"I already have what I want—you," he replies, his fingers tracing soft circles on my arm.

"Yes, you have me. What else?"

"I don't need anything else."

"Well, if you don't give me ideas, you're going to end up with a pile of ties."

"I'd love every one of them," he chuckles.

"Oh, speaking of Christmas, my mom wants to know what our plans are for Christmas Day. I usually go home, but I wasn't sure what your family does. And I didn't want to take you away from your traditions for mine. I mean if you want to go with me that is. You don't, but I...." Ethan's lips press to mine, cutting off my rambling.

"I'm sure we can do both," he says, sitting up and immediately calling his mom. The man wastes no time when it comes to planning.

After a quick conversation, he proposes we spend Christmas Eve with his family and then head to my parents' place for Christmas Day. I call my mom to confirm, and she agrees on the condition that we stay the weekend. It's almost too easy.

As we settle back into the couch, I yawn, "I still need to finish shopping for my family and pick up something for your family too."

"Why don't we take Friday off and go shopping to-gether?" Ethan suggests.

"I love that idea. I'm sure Paul will be okay with me tak-ing the day off."

"Done," he says, wrapping his arms around me.

"I wish all decisions could be this easy," I murmur.

"With you, they seem to be," he replies softly, pulling me closer as I drift off in his arms.

Chapter 32

Monday and Tuesday fly by, and since Ethan will be working late again, I decide it's the perfect time to finish shopping for his presents. Charlie is more than happy to drive me around and even gives me some suggestions along the way.

I find some beautiful ties in a shop, and even though I can't decide on just one, I end up buying all five. What started as a funny idea is now a real gift, and I feel good about it. But after wandering through a few more stores, I hit a wall. What do you buy the man who has everything? A boat? I'm pretty sure he doesn't have one, but that might be overkill. And not that I could afford it, but now I'm curious if he has one, so I send him a text.

Do you have a boat?

No, do I need one?

I was just checking. I'm shopping.

Shopping for a boat?

No, shopping for you. I was going to buy you one, since you have everything else.

I have no place to store a boat at the house.

True. Ok, no boat. Got it. Carry on.

Have fun. See you after work then.

Yes, you will. Bye.

Ok, no boat. That's good to know. And now I'm back to where I started with no idea what else to get him.

Just as I'm about to give up, I spot a small antique store with a quirky collection of items. It's not exactly Ethan's style, but something about it pulls me in. The place is filled with old records, posters, mirrors, and vintage lamps. As I browse, my eyes land on something sitting alone in the middle of a glass case. It's perfect, and I don't even care how much it costs—I have to get it for him.

Feeling excited with my finds, I head back to the apartment. Since Ethan's still not home, I sneak everything into my office and wrap it all up, labeling the packages carefully, and tying them with bows. This is going to be an amazing Christmas.

Just as I'm finishing tucking them under the tree, Ethan walks in carrying a huge stack of presents himself.

"What is all that?" I ask, raising an eyebrow.

"I couldn't help myself," he laughs, placing the gifts under the tree.

"I thought we agreed on just a few," I tease, but his grin gives him away.

"This is a few," he says, trying to defend himself. "And honestly, I didn't think you were home yet, so I was trying to sneak these in."

"Well, that makes two of us. I've been wrapping yours." We laugh together, standing in front of the now-overflowing pile of gifts beneath the tree.

"You know, this is going to be the best Christmas of my life," Ethan says, wrapping an arm around my waist and pulling me in close.

"I hope you like what I got you," I say, suddenly feeling a little nervous.

"I will."

"You better."

"Miranda, anything you give me will be perfect."

"I feel the same way." I smile, leaning into him.

"Now, come here and kiss me," he says, pulling me closer for a sweet kiss before scooping me up and carrying me off to the bedroom as we laugh.

Later that night, as tiny snowflakes start to fall outside, I lie in bed, listening to Ethan's deep, steady breathing. His hand is resting on my stomach, and I'm about to drift off, but something about the soft glow of the snow calls to me. Gently moving his hand, I slip out of bed and go to the window, watching as the snow begins to stick, illuminated by the moonlight.

"Miranda?" Ethan's sleepy voice calls out. I turn to see him sitting up, looking for me. When his eyes find me, even in the dark, I know he's smiling.

"What's wrong?" he asks as his tone changes to one of worry.

"Nothing, it's snowing," I reply, my voice soft as I turn back to the window.

"Oh, it is. Come back to bed," he says, his voice heavy with sleep.

"In a minute. I'm just watching it," I answer, my eyes still on the snow falling quietly outside.

Moments later, I feel his warm arms wrap around me from behind, and I lean into him.

"It's beautiful up here at night," I murmur. "You can see the whole city below as the snow falls. It's like being in a tower."

"Fit for a princess," he whispers against my neck.

"More like a king in his ivory tower."

"Then you're my queen," he answers softly.

"I can get behind that."

We stand there in silence for a few minutes, watching the snow together, before he effortlessly picks me up and carries me back to bed. I settle back into his arms, the warmth of his body lulling me into a peaceful sleep.

Friday morning, I wake just before sunrise. Ethan is still curled up next to me, fast asleep, his face calm and peaceful. I can't help but smile as I watch him, wondering how I got so lucky. It all seems too good to be true sometimes, like a dream. But as I stare at him, doubts begin to creep into my mind. *What if he realizes how ordinary I am? What if he wakes up one day and wants something—or someone—better?*

"Whatever crazy idea is in your head, stop," Ethan's voice cuts through my thoughts. His bright green eyes open, locking onto mine.

"What?"

"You can't lie to me, Miranda. I see it on your face. What's got you worried?"

"Nothing," I mumble.

"Miranda, I know the look."

"It's just my stupid brain."

"Your brain isn't stupid. It's beautiful—just like you. Now, tell your king what's wrong." His teasing makes me laugh, easing the tension building inside me.

"It's nothing," I try again, but he's not buying it.

"I can't make it right if you don't tell me."

"I don't need you to fix this. It's just… me."

He shifts onto his side, pulling me closer to him. "What's bothering you?"

"I…" I hesitate, unsure if I should even say it. But his eyes are soft and patient, and I know I can't keep it from him. "I have this tiny fear that you might wake up one day and realize you want someone else."

"Miranda," he says firmly, his hand cupping my face. "No. Never. Not in a million years. I swear to you, I don't want anyone but you."

"I know, it's silly. It's just my past, and then there was the whole thing with the redhead, and the conversations last night… I told you it was stupid."

"It's not stupid. But Miranda, you mean everything to me. I thought I made that clear to you. I don't want anyone but you. From the moment I met you, I knew it. Those boys from your past have nothing on me. I'm going to keep you here with me forever."

His forehead presses against mine, and he exhales slowly, grounding me with his steady presence.

"You promise?" I ask, my voice small but hopeful.

"I swear," he whispers before kissing me softly.

I close my eyes, feeling safe in his arms, the doubts fading away as I hold on to the man who has given me everything that I never knew I needed.

"When you left my office that day, I wanted to chase after you, but Jason stopped me at the door. He said I'd only make things worse, so I just stood there...and then I collapsed to my knees. I thought I was going to die. My chest hurt in a way I'd never felt before, and that's when I knew for sure that I loved you. I went back to my office, stared at that broken photo, and cried harder than I ever thought possible. I couldn't breathe. But do you know what I did next?"

His voice softens, drawing me closer.

I shake my head, barely whispering, "No."

"I decided I wasn't going to let you go. So, I pulled myself together and went after you. And then... I waited. I waited those long, painful days, holding on, trying again and again. Do you know why?"

I'm silent, caught in the emotion of his words.

"Because you're my forever," he says, his voice breaking through the silence. "You always have been."

"Am I?" I murmur, the weight of his words pressing into me.

"You are," he confirms, his eyes locking with mine. "And you know what? I'll keep waiting for you, again and again, if I have to. I will always be here for you. The truth is, I was more terrified of losing you during those six days than anything else in my life. I begged God for you twice, and somehow, he brought you back to me. Now that I have you, I'm never letting go. You're mine, baby. And I'm yours."

As his lips meet mine, every fear, every insecurity, every doubt dissolves. He loves me—completely, utterly. Me. And if this isn't a real-life fairy tale, then I don't know what is.

Without another word, I pour every bit of myself into him, into us, as we come together, knowing this is where I belong.

"I think we have enough!" I laugh as Ethan tosses yet another item into the cart. We bought presents for everyone—Sophia, Tristen, Emma, Joe, my parents, his mom, Isabell, and even his sister Elizabeth, whom I haven't even met yet. He's like Santa on a shopping spree, only worse.

"Never enough!" he calls, pushing the cart faster, making me giggle as I try to keep up.

After stuffing everything into the car—literally to the brim—I realize I haven't had this much fun shopping in ages. He's wild, but I love every part of him. As we settle into the car, I rest my hand on his leg, feeling the warmth through his jeans.

"You know," I say, "even though you paid for 90% of this madness, which still drives me a little crazy, thank you for not making an issue when I insisted on paying for some."

"And thank you for letting me handle the rest." He takes my hand, kissing it softly. "I think we're starting to figure this thing out." He adds, rubbing my knuckles against his scruffy face. I've been teasing him all day about that stubble, and he's clearly enjoying using it as a weapon.

"Just picking my battles," I tease back, glancing over at him.

With a wink, he starts the car, and we drive off, exhausted but happy. After dinner at a cozy little place nearby, we head home, needing three trips up to the apartment to get all the bags inside.

"We bought too much," I declare as we drop the final bags onto the living room floor.

"It's Christmas," he says, slipping his arm around my waist and pressing a kiss to the back of my neck. "I've never had kids to buy for before, so let me have this joy."

"They're going to love you," I sigh, leaning back into him as he finds that sweet spot right behind my ear that makes me melt.

"Let's go to bed," he growls playfully, pulling me closer. "I have some unwrapping to do."

"Actually," I counter with a mischievous grin, "I think it's my turn to do the unwrapping."

He raises an eyebrow, but before he can respond, I turn in his arms, running my hands down to his waistband, feeling the heat between us rise. His breath hitches as I move closer, my fingers teasing him, the anticipation building as I drop to my knees.

"Miranda, you're going to..." Ethan's words trail off, replaced by a deep moan as I press my lips to him through his clothes. His body tenses, and I feel him shudder under my touch, but I'm not done teasing him yet. My fingers find the waistband of his boxer briefs, slowly peeling them down to reveal more skin, warm and firm beneath my lips.

"Have I told you how sexy these boxer briefs are?" I murmur, pausing between kisses.

"No…" His voice is low, strained.

"They hug you so perfectly," I whisper, running my lips up his length. His knees bend involuntarily as I move higher, loving how I have him at my mercy. "They show me every inch of you," I continue, letting my tongue flicker lightly across his skin, savoring his every reaction.

He groans deeply, gripping my hair, his body trembling as I explore him with my mouth. I take my time, loving the way he's losing control, every movement pushing him closer to the edge. He whispers my name, but I keep going, drawing out his pleasure, my touch slow and deliberate.

"Miranda, stop… I can't…" He tries to pull me up, but I'm not letting him go just yet. I want him undone, completely. His breath comes faster, every moan vibrating through him, and just as I feel him about to break, he calls out my name, his body surrendering as I take him over the edge.

When it's over, I stand to meet his gaze, and his eyes, heavy with satisfaction, lock onto mine. "Mind-blowing," he breathes, pulling me into a kiss. The taste of him lingers on my lips, and I can't help but grin as he groans against my mouth. "I taste myself on you," he whispers.

"And you taste so sweet," I reply softly, kissing him again.

He chuckles, still catching his breath. "I think I may have just seen heaven."

"I'm glad I could help with that," I laugh softly, feeling a sense of pride, knowing I've completely unraveled him.

"You should've stopped," he growls, his voice husky as

he pulls me closer, his hands tightening in my hair. He kisses me harder this time, his desire still simmering just beneath the surface.

"No chance," I tease, biting back a grin. "You never let me finish like that, and I wasn't about to stop until I had you right where I wanted you."

"That's sexy as hell," he groans, his hands roaming my body again, and just like that, the heat between us flares back to life.

In one swift movement, he spins me around, pulling my shirt over my head before unbuckling my jeans and slipping them down. His hands are all over me, possessive and hungry, sending shivers through my body. I can barely think, my breath catching as he presses against me, his lips at my ear.

"Walk forward," he commands, his voice low and demanding. I do as he says, feeling his hands guiding me around the back of the couch. With one firm push, he bends me forward, my body arching as he pulls me back against him.

Every inch of my skin tingles in anticipation as his hands trail over me, taking his time, teasing me with what's to come. My heart races as he leans in, whispering softly in my ear, "Now it's my turn."

Ethan slides my panties down my legs, his breath warm against my skin. As he reaches my thighs, he presses soft kisses along the way, sending shivers up my spine. "You're irresistible," he murmurs as his hands travel slowly over my body, igniting every inch of my skin.

"Ready?" His voice is deep in my ear, and all I can manage is a soft, breathless "yes." His fingers trace the curves of my body before he positions himself. I hold my breath, feeling the heat radiate between us as he enters me gently, pausing just enough for me to adjust. The sensation of him, so close, so connected, sends a wave of warmth through me.

He starts to move, gradually picking up speed until the rhythm becomes an intoxicating blend of pleasure and tension. Each movement pushes me further into a haze of sensation, making me gasp for air. His hands grip my hips, his strength guiding me closer as he thrusts deeper, making me lose control.

I feel the build of tension spiraling within me, and before I know it, I'm overwhelmed by the intensity, crying out his name as the world around us fades away. Ethan doesn't stop; he drives forward, matching every pulse of pleasure with even more intensity, bringing me to the edge once again. My legs threaten to give out, but he holds me steady, supporting me in his arms.

"I love you," he growls, his voice thick with passion as we reach that final, sweet crescendo together. The room feels electric as we both collapse, breathless and spent.

He kisses my shoulder gently, his hands still tracing lazy patterns on my skin. "You're my everything, you know that?" he whispers, pulling me close as the last waves of our shared moment settle. I melt into his embrace, feeling utterly connected to him, body and soul.

"Yes. Yours. Always. I love you," I whisper, too tired to say much more, but he understands. He always does.

With a delicate kiss to my forehead, he picks me up and carries me to bed, cradling me as if I'm the most precious thing in the world.

Chapter 33

We spend Saturday wrapping presents and dividing them into piles for each family as we go. I'm amazed at how many gifts we've accumulated, especially for the kids. I remind Ethan, again, that we might have gone a little overboard, but he just laughs it off, insisting, "There's no such thing." I shake my head, disagreeing, but let him have his fun. Seeing him this excited brings me so much joy, so who am I to argue?

Once everything is wrapped, packed, and sorted, we decide to order dinner in and settle by the fire. I can't help but look over at the pile of presents and smile, imagining Ethan tearing into them. He's been like a little kid all day, sneaking glances and trying to shake the boxes. It's adorable, and honestly, I can't blame him, I'm just as excited to open mine. I have no clue what he's put under the tree for me, but I'm sure I'll love every single thing.

Now, as we lay on the couch, wrapped in a blanket, in our pajamas, watching *A Christmas Story*, I feel an overwhelming sense of happiness. This is already the perfect Christmas, and we haven't even opened gifts yet. I'm drifting off to sleep, snuggled up next to Ethan, when he suddenly sits me up, his expression more serious than usual.

"I have something for you," he starts, his tone quiet but filled with a slight sense of excitement. "But before I give it to you, I need you to promise me something."

The way he's looking at me sends my body into high alert, butterflies are suddenly taking flight in my stomach. "Okay," I reply cautiously, watching as he moves toward the mantel. That's when I notice it—a small box tied with a ribbon. My heart skips a beat. How did I not see it there before?

He picks it up, turning to me with a grin, but I can see something more serious behind his smile. The box is small and flat, giving me no clue as to what is inside. My mind races with possibilities, and I can't quite figure out if I should be excited or nervous.

"Promise me," he says, his voice steady, "that no matter what you're thinking, you won't say anything except 'thank you' and 'I love it.'"

I narrow my eyes at him playfully, trying to figure out what he's up to. "Promise me, Miranda," he repeats, this time with a mock sternness in his voice, though the twinkle in his eyes betrays him.

"Alright, alright, I promise," I laugh, but my curiosity is definitely piqued. "Okay, give it here."

He hands me the box, and it's slightly heavier than I expect. Slowly I untie the silver ribbon, my hands shaking slightly as I wonder what is inside. The moment feels so charged, and I can't help but glance at him as I peel back the wrapping. The box opens, and nestled inside is something I never expected—a car key.

I blink, trying to process what I'm seeing, holding the key up in disbelief. "Ethan, what...?" I stammer, my voice trailing off.

"The rest of it is downstairs, in the garage," he says, his grin now full-blown as he watches my reaction.

I gape at him, my mouth hanging open. "Please tell me you didn't buy me a car?"

His smile turns into a mischievous one. "I might have."

For a moment, I'm speechless, a flood of emotions rushing through me. "Ethan! We talked about not going overboard with expensive gifts!" I say, shaking my head, but he cuts me off.

"You promised," he reminds me, raising his eyebrows in a challenge. "Besides, it's not a Christmas present, it's just a gift, from me to you."

I can't help but laugh at the absurdity of it all—he bought me a car. A car. Without another thought, I jump up from the couch and make a beeline for the elevator.

"SHOES!" he calls after me, still laughing as he grabs our coats and rushes to catch up.

By the time we reach the garage, I'm practically buzzing with excitement. We step out of the elevator, and there it is—a sleek, dark gray Genesis G80 Sport with a huge red bow on the hood. My hands fly to my mouth as I stare at it, stunned. "Ethan... I... I can't believe you did this!"

He steps closer, slipping the key into my hand. "I noticed you checking out the Genesis at dinner the other night, so I decided to make it happen."

I turn to face him, and despite my instinct to scold him for going over the top, I feel tears welling up. "I don't know if I should be mad at you or kiss you right now."

Ethan takes the key from my hand and opens the car door with a grin. "Get in." I just stand there for a moment, taking it all in, the shy smile on my face growing wider.

"You promised," he teases, but his voice is softer this time, playful.

With a laugh, I stretch up and plant a gentle kiss on his lips. "Thank you. I love it," I whisper, and his face lights up, his grin spreading as wide as possible.

Sliding into the driver's seat, I start the car, and it purrs like a dream. I run my hand over the sleek dashboard, the smooth steering wheel, and the pristine console, trying to process all the emotions swirling inside me. It feels surreal—this car, this moment. My eyes threaten tears as Ethan joins me in the passenger seat.

"It's the top of the line with everything," he explains, watching me with that satisfied look he gets when he knows he's outdone himself.

I lean over and take his face in my hands, kissing him tenderly. "You are too much. This is way too much... but I love it. And I love you." I pepper his face with kisses, and he laughs, trying to squirm away.

"You can take it for a spin in the morning," he chuckles, "when you're not in pajamas, and it's not freezing."

I play with every gadget, pressing buttons and exploring the features, still in awe. I can't believe he bought me the car I wanted, and it's even the right color!

All the way back to the apartment, I shower him with hugs and kisses, thanking him repeatedly. "I'm glad you kept your promise," he says as he pulls me into the elevator.

"I thought about punching you for spending so much," I joke, shaking my head, "but I couldn't. It's perfect, and I love it. Thank you. But you know, I'm paying for—"

He cuts me off with a kiss. "No. It's done. It's a gift for my amazing girlfriend, who's made my life better in every way. You've given me so much, Miranda. Let me do this for you." He nuzzles into my neck, and I feel a rush of warmth as I hug him tight.

"Thank you," I whisper again, my head resting against his chest as he murmurs something soft against my neck.

In one swift motion, he bends down, scoops me up, and throws me over his shoulder. "Now," he says, smirking, "you can thank me properly." He smacks me playfully on the backside, and I dissolve into a fit of giggles as he carries me toward the bedroom, tossing me onto the bed with a laugh.

And I do thank him—over and over, filling the night with our shared joy and laughter, feeling closer than ever.

Chapter 34

"Wake up, sleepyhead." Ethan's lips are gently brushing against my shoulder, his excitement palpable.

"I'm awake," I mumble into the pillow, my voice muffled by sleep.

"It's Christmas Eve!" He sounds like a child on Christmas morning. "And?"

"We agreed to open presents today!" He's practically bouncing on the bed like a five-year-old, waiting for his parents to wake up.

"OKAY, I'm getting up." Before I can even fully wake up, he jumps out of bed, pulling me along into the living room.

He quickly grabs a Santa hat, slipping it on before he hands me a hot cup of coffee, grinning from ear to ear. I watch as he starts pulling out presents, stacking mine in front of me, while making his own pile next to it. He places four small presents for Kasey on the rug by the fireplace, and Kasey meows, already intrigued by his pile.

"You can't just tear into them! One at a time," I laugh,

watching Ethan as he eagerly shakes the boxes in front of him.

"Okay, open this one first," he says, handing me a smaller box with 'wear' written on it, which makes me giggle. I shake the box, curious as it rattles lightly. Carefully, I pull off the silver and blue wrapping paper and open the velvet box inside to reveal a simple yet beautiful silver locket. Inside is a picture of the two of us.

"Oh, Ethan, I love it," I say, my voice soft as I admire the locket. I put it on immediately. "It's perfect."

"Your turn!" I point to one of the larger boxes in his pile, and without hesitation, he rips into it. He pulls out the Blackhawks jersey and flips it over. His face lights up when he sees his name printed on the back.

"It has my name on it! I love it!!!" His excitement is contagious, and I can't help but giggle as he slips it on, smoothing it out with pride. I grab my phone and snap a picture of him grinning like a kid, looking absolutely thrilled.

"That one next!" Ethan points to a box in my pile, and I pick up the heavy one marked 'want.' I tear into the paper and gasp. It's the Keurig I had been eyeing for weeks.

"It's the one I wanted too! Thank you!" I laugh, hugging the box tightly. He takes a picture of me holding it, grinning from ear to ear.

"The silver one," I say, giggling again. Ethan opens the box to find five smaller packages inside, all wrapped individually.

"Oh, it's going to be like that?" he teases, as he starts unwrapping the first one. It's a tie.

"A tie?" He chuckles.

"I told you if you didn't tell me what you wanted, I was buying you all ties," I laugh as he playfully tosses the wrapping paper at me. He unwraps the rest, revealing five different ties, all perfectly chosen.

"I actually love all of them, thank you," he says, smiling. "I'll wear them with pride." He leans in and kisses me, making my heart flutter.

"You have to get the purple one next," he says, pointing. I shuffle through the pile and pick up the small box with 'want' written on it. I unwrap it to find a gorgeous silver watch with a pink face.

"It's beautiful," I say, admiring it.

"Turn it over," he prompts, and I do. Engraved on the back are the words:

Time stood still the day I met you.
~Ethan.

"It's a Breitling, the same brand I wear. It's a great watch, and it'll last a lifetime," he explains with a wink. I blush at the hidden meaning behind his words.

"I love it," I whisper, my voice full of emotion. As I fasten it around my wrist, he snaps a picture of me, and I shake my head, laughing softly.

He grins as I admire the watch, reminding me of the next present. "Gold one."

"Don't shake it," I warn playfully. He unwraps it carefully, revealing two framed photos. One is a 5x7 of me standing at the pier, looking out over the water, and the other is an 8x10 of the two of us that I took while we were shopping.

He holds them up, grinning. "You wanted me," I shrug, feeling a bit shy.

He laughs and shakes his head. "Miranda, I love them. They're perfect." He stands up and walks the photos over to the mantel, placing them next to the others there.

"I wanted to give you a new one of us, since I broke the last one," I say, feeling my cheeks heat up as I remember that awful day.

Ethan walks back over and cups my face in his hands, kissing me softly. "I love them, and I love you. Now you can keep me company every day here, and at the office. Only you." He winks and then sits back down on the floor to the rest of his packages.

"That one next." He points to another purple box with a big shiny bow. It's very heavy, and I see that 'read' is on this tag. I open it to find three hard cover books by Julie, the author we had dinner with. I'm so excited. Ethan tells me they are all first prints of her series and she has signed each on to me. They are perfect!

"Ok, you have to open your read box next." I wave at that box, and as he starts to unwrap it, I freak out. "No, never mind, I changed my mind." I try to take it, but he pulls it away with a laugh.

"Nope. It's mine. You gave it to me and no take backs." As he opens it, I hide my face in shame, as he reads the first page.

"Miranda, what is this? Did you write a book?" He looks up in surprise.

"I did. A long time ago. No one has ever read it, and I thought maybe…I was…Oh God, just give it back." A wave of embarrassment washes over me and my face burns.

"No way. You wrote this?" He flips the yellowed pages, and I'm mortified.

"I did, and well, I thought, maybe you would like to be the first to read it. I mean as my boyfriend, not as your job or anything. I wanted to share it with you, as part of me, and something I have never shared with anyone else." I admit, my smile forced as uneasiness settle in my stomach.

"Miranda, I would be honored." He reaches out, takes my hand, and kisses all my knuckles before tugging me down to his lap for a quick kiss.

He hands me my next box, and after unwrapping it, I find a men's shoe box, which makes me laugh. He tells me to keep going, that it's just a box, but he chuckles when I find a small box inside that stuffed with tissue.

Inside I find a silver engraved key chain that says Bradley. It has a single key on it and I hold it up confused.

"That is your own house key. And if I remember correctly, you asked for a keychain." He gives me a wink and a boyish grin. And as I agree, it hits me that I officially live here now.

"You are too much, but I love it all. Thank you." I mutter in between kisses.

"I love you and nothing is ever too much for you. I told you, I would give you the world." He holds my head, looking deep into my eyes, and I feel it to the ends of my soul. He's perfect.

"Wait! You have one more. The most important one." I jump off the couch and search for the small green box on the floor among the discarded paper. "Here." I smile as he takes the box and shakes it. I watch as he tears off the paper, opens the lid, but then stops as he studies it for a long minute, not even taking it from the box.

"How?" He looks up at me and I snap a picture of the shock on his face. He's speechless and I'm confused at his reaction. His hand runs over his chin, but still he says nothing. He makes a noise, and then finally delicately takes out the vintage tie tack with the "E" on it.

"It's just like…" He runs his finger over it again and shakes his head without finishing his thought. He stands and walks over to the photo on the mantel, and I watch him turn over the pin in his hand.

"Where did you get this?" His voice is strained.

"I found it in an antique store. I saw it and thought it looked similar to the one your dad is wearing in the photo. That's why I thought you would like it. I'm sorry, you don't have to keep it." I stand there, heartbroken, but he suddenly takes two giant steps and pulls me into a hug, crying into my hair.

"Ethan? What's wrong? I didn't mean to upset you." He pulls back and kisses me hard, his tears wetting my cheeks.

"Ethan?" I ask again, confused. Is it the thought of his dad? He's so upset, and I want to cry. He looks at me and smiles, getting himself under control and clearing his throat.

"This was my dad's," he whispers.

"What?" I ask, bewildered. He turns it over and shows me the scratch marks on the back.

"I did this. I scratched my name in it when I was about six. This was his. My mom gave it to him, and he wore it everywhere he went until he lost it a few years before he died." He looks up at me again, his eyes red but a huge smile on his face.

"Oh. I just thought they were similar." I'm stunned as he hugs me again. "I can't believe you found this." He squeezes me so tightly I can barely breathe. "This is the best present I have ever received. Thank you." He kisses me hard, repeatedly.

Okay, he doesn't hate it then.

"I don't even know what to say. I'm so glad I bought it. I wanted to get you something for those ties, since I know you like that stuff. When I found it, I knew I had seen something like it before, but I just couldn't figure it out. After I got it home, I looked through your tie pins, and it wasn't one of yours. Then I saw the picture, and I knew it was similar. I guess it was just fate."

"Thank you." He kisses me again.

"You are welcome."

"This is the best Christmas ever," he says, brushing his thumb over my lips.

"I would have to agree, Mr. Moneybags. I said 'not expensive,' and you bought me a $70,000 car and a really expensive watch!" I smack his arm, but he barely flinches.

"Actually, $90,000, and the watch was only $4,800." His wink shocks me, and I glance at the watch, exhaling loudly.

"Holy shit! Now I'm going to have to chain it to my arm! Ethan!" My groan makes him laugh, a new gleam in his eyes.

"I think what you just gave me is priceless." He kisses me again softly, rubbing his thumbs over my cheeks as he gazes at me.

"I still think I came out ahead," I admit.

"Nope, I did. I got you. Plus, I have a jersey with my name on it!" He chuckles.

"I love my locket and coffee pot, too!" I touch the locket around my neck.

"And I love my ties, my photos, and that book I can't wait to read. I couldn't be happier right now." He kisses my nose, and I reach up to wipe away the dampness from his tears. I don't need to say it, I can see he feels it.

We help Kasey open his presents of catnip, toys, and a new bed. Then I grab a trash bag to clean up the paper and boxes, while Ethan carries the coffee pot to the kitchen and places it on the counter, ready for me to switch out later. He fills up our coffee cups and returns to the living room.

"Wait, I think there might be something else that I forgot," Ethan says, setting down the cups and glancing around the room.

"No! You cannot give me anything else," I warn him.

"Wait here," he replies.

"Ethan, no!" I protest, but he's already walking behind the couch, disappearing into his office as I laugh. "Ethan! No more!" I call after him, knowing it's pointless. He's too much.

A moment later, he returns with a small gift bag decorated with puppies in Christmas hats. I give him a look, and he laughs.

"Open me…" he says in a silly voice, handing it to me. It's really light, and the tag reads, "Wear me." I pull out the tissue paper, revealing fuzzy socks.

"Fuzzy socks! You did it! This is even better than the car!" I collapse onto the couch, laughing so hard I can hardly breathe. I love the playful smile on his face as I look up at him. "Thank you." I clutch the socks to my chest as I watch him walk to the mantel, set down his phone, and pick up a remote. He presses a button, and music begins playing through the sound system. I expect Christmas music, but then I recognize the song.

"Wait, this is the song the guy played on the pier!" He found it! Ethan nods and walks back to me, pulling me off the couch to dance, holding me close. I lean my face against his chest, feeling like life couldn't get any better. My exhale makes him pull me even closer.

Halfway through the song, he suddenly stops and steps away, walking back to the couch. He picks up the socks and hands them back to me.

"I think you missed something," he says.

I give him a curious look and feel inside one of the socks. There's something in it. I reach in and pull out a ring, my heart stopping. Before I can react, Ethan takes the ring from my hand as I stand there, frozen.

"Miranda, my life changed that day I crashed into yours, and it's never been the same. I came to life with that first kiss, and I want every single one of them from this day forward. You make me a better man, and you've taught me that the best things in life truly are free. I never thought I could love someone like I love you, and I never want to live another day without you by my side." He takes my left hand, kneeling down on one knee, and my hand flies to my mouth as I try to hold in my breath.

"You once asked me to stay with you. Now, I'm asking you to stay with me. Forever." His voice cracks, and I hold my breath. "Miranda Grace Michaels, will you be my happily ever after?" He holds up the ring, and tears begin to blur my vision.

"YES!" I cry, my voice breaking as the dam finally bursts, and he slips the ring onto my finger. It fits perfectly.

Ethan stands and kisses me as happy tears run down my cheeks. "I love you so much, and now this is the perfect Christmas. I truly have you," he whispers against my lips, and I kiss him over and over, unable to stop.

"Ethan," I murmur, looking down at the ring on my finger, unsure what else to say.

"Do you like it? I was really nervous that you wouldn't, or that it might be too much."

"It's perfect. Just what I would have chosen for myself." He cradles my face in his hands, his eyes welling up again, which only makes me cry harder.

"Okay, maybe a little smaller though," I tease, throwing my arms around him. He laughs and swings me around, our laughter filling the room. "I do think it's perfect," I whisper in his ear as he holds me tight.

"I need to call my mom and Emma!" I exclaim, pulling away from him and searching for my phone.

"Right now?" he asks playfully.

"YES! The biggest moment of my life has to be shared with my sister!" I respond, finally finding my phone and video-dialing Emma, trying to compose myself as she answers.

"Hey, Sis! Merry Christmas! Nice to see your beautiful face," she says, winking, but then moves the phone closer, instantly concerned. "What's wrong? Why are you crying? Miranda, tell me right now," she demands, her voice filled with urgency. I can't help but smile.

"Merry Christmas to you, too. And nothing's wrong. Where are you?" I ask, trying to ease her panic.

"Mom and Dad's. Why?" she asks suspiciously.

"Where's Mom?" I ask again, dodging her question.

"Rana, what's wrong?" she presses.

"Nothing, just get Mom. It's all perfect," I assure her.

"Miranda?" she questions one last time.

"Just do it," I say with an eye roll. This time, she starts walking through the house, calling out that I'm on the phone and I need to talk to Mom.

Emma returns to the phone, standing next to Mom so I can see them both.

"Hi, sweetheart. How are you?" Mom asks, her voice warm and comforting.

"I'm great! I wanted to tell you both first. Look!" I say, holding up my hand and showing off the ring. Their eyes widen, and Emma screeches my name.

"IS THAT WHAT I THINK IT IS?" she shrieks again.

"It is! Ethan asked me to marry him, and I said yes."

"Oh my God! Was it so romantic?" Emma jumps up and down, while Mom begins to cry.

"Yes! It was incredible," I say as tears well up in my eyes once more.

"Honey, I'm so happy for you," Mom finally says, her voice trembling with emotion. We're all bouncing with excitement, and I can hear Dad talking off-camera to Emma. She turns the phone towards him.

"Hey, Miranda! What's going on with all the screaming?" Dad asks, looking confused.

"Ethan asked me to marry him, and I said yes!" I manage through my tears, as Dad grins.

"I know. He called me earlier this week," Dad says calmly, shrugging and laughing. I turn to Ethan, who's now snuggled against me on the couch, peeking at the phone.

"Hi, Dad," Ethan greets him with a smile, and Dad chuckles.

I immediately punch Ethan in the arm as Mom yells at Dad.

"I'm going to die! He even asked dad!" Emma is a blubbering mess.

"He did! And after a long conversation, I gave him my blessing. Miranda, he's a good man, and I know he'll treat you right," Dad says, winking at me.

"Thank you, Dad. I love you all." I blow a kiss to everyone from my side of the phone.

"We'll see you tonight! Merry Christmas!" Ethan chimes in as we all wish each other a Merry Christmas Eve and say our goodbyes.

"You called my dad?" I ask, surprised.

"I did."

"You amaze me."

"As do you. Now get back over here and amaze me some more," he teases, wiggling his eyebrows as he pulls the blanket over me.

"I can't believe you asked my dad!" I say, still in disbelief.

"It was only proper. I wanted to make sure I had his blessing before I took his little girl."

"You've already taken me multiple times," I tease.

"I have, but not in the way I want. Now, enough talking, more doing. I need to spend some time with my fiancée," he says, pulling me under him and kissing me sweetly.

"I don't want to move," I murmur, snuggling closer to him.

"Me either. I've just had the best sex with the most beautiful woman, who also happens to be my future wife. But we should probably get up, shower, and get ready to head to my mom's. It's almost 10," he says, holding me tightly.

"I can't even process what you just said. I'm still reeling from the amount of money I'm wearing on my body right now," I mumble against his shoulder, as I glance at the ring for the twentieth time. "And that car. Good Lord, Ethan. What if I wreck it?"

"Just don't lose the ring. It's worth more," he says, making me groan.

"I think I'm going to hyperventilate!" I whine.

"Don't do that. No more hospitals for you!" He kisses the top of my head, and then a thought pops into my mind.

"What if we have kids?" I ask suddenly.

He sits up abruptly, dumping me onto the couch. "Are you pregnant?!"

I fall off the couch, laughing. "No! I just meant I'd have to go to the hospital for that!" I laugh harder, tears streaming down my face as he groans in frustration, falling back onto the couch.

"You scared the hell out of me," he says, sounding genuinely rattled, which makes me laugh even more.

"You do want kids, right?" I ask, suddenly worried.

"Of course! Just not this minute," he assures me.

"Okay, good," I say, relaxing again.

"Woman, I've had more emotions today than I can handle. No more," he says dramatically, crawling over to me. Looking down at me, his eyes sparkle with amusement as he kisses my nose.

"Remind me on Monday to take out a very large insurance policy on myself so that when I do stroke out, you can collect," he jokes. I giggle uncontrollably as he pulls me up.

"Let's shower," he groans as I skip off to the bathroom, leaving him to follow.

I dress in slacks, black boots, and the beautiful red sweater Ethan bought me on Friday. He's wearing black pants, a white shirt, and the emerald green tie I got him.

"You look hot," I say as he walks past me.

"So do you," he growls, his hand sliding across my ass.

"Thanks." I wink, then focus on finishing my outfit.

I put on my watch and locket, fluff my hair in the mirror, and after one more long look at my ring, I'm ready. When I turn back, I see Ethan struggling to put on the tie pin, his hands shaking slightly. I walk over and gently take it from him to help.

"I still can't believe you found this. And you didn't even know what you found," he says softly, his eyes meeting mine.

"I still can't believe you bought me a ring that costs more than my car!" I exclaim, then suddenly ask, "Ooo, can I drive my car?"

"Yes," he nods as I finish fixing his tie pin.

"Cool. Then let's go," I say with a wink, and he follows me, still absently touching his tie.

We carry the bags of gifts downstairs, and after loading them into the trunk, I take a bunch of pictures of my new car. Ethan pulls off the huge bow that's been adorning it.

"Can you put that in the backseat? I'm going to put it to good use later," I tease, wiggling my eyebrows.

He just shakes his head, knowing exactly what I mean. I love it.

Chapter 35

The car is incredible to drive, and I think I've told Ethan a hundred and twelve times how much I love it. I'm sure he's getting tired of me gushing, but he just smiles and says something sweet each time. We arrive at Eloise's house in no time, and I'm a little bummed to stop driving so soon, but I'm also excited to get the day started. Ethan tells me to park out front, and I notice the large number of cars already there.

"Miranda, I haven't told my family yet, and I'd like to do it myself if that's okay. I want to surprise them," Ethan says just before we get out of the car.

"Okay, that's fine with me. But I don't know how I'm going to hide this rock that's brighter than the sun!" I laugh, showing him my hand.

"I'm sure you'll manage," he says with an adorable wink as he takes my hand, and we walk up to the porch, where Isabell is already waiting for us.

"Merry Christmas!" she yells, bounding down the steps to give Ethan a big hug before turning to me for mine. "I'm so glad you both are here! Nice car. Is this yours?" she asks, eyeing the sleek new vehicle.

"Yes. Santa brought it to me," I say with a playful smile at Ethan.

"No, it was not a Christmas present," Ethan clarifies with a laugh.

"Holy cow, you must have been extra nice this year!" Isabell laughs.

"No, just a crazy over-the-top boyfriend with more money than sense. But I do love it," I say, chuckling.

"What did Santa get you?" Isabell asks Ethan.

"Ties," he says casually, and Isabell stops, looking at me before we both burst out laughing.

"He got more than that, don't let him fool you," I blush, shaking my head, and Ethan takes my hand again.

We barely step inside the front door before a taller version of Isabell comes rushing up, practically jumping on Ethan and hugging him like mad.

"Elizabeth," Ethan greets her, kissing her cheek as she squeezes him tightly. "This is Miranda," he announces as soon as she lets him go.

Elizabeth turns to me, taking hold of my arms and giving me an appraising look. "It is so good to meet you! Mom and Izz have told me all about you," she says, pulling me into a surprisingly strong hug.

"It's great to finally meet you, too," I reply, hugging her back, trying to keep my ring hand out of sight.

Ethan takes my coat and hands it off to a man waiting by the door. Then, to my relief, he takes my left hand again—probably to help hide the ring—and leads us into the sitting room, where all eyes immediately turn toward us. There are far more people than I expected, and feeling a bit shy, I instinctively step closer to Ethan. The room's attention is entirely on me, and I'm not sure what to do with myself.

Eloise comes over, wrapping me in a warm hug, but Ethan still doesn't let go of my hand.

"Miranda, Merry Christmas!" she exclaims.

"Merry Christmas," I reply with a smile.

"Ethan, sweetheart," she says, kissing his cheek.

"Merry Christmas, Mom," he says, returning the kiss.

"Miranda, let me introduce you to the family," Eloise offers with a smile. I glance at Ethan, who just grins and shrugs as she pulls me away from him. "Come on, dear," she insists, and I nervously pull my sleeve down over my hand, trying not to giggle.

Eloise takes me around, introducing me to her sister Helen, who gives me a hug and then kisses Ethan's cheek. "She's so pretty!" I hear Helen say to him, and I can feel my cheeks flushing again.

Next, I meet Helen's husband—though his name escapes me almost immediately—and their two kids, one of whom is married and has a new baby. Eloise moves so quickly through the introductions that I can barely keep up with all the names. Then, we meet Ethan's uncle Arthur, and I do a double take, glancing between him and Ethan, which makes Eloise laugh.

"Arthur is Edward's brother, Ethan's father. And yes, they all look alike," she says with a pat on my arm, clearly amused by my reaction.

Suddenly, she pauses and pulls up my sleeve. "You had your cast removed! That's wonderful! Ethan didn't mention that when we spoke yesterday."

My cheeks darken even more, and I feel like I'm going to be blushing all day at this rate.

"Thank you. It's been a crazy few days, with so many more important things going on that I'm sure he forgot," I manage to say to Eloise, who accepts the explanation with a nod as we continue making our rounds of introductions. We're nearly back to the start when suddenly, Isabell yells out.

"WHOA! HOLD UP!" she shouts, and the room falls silent as everyone turns to look at her. She marches right in front of me, and before I can react, she grabs my left arm. I glance at Ethan, who tries to intervene, but it's too late. She pulls up my sleeve, revealing the ring.

"HOLY SHIT!" Isabell exclaims, and a huge gasp comes from Eloise as the room erupts in chatter. Ethan raises his hands to calm everyone down while I close my eyes, feeling like I might faint.

"Thanks for ruining the surprise, Isabell," Ethan teases, laughing, and Isabell looks embarrassed. "Well, since the cat's out of the bag, I want everyone to know that I asked Miranda to marry me this morning, and she said yes," Ethan announces, his voice full of pride.

There's a round of applause and congratulations, but I'm still staring at the floor, overwhelmed by the sudden attention. Ethan tugs gently on my arm, and when I look up, he mouths, *I love you.* The hugs and kisses start flowing in right after that.

Eloise is the first to embrace me. "Oh, Miranda, I'm so happy. Congratulations! I'm so excited to have you join our family," she says, kissing me on the cheek before starting to cry. "Oh, bother," she mutters, hugging me again before excusing herself from the room. I stand there, still in a bit of a daze, half-expecting some resistance because things are moving quickly, but no one seems concerned about that.

"I'm so sorry I ruined the surprise," Isabell says to me.

"Oh, no, please. I'm actually glad you did. I was dying trying to hold it all in," I admit, laughing as we exchange a tight hug.

Isabell grabs my hand to admire the ring again. "It's gorgeous," she says, turning my hand to see it sparkle in the light. "Thank you. It's so big, I'm a little scared to wear it," I confess, and she laughs with me.

Ethan walks over, pulling me into his side, holding me close. I've noticed over the past few days that he's been more affectionate, almost like he's been nervous about something, and now I know why.

"Ethan, I'm so happy for you," Isabell says, hugging him tightly.

"Thank you. I'm pretty happy, too," he replies, smiling down at me.

"So, she gets a car *and* a ring? Nice. Great presents," Isabell teases.

"They're nothing compared to what I got—the woman of my dreams," he says, kissing my cheek, and I feel like I might melt on the spot.

"Aww, you're so mushy now!" Isabell teases, poking him in the ribs.

"All her," Ethan says, laughing.

"No, all him. He's like a teenager," I joke, which gets another round of laughter from everyone.

A moment later, Eloise returns with a bottle of champagne, followed by two girls carrying trays of filled glasses. They pass them around to everyone.

"I propose a toast to my son and his beautiful bride-to-be. Merry Christmas, everyone!" Eloise announces, raising her glass. We all toast and sip champagne, and I keep pinching myself to make sure I'm not dreaming.

After the rounds of toasts, Eloise comes over to admire my ring more closely. "It's very beautiful," she comments.

"Thank you. I think so too," I reply, beaming with pride.

"Platinum? And what, 3 or 4 carats?" she asks, turning the ring to inspect it.

I glance at Ethan because I have no idea. "Yes, platinum. Three carats on the main stone and another three-quarters in the side stones. Ideal IF E," he says, clearly knowledgeable in diamonds.

I feel faint. That's huge. I don't even know what the other technical terms mean, but I'm certain it's very expensive.

"Very good. Great investment. Well done," Eloise says, winking at Ethan before patting my hand.

"I think we're overwhelming my fiancée," Ethan says with a gentle smile.

"I'm good," I reassure him with a smile, though I do feel a bit overwhelmed.

Eloise pats my hand and turns to Ethan. "I can't tell you how happy I am. I have never..." she starts, but suddenly her words trail off as she reaches for Ethan's tie, her fingers brushing over the pin. "Ethan?" she says, her voice filled with surprise.

"Yes, it is," Ethan says, choking up slightly. "You won't believe it, but this angel of mine found it in an antique shop and gave it to me for Christmas," he adds, looking at me with so much love.

"How did you know?" Eloise asks, glancing at me with tears in her eyes.

"I didn't know," I admit softly. "Honestly, it just looked like the one in the photo on the mantel that his dad was wearing. I had no idea it was the same one. I just thought it was a beautiful piece that he'd love. I mean, what do you buy the man who has more money than sense?" I laugh, but neither of them joins in, they are too lost in their emotions.

"Are you sure?" Eloise asks Ethan, her voice filled with uncertainty.

"Yes. My name is still scratched on the back," he replies softly. She runs her finger over the "E" once more, then suddenly pulls me into a tight embrace.

"Not only did you win this boy's heart, but you found something that has been missing from our family for over ten years. I think you are an angel too," she says, hugging me so tightly I can hardly breathe. Over her shoulder, I see Ethan wiping away a tear.

Finally, Ethan gently pries her off me, and she clears her throat, patting my cheek before announcing it's time to eat. She quickly moves away to help seat the guests. Ethan's fingers find mine, intertwining them as he pulls me close again.

"You have no idea how much this little thing means to us all," he whispers, kissing me softly.

"I really had no idea," I admit.

"That makes it even more perfect," he says, his eyes filled with love as he leads me into the kitchen. We enjoy a fantastic feast and more conversation than I can keep up with. By the time we've had dessert and coffee, I'm absolutely stuffed as we move to the family room to open presents.

As we watch everyone open gifts and enjoy each other's company, Ethan keeps one arm around my shoulders, and the other occasionally brushes his finger over the band of my ring, sending flutters through my heart every time. His smile hasn't faded all day, and I don't think mine has either.

I watch Ethan open his gifts: a funny t-shirt, a travel tie case he's excited about, and an amazing new Breitling watch from his mom—the newest model, not even available yet. The man loves his watches, and I trace my thumb over my own as I watch.

When it's my turn, I open a beautiful scarf from Isabell, a hand-carved wooden bracelet from Elizabeth that she brought back from Africa, and black leather driving gloves from Eloise. Ethan must have told her about my new car, and she found the perfect gift. I love them all.

His sisters love the cat scarves and matching mittens, and they laugh at the silly t-shirts we got them. Ethan had to explain the family tradition of giving awful t-shirts and funny gifts every year. The best (or worst) part is, they actually wear them! I find it endearing that, despite their wealth, they keep things light and fun with this tradition. It's touching to think that I'll soon have two more sisters in my life.

Eloise suddenly comes over and sits beside me, pulling

me out of my thoughts. "I have something for you. I hope you don't think it's too much," she says, handing me a long, flat box.

I unwrap it gently and find a stunning diamond solitaire necklace inside. "Oh, Eloise, it's gorgeous. Thank you so much," I say, admiring the simple elegance of the piece.

"Ethan mentioned you don't have many diamonds, so I wanted to give you something to start your collection," she says, looking a bit bashful, which surprises me.

"It's so beautiful," I reply, holding back tears.

"It is. Now, it's only a carat, but it's a good starter necklace," she says with a wink.

I stand up and hug her tightly. "Thank you. I will always treasure it."

I hand the necklace to Ethan, and he carefully fastens it around my neck. It rests just above my locket, as though it was meant to be there. Eloise pats my hand and moves on to spoil someone else.

Ethan gives me a knowing smile as I bite my tongue. "You know, you're going to have to insure me before long. I'm wearing more than everything I've ever owned in my life combined," I whisper to him. "I'm terrified of losing this ring."

"Everything is insured. Get used to it because I'm going to spoil you every chance I get," he says, smiling like he couldn't be happier.

"You know I don't need anything flashy. Just you."

"You have me," he whispers, brushing his lips against my ear, sending shivers down my spine.

Eventually, after everyone has opened their presents, Ethan announces, "We should get going. We have a long drive tonight."

"We don't have to rush. I'm having a great time," I protest, genuinely enjoying spending time with his family.

"We still have to stop by home to pick up the rest of the gifts, and I want some alone time with you," he whispers, his voice low and full of promise.

I can barely suppress the shiver of anticipation. "Okay," I reply, more than willing to give in to that plan.

"Did you have a nice time?" Ethan asks as I pull out of the driveway.

"I did. Your family is great. I am sort of surprised, though, that your mom took it so well. I was really afraid she might not," I admit, glancing over at him. Out of the corner of my eye, I see him turn toward me, clearly confused.

"What makes you say that?" he asks, his tone serious.

"Um, we've only been officially dating for a month and have known each other for two. And, well..." I glance at him again, feeling nervous about voicing my thoughts.

"Miranda?" His tone grows more stern, and I know I need to answer.

"The first time I met her and Isabell, they both warned me separately not to be after your money. I was just expecting them to think I forced you into something since it's happening so quickly." I realize how ridiculous it sounds out loud, and I hope I didn't hit a nerve.

Ethan is quiet for a moment before responding. "I'm sorry about that. I didn't know they had approached you like that. But, as I've told you before, Mom has always been suspicious of the women I've dated, thinking they're just after money. So, it doesn't really surprise me. But I did talk to her before I made this decision, told her how I felt about you, and that I knew you were the one. She brought up the subject of money, but I told her straight out that it wasn't an issue. You literally fight me every time I try to pay for anything, which drives me crazy, by the way. But I also know, without a doubt, that you don't want my money. After that, she told me not to let you get away. Miranda, I know in my heart that you are my forever." He takes my hand, kisses it softly, and runs his nose over my knuckles, making my heart flutter.

"And if I had to lose it all for you, I would," he adds.

"Ethan," I say, feeling tears welling up in my eyes. I shake my head to control them while I drive. "I feel the same way about you. I didn't even have to think when you asked. I just knew it was right. Honestly, I was shocked it happened so quickly, but it doesn't matter if I have a ring now or in a year. I'm yours." I smile, and he kisses my hand again.

"I couldn't wait that long. Once I realized my heart fully belonged to you, I had to make it happen. It will only ever be you for the rest of my life," he says, his voice full of emotion. With that, there's no more need for words. We ride the rest of the way home in comfortable silence, holding hands and stealing glances at each other.

We barely make it through the front door before Ethan has me stripped, and we make sweet love on the couch. It's becoming my favorite spot. We can never seem to get enough of each other, but every time feels so right, so perfect. I exhale contentedly into his chest as we lay there, wrapped up in a blanket, basking in each other's warmth.

"That sounds like a contented sigh," Ethan whispers, his hand brushing over my back.

"Very," I murmur against his skin.

"Me too," he says, holding me tighter. We lay there for a while longer before I reluctantly start to move.

"We have to get going if we're going to make it to Emma's before midnight," I say, kissing his chest as I go.

"Careful," he warns with a smirk. "You're naked, I'm naked, and kissing leads to..."

"Stop it," I giggle, hitting his arm, but as I get up, I feel his erection brush against my leg.

He groans as he throws the blanket off and grins mischievously. "Ethan!" I exclaim, shaking my head at his now fully naked body.

"I can't help it! I just had your beautiful body lying on me," he teases, reaching for me, but I take off running, nearly tripping over Kasey, who's loyally trailing behind. Ethan leaps off the couch and chases after me. I'm giggling uncontrollably as I round the bed, but I have nowhere to go. He's so much faster than I expect.

He catches me, and we tumble onto the bed, laughing as he pins me down and kisses my neck. "Ethan James!" I try to protest, but his hands and lips are everywhere.

"Miranda Bradley," he murmurs, nuzzling my neck. "It has a nice ring to it." His words make me pause, and I smile up at him. It's the first time I've thought about my name change, and it sounds so sweet. Seeing my huge smile, he says it again softly. "Mrs. Bradley. I like it." He growls playfully into my shoulder, and I can't resist giving in to him again.

"Okay, twice is enough. We have to go," I finally manage, pushing him off my shoulder as he groans in protest.

"I don't want to," he says, kissing me again.

"You don't want to go?" I ask, surprised.

"Yes, I want to go. But no, I don't want to get out of this bed with you yet," he admits with a playful smile that nearly makes me cave.

"We'll be back in bed in a few hours, and I'll make it up to you," I promise, trying to slide off the bed.

"Deal," he grins, getting up and pulling me with him as he heads to the dresser.

"That was easy," I tease, opening the drawer beside him and pulling out a pair of red lace panties, making him growl.

"No, Ethan," I warn with a grin.

"A promise of more sex with you is the best bargaining chip ever," he says, playfully smacking my bare ass.

"I'll remember that," I reply with a groan, heading into the bathroom.

We get dressed, load up my car with the mountain of presents, and grab our bags and Kasey. Ethan hands me my keys as we step into the elevator, and I smile at the keychain, running my fingers over the engraved "Bradley." Suddenly, I realize it's not just a keychain—it's a hint. I hold it up, looking at him in shock.

"Took you long enough," he chuckles.

I swat his arm as he laughs. "Pretty slick."

"I thought so," he says proudly, beaming at me.

I drive for the first two hours, and we stop for coffee and a bathroom break before Ethan takes over, as I'm getting tired. We're making great time, and I thank him again for the car.

"Why don't you lay your head back and rest? I can see how tired you are," Ethan says as we get back on the highway.

"I am, but I want to stay awake with you," I try, but a yawn betrays me.

"Rest. I've got this. Directions are in the GPS, I've got coffee, and I feel great. I'll wake you when we're close."

"Are you sure?" I ask again, my voice sleepy.

"Yes, very sure."

"Okay, I'm just going to close my eyes for a bit. Don't let me sleep the whole time, though," I mumble, knowing full well that he won't wake me.

"Okay," he agrees, smiling.

The next thing I know, I hear him softly talking. I blink my eyes open, still cozy in the seat. "Hey, sleepyhead. We're almost there. Wake up," he says, squeezing my knee.

I stretch and sit up, only to realize we're more than almost there—he's pulling down their street. I straighten myself up and glance in the mirror to check my face.

"You're still beautiful," Ethan chuckles.

"I need to call Emma," I say, reaching for my purse, but he stops me.

"I already did. They're waiting for us."

I smile, leaning back in my seat. "You always take care of everything."

"I do. Remember that," he says, taking my hand, and I know in my heart he always will.

We pull into the driveway, and before I can even get out of the car, Emma and the kids are running towards us. I'm not sure who's moving faster, her or the kids. As soon as I step out, Emma grabs my hand, her eyes immediately zeroing in on my ring.

"OH MIRANDA, IT'S HUGE!" she shouts, pulling me out of the car and into a tight hug. "I'm so happy for you!" She pulls back slightly, kissing my face all over like an excited puppy.

"So *that's* where you get that from," Ethan says with a laugh as he joins us.

"Oh, Ethan!" Emma exclaims, pulling him into a hug as well. "I'm so happy for you too. Congratulations! I'm so excited for you guys!" She gives him a couple of kisses on the cheek before finally releasing him.

Inside, my mom, dad, and Joe give us hugs and congratulations. Mom can't stop staring at my ring, and Sophia, with her childlike wonder, declares that it's almost as big as her head. Ethan looks a little overwhelmed by all the attention, but he doesn't complain, graciously accepting the hugs and kisses.

After settling in, Mom fixes us some sandwiches since we didn't have dinner, and we all sit around catching up while sipping beer. Emma perches on the arm of the loveseat next to me, eagerly listening as I recount how Ethan proposed.

"That is so romantic," she sighs, wiping tears from her eyes, which sets me off crying, too. Tristen, clearly used to his mom's emotional outbursts, hands her a box of tissues, earning a laugh from everyone.

"She cries over everything," he grumbles, and we all laugh harder.

"What's the song?" Emma asks, curious.

"Oh, I don't know the name of it," I admit, turning to Ethan.

"Funny enough, it's called *Yours*. I tracked down the musician on the pier to find out," Ethan says, causing me to tear up again.

"You guys are so sweet together," Emma says dreamily.

"I think so too," I reply, leaning back into Ethan's chest, feeling completely content.

"So, have you picked a date?" Mom asks, and Emma quickly jumps in.

"Or a location? You should have it at that winery you love so much. You always said it would be perfect for a wedding," she adds.

"Slow down, it just happened this morning, remember?" I groan, making Ethan chuckle as he squeezes my shoulder.

"Wherever you want to have it, and as big or as small as you want. I'm on board with anything," Ethan says, kissing my forehead, which makes my cheeks flush.

"Well, that sounds like we need to schedule some time to start planning!" Emma exclaims, practically bouncing with excitement.

"Let's not get ahead of ourselves! Can I enjoy being engaged for a day, maybe two?" I plead.

"Of course, of course. I'm just so happy for you!" Emma

says, smothering me with kisses again until I push her away, laughing.

"See? It's crazy, isn't it?" Ethan teases.

"I don't slobber on you!" I groan.

"Oh, I think you do sometimes," he replies with a mischievous grin, and everyone bursts into laughter again.

"Actually, I need something from you now, before we plan anything," I say, turning to Emma with a serious tone.

"A notebook?" she jokes, her eyes twinkling.

"No, a maid of honor," I say, watching her face as she registers my words.

Tears immediately fill her eyes. "YES!" she shouts, tackling me into a hug so forceful we fall off the couch. Ethan tries to catch us, but we all end up on the floor in a heap, laughing.

"Sophia, Tristen, I want you guys in it too!" I manage to say between giggles, and suddenly the kids jump on top of me, and Ethan piles on, too. We're all laughing, and I've never felt more blissful or surrounded by pure love in my life.

After a few more beers and endless laughter, Ethan and I finally crawl into bed. He pulls me close, as I whisper, "I'm so happy I think I might explode."

"Don't do that, I just found you," he says, kissing my nose. "You plan the wedding of your dreams. Don't worry about the expense. I want it to be perfect," he says, his voice soft and sincere.

"As long as you're there, it will be," I reply, kissing him back.

He continues, "We can do it here, or at home, somewhere tropical, or even in Ireland. Whatever you want."

"I don't want crazy. I want simple and beautiful. Maybe in the fall or spring, with pink flowers… or red…or yellow. A simple white gown, you in a tux, and our friends and family there. If it's spring, we can do it outside," I muse, picturing it in my head.

"It sounds beautiful already," he says, rubbing his nose against mine.

"What about you?" I ask, curious. "What did you picture when you thought about getting married? This is for both of us."

"Honestly, I never thought much about it. I didn't think I'd get married for a long time, and it wasn't something I cared about. Until you." His smile melts my soul.

"And what do you see now?" I press, wanting to know.

He leans his head back, closing his eyes. "I see myself standing at the end of the aisle, watching you walk toward me in a flowing white dress, a veil covering your face, but I can still see your eyes as you get closer. We're outside, and I hear birds chirping, the sun shining behind you. You're breathtaking, and our families are standing around us," he says, his voice full of warmth and love.

I swallow hard, fighting back the tears as his vision of our wedding plays in my mind. He's so romantic.

"I agree, outside," I whisper.

"What time of year?" he asks.

"Spring."

"This coming spring—it's closer," he says with a grin.

"That's not much time to plan," I point out, raising an eyebrow.

"No, but I know you can do it. We can fly you down here, or Emma can come up to us, and you two can plan away." His answering smile makes me smile bigger.

"It'll be hard to find somewhere available so soon, and it'll be expensive," I say with a sigh.

"Miranda, I've told you before, money is not a problem. What's mine is yours. You'll never want for anything as long as you live." He exhales as he kisses me deeply. I know I won't, but that's not important to me.

"I don't want your money," I say between kisses.

"I know, and that's why it's all yours," he murmurs, kissing me again, effectively silencing any further protests.

"Not mine," I say, pulling back from his kiss.

"It will be. The day you take my name," he insists, biting playfully at my lip.

"No," I say, trying to sound firm.

"Yes. All of it. Everything," he says, attempting to kiss me again, but I turn my head so his lips land on my cheek instead.

"You are so hardheaded! I don't want your money. We do this together," I argue, trying to keep my resolve.

"Together with our money," he says, kissing me again. I can only groan in frustration.

"You are impossible," I pout.

"Yep, get used to it," he teases, nuzzling into me. I'm losing this battle fast, so I change tactics to stay on top.

"Fine. I want something in writing that says I won't get your money if something happens between us. I don't want half of anything either," I say seriously.

He pulls away from my neck, clearly taken aback. "Miranda, you want a prenup?" His voice is filled with surprise.

"Yes."

"No."

"Yes."

"Absolutely not."

"Ethan, I don't want anyone thinking I'm marrying you for your money or your companies or whatever else you have. I just want you," I plead, hoping he'll understand.

He stares at me for a moment, thinking before he responds. "You are something else. I'm marrying you, and you will be my wife. Everything I have will be yours too. Period. And if something happens and you leave me, you might as well take it all because I'll die on the spot." His voice is sad, and I can see this is difficult for him, but I can't let him dismiss my feelings.

"Ethan, we need to talk about this. I'm serious," I insist.

"So am I," he replies, brushing the hair behind my ear.

"Can we compromise somehow? I don't want people thinking I'm in this for the money, and I want to protect you too..." I begin, but he cuts me off.

"I don't care what people think. I protect you, Miranda. I don't want to fight about this," he groans.

"We're not fighting, we're discussing. Can you see my point, though?" I ask, hoping for a breakthrough.

"No, I can't," he admits bluntly.

I sigh. "Okay, I know nothing I say will make you fully understand, but I'm going to try. Listen, I grew up in a middle-income family. We lived comfortably. We had vacations, but not to tropical islands. We had a nice house, but it wasn't extravagant. It was perfect for us. I've worked hard for what I have, and I make good money now, but I'm still the same. I've never dreamed of being rich. Maybe in some fantasies sure, but I'm just a regular girl with regular dreams. All I want is love and happiness. That's all I need. I don't need money for that. Just you," I explain, hoping I'm getting through to him.

He studies me for a moment. "I see your point," he says, surprising me.

"You do? Really?" I ask, genuinely surprised.

"Yes. However, I grew up differently. I've never had to worry about money. It has always been a part of my life, part of my job. My world revolves around it. I work hard for it, and I don't know how to live without it. Can you see my point?" he asks, his fingers tracing the outline of my face.

"I can," I admit, understanding now how deeply ingrained this is for him.

"Okay, neither of us wants to budge, but I don't want people thinking I'm after your money, and you don't want me to go without. So, how about we sleep on it and discuss it again later? Maybe we can come up with a compromise, like, after a certain number of years, the prenup goes away. I protect you, you take care of me, and we both agree," I suggest, hoping it makes sense to him.

"I think we can work with that," he nods.

"We can?" I feel relieved.

"Yes. I just want you to be happy. I know all of this is overwhelming, and I don't want that. I'll talk to Jason, and we'll figure something out that works for both of us. However," he adds with a playful grin, "you do *not* fight me on this wedding. I want it to be everything you've ever dreamed of. We don't worry about costs—just about making it perfect. Promise me that, and I'll agree to your demands," he says, his eyes twinkling.

I know he's giving in more than he'd like, but I smile and agree anyway. "Deal."

He pulls me on top of him, kissing me deeply and running his hands down my sides. "You drive me crazy sometimes," he groans, his voice vibrating through me.

"Well, you make it hard not to," I reply, kissing his chin and nose.

"I'll show you hard," he growls playfully, pulling me so I'm straddling him. He's already more than ready, and I laugh as we lose ourselves in each other again.

After we make love, we lie wrapped up in each other's arms, utterly content.

"May or June?" he asks, his fingers tracing patterns on my arm.

"Hmm?" I murmur, half-asleep.

"The wedding. May or June?" he asks again.

"May. Pink flowers. Maybe some gray in there. Outside. With you," I say dreamily.

His chest rumbles with a soft chuckle. "Pink and gray? I like it."

"Me too. I love you," I whisper.

"And I love you more than the world," he replies, kissing the top of my head as we drift off to sleep together.

Chapter 36

I wake to the sound of excited yelling and the thundering footsteps of kids running down the hall. Before I can even fully open my eyes, the door flies open, and Sophia and Tristen jump onto the bed. Behind them, I hear Emma trying to rein them in, telling them to knock, but it's already too late.

"Aunt Rana, Uncle Ethan, wake up, it's Christmas!" Sophia shakes me eagerly.

"I'm awake," I reply, looking over at Ethan, who is squeezing his eyes shut, trying not to smile. "Is the sun even up yet?" he grumbles.

"Yes, now get up. We have presents!" Tristen's infectious laughter fills the room.

"We do?" Ethan asks, opening one eye. Sophia bursts into giggles.

"Yes! We have some for you, too!" she squeals.

"Well, in that case, I better get up. I love presents!" Ethan teases, grabbing Sophia and tickling her as she shrieks with delight.

Emma leans in the doorway, watching the scene with a huge smile on her face. She looks genuinely happy.

"OKAY, out! Both of you," she finally says. "Let them get up." Ethan releases Sophia, and she skips out of the room with Tristen.

"Good morning, and Merry Christmas," Emma says with a wink.

"Merry Christmas!" Ethan and I call out together.

We make our way to the kitchen, where Mom is already busy preparing breakfast.

"Good morning, Merry Christmas!" she greets us warmly. I give her a kiss on the cheek, and she touches my face, beaming.

"I love seeing you so happy," she whispers.

"Me too," Emma adds, grinning beside her. Ethan strolls over to give my mom a hug and kisses her on the cheek, making her blush. He's so different than what I expected, and I'm so happy that he is.

We enjoy a wonderful breakfast filled with the warmth of family and holiday cheer. Afterward, it's time to open presents, and the kids are practically bouncing with excitement at the sight of their pile of gifts.

"Too much," Emma mutters to me, shaking her head.

"Blame him!" I point to Ethan, who grins unapologetically.

"They're kids. They're meant to be spoiled," he says, throwing up his hands in mock surrender. I can't help but laugh. God, I love him.

"Emma, I said the same thing and look what happened." I gesture to my ring, my watch, and my locket and point outside toward my car. Ethan just laughs at me.

"Hey, I stuck to the 'want, need, wear, read' thing, so don't kill my joy," Ethan says with a wink, tossing another gift to Sophia. The kids eagerly tear into their presents, squealing with joy as they uncover clothes, gift cards, books, and socks. But the real screams of excitement come when they open their VR headsets.

"Miranda! Ethan!" Emma yells her voice somewhere between shock and amusement.

"Shhhh, it's the joy of Christmas," Ethan says, holding up a hand, completely unbothered.

The kids return the favor by giving Ethan a huge box filled with Kit-Kats of all different sizes and varieties. He dramatically pretends to weep.

"BEST PRESENT EVER!" he declares, making the kids burst into more laughter.

We finish unwrapping the rest of the gifts, and it's truly been an amazing Christmas.

Later, Ethan, Joe, and the kids are fully immersed in their VR games, stumbling around and laughing, while the rest of us watch the hilarity unfold. Emma moves over to sit beside me on the couch, resting her head on my shoulder.

"He's amazing with kids," she says softly, watching Ethan with admiration.

"I know," I reply, my heart swelling with pride.

"You're going to be so happy. You'll have lots of kids and live your happily ever after," Emma says, taking my hand.

"I know," I say, smiling so wide I can't contain it.

"And to think you doubted me!" Emma teases, giving me a playful elbow in the ribs.

"Ouch," I giggle, nudging her back.

Ethan looks over at us with his signature silly grin, and I can't help but feel overwhelmed with love. "He really is my hero, you know," I say, my voice catching with emotion. "He makes me more than happy. He makes me whole."

"He's your soulmate," Emma whispers, squeezing my hand.

"I know," I say, tears of happiness welling in my eyes as I watch my future husband laugh and play like a kid himself. This moment—this simple, joyful moment—is my fairy tale.

It's my happily ever after.

Author Bio

Kim Love is a mother, wife, entrepreneur, and the author of her debut novel, *Yours*. When she's not writing, you can find her volunteering in her community, working at a local dog rescue, or spending time with her family. Kim lives in St. Louis but loves to travel, especially enjoying cruises with extended family and friends. She plans to complete her second novel in 2025—if she can stop reading everyone else's books!